Tomorrow...is another Trial:

a woman's inspirational life journey

明日又天涯

Phoebe Sayers 馮友梅

This page is left blank

Title	Tomorrow Is Another Trial
Sub Title	A woman's inspirational life journey
Author	Phoebe Sayers
eMail	Phoebe.sayers@gmail.com
Bookcover Design	Ruth Lock
	ruthlock@ERLdesign.com
Publisher	Sharewin Pty Ltd
Place of Publisher	Australia
Date of Publication	December 2015
Version	1.0
Distributor	Ingram
Paperback ISBN-10	0-9875865-05
Paperback ISBN-13	978-0-9875865-0-6
ePUB ISBN	978-0-9875865-1-3
Mobipocket ISBN	978-0-9875865-2-0

版權所有　翻印必究

如有雷同　實屬巧合

DEDICATION ←

I dedicate this book to the loving memory of my dear Mummy whom I never knew very well, and at times misunderstood. When I reconstructed her life from her writing, I discovered what a determined and strong lady she was. It is from her that I inherited the discipline, determination and tenacity in my approach to struggles and everything I do.

I want to share this story of my Mummy's life with my family, friends, and the world. To honour this exceptional lady who managed to triumph over all the trials and tribulations that life's bad fortune dealt her.

ENDORSEMENT

Robert Lewis Galinsky was born on July 1, 1953 in Sioux City, Iowa, USA. He is a producer and writer, known for producing Prey, his other achievements are Dreamtime's Over (2009), The Bodhi Tree (2015), and Dust and Glory.

Tomorrow is Another Trial is a magnetic love poem to two generations written by the woman detailing the 'trials and tribulations' of a most challenging and ultimately triumphant life of her mother's journey from child in China to the end of her life in Australia. The seeds sown by the author's grandmother that set the stage for the young female scion's rise and fall, and further fall before finding love and salvation through incredible adversity is both heart wrenching and in some ways quite clinical look back at what was an unthinkable road to travel for a genteel Asian women after the turn of the 20th century.

Phoebe Sayers has poured her heart into telling 'her mummy's story' against the odds and without the typical path of a trained writer. Yet her story is one that can't be put down, whether the reader is a student of history, a chronicler of family, or simply someone who believes that even the darkest and most difficult life can lead to love and hope when the mind and soul are open to new experience and looking towards the light.

Phoebe would say 'it's her mummy's story' when she describes her grandmother's lifestyle when her mother was born and what happened when all luck and fortune went away. But really, it's Phoebe's story... She has brought this tome to life, to bring us hope and entertainment from what was an astonishing collection of notes and detail and material that would have remained otherwise undiscovered.

Ms. Sayers is not pretending to be a candidate for the Miles Franklin Award or literary history, rather---she has taken a century of milestones and beautifully and painstakingly collected and woven them into a story of heartbreak, determination, and historical imagery we won't put down, and will never forget.

Table of Contents

ACKNOWLEDGMENTS

I have many good friends and relatives who guided me in the writing of our family saga. I am deeply in debt for the time and effort they have spent meticulously correcting my many errors and grammatical mistakes.

I would like to thank Alex Fung my nephew, and Belinda Elliott my daughter and Simon James Smith my son, for writing the prologue because I know it comes straight from the heart. I am touched. Also special thanks to my brother Hubert Fung (Kai Son) and my late brother Peter Fung (Kai Ming) who helped to fill in some early memories of our family which have enriched this story.

A big thank you goes to Kay Winter, my sister-in-law, David Sayers, my brother, and Erin Sayers, my niece, who spent precious time proof reading my story a number of times and provided me with constructive feedback.

Another big thank you goes to Teresa Mascenon, my sister, and Belinda Elliott, my dear daughter, who spent a lot of time proof reading my story and provided valuable contributions to the story.

A very special thank you has to go to Jill Elizabeth Spooner. Jill is a retired English teacher who had the hardest task of editing my original manuscript in English. For that I am deeply grateful. I thank her for her meticulous corrections and advice to improve the readability of my story.

A big thank you goes to Elizabeth Alma Fennell and Susan Marian Berry who spent their precious time combing through my story to improve syntax and coherence.

Another thank you goes to David Michael Wicken, and my dear son Simon James Smith, who spent their time scrutinising the proper use of references to improve the flow of citation throughout the story.

Another special thank you goes to Mycah Chavez, a professional editor and an English Professor in Manila, who ploughed through my manuscript to give the story the polished language that it needed.

Another very special thank you goes to Ruth Lock for the book jacket design. She was able to capture the spirit and the feeling of the story and present it in such an artistic way that is reflective of my Mummy's life story.

I am grateful to Julie Stroud, the well-known editor from Penguin Book and Robert Lewis Galinsky, the experienced scriptwriter and film producer for their valuable time to plough through my manuscript and give me precious feedback with story writing insight which I have taken on board.

Robert Lewis Galinsky who is the screenwriter and producer for the movie 'Dust and Glory' is in the process of adapting this story into a TV series.

This book will not be here without the assistance of many who generously guided me and gave their precious time to edit my manuscript. I give them my humble gratitude.

PROLOGUE

Kwan Mee See was my grandmother and Bob Sayers was my grandfather on my Dad's side (Gri Sen). Shortly before she left this world for good, my grandmother told me her life story.

As one of the younger generation, I was touched by this story and was astounded at the detail and colour that filtered through grandma and Ah Tai's life. I had heard the rumours of a South American heritage. Dad had always told me about his family's past wealth, but nothing could prepare me for this tale of bravery, struggle and courage.

Grandparents always have fantastic stories, and for me, this book is a treasure trove of history and of where I came from. I sincerely thank Goo Ma (Yau Mui) for going into the depth of detail that she had to write with ink on the pages. It seems we owe a lot to our ancestors and what better way to thank them than to tell their life story in vivid detail.

To me, grandma always seemed a very strong matriarch of the family, and now I can see why. She followed her mother's example of fighting for justice and keeping her family together no matter what the personal consequences were for her. She always used to tell me, "Speak Chinese, you need to know your ancestral language." Little did I know that she, on the other side was always trying to learn better English. I thank her for always drilling that into me as I can speak fluent Cantonese now. I feel like I've inherited so much of my cultural tapestry from her influence, and am very thankful for the sacrifices that she had to make. But I'm also very thankful for the angel that came along in grandpa Bob. In life there are trials and tribulations, best friends who become family, and sisters or brothers whom we need to stay connected to. Hug them a little closer, tell them that you love them and help everyone through that journey we call life.

From Alexander Fung 馮文偉 July 2013

Every person has a story to tell... The proliferation of biographies and autobiographies from Communist China in recent years is evidence of this. I read *Wild Swans: Three Daughters of China* by Jung Chang as an impressionable teenager and hoped one day someone would record our family story which spans a similar time in China's tumultuous history. Little did I know, it would be my mother's task.

When my extended family came together for a 'relo bash', which was fairly regularly during my childhood, we cousins would hear fragments of the Fung family history. Like shards of a broken vase, these whispers were difficult to piece together. There were tales of astonishing wealth – a summer house and a mansion in Canton; jewels that were tossed aside because they were mere trifles, rich silks and delicate trinkets. Then there were anecdotes from Macao – moving house because the rent increased, finding coins in a phone box to buy a sweet bun, a rare treat. How did a prosperous family fall on such desperate times? I remember being told Grandma had forged documents to escape from Communist China to Hong Kong, one more fact to add to my accumulating understanding of my mother's life. I am thankful that at last all of the shards have been painstakingly pieced together to tell a heart breaking but inspiring story.

Strength and determination is a family trait in the Kwan women. My mother, Grandmother and Great-grandmother have faced many hardships but they have endured with dignity and through sheer tenacity. Our generation owe so much to our Grandmother who did what was necessary in order to hold her family together, no matter what trails she faced. We can never fully appreciate the despair she felt and the sacrifices she made but we can honour her by instilling in our own children the same determination and values she learnt from her mother. I can only hope my daughter and son emulate their ancestors by seeking justice, respecting all people regardless of rank and putting their neighbours' needs ahead of their own.

Belinda Elliott 15 July 2014

Growing up as kids, we heard stories about our grandparents and great grandparents of how much of a struggle it was growing up and of having to give up so much. I had seen movies and read books of adventure and tales of riches but had not expected that my own family history would play out in a story that was comparable.

Reading this book has given me a deeper insight and appreciation of my grandparents. We often don't realise what we have and how much has been done for us, until it's too late. I'm thankful to have known them when I have had the chance.

From this story about my grandmother I can see in my mum, the inner strength and determination, tenacity, and hope in the face of hardship that seems to be a trademark of all the women in our family.

Thank you mum for sharing this story with us.

Simon James Smith 1 November 2015

KWAN MEE SEE'S FAMILY TREE

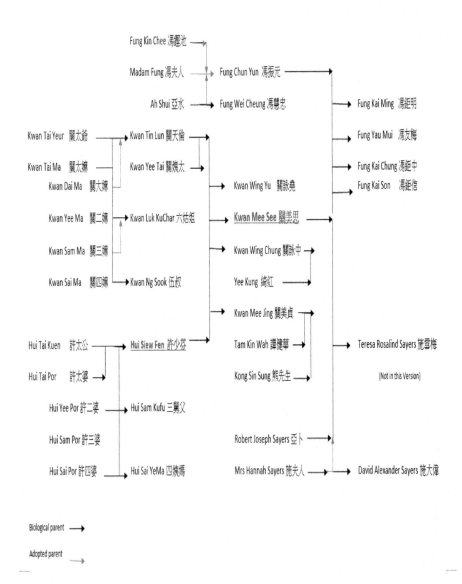

Kwan Mee See's 關美思 Family Diagram

MEE SEE AND SIEW FEN'S LIFE JOURNEY

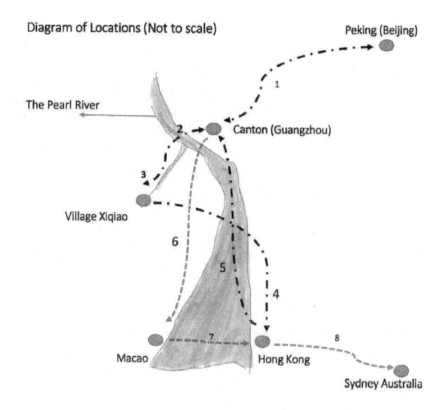

Diagram of Locations (Not to scale)

Legend:

1. Siew Fen was brought up in Peking as a boy till her late teens.
2. Siew Fen went to Xiqiao to sell properties in financial settlement after seven years law suit.
3. Escaped from Japanese occupation in Canton, to Xiqiao, Siew Fen worked as a teacher in a village school.
4. Master Hui requested Siew Fen and children to return Hong Kong, Madam Hui was seriously ill.
5. Japan occupied Hong Kong, Siew Fen took family home to Canton.
6. Mee See took family to escape to Macao to avoid embezzlement investigation.
7. Mee See's last option to work in Hong Kong.
8. Mee See and family migrated from Hong Kong to Australia (not in this version).

Part One – Mee See's Childhood

The Kwan Family

Having amassed a large fortune as a successful businessman in Peru, South America, Master Kwan Tai Yeur (關太爺) decided to return to his homeland China with his Incan wife Madam Kwan Tai Ma (關太嫲) and their son Kwan Tin Lun (關天倫). They settled in his hometown of Canton (now Guangzhou) in the Kwan family mansion.

Master Kwan established a family home that was a grand manor within a large walled residence, consisting of a number of brick cottages, each with its own courtyard opening onto a central garden. They lived in the largest cottage, a modern garden mansion with four lounge rooms and seven bedrooms downstairs and the same area on the top floor. In the centre of the estate, there was a huge Chinese-style garden with two sizeable fish ponds joined by a red wooden foot bridge leading to a short pagoda which was a feature of the garden. There were a couple of garages where sedan chairs were housed. They employed a team of maids, servants, chefs, doormen, butlers, and footmen to cater for the family's comfort within this huge estate.

Master Kwan purchased numerous properties on several streets in various suburbs of Canton that provided a stable rental income. And so they prospered.

Master Kwan's ancestral village was at Xiqiao (西樵), which was in the picturesque fishing village of Kun Shan (官山墟) along the Pearl River (珠江), about half a day's ferry journey south of Canton. Master Kwan rebuilt the grand Kwan family shrine and reinstalled all the Kwan ancestors' plaques into this shrine for all the Kwan families who lived in Xiqiao. He also rebuilt the village wharf with a long jetty that stretched out onto the Pearl River for all the villagers to use. Villagers and children could walk out to fish along the jetty and fishing junks and ferries could drop off travellers at this jetty.

Behind the family shrine, Master Kwan rebuilt the huge ancestral home as a holiday residence for his family to escape the oppressive heat of Canton in the summer. He also bought many plots of farm land, the local fishery and a number of fishing junks to rent out to the villagers. Villagers could opt to pay their rent using their products instead of cash. He was beloved by all in the area as he was a kindly man. Several times when natural disasters like floods struck the area, Master Kwan would waive the rent and help the villagers re-establish their livelihood. All the villagers were grateful for Master Kwan's generosity.

Madam Kwan Tai Ma was not accustomed to life in China. It was a very different culture from her country of birth. As an Incan lady from Peru, she found herself out of place in the huge Kwan family with an army of servants that she was expected to control. She found life in the city of Canton very different and demanding, and she disliked the simple village life at the summer residence at Xiqiao. Madam Kwan Tai Ma opted to return to her home in Peru alone. Sadly, she had to leave her son Tin Lun in China with his father.

Soon after, Master Kwan married Dai Ma (關大嬤), a lady from a wealthy family in Canton. She was a very determined lady and demanded to be treated as "the supreme wife". She did not bear any children of her own and treated Tin Lun as her own son. She forbade the family to mention Master Kwan's previous wife.

Madam Kwan[1], as she wanted to be called, was a very capable and well-organised lady and soon commanded the whole household with firm control. As Master Kwan had retired from his successful business, having established his wealthy position in Canton and Xiqiao, he

---

[1] Madam Kwan was the exclusive title reserved for the first wife, supreme ruler of the household. Dai Ma was the second wife in rank. However, she insisted on being called 'The Madam' raising her rank in the family hierarchy.

retreated to live a quiet leisurely life. He gladly left all family affairs in the capable hands of Madam Kwan.

Madam Kwan employed a property manager to assist her with all the rental arrangements in Canton and in the village Xiqiao. The property manager collected rent from the villagers, or products in place of their rent. He organised the transport, storage and sale of the food provisions collected from the villagers. Madam Kwan often came up to Xiqiao village with the property manager unannounced to collect rent and to keep a close watch on the team of servants and workmen. The property manager entered all transactions into a register for Madam Kwan who went through the book meticulously each month.

During summer the Kwan family would visit the Xiqiao country residence to escape the humid summer heat of Canton. All the villagers knew each member of the Kwan family and bowed to pay them respect. They were treated as lords in the village.

Although Madam Kwan could not bear any children of her own, she would have liked to have a few siblings for Tin Lun to keep him company and to bring more joy to Kwan's household. Most importantly, the Kwan family needed to have more sons to carry on the Kwan name. Madam Kwan carefully selected a number of girls from good families as concubines [2](妾士) for Master Kwan. They each lived in a separate brick house inside the Kwan estate. It was hoped that the concubines would produce a number of sons to carry on the Kwan's family name. In the Chinese household, all the children were ranked in order within the family structure according to when they were born. Girls and boys would rank separately. Lots of babies did not survive in those days for various reasons. However subsequent children would continue the family's numeric ranking along the bloodline.

Madam Kwan had chosen three concubines for Master Kwan over a

---

[2] Concubines 妾士 were common in a wealthy household. The master usually had a number of other lesser wives selected by the supreme wife.

16

number of years. All the concubines dined with and paid Madam Kwan respect every evening in her quarters. Second wife, Yee Ma (二嫲) only bore a son who died before the month was out. Yee Ma spent half her life in misery, missing the son who had passed away. Later, she adopted Third wife Sam Ma's daughter Luk KuChar (六姑姐) and spent her life bringing her up as her own child. Third wife Sam Ma (三嫲) gave birth to a daughter, Luk KuChar in the first year of her marriage into the Kwan household. She did not get on with Madam Kwan because she did not produce a son. Unhappily she returned to her parents leaving her daughter in the care of Yee Ma. Madam Kwan gave Master Kwan a fourth wife, Sai Ma (四嫲), to celebrate his fortieth birthday. Sai Ma just turned fifteen when she was married into the Kwan household. She gave birth to Master Kwan's second son Ng Sook (伍叔) years after Tin Lun, Kwan's eldest son, was married and had started his own family.

Tin Lun, was half-Incan. However, no one dared talk about his South American background. He was over six foot tall, handsome, with thick black hair and bright, light brown eyes and a deep olive complexion. For many years, he was the only son and heir. He was spoiled by his stepmother who granted his every wish. Tin Lun never needed to consider anybody and could never see anybody else's point of view. Tin Lun never needed to study nor did he want for a career. Madam Kwan had scholars come to the Kwan's house to teach Tin Lun scholastic disciplines like reading poetry, drawing, writing calligraphy and water colour painting to keep him interested. He reckoned because his father had such great wealth he would never use up all the money his father had accumulated. Tin Lun lived a life of debauchery, gambling on horses, dog racing and cock fighting, dancing, drinking, visiting opium dens, brothels and the like. Life, to Tin Lun, was simply one long joyous session from one entertainment house to the next. Madam Kwan gave Tin Lun a generous allowance that was expendable. He had a large contingent of friends who joined his escapades. Often, he would settle all the expenses for his friends wherever they went.

Tin Lun was twenty when Madam Kwan felt it was time for Tin Lun to get married. Madam Kwan spoke to Master Kwan.

"Lau Yau[3](老爺), as Tin Lun is already twenty years old, it is time for him to marry a girl from a good family. You would like to have a few heirs to the Kwan name, wouldn't you? Grandchildren would bring a lot of joy to the household."

Since retiring from business and with Madam Kwan looking after everything in the household, Master Kwan spent his day leisurely visiting tea houses with his favourite pet bird in a gold-gilded cage. He joined his friends playing Chinese chess under the huge banyan tree by the tea house. He frequented a number of smoking houses to smoke a water pipe as part of his daily past time.

Master Kwan smiled at Madam Kwan and said, "You are right! As you are so capable with all these household matters, I shall leave everything to you. Yes, go ahead and find Tin Lun a suitable match."

Madam Kwan employed a famous match maker Mei-Yan-Por (媒人婆) to find a girl who was suitable as the supreme wife for the Kwan family's only son and heir.

Match maker Mei-Yan-Por wore her hair as a bundle tied up on the top of her head with several scented yellow magnolias on the side of her head. She laughed with the broadest smile and looked most engaging and was eager to please. She covered her mouth with her red handkerchief to hide her uneven tarnished teeth as she told Madam Kwan, "This is such a co-incidence! Master Hui who was a chief judge in Peking, serving the highest court in the Capital City, has now returned home and retired to Canton. The Hui family have a single daughter who has not been spoken for just yet. This is absolutely timely…. let me make an enquiry for you."

Mei-Yan-Por added, "The Hui family is ever so wealthy and powerful. The Hui family owns many streets of properties in down town Canton.

---

[3] Lau Yau 老爺 was a respectful way to address the head of the household in those days

Hui's daughter has just turned eighteen and is an absolute beauty! Her skin is white and as soft as silk; she has bright eyes and shiny hair. She has been educated in a private college in Peking, and she is one of the rare beauties who can actually read and write poetry."

Mei-Yan-Por paused and then added, "Hui's only daughter and Kwan's only son is a match made in Heaven!"

The Hui Family

Master Hui Tai Kuen (許太公) had been a chief judge in Peking (now Beijing) for most of his life. He had a reputation for upholding justice and had a successful career in the courts. Madam Hui Tai Por (許太婆), the first wife supreme, only bore a daughter named Siew Fen (少芬). For many years Master Hui worked in Peking while Madam Hui remained at Canton. Master Hui was a caring husband and a loving father. Madam Hui insisted on seeking for Master Hui a number of suitable concubines, hoping that they could produce sons to carry the Hui family name.

Madam Hui pointed out to Master Hui, "Lau Yau (老爺), unfortunately I have not been blessed to produce a son for you since Siew Fen arrived. The Hui family needs at least an heir to carry on the family name and fortune. Besides, Lau Yau would lose face, if Lau Yau did not even have a few concubines to care for your comforts. Every one of your colleagues at court has a number of concubines. Lau Yau should have at least three or four wives in the household to look respectable in front of your friends and colleagues."

Madam Hui found three suitable concubines to marry into the Hui household. Second wife, Yee Por (二婆) was married to the Hui family for many years before she produced two sons. The first son died within the first twelve months. The second son, Sam Kufu (三舅父), was the only son and heir of the Hui family. Third wife, Sam Por (三婆) never produced any children. She lost favour from Master Hui and died in her early twenties. Fourth wife, Sai Por (四婆) only produced a daughter, Sai YeMa (四姨媽), soon after she was married into the Hui family.

Over the years, Master Hui purchased several streets of properties in Canton. Madam Hui assisted in collecting the rent while he was working in Peking. At the time, foreign influence in building construction was in vogue in Canton. Inside the Hui family's walled ancestral home Master Hui built a brand new modern garden mansion facing the corner of Chin Wah Lane (青華里), the wealthy side of Canton. His concubines each occupied a separate mud brick cottage within this walled estate, while Madam Hui, Siew Fen and Master Hui moved into this huge modern garden mansion. This mansion had two storeys. Each floor had three lounge rooms and six bedrooms decorated with sets of the best Shun-Chee[4](酸枝) dark wood furniture. Each set of Shun-Chee furniture was inlaid with mother-of-pearl and other precious stones in patterns that depicted the four seasons. In the middle of the walled estate was the huge central garden. There was a fish pond with a tall rockery against the back drop of a low two-tiered pagoda. There were a number of court yards that connected with the network of mud brick cottages. The walled estate had an imposing iron gate at the entrance. At that time, Hui's residence was considered modern and located on the rich side of town.

Madam Hui only saw the other wives at dinner when all the concubines came over to the garden mansion to dine and to pay their respects to the supreme wife and Master Hui, whenever he happened to be home for dinner. The family under Madam Hui's direction lived in harmony. Everybody had a role in this household and everyone knew their place. She managed the Hui family matters in a strict, traditional way and kept the family finances firmly under her control.

Madam Hui had her feet bound. Her tiny feet were referred to as her

---

[4] Shun-chee 酸枝 was a dark hard wood used to build better quality furniture for the wealthy families.

"three-inch golden lotus[5] (三寸金蓮)", which made it virtually impossible for her to get around. She enlisted the help of two Hui-uncles to assist her to manage the large portfolio of the Hui's family wealth. The Hui-uncles reported to Madam Hui the dealings that they each handled in a separate register. She kept a very close eye on all the transactions in these financial registers. At Madam Hui's direction, the Hui-uncles would swap registers at certain times to get familiar with each other's portfolio. She often referred to the Hui-uncles as her left and right hand men to affirm their importance. However, she was quite capable of reassigning their role to a more deserving member of the Hui family if she so pleased.

Siew Fen was the only child in the Hui family until she was in her late teens when her other half-siblings arrived. She escaped the fate of having her feet bound because she was brought up as a boy throughout her childhood. Dressed as a boy from the very beginning, her father brought her to Peking. She used to sit by Master Hui's side at his law court to watch her father deliver justice. At twelve years old, she was given her own water pipe to smoke alongside her father. Using her father as a role model, she learned to be fair and just with all her dealings, always seeking to get to the bottom of the truth and insisting on helping people around her. She learned how to deal with servants to get the best out of those under her. She would not hesitate to fist fight her opponents to maintain justice. She also learned from her mother how to keep discipline at home and to manage their financial affairs.

Despite a disciplined and lonely childhood, Siew Fen was well educated. Her parents brought in scholars to the Hui estate to teach her Chinese literature and both ancient and modern history. She even learnt Sun Tzu the Art of War[6] (孫子兵法), the ancient war strategy. Her play mates were sons of her father's judicial colleagues. In Peking, she also

---

[5] Three-inch golden lotus 三寸金蓮 was the custom of applying painfully tight binding to the feet of young girls to prevent further growth. The practice originated among upper-class families. The tiny narrow feet of the ladies were considered beautiful.
[6] Sun Tzu the Art of War 孫子兵法 an ancient book on strategy and military tactics in war which is the most important military treatise in Asia.

attended school with them. Her favourite subjects were chess, strategic war games, poetry, and composition. She could write beautiful calligraphy and composed her own poetry. Influenced by her father during her formative years, she had no fear of anyone. She would not give an inch when she thought she had justice on her side.

She did not learn embroidery nor did she learn about floral art. She would not indulge in face powder and rouge to highlight her pale and beautiful face. There was no lipstick on her lips. She was fortunate to have escaped the fate of having her feet bound. Instead, she had special embroidered shoes made for her full size feet. She would only wear the best silk and the most expensive jewellery. She had seven servants at her command at all times. Siew Fen only knew and lived a life of absolute luxury and extravagance.

When Siew Fen turned eighteen, there were two very young siblings from the stepmothers. However, she was not interested in playing with them. Once Master Hui had retired as a high court judge and settled in Canton for good, Madam Hui knew that she had to prepare Siew Fen to live as a girl once again.

Siew Fen was re-educated to be refined and ladylike, which was different from the fist fighting and boisterous pursuits that she knew while growing up with her father.

With seven servants at her command, Siew Fen had one servant whose sole purpose was to look after her hair and teach her how to apply face power, highlights, and lipstick. Another servant would guide her to dress in the latest fashion. She learned to mix and match different garments with different colours to create a graceful outfit for a lady of her standing. She was also taught how to change her hair style to suite her disposition. Siew Fen wore her black hair in a bob with a fashionable fringe which complimented her oval face. Her eyes were bright and penetrating with a determined gaze. As a boy, she favoured using eye contact, looking directly into the eyes of the person she was communicating with. However, as a girl, she was taught to hold her head lower and to look down and sideways without being too confronting. She was always elegant; she preferred dark monochrome silk half Qipao[7] (旗袍 Chinese Cheongsam) tops with a pair of matching pants. It was unusual for a young miss of a wealthy household to wear silk trousers. However, Siew Fen was brought up wearing boy's attire. She disliked the restricting full length Qipao that ladies of her position were expected to wear. Her ears were adorned with exquisite stud diamonds and jade, never pearls. Siew Fen was surprised to see her own transformation. However, she was grateful that her mother had paved the way for a good future as a supreme wife in a wealthy household.

Madam Hui spoke to Master Hui, "Lau Yau, Siew Fen is at the age she should be married. We need to make sure she will be married to a family of equal status to match her affluent upbringing."

Master Hui had been a caring husband to his wife. He always showed due respect to Madam Hui, who was a good role model of a supreme wife. Siew Fen had an expectation of what her future husband should be like. She also had a vision of what it would be like to be the supreme wife of a family of the same class and hierarchy in society. Siew Fen felt confident that she could take up the challenge. Little did Siew Fen know at the time that life was not meant to be so straight forward, even for the wealthy!

The matchmaker Mei-Yan-Por told Madam Hui, "The Kwan family is a family of a successful and wealthy merchant from South America. They are one of the richest and best-known families in Canton. The Kwan family's only son has never married and the Kwan family is looking for a gracious girl as the supreme wife to their only son and heir. They will only consider a girl brought up in a disciplined, wealthy household with a good family background."

Mei-Yan-Por paused and then added, "The Kwan's only son and the

---

[7] Qipao 旗袍 was a stylish body-hugging one-piece Chinese dress for fashionable socialites and upper-class women

23

Hui's only daughter is a match made in Heaven!" Under the extreme hard sell of the matchmaker, the Hui family agreed to let their only daughter, Siew Fen, marry the Kwan family's only son and heir, Tin Lun.

In terms of wealth, power and respect, the Kwan family and the Hui family were a perfect match. They were equally wealthy, similarly powerful and just as well known in the city of Canton.

Marriage of the Kwan and Hui Family

At the age of eighteen, Siew Fen entered into this arranged marriage through the matchmaker Mei-Yan-Por, which was an accepted way for families to find a match from an eminently suitable family for their offspring. They must be "men dang bu dui(門當戶對)"[8] with the saying "bamboo door to bamboo door frame and wooden door to wood door frame (竹門對竹門, 木門對木門)", which carried the meaning of the appropriate door would fit the frame of the correct house. The Hui family was a good match for the Kwan family.

It was quite an occasion as both families were wealthy and lived in the rich neighbourhood of Canton. There was a lot of commotion in the two households, trying to get ready for this joyous occasion. Each family's colourful banners were flying high at the front and back entrances of the family alcove.

The Hui family's dowry was remarkable. There were three complete sets of Shun-Chee hardwood furniture to fill up several rooms. More than twenty large size camphor chests of clothes were brought over to the Kwan family. The twenty camphor chests were filled with dresses and suits for the new bride. There were traditional Qipaos, beautiful tailored Cheongsams, traditional full length Chinese trousers, embroidered silk robes, dress suites decorated with beads and pearls, and sets of shoes to match each outfit. In addition, there were sets of jewellery with a

---

[8] men dang bu dui 門當戶對 usually refers to the marriage of the offspring from families of the same standing in society.

mixture of precious stones, necklaces, bracelets and matching earrings. The jewellery was set in 24-carat yellow and white gold with rubies, sapphires, pearls, emeralds and diamonds. There were also countless pendants and hair clips made of the most precious translucent green and white jade. There was even a butterfly hair clip made of real jade in shades of pink and peach.

The Hui family generously gave the seven servants who had been serving Siew Fen, as a gift to accompany her when she married into the Kwan family.

In the Kwan family, there was a lot of fanfare in preparation for the upcoming wedding. There were countless presents: a number of suckling pigs, baskets of cakes and exquisite delicacies brought over to the Hui family to honour the parents of their future daughter-in-law.

A section of the family estate was refurbished and newly decorated to welcome the newlyweds. Accommodation for the seven additional servants were provided close by to show how the Kwan family valued the new supreme wife.

The upcoming wedding was a fairy tale marriage that became the talk of Canton. Both families tried hard to show their generosity to celebrate the union of these two very wealthy families. Even the newspaper reported the progress of this prosperous wedding as each family offered the other extravagant gifts. Both families displayed their wealthy status publicly and unashamedly.

On the eve of the wedding, Siew Fen was summoned to her father and mother's presence. Madam Hui instructed Siew Fen, "Tomorrow you will belong to the Kwan family. From now on the Kwan family home is your home. You can contact us only with your husband's permission. Your duty will be to please him and your in-laws. Bear them many sons and subjugate your own desires. You must be willing to serve the Kwans obediently and we will be proud of you."

Siew Fen looked up at her father and mother thoughtfully. This teaching was unlike what she was used to. Siew Fen responded, "Only if I am treated fairly, then I will serve the Kwan family whole heartedly. Pa Pa[9](爸爸), you have maintained justice all your life at the highest court in China. You will support and maintain justice for your own flesh and blood, won't you?"

Madam Hui added, "Siew Fen, this Kwan family is wealthy and well-known in Canton. They have an only son and they have deliberately sought out our family to tie this marital knot. You are the supreme wife of the heir to the Kwan family fortune. How would you be treated unfairly? When you bear them sons, your position will be further elevated. As the supreme wife, you have to be wise and exert your position in the Kwan household."

Madam Hui paused and then continued, "Controlling the finances of the family will make sure your position will not be diluted in any way."

Siew Fen leaned against the pagoda adjoining the fish pond and the rockery around the pond. As Siew Fen fed her favourite gold fish for the last time, several colourful gold fish swam towards her. With a couple of rain clouds in the sky, the bright moon was reflected in the still water of the pond. Siew Fen did not know what was ahead. She felt that her life was beginning a new chapter that she had very little control over. However, with the positive upbringing as a boy in her formative years, she was determined to learn to take control of her life somehow.

The next day Siew Fen was a trembling bride, dressed in a red silk gown that was embroidered with gold threads in the image of a phoenix. She wore a red and gold headdress with a red silk scarf covering the headdress and her face. She was carried to the huge Kwan family estate in a red and gold sedan chair. Her servants walked in a line behind her to make sure the young bride was attended to on the way. The sedan chair was painted gold and red with a dragon and a phoenix befitting the Kwan and Hui family's wealthy status at the union of their offspring.

---

[9] Pa Pa 爸爸 an endearing address to one's father.

The wedding procession was a colourful and noisy affair accompanied by bright red lanterns, colourful family banners, gongs clanging and trumpets blowing. It was a point of honour for the families to display lavish expense on such occasions. There were footmen who scattered coins all the way. Children and beggars rushed forward to pick up the coins from behind the sedan chair. They were clapping and cheering happily following behind the procession all the way from the Hui estate to the Kwan mansion.

At the Kwan family home, there was a lavish wedding banquet ready for the many friends, business associates, relatives and family elders. The newlyweds followed the master-of-ceremony's instructions, who officiated the wedding in an extravagant Chinese traditional. At the tea ceremony they offered tea to all the Kwan elders starting with Master and Madam Kwan. The maid in waiting supported Siew Fen as she and Tin Lun got down on their knees to kowtow[10] (叩頭) to show respect before all the Kwan elders according to their rank in the family hierarchy. As the newlyweds offered tea, Madam Kwan, followed by the other mothers-in-law gave sets of jewellery to Siew Fen, draping her neck with multiple necklaces. Siew Fen's maids-in-waiting assisted in putting on all the matching necklaces, bracelets and rings, to show respect and gratitude for the precious gifts from the elders. Each elder also gave the new couple a red pocket Lai-See[11] (利是). Siew Fen handed them over to her maid to collect and put away for her.

Then followed drinking at each table to show appreciation and thanks to all the relatives, friends and business associates who attended the wedding celebration for their good wishes. Friends and relatives gave Lai-See to show their respect of Master Kwan and to give good luck wishes to the newlyweds. Siew Fen's maids-in-waiting helped her to gather all the Lai-See.

---

[10] Kowtow 叩頭 at the tea ceremony at wedding was an act to kneel and touch the forehead to the ground in expression of deep respect, and submission to one's elders.
[11] Lai-See 利是 money in red pocket to give good luck blessings and prosperity at happy occasions like wedding, birthday and new years.

It was long into the night before Siew Fen and Tin Lun retired to their quarters that had been newly decorated with red and gold drapes. The red and gold word of "Double Happiness (囍)" hung from every pole and window. Red lanterns and red candles burned brightly, leading the way through the corridors and the court yards all the way to the newlyweds' living quarters. The suite was decorated lavishly with Ming pottery, Tong screen painting, and watercolour paintings by well-known artists.

It was the first time the newlyweds set eyes on each other on their wedding day. Siew Fen was quietly happy with Tin Lun who stood six foot tall and was good looking. She recognised the Shun-Chee furniture inlaid with mother-of-pearl and other precious stones that were installed in her rooms. She found some of her camphor chests in her quarters. She was comforted to have all her servants around her to give her the help and support that she was accustomed to.

Siew Fen found her surroundings acceptable. Marriage was not so bad after all, Siew Fen thought.

Siew Fen and Tin Lun lived in a spacious modern family home within the Kwan's estate. They had their private study area, dressing rooms, and sleeping quarters upstairs while several lounge rooms, a games room, and greeting rooms were located downstairs with an annex to their servant's quarters.

In the Kwan household, Madam Kwan controlled all the family affairs. Siew Fen was used to helping her mother with the finances of the family property portfolio. However Madam Kwan would not let Siew Fen or any of the concubines help with the family's finances. There was very little that Siew Fen could do around the house. She was not keen on embroidery and knew nothing about floral art or other lady's leisure pursuits. She spent her time writing poetry and using a big brush to write calligraphy.

Siew Fen produced two sons in three years. That pleased Madam Kwan and Master Kwan very much. It was a pleasant change to have the sound of babies around the usually quiet household. The eldest son was called Wing Yu. Unfortunately the second son died soon after Siew Fen's third child, a girl named Mee See, was born. Madam Kwan called Mee See a 'sweet mandarin' because the Kwan family lost an orange but gained a mandarin to replace it. It was Madam Kwan's practical analogy of the sad reality - losing a son but gaining a daughter. Mee See was followed by a third son named Wing Chung and a second daughter named Mee Jing.

All the children were born in a well renowned private hospital in Canton. They were delivered by the most eminent obstetrician at the time. The supreme wife from a wealthy family did not breast feed nor attend to the daily needs of her own babies. Each child was taken care of specifically by their own Sup-Ma (濕媽)[12] and a Kon-Ma (乾媽)[13].

A Sup-Ma was a nursing mother brought in with her own baby to live in the household. The nursing mother was well fed and well rested so she could produce the best quality milk for the young miss or master. Her only duty was to produce the milk to feed the Kwan offspring under her care. She would feed the little Kwan baby before she could feed her own child. She would stay in the family until the Kwan baby was weaned.

A Kon-Ma was a maid brought in to do all the chores for each new baby. She would be on hand at all hours to look after the baby's every need until such time when she was discharged. Some Kon-Mas stayed with their charges until the children grew up and married. The Kon-Ma would bring the Kwan baby to visit the grandparents and parents after the baby was well fed, well rested, changed, and contented. The Kon-Ma was always nearby just in case the baby needed nursing and comforting while spending time with their parents or grandparents. As the supreme wife in the Kwan's household, Siew Fen did not need to care for any of her children's physical needs. She would nurse and play with the babies

---

[12] Sup-Ma 濕媽 a nursing mother brought in to breast feed the new born in a wealthy family.
[13] Kon-Ma 乾媽 a maid employed to care for the new born in a wealthy family.

when the Kon-Ma brought them to visit her during the day.

As the children grew older, Siew Fen felt she had lost control of the upbringing of her children. Being the first grandson and heir of the Kwan family, Madam Kwan spoiled Wing Yu the same way she did Tin Lun. Wing Yu was allowed to have whatever he desired. At five years old, Wing Yu's Kon-Ma would still dress him in bed every day. She would chase him around the dining room to spoon-feed him.

Siew Fen protested to Madam Kwan but was told, "Wing Yu is the future of the Kwan family. He deserves to have special treatment from the rest of his siblings."

At last, Siew Fen took it upon herself to care for her children and sent away three of the four Kon-Ma, discharging them quietly. She took up the duty to discipline the children. Wing Yu was shocked when Siew Fen picked up a stick and hit him hard for being disobedient. Wing Yu was so surprised that he actually for once, stopped screaming and started to behave himself. It was too late for Madam Kwan to do anything when she found that Siew Fen had discharged her children's maids.

Madam Kwan was not happy with her daughter-in-law who disobeyed her supreme orders. Very few people dared contradict Madam Kwan. However, this daughter-in-law would argue with Madam Kwan using a list of reasons from a different point of view. Siew Fen wanted to bring up all the Kwan children according to the principles she learnt from Master Hui, her father. She wanted to bring up her children with good virtues.

It was surprising that the children behaved better under Siew Fen's teaching. They stopped fighting and yelling when they were with adults. Madam Kwan, whilst unhappy with the daughter-in-law, did not have any reason to find fault in Siew Fen's new approach with the discipline of her children. Even Wing Yu was well mannered when greeting his grandfather and father. He respected all his grandmothers. When Wing Yu turned five, Siew Fen engaged a scholar to come into the Kwan family home to teach all the children reading and writing. Even though the other children were not old enough, Siew Fen made all the children sit around and listen quietly at one side. Each child's maid would sit with them to make sure they would not disturb the teacher.

Shortly after Siew Fen and Tin Lun had their third child, Tin Lun wanted to return to the free and leisurely life of his bachelor days. Once again, he joined his wealthy friends and lived his pre-marital lifestyle. He would come home at all hours half-drunk and threw up wherever he happened to be. Servants would follow him to clean up the mess. He had little time for the children because he had lost interest in them. Siew Fen found Tin Lun's behaviour unacceptable. Comparing Tin Lun with her loving father, she was not happy with him as a father or as a husband. She was disappointed with what this marriage had to offer. From a young age, Siew Fen believed that one should fight for justice and speak out when things were wrong. She decided to bring up the subject with Tin Lun when he came home one night.

She waited and waited until long after midnight. As Tin Lun waddled up the stairs onto the landing, Siew Fen could hardly contain herself any longer. She held her temper using the most even tone of voice to ask Tin Lun, "Where have you been till this late at night? Madam Kwan and the children were waiting for you to have dinner together to celebrate Wing Yu's fourth birthday."

Inebriated, Tin Lun gave a heavy, smelly hiccup and sneered at Siew Fen with displeasure. He turned around and walked into his room. Siew Fen could not contain her anger any longer. She ran to grab his Cheongsam robe to turn him around to face her. She raised a fist and, wham, hit him on his chest as she was not tall enough to hit his face. Tin Lun was surprised at being struck. He turned around and yelled out some obscenity. He walked into his bedroom, threw himself on the bed and went to sleep, leaving Siew Fen standing at the doorway fuming.

Siew Fen went to the Hui family home to discuss with her parents what she could do to change the situation. She told her father about how unfair her husband had been to her and the children. She implored her father to judge the situation and pleaded for his intervention, begging him to come over to the Kwan home to talk to Tin Lun. She was hoping that her father's intervention might remind Tin Lun that he was expected to be the head of the Kwan household one day. She wanted him to give up his irresponsible lifestyle to prepare for the charge as head of the family. Master Hui came over to talk to Tin Lun giving reasons why he should change his behaviour. In order to get rid of the father-in-law, Tin Lun agreed to change his behaviour. He agreed with everything that Master Hui suggested. He thought it was good riddance as he walked the father-in-law out of the main gate, feigning respect.

Since that night, there were verbal arguments whenever Siew Fen and Tin Lun met. Then, it was fist fighting each time there was an argument. Siew Fen would call her footman, "Go fetch Master Hui here to reason this." Each time Master Hui turned up, he delivered another lecture about good behaviour, one more lesson on responsibility, and another talk on setting a good example to the children.

Tin Lun had heard them all before; he was not interested. He was not about to listen to advice and reform his behaviour. As soon as Siew Fen called out for the footman to fetch Master Hui, Tin Lun quickly slipped out of the Kwan estate from the rear exit. He found refuge at Chang's brothel and stayed there for days at a time. Then it was for months at a time. It was rumored that he sold a street of properties to spend on the most famous escort at the Chang's brothel.

Displeased with Siew Fen for bringing her father to lecture Tin Lun, Madam Kwan said sarcastically to Siew Fen, "It is the right of the master of the house to entertain his business partner. A good obedient wife should support her husband instead of causing arguments in the household."

Tin Lun decided to bring the top two prostitutes home as concubines to live in the Kwan estate in a separate mud brick cottage called Cloud Pagoda. He had workmen repaint Cloud Pagoda and hang new red lanterns with rich red and gold colour drapes everywhere. One night he quietly brought home the two girls from Chang's brothel, and had every intention of installing them publicly as second wife, Yei Yee Tai (二姨太) and as third wife, Sam Yee Tai (三姨太). He moved over to Cloud Pagoda to live with the girls. He even used Siew Fen's personal maids to take care of the two Yee Tai Tai[14](姨太太).

Siew Fen was furious that Tin Lun had brought home two prostitutes without her permission. She took it up with Madam Kwan and said, "Dai Ma, Tin Lun has brought two prostitutes from Chang's brothel in the middle of the night and installed them as Yei Tai Tai. The Kwan family will lose face if people hear we allow such lowly women to be installed as concubines in our household."

Madam Kwan defended Tin Lun. She pointed out to Siew Fen the duty of a wife and said, "Which husband does not have more than one wife? It is the right of a husband to have several wives. A dutiful wife should bare many sons. She should be obedient and respectful of her husband. She should help her husband to install a number of Yee Tai Tai. A dutiful wife would do anything to keep a harmonious household. "

Madam Kwan was using this opportunity to lecture Siew Fen and to reflect on her disobedient and uncooperative approach. In fact, Madam Kwan was happy to have Tin Lun move back home again. He didn't need to hide at Chang's brothel anymore. She was overjoyed to see her son home for dinner each night. As the prostitutes were not properly installed as wives, Madam Kwan did not need to acknowledge their presence. She didn't demand their attendance at the dinner table, as long as they stayed in their own quarters.

However, in Siew Fen's upbringing, the supreme wife was the one who should install all the concubines for her husband. Prostitutes from

---

[14] Yee Tai Tai 姨太太 referred to two concubines, second and subsequent wives in a wealthy household.

Chang's brothel were too lowly to be elevated to be the Kwan family's concubines. These girls entered the Kwan house in the middle of the night. They had no manners, paid no respect to Siew Fen, and did not know how to behave in a well-disciplined household.

Siew Fen retaliated, "Dai Ma, I can't agree with you on this matter. I have born two healthy and strong sons for the Kwan family. I have done more than my fair share as a dutiful wife. Some supreme wives can't even produce an egg for the Kwan family in their life time! They only adopt another wife's' son to call their own."

Madam Kwan sensed Siew Fen's insinuation and cursed Siew Fen under her breath. However, she did not want to continue this conversation, she remained silent to sheath Siew Fen's razor sharp tongue in case she brought up more unsavoury truths that she was trying to hide from the family. Siew Fen could see that she was winning the verbal crossfire and continued, "According to the Kwan family's standing in society, Tin Lun should have many concubines. But they should be ladies from a family of good reputation. These two slugs from the brothels have no manners and no style. They are lowly by birth. They should never be part of the Kwan family." Siew Fen affirmed to Madam Kwan, "As long as I am supreme wife of the Kwan family, I will never allow them in."

Madam Kwan hated this daughter-in-law who would never give an inch. Siew Fen had a long memory. Her words were sharp and to the point and she would never forgive or forget. The worst fact was Siew Fen meant everything she said. Madam Kwan wished that she had never brought Siew Fen in and installed her as her son's supreme wife. She could not get rid of Siew Fen because she bore two sons to carry the Kwan family name. Siew Fen never dishonoured the family name. Madam Kwan could not find a reason to disown Siew Fen. She simply wished she could wave a magic wand to make this daughter-in-law disappear.

Unfortunately, Tin Lun succumbed to the three vices common to Chinese men at that time; opium, gambling, and brothels. He reckoned the family was so wealthy that Siew Fen could have all the comforts and honour being the supreme wife. He could not understand why his wife should stop him from enjoying life, as the son and heir of this wealthy family. He thought Siew Fen was most unreasonable.

The more Siew Fen thought about the situation, the more she was incensed with Tin Lun and Madam Kwan. She felt that she had to take matters into her own hands to make things right. According to her, it was a gross injustice that Tin Lun brought in prostitutes without asking her permission. What was more, the prostitutes never took notice of Siew Fen as the supreme wife and yet they stayed in her household and used her personal maids.

Her opportunity came one day when Tin Lun was away with his group of friends gambling on horse races and lounging in opium dens. Siew Fen took the sharpest pair of tailor's scissors. She arrived at Cloud Pagoda while both Yei Yee Tai and Sam Yee Tai were arranging flowers in the garden pagoda beyond the fish pond on the other side of the huge garden. Siew Fen walked into their bed chamber. She opened their camphor chest and found their beautiful robes. There were Qipao made of silk, embroidered with beads and pearls in beautiful colours. Siew Fen sailed through those dresses with her sharp scissors. She tore them to pieces and threw them on the floor. Beads and pearls dropped from broken thread and rolled all over the floor. There were green Qipao, red Qipao, pinks silk robes, blue silk pajamas and silver silk gowns. She kept cutting and tearing as her temper rose higher and her anger grew hotter. She was venting her long held anger and frustration through her scissors.

This commotion disturbed some of the maids in the quarters. They ran to fetch the two Yee Tai Tais, who turned up and saw their beautiful Qipao and silk gowns all cut, torn and scattered around the floor as Siew Fen continued with lightning speed to destroy the rest of their beautiful gowns.

Siew Fen stood up, looked straight into the eyes of Yei Yee Tai and Sam Yee Tai and told them, "As the supreme wife of the Kwan household, you have no place in my estate. Who installed you to be the Kwan family's Yee Tai Tais without my authority? How dare you, enter into the Kwan family without my permission!?"

As she walked across the room, she yelled at the maid Sai-Mui to summon Luk-Por and Ah-Din. Sai-Mui, Luk-Por and Ah-Din were the Hui family's most faithful servants, who followed Siew Fen when she married into the Kwan family. The servants came running at Siew Fen's summons with their heads bowed to show respect to the supreme wife, waiting for instructions.

Siew Fen did not even look at the Yee Tai Tais and told Ah-Din, "Take these street girls out of the Kwan estate back to Chang's brothel where they belong. Sai-Mui, Luk-Por I want this place tidied up; get rid of everything that does not belong to the Kwan family."

As Siew Fen talked, she walked out of the Cloud Pagoda, leaving the Yee Tai Tais crying over their loss. Ah-Din used a double sedan chair with two footmen to escort the Yee Tai Tais back to Chang's brothel.

With her head held upright, Siew Fen walked across the garden, over the red wooden footbridge between the two fish ponds. She took a deep breath and knew she had at last exerted her rightful authority as the supreme wife of the Kwan family.

As expected, Tin Lun returned home half-drunk after a good day gambling on horse racing. The whole group of friends finished with a double session at a famous opium den. He walked into Cloud Pagoda and found the entire place cleaned up. There was no trace of Yei Yee Tai and Sam Yee Tai. Tin Lun summoned the servants charged with serving the Cloud Pagoda; they revealed that it was Siew Fen who sent them back to Chang's brothel.

Tin Lun rushed to Siew Fen's quarters in anger. He yelled out as he was rushing up the stairs, "You have no right to send my concubines away. I will bring them back in the morning."

Siew Fen retaliated, "You are talking about rights! I am the Kwan family's supreme wife and this is my domain, my household. You brought in lowly girls from the brothel right under my nose and expected to install them as Kwan's concubines without my permission. Are you talking about rights? "

Siew Fen had been quiet and obedient for so long. That afternoon she found an inner strength that she forgot she ever had. This incident reminded her of when she was a teenager and dressed as a boy who upheld justice. This time she could no longer contain her anger. She was brought up to fight for justice. Whatever was wrong, she ought to speak out and make it right.

Tin Lun yelled back, "I want them here, and they will be my supreme wives and you …. you… you can go home to your parents and from now on you are discharged to your family."

Before he finished speaking, Siew Fen punched his face as he was rushing up the stairs. She missed and hit his nose. Tin Lun's nose bled profusely. He rushed over and the two got into a tangle as they fist fought until Tin Lun saw his blood all over his sleeve. He was still bleeding as Siew Fen rushed in and found a knife to protect herself. Tin Lun saw her lashing out with a knife in her hand; her eyes were sharp and her face was filled with determination. He turned around and jumped down the stairs two steps at a time. Tin Lun was used to running out of the Kwan estate via the rear exit. Tin Lun ran off to Chang's brothel and hid there for days. He came home to see Madam Kwan only to get more allowance to sustain his living away from home.

Madam Kwan was broken-hearted that Tin Lun returned to Chang's brothel and stayed away from his home. She blamed the daughter-in-law for causing the family break up.

Although Madam Kwan disliked Siew Fen, the other mothers-in-law found Siew Fen well-mannered and respectful. Being nearly the same age, Siew Fen was friendly with her second mother-in-law Yee Ma. Yee

Ma's adopted daughter Luk KuChar was a similar age as Siew Fen's elder daughter Mee See. The two girls played well together and Yee Ma and Siew Fen had a lot of common interests. Sai Ma was only fifteen when she married into the Kwan household as Master Kwan's fourth wife. Siew Fen paid Sai Ma due respect as her mother-in-law even though Sai Ma was much younger than herself. Siew Fen continued to join Madam Kwan for dinner and to pay respect to all the mothers-in-law.

Siew Fen was left at home with her children, servants, and footmen. She knew then, there was nothing she could do to rescue the marriage. She gave up trying to please Tin Lun and make him return home to be a responsible husband and a caring father. She focused on bringing up the Kwan children and provided them with the upbringing that was befitting their position. As Tin Lun could not be a good provider without his father's financial backing, Siew Fen knew that she had to stay at the Kwan family to fund the cost of living and education for her children.

Siew Fen was now twenty-four years old.

The moon shone onto the peaceful fish pond, as a few dark clouds gently drifted across the sky to block the moonlight. There was not a ripple on the pond. Siew Fen was leaning against the pagoda as she looked out into the still of the night. She reflected on the recent events. She knew that Madam Kwan disliked her and Tin Lun could not stand the sight of her. Her future only relied on the fact that she had bore two boys who would carry on the Kwan name. Siew Fen suddenly felt insecure. Tears rolled down her cheeks like pearls from a broken string. Without a reliable husband whom she could lean on, her children were vulnerable and her future was uncertain. She felt helpless and hopeless. She wished she hadn't married into the Kwan family. She was considering what she could do to secure her future. How was she going to spend the rest of her life in this loveless situation? What would tomorrow bring?

The Yellow Knot Curse

Chinese Lunar New Year was the most important time of the year. It was referred to as the Spring Festival[15] (春節). The Kwan household held many of the festivities over the entire month prior to and after New Year's Day. Madam Kwan provided the property managers and heads of servants in the household with extra money to buy presents, decorations and all of the food for the festival.

With the New Year approaching, it was the custom to sweep away any ill-fortune and to make way for the incoming luck and fortune. A team of butlers, maids, servants, footmen, chefs, cooks, and gardeners spent the whole month prior to the New Year scrubbing, cleaning, and wiping every cottage and quarter in the estate. The gardeners were busy trimming winter plums and cherry blossoms to make sure they bloomed at the precise time when all the visitors would come to pay respect to Master Kwan and to admire the Kwan's well-known winter blooms. Even the two fish ponds received special attention to make sure the well-fed gold fish were alert, plump and healthy.

No expense was spared to prepare the Kwan estate for this important festive season. Everywhere in the Kwan household was decorated in red and gold, the colours of good fortune. Decorations like paper-cuts and wall-hangings in gold and red with the words 'good fortune (福)', 'prosperity (祿)' and 'longevity (壽)' were hung on every possible beam, window or doorway. They swayed and danced as they blew in the wind, blessing each passer-by with the popular theme word.

On the eve of Chinese New Year, a feast called Tun-Lean-Fan [16] (團年飯) was held, which was the most important dinner in the year for all living

---

[15] Spring Festival 春節 it usually lasted over the month prior to and after the Lunar New Year Day.
[16] Tun-Lean-Fan 團年飯 a cultural practice at New Year's Eve when the whole family got together to partake in a dinner.

in the Kwan family estate. The chefs used the best ingredients for this special feast. They supervised the team of cooks to excel themselves with all sorts of delicacies prepared especially for the festival. There were suckling pigs, geese, chicken, pork, fish, sea cucumber, abalone, and several special vegetable dishes. There were also typical New Year sweet delicacies. All family members joined in this special Tun-Lean-Fan dinner at Master and Madam Kwan's quarters. Seating was arranged in accordance to a person's rank in the Kwan family hierarchy. Maids surrounded their masters and mistresses to wait on them diligently.

The family started the afternoon with the ritual of paying respect to Kwan's ancestors in the family shrine. Each family member took turns to kowtow and burn incense to give thanks for the blessings they received during the year. The family ended the night with lighting colourful lanterns, fireworks, and firecrackers in their huge garden and court yards.

The end of the year was also the time for the Kwan masters to show their appreciation to the servants for their effort during the year. Madam Kwan gave each servant a sizeable Lai-See, to reward their good efforts throughout the year. Usually this Lai-See was worth the entire month's wage as a reward for jobs well done during the year. Each household mistress also gave extra Lai-See to the servants serving their quarters. With all the extra Lai-See being handed out from different mistresses, New Year was a prosperous time for all of the servants.

Outside the Kwan estate, beggars, unemployed people, and street kids surrounded the Iron Gate, carrying a picture of the 'God of Wealth (財神)' shouting "Choi-Sun-dao (財神到)!" meaning "The God of Wealth had arrived!" The Kwan family's footmen were instructed to hand out Lai-See to receive the picture of the 'God of Wealth (財神)' to bolster the wealth of the Kwan family fortune.

It was important for everyone to have a brand new outfit to wear on New Year's Day. At midnight of New Year's Eve, servants put out a new outfit, new socks, and new shoes on top of a camphor chest ready for each master and mistress to wear at daybreak.

Early in the morning on New Year's Day, maids helped the children dress in their brand new outfits. They each greeted Siew Fen by wishing her "Kon Ha Fat Choi (恭喜發財)[17]", meaning: "Wishing you lots of prosperity." Siew Fen gave each child a Lai-See but forbade them from opening their red pockets in front of her. In the Chinese custom, it was considered rude to open presents immediately in front of the person who gave the gift. Children were told to bow their heads to express gratitude on receiving the gifts and to wait until they got back to their quarters before they could open their Lai-See. They could express thanks again for the gift the next time they met.

The Chinese New Year tradition was an opportunity to reconcile, to forget all grudges, and to sincerely wish for peace and happiness for everyone. Most importantly, the first day of the Chinese New Year was a time to honour one's elders. Families would visit the eldest and most senior family members in hierarchical order.

Much fanfare was made of the tea ceremony where Master and Madam Kwan led the concubines to accept all well wishes and drink the tea offered from the junior Kwan members. Siew Fen and her four children took their place following Tin Lun. She accompanied each of her children and taught them to kowtow to their grandparents starting with Master Kwan, Madam Kwan, Yee Ma, Sam Ma and Sai Ma. Siew Fen's favourite maid, prepared cups of tea with a dried red plum in each cup. Tea was offered to each elder as the children spelled out their good wishes. On acceptance of the cup of tea, each elder gave a Lai-See in return.

Madam Kwan gave Siew Fen a nice big Lai-See which Siew Fen put away into her inner pocket. All the children were well behaved and received lots of Lai-See on New Year's Day. Siew Fen's four children were brought

---

[17] Kon Ha Fat Choi 恭喜發財 A saying that is used during new year wishing everyone prosperity throughout the year.

up in this tradition. Mee See was most keen to follow her mother and observed every detail.

The Kwan family also invited a team of musicians and a lion dance troupe as a symbolic ritual to evict bad spirits from the premises and to usher in good fortune and prosperity for the New Year. Wing Yu and Wing Chung lit firecrackers while Mee See and Mee Jing watched on with hands over their ears to block the explosive sounds. Within the walls of the Kwan estate, festivities were held in the middle of the huge central garden. There was music, gongs, trumpets, arias from famous Chinese operas, lion dancing, and firecrackers all mixed up with lots of laughter and noise to usher in the beginning of another prosperous year.

Ever since the incident when Siew Fen sent away Yei Yee Tai and Sam Yee Tai back to the Chang's brothel, Tin Lun continued to stay at Cloud Pagoda whenever he was home. Tin Lun went back to his quarters after paying respect to his parents. Later he went back to the Chang's brothel to stay.

The New Year celebrations were tiring. Siew Fen and her children retired to her quarters. The children surrounded Siew Fen as they opened their red pockets, comparing the money they received. They were going to buy some marbles and a kite when shops opened after the New Year. As Mee Jing was still a toddler, Siew Fen put all her Lai-See money into Mee Jing's camphor chest for when she grew up.

Siew Fen opened the red pocket that Madam Kwan gave her that morning. She could feel through the red pocket that it was rather thick with a hard centre. Siew Fen shook the object out expecting a thick pile of Tai-Yuan dollar bills. To her surprise, she found a brand new yellow string, twisted and tied tightly like a coin in the middle with strings dangling from opposite ends.

Mee See picked it up and said, "Ah-Tai[18] what is this little string?"

Siew Fen was bewildered and said, "It must be a mistake. Your Dai Ma must have put this in the red pocket by mistake. It should be several Tai-Yuan bills of lucky money as in previous years. Let me go and ask Yee Ma what to do with this string."

Yee Ma had always been friendly with Siew Fen and she also knew that Madam Kwan was not happy with Siew Fen. She held the yellow string in her hand and said, "This is a strange thing to find in a Lai-See! It must be a mistake. But we better find out for sure before you question Madam Kwan. I know an old fortune teller at the temple who may have seen this sort of string."

On the second day of the New Year, Yee Ma and Siew Fen took the sedan chair to the temple so they could burn incense and candles to make wishes for the New Year. They also went to the temple to seek help from Yee Ma's family friend who was a fortuneteller. Accompanying them were Siew Fen's maid Luk-Por, butler Ah-Din and two footmen. As many people went to the temple to worship and burn incense to their Guanyin [19](觀音) Buddha during this festive season, the temple was filled with smoke and was full of people worshipping.

The old lady fortuneteller had wrinkles all over her face; she looked as though she had many years of experience in different matters. With her scrawny and wrinkly hands, she picked up the yellow string, turned it round and examined the knots that were tied tightly all around a metal ring.

She stopped and said, "Pray, who did you offend young Madam Kwan? You have been given a death curse. This is a death knot. This knot will strangle your neck and you will be dead in seven days."

---

[18]Ah-Tai 亞大 The Kwan family called their mother who was the supreme wife of the family as Ah-Tai.
[19] Guanyin 觀音 Buddha goddess known as the Goddess of Mercy.

Siew Fen was shocked and speechless. She did not know how to respond. She thought of her four young children, what would become of them if she passed away so young? Tears streamed down her face as she wept uncontrollably.

Yee Ma eagerly asked, "What can we do to break this curse? Our young Madam of the Kwan family from Chin Wah Lane is so young. She has four children and two of them are sons and heirs of the Kwan family. She is so young and inexperienced. She might have offended somebody without even knowing."

Yee Ma looked at Siew Fen's teary face and continued, "Please have mercy on our young Madam Kwan.... please, can you help her to break this curse and save her from this ill fate? The Kwan family will be forever grateful."

The old lady frowned and turned around looking at the tearful Siew Fen and said, "This is a death knot, a very strong curse from a very powerful master. There is no way I have the power to reverse this curse."

The old lady further examined the yellow strings. She was deep in thought, then slowly she added, "There may be one way...The only thing you can do, young Madam Kwan, is to acknowledge you know about the curse but you will not accept this curse, do this by returning the object in the same Lai-See that it came in. You must give it back to the hands of the person who gave you this Lai-See. As soon as you have done that, you must leave immediately and go back to the safety of your quarters. There you will stay for seven days and seven nights quietly. With some luck, this curse may pass you by."

Yee Ma and Siew Fen both bowed deeply to thank the old fortuneteller. They left her a sizeable Lai-See with a number of ten Tai-Yuan dollars in it for advising the young Madam Kwan.

As soon as Siew Fen got home, accompanied by Luk-Por, she went straight to Madam Kwan's quarters to pay her mother-in-law respect. Madam Kwan thought Siew Fen was very respectful to greet her again on the second day of New Year. She ordered her servant to serve Siew Fen tea at the round table in her tea room.

Siew Fen took the same Lai-See with the yellow string knots and returned it to Madam's hand. To hide her fright, she smiled nervously and said, "Madam Kwan, this is not meant for me. You have given this to the wrong person. I now return it back to you." As soon as she said those words, she turned around and walked out of Madam Kwan's quarters with Luk-Por. They both walked swiftly, without running, over the threshold into the courtyard, through the garden back towards Siew Fen's own quarters.

Madam Kwan was surprised to receive in her hand the Lai-See she gave to Siew Fen. She called out, "Dai-So (大嫂)[20], come back! It is the festive season. Stay, Dai-So, and have tea and some Lin-Ko (年糕 New Year's cake) with me."

Siew Fen didn't dare turn her head and kept walking with Luk-Por. Once out of the garden, they both rushed home and closed the gate. Once inside her quarters, they shut the door and bolted the entrance and closed the shutters. Siew Fen and Luk-Por both breathed heavily, Siew Fen took a breath of fresh air and tried to still her shaking body. There Siew Fen stayed quietly and nervously over the next seven days and nights. Luk-Por organised all her meals to be brought into Siew Fen's inner quarters. Even the children were brought to see their mother during the day.

After seven days, unexpectedly, Madam Kwan collapsed on the floor. She never woke again. It was so sudden, the whole family were grief-stricken. Siew Fen, Yee Ma and Luk-Por all knew what had transpired but they did not tell anybody. No one knew about the incident of the yellow magical knot for a long time.

Madam Kwan was buried with full ceremony befitting her supreme

---

20 Dai-So 大嫂 a respectful way to address the eldest daughter-in-law.

position in the Kwan family. Each member of the family dressed in mourning attire that was according to the rank in the family hierarchy. They each paid respect to honour the loss of their supreme Madam Kwan. Master Kwan had a master of ceremony organise the funeral with all the lavish trimmings to make sure Madam Kwan had a smooth journey to the other world.

Madam Kwan's passing was most unexpected. It put the whole family into a crisis. She had such a tight control over everything in the house that nobody, not even Yee Ma and Sai Ma knew how she managed the Kwan family affairs. Since his retirement, Master Kwan completely relied on Madam Kwan to control every detail of the household. He had to find someone reliable and capable to take up this important task. He demanded to see Tin Lun and discovered that he spent most days at the Chang's brothel. Master Kwan summoned Tin Lun and Siew Fen to his quarters. Siew Fen hurriedly sent Ah-Din to fetch Tin Lun home from Chang's brothel.

Master Kwan said to the couple, "I need you, Tin Lun, to look after the family finances and I need Siew Fen to take charge of the Kwan family household."

All his life, Tin Lun only knew comfort and leisure. He had no clue where his allowance came from, let alone how the family finances were handled. Madam Kwan had such tight control on everything that nobody in the house knew anything except for the fact that she kept a ledger, and the property manager helped to collect rent from the properties in Canton and rent or products from the villagers at Xiqiao.

Tin Lun protested, "I have no idea how or what to do! This task is too hard for me to manage."

Master Kwan was aware that Tin Lun had done nothing with his life except pursue leisure. He regretted that Madam Kwan had not prepared him to take over the running of the family.

Siew Fen calmly said to her father-in-law, "Lau Yau (老爺), I am honoured to be trusted to take charge of the Kwan family matters. I will do my very best."

Siew Fen continued, "At home, I was given the task to help Madam Hui look after the family's property portfolio. I am also aware Madam Kwan kept a ledger, and the property manager has been collecting rent and recording details in a register. I might be able to work out how Madam Kwan controlled the family finances using the family ledger and the rental register. Perhaps Tin Lun and I can manage the family's finances together."

Master Kwan thought Siew Fen was the most suitable person to take up this duty. As she had learned from Madam Hui how to manage a household of similar wealth and prestige, she would know more about managing than Tin Lun. Master Kwan was happy to hand over Madam Kwan's family ledger and the rental register to Siew Fen, who after all, was the supreme wife of his son and heir.

Tin Lun was most relieved that he did not have the responsibility of running the Kwan family. As long as he continued to have his allowance and he was free to continue his lifestyle, he was happy to let Siew Fen pick up this duty. He could also blame her if anything went wrong.

Siew Fen was elevated to be the new Madam Kwan and accepted the Kwan's family ledger and the rental register. Now she had the authority and the responsibility for running the Kwan family affairs. Siew Fen studied Madam Kwan's ledger in detail. She also consulted with the property manager to find his role in the compilation of the rental register. With the background details at hand, she set out to do a fact-finding trip with the property manager. Two footmen carried her sedan chair and her servants Luk-Por and Ah-Din accompanied her. It was her intention to examine the Kwan property portfolio in Canton, she renegotiated rental levels with all of the tenants. The party also went to Xiqiao village to meet all the tenants and the villagers. Siew Fen brought her four children, Luk-Por, Ah-Din, her favourite cooks and maids, and the children's Sup-Ma and Kon-Ma to serve her while she was in the village. They stayed at the summer residence in Xiqiao.

Siew Fen was fair and exact with all of the tenants. When they experienced hardship, she was compassionate and gave them assistance. Soon the young Madam Kwan won the admiration of all the people she dealt with, both in the city of Canton as well as in the village of Xiqiao. They all admitted the young Madam Kwan was not only efficient but she was also fair and understanding in her dealings with everyone. The property manager continued his task of updating the rental register with the new rental rates. He continued to work as the rent collector under Siew Fen's direction.

Siew Fen recorded in the ledger all the allowances that she gave to each family member as well as the extra allowance that Tin Lun demanded at various times. She also catalogued the wages she gave to each servant within the entire Kwan estate. After she updated the status of the ledger and the rental register, she reported to her father-in-law. All her recorded items were clear and concise.

Master Kwan was surprised and delighted with Siew Fen's ability to manage the Kwan family finances. He was comforted that this daughter-in-law was intelligent and reliable, and he was glad that he had picked the right person to oversee the family matters. Secretly Master Kwan was aware that he should not have suggested giving Tin Lun this task. He was happy to return to his peaceful life of retirement. Tin Lun was happy that he did not have to do anything on the home front. He continued to enjoy the generous allowance and returned to his leisurely life away from home with his Yee Tai Tais.

Siew Fen found her niche in managing the Kwan household. For the first time since her marriage into the Kwan's household, Siew Fen felt that there was a purpose in her life.

Seven-Year Court Case

Within a couple of years of Madam Kwan's passing, Master Kwan also passed away, he was forty-six years old. Tin Lun became the head of the Kwan family because he was the eldest son from the supreme wife. In the Kwan family tradition, only sons had the right to a share of the family fortune. Girls born to the family were meant to be married off and they would take on the surname of the family into which they married. Therefore girls were never considered to have a share of the family inheritance. However, until the girls were married, they continued to enjoy the upbringing befitting girls of the wealthy Kwan household.

When Master Kwan passed away he left behind his first son and heir Tin Lun and his supreme wife Siew Fen and their four children, Wing Yu, Mee See, Wing Chung and Mee Jing. There was Master Kwan's widow concubine second wife Yee Ma, who was in her late twenties and their eight-year-old daughter Luk KuChar. And Master Kwan's other widow concubine, fourth wife Sai Ma, who, was in her early twenties. She was pregnant at the time and soon bore a boy, Ng Sook, who was the second son and heir to the Kwan family. The young widows and their children were Tin Lun's stepmothers and siblings. As they had no other means of living, they were dependant on the Kwan family. Siew Fen and Tin Lun's four young children also needed to be provided for as the Kwan direct descendants.

Tin Lun and Siew Fen had come to the point of their marriage where they seldom talked except for matters relating to the family or if Tin Lun wanted extra allowance for his extravagant lifestyle outside of the Kwan estate. The Kwan immediate family was not a big family; there was plenty of wealth in the family to keep one and all in comfort for their lifetime.

Soon after Master Kwan's funeral Tin Lun demanded, "Now that I am the Master of the Kwan household, I want to take over the running of the family finances. I want the family ledger and the rental register today."

Siew Fen said calmly and quietly, "What plans do you have for your two step mothers, your brother and sister, our four children and me?"

Tin Lun had not considered these issues. He simply wanted the freedom to use the Kwan wealth at will, so he would not need to let Siew Fen know what he was doing with his father's estate. Tin Lun forgot that he now had a younger brother. This baby brother, by the family tradition, deserved half of the family's fortune. There was also Wing Yu and Wing Chung, who were entitled to a share of the estate because they were sons in the direct bloodline. Tin Lun reckoned that being the heir of the family, he should keep everything. It would be out of his mercy if he was to share this vast wealth that he inherited with anyone at all. He had been waiting for a long time to settle the score with Siew Fen for sending away his beloved Yee Tai Tais from the estate.

Tin Lun hesitated, and then said, "Ng...ng ...Yee Ma and Sai Ma can continue to stay in their quarters. You and the four children can move into one of the larger cottages on the other side of the estate. I want to bring my Yei Yee Tai and Sam Yee Tai into these quarters because I need the space."

Tin Lun had underestimated Siew Fen's knowledge of the law of the land and family inheritance disputes. He had no idea of Siew Fen's strength, her willpower, and her determination to fight as long as she had the law on her side.

Siew Fen told Tin Lun, "According to the family tradition, your brother deserves the same inheritance as yours from the family estate. My two sons, being Kwan family direct descendants, also deserve a big part of the inheritance. Living within the Kwan estate will not be sufficient to take care of all the Kwan children. What provisions do you have for their future and education as they grow older?"

It had not occurred to Tin Lun that anybody else should have a share of his father's estate except himself. He demanded, "What brother are you talking about? He is only a baby. I am the heir of the family. I should take charge of my father's inheritance, not you, not anyone."

Siew Fen retaliated, "Lau Yai gave me the family ledger and the rental register to look after the family affairs. You also agreed as long as you could have the allowance whenever you have the need. You have had all the allowances you demanded. Now that Lau Yai has passed on, I will continue to manage the family matters until such time that the estate is divided."

Siew Fen stopped, took a deep breath, and continued quietly but firmly, "If you want to share out the family estate, we can do that legally, provided our widow mothers, your brother, your sister, my four children, and I are provided for with our fair share." There was no way Siew Fen would hand over the family ledger and the rental register. Tin Lun never took any interest in the family's wealth. He had no idea where the family had properties and what rental they were getting. He did not even know where their daily food came from. Siew Fen knew that Tin Lun would not take care of the family if he got the inheritance all to himself.

Tin Lun had already installed his Yei Yee Tai and Sam Yee Tai in one of the Kwan cottages outside the Kwan estate. Siew Fen would not allow them to set foot into the Kwan estate and warned Tin Lun she would repeat the same ugly scene if ever he tried to bring anyone home without her permission. For that, Tin Lun hated Siew Fen and wished he could vent his anger and throw her out of her quarters as revenge.

Tin Lun could not get any pleasure from Siew Fen, he was frustrated and left the Kwan estate to go home to his Yee Tai Tais infuriated.

Siew Fen went to consult her father on the rights of the descendants in case they were to get into a legal battle. Master Hui had many contacts in the courts throughout Canton and all the way to Peking. Siew Fen wanted to formulate a reasonable settlement so that all the members of the Kwan family had a share of the Kwan inheritance to ensure their future was secure.

Master Hui warned his daughter, "Your case is to maintain justice for the Kwan descendants. I agree with your idealism but you must be prepared for substantial fees. It will cost the Kwan family a lot of money to fight with each other in court publicly. I suggest trying mediation first using one of my associates. I must keep out of all proceedings, and advise you only when needed."

At the mediation, Siew Fen suggested a split of the family wealth in four ways; Yee Ma, Sai Ma, Tin Lun and Siew Fen each took one share. Tin Lun would not accept the idea of giving up anything to anyone. He offered to release Siew Fen and her children home to her parents. He promised to look after the stepmothers and his siblings. Tin Lun's suggested resolution was to keep the entire inheritance himself. He was determined to take revenge, and refused to give Siew Fen and her children anything to satisfy his hatred. They decided to fight it out in court. Tin Lun preferred to use the family's wealth that he believed should have been all his to fight Siew Fen, rather than to share it with her and his siblings.

For seven years, Tin Lun and Siew Fen fought in courts over the family's inheritance. Both camps spent a lot of money to employ teams of the best-known legal councils; hence the most expensive solicitors, to represent their case from the lowest level to the highest court in Canton City.

The educated Siew Fen begged her father to help her at each step of the way. To continue the fight, Siew Fen even sold some of her own jewellery to fund the lawsuit. She had to fight on because if she lost, all of Kwan's descendants would be in jeopardy. Their future would be very bleak if Tin Lun got the major share of the inheritance.

The judgement from the highest court in Canton was a fair and final settlement. The Kwan wealth was to be divided into six shares. Yee Ma and her daughter took one share, Sai Ma and her son took one share, Tin Lun took two shares and Siew Fen and her four children took two shares. It was a great relief to all parties to reach the final decision. As Master Kwan had selected Siew Fen as the financial controller, the court ordered Siew Fen as the executor of the Kwan estate.

It was such a public dispute that their lawsuit was well reported in the newspapers. People were interested to follow this family struggle and the spectacle of the bitter fighting between husband and wife. It was unheard of for a wife to fight her husband over a family inheritance and to share the estate with her mothers-in-law and her husband's siblings. Siew Fen was reported as a most courageous and remarkable lady. At such a tender age, Mee See observed how her mother conducted herself. She admired her mother, and she wanted to be like her.

During these seven years, the Kwan family had to sell a number of properties and Siew Fen sold a lot of jewellery to finance the legal battle. It was such a pity that they could not settle with mediation. Siew Fen maintained that it was worth all the money spent because the right decision was handed down by the court. She was happy there was still plenty of wealth from the inheritance to share around accordingly.

Yee Ma and Sai Ma were two defenceless widows with very young children. They knew that Tin Lun would have sent them back to their respective parents with the Kwan children. They would be left to fend for themselves and they would not have the means to support themselves and their children. The widows were very grateful that Siew Fen fought on their behalf. Siew Fen also knew that if she did not fight on, Tin Lun would also have sent her back to the Hui family with all of her children. Siew Fen would lose face in the Hui family if she was to be sent back by her husband to her parents' home. All the Kwan children should be brought up in the way that was befitting the Kwan's standing in society. Siew Fen was honoured by her mothers-in-law for getting an impartial resolution for them all.

Justice was served at long last in spite of the high cost!

Tin Lun was furious at the court order. However, he had no other way to appeal. He was not going to help in the settlement process. It was up to Siew Fen, the executor, to explore how she could share the family fortune in accordance with the court order.

Siew Fen had to liquidate some of the assets in order to divide the Kwan estate. It was decided that some of the established ancestral family homes were not for sale. Only those purchased by Master Kwan after his return to China were for sale. Siew Fen took the children with a number of servants to Kun Shan village at Xiqiao. At the time, Wing Yu was thirteen, Mee See was eleven, Wing Chung was ten, and Mee Jing was nine years old. The children looked on and played with their toys quietly as their mother conducted the meeting with the villagers. Mee See was most impressed with her mother's actions.

In recent years Siew Fen had visited Xiqiao Kun Shan village with her children many times to collect rent with her property manager. All the villagers knew that Madam Kwan was the Kwan family's financial controller. A few times when floods washed off some of the villagers' crops, Madam Kwan had allowed these tenants free rental. She even provided help to re-establish their seedlings for planting the next crop. She was well respected by the villagers.

Ah-Din set up a table, a chair, and a platform for Madam Kwan in front of the Kwan ancestral shrine by the Pearl River. Madam Kwan sat down calmly with the court order documents on one side of the table. The property manager with a register under his arm stood at attention next to Madam Kwan. All her children and their servants sat on wooden stools close by.

Ah-Din hit the gong to summon all the villagers to a meeting with her. They gathered by the family shrine in a circle surrounding Madam Kwan. Many villagers bowed to Madam Kwan as they drew closer. Groups of villagers were chattering with one another. Some villagers looked perplexed, wondering what it was all about. Madam Kwan slowly stood up, walked by the table, and waited until the villagers had stopped their conversations. They stood to hear what she had to say. Madam Kwan, who stood only five feet climbed onto the platform to have eye contact with the villagers. She stated that since Master Kwan's passing, it was time for the Kwan family to sell most of the properties, the fishery, and the fleet of fishing junks at Xiqiao. Shortly the villagers would be meeting their new landlords. She would attempt to put forward to the new owners the long-time rental arrangements that the villagers had with the Kwan family. However, she could not guarantee the rental arrangement would be the same. It was up to the villagers to negotiate with their new landlords. If any of the villagers would like to purchase the property they were renting, they should discuss this with Madam Kwan. She concluded by thanking all the villagers for being the best tenants any landowner could ever want.

At once there was commotion among the villagers. This came as a surprise, as Master Kwan had been their master and landlord for as long as they could remember. The uncertain future was a most unwelcome message for all the villagers. The villagers started talking all at once: some were pointing their fingers; others were shaking their heads; others were tightening their fists; yet others looked up at Madam Kwan still wondering what it all meant for this village.

One of the oldest village elders stepped forward and said, "According to the Kwan family tradition, only the master of the family has the authority to sell the properties. Women folk usually do not have the right to conduct such an important and complicated undertaking. Without being disrespectful, Madam Kwan, why don't we wait until Master Kwan's return to the village for us to hold this discussion?"

Siew Fen was sure that all the villagers were aware that for many years, she was the financial controller of the Kwan family. Master Tin Lun only came to the villages on odd occasions during summer seasons. Now Siew Fen had the court order from the highest court in Canton, it stated she was the executor of the estate. The villagers had no choice about the settlement process that she was instigating. However, Siew Fen was aware that the elders had influence over the villagers. She could not upset these elders because she wanted the best sales outcome from these properties. She needed to win them over so they would be cooperative in the selling process. She could not fail, nor did she want to be ridiculed by the villagers.

Madam Kwan got down from the platform to walk to the table. She picked up the thick pile of documents with her hands. She faced all the villagers and looked into each of the elders' eyes. Madam Kwan paused and said calmly, "In my hands, is the court order from the highest court in Canton. The court ordered me to be the executor for the settlement of the Kwan estate."

She slowly stacked the documents on one side of the table and left them there.

Looking directly at the elders' groups, Madam Kwan stood by the table and continued, "I can't agree more with our village elders. I have the highest regard for the Kwan family tradition. I deeply respect our elders' reminding me of the responsibility and authority of Master Kwan. In other families, the Master of the household would have taken up the responsibility to execute this important matter. There would never be the need for a defenceless woman of the Kwan family to carry out such a complicated and difficult task."

Madam Kwan waited, and then continued, "I highly respect our elder's suggestion. The Kwan family needs to sell the properties in order to raise the Kwan children and give them an education. Why don't I leave the Kwan children with the elders and let them raise the Kwan children and help educate them. I shall go back to Canton while we all wait for Master Kwan to come to Xiqiao for this discussion."

When Siew Fen finished speaking, she went to Wing Yu and took his hand. She walked him to the oldest elder who spoke earlier and handed Wing Yu's hand to him saying, "Wing Yu, from today, you stay with

Kwan Kon Kon[21]. I want you to be a good boy. I want you to continue to study. You obey Kon Kon. I am going back to Canton now."

Madam Kwan repeated the same action with Mee See to another elder, and Wing Chung to a third elder and Mee Jing with a fourth elder standing in front of the platform.

It was such an unexpected development that everyone was surprised at Madam Kwan's action. The children were scared of the elders, and all started to scream and cry uncontrollably. Each of the children shook their hands free from the elders and ran towards their mother. They hung on to Siew Fen's dress and would not let their mother go. Siew Fen consoled the four children wiping the tears from their eyes. Some villagers scattered into their own groups, all talking at the same time. It was quite a commotion outside the family shrine.

A younger elder walked to Madam Kwan in front of all the villagers. He eyed each of the other elders to gain approval and spoke on their behalf, "Madam Kwan, we, the elders of the village do not mean to separate the Kwan children from their mother. Our suggestion just now was only a view about the Kwan family traditions. Madam Kwan has the instruction from the highest court in Canton to execute the court order. We, the village elders, do not have the authority to stop the court order. We would not dare stop any Kwan family decisions. We hope that our Madam Kwan would not misunderstand us."

From then on, nobody dared stop Siew Fen from selling the properties of the village. The story of this incident was talked about in the neighbouring villages surrounding Xiqiao. The villagers all thought Madam Kwan was a brave and decisive lady. They all admired her courage and her upright approach. Siew Fen managed to sell all the properties, the fishery, and the fleet of fishing junks except for the ancestral summer residence.

---

[21] Kon Kon 公公, a respectful way to address an elder not necessarily a close member of the family.

After Siew Fen sold the properties, she disbursed the Kwan estate according to the court order in a fair and equitable manner. Her calculations were clear and precise so each party could see how the estate was divided accordingly. She was glad to be sorting out the estate because she was the only one who could conduct this with the utmost honesty and fairness to all.

Tin Lun settled the score by demanding he would keep the huge ancestral home where the stepmothers, Siew Fen and all the Kwan children were living. He took his two shares and went off without seeing any of his children. He never paid respect to his stepmothers, nor did he visit his siblings. He had already set up his home with his Yei Yee Tai and Sam Yee Tai at one of the Kwan's ancestral homes well before the court case. He continued with the lifestyle to which he was accustomed, spending his days and nights entertaining his friends.

As it was decided none of the ancestral homes were for sale, Siew Fen and the children kept the summer residence at Xiqiao and a number of ancestral homes in Canton, plus a number of investment properties for rental to provide an income for the Kwan family. Yee Ma and Sai Ma each got their share of the settlement. They were grateful for Siew Fen's honesty and her dealings with the two widows. They kept their share of the disbursement in property, jewellery and cash. As they had no experience managing finances, Siew Fen showed them how to manage their rental properties.

Siew Fen and the four children, Yee Ma and her daughter, Sai Ma and her son moved out into another large ancestral home in Canton Sharmeen (沙面)[22] Chin Ping Road to live. It was a two-story garden mansion. Each floor had four lounge rooms and seven bedrooms. To cut down costs, Siew Fen dismissed most of the servants, keeping only her most trusted servants, Ah-Din and Luk-Por, two cooks Sai-Chai and Sam-

---

[22] Sharmeen 沙面 was an area in Canton, where many embassies were located. It was also near the foreigner's area and near the Kwan family home at the rich side of town.

Chai and two servants Sai-Mui and Sai Por to keep the house clean and functional for the nine family members.

The rental income from the investment properties was more than sufficient to cover all of their expenses. Siew Fen was taught at a young age that paper money could not hold its value in time of war or uncertainty. She believed in carrying her savings in gold nuggets. Siew Fen saved all the excess cash to buy gold nuggets. She taught the widow stepmothers this very useful method of accumulating wealth.

Siew Fen wanted all the children to have a good education. Above all, she wanted the children to learn English. At that time, foreign language was in vogue. Foreigners, who had been seconded to work in Canton, held executive positions. Those Chinese who knew the language got first priority in employment at these institutions. A number of Christian missionaries were stationed in major cities in China and they set up schools to teach English in the foreign quarters in Canton. Siew Fen decided the Kwan children would get the edge over other children by being bilingual. The six children went off to school hand-in-hand. They all attended Canton 45 Primary School to study Chinese. In addition they attended East Bridge Private School (東橋私塾) to learn English. In those days, it was rather innovative to send children to learn a foreign language.

East Bridge Private School had over 50 students in a class. There were several French nuns teaching English classes. Except for four Portuguese students, the rest were Chinese students from wealthy families living around the Sharmeen area. Wing Yu, Wing Chung and Ng Sook were not interested in studying English. They were very shy about learning a new language and would not practise nor do homework. Mee See, Luk KuChar and Mee Jing, on the other hand, were hard working. They practised talking English amongst themselves. There were very few girls learning English at the time. As the three girls were bright and eager to learn, the French nuns were particularly interested in giving them extra lessons.

The years went by happily whilst living in Canton. The children had a happy childhood with their mother and grandmothers even though they did not have a male role model during their entire childhood. The children played well together and they were well disciplined. They finished primary school and went onto high school. Wing Yu and Win Cheung were so far behind with their English that at last, they had to give up their extra class. Ng Sook continued English lessons with the girls. To their delight, Wing Yu and Wing Chung had extra time to play marbles, fly kites, and play card games at home while the girls and Ng Sook continued with their extra English lessons for quite a few years.

Mee See in particular wanted to do well in school to please her mother and to set a good example for the girls. Little did they know that learning English would help pave the way for their future, giving them the edge over other colleagues.

Good Karma or Bad Karma

Tin Lun was a not a loyal friend. He would circulate with different groups of friends depending on who took his fancy at the time. He had explored thoroughly his three vices: gambling, opium and the brothels, which most wealthy Chinese men did at that time. Tin Lun spent his entire life soaking in these three vices spending money as though there was no tomorrow. His inheritance was wasted on his leisure and extravagant pursuits. His hanger-ons deserted him as soon as he could not afford to pay for their leisure. He sought friendship with those, who would only be around when he had money and was paying. Tin Lun always held the belief that he would never run out of money with his father's opulent bequest.

In his early forties, Tin Lun fell gravely ill and never recovered. He passed away at an even younger age than his father. He left behind his one true love, Yei Yee Tai from Chang's brothel. She had been Tin Lun's concubine for many years.

Yei Yee Tai did not have the money for his funeral. Even the ancestral home in which they were living had been mortgaged to Master Chang of Chang's brothel. When Tin Lun passed away, Master Chang came to give Yei Yee Tai her eviction notice. She was offered her old job as an escort mistress at Chang's brothel. Tin Lun never knew how to save and Yei Yee Tai never knew to put away money when Tin Lun was generous and had plenty to spend. Now there was no money to pay the funeral parlour to give Tin Lun a proper burial. Master Chang would not advance any more money to Yei Yee Tai because he knew there was no way she could repay him this time.

On a dark rainy day, Yei Yee Tai stood under the cold iron front gate and huddled under the tiny iron shade to avoid getting thoroughly drenched. The rain came down on her face mixing with the tears which ran down the contour of her once beautiful, almond shaped face. Yei Yee Tai went to ask Madam Kwan to pay for the funeral. Ah-Din told Yei Yee Tai that Madam Kwan was too busy to see her. Madam Kwan said that she had nothing to say nor any reason to see the woman. Yei Yee Tai stood there begging, and she told Ah-Din that she would wait there until Madam Kwan had time to see her. The rain kept pouring down. It was cold, and it was getting dark. Yei Yee Tai must have stood there for hours. Ah-Din came back to let Madam Kwan know that Yei Yee Tai was still waiting outside in the rain. She would wait outside until Madam Kwan had time to see her.

Siew Fen sensed that the reason she had come was to ask for money to help Tin Lun. There would be no other reason that she would be at their door. To get rid of Yei Yee Tai, Siew Fen thought she would stop the idea of handouts once and for all. The thought of Tin Lun's displeasure welled up in her mind and Siew Fen's anger started to rise up within her. She was ready to give Yei Yee Tai a mouthful. She would not give one coin to help Tin Lun. She was ready to send her off empty handed so that she would never come again.

She thought, "Where the hell is Tin Lun? How dare he send his Yei Yee Tai? He is not a gallant man to let his concubine come and call on me for money! He is despicable!!!" Siew Fen was determined to never give an inch as Yei Yee Tai walked in.

Yei Yee Tai was drenched. She was pale and thin, red-eyed with tears all over her face. Siew Fen was staggered to see her without a shadow of that beautiful powdered face that she remembered.

Yei Yee Tai knelt down in front of Siew Fen and her tears welled up as though a river had burst its banks. Yei Yee Tai wept as she said, "Master Kwan passed away after a short illness five days ago. I don't have any money for his funeral. I beg you Madam Kwan to allow him a proper burial." Yei Yee Tai went onto the floor to kowtow a number of times saying, "Please have mercy on Master Kwan – he is your children's father. Have mercy…, have mercy and let the children's father have a proper burial. Have mercy Madam Kwan, have mercy and do a kind deed and the Buddha will reward you. Good karma will fall on you and the Kwan descendants. Have mercy…" Yei Yee Tai kept kowtowing to Madam Kwan. Her forehead became red and raw after the countless times that she hit it on the floor. She knew that this was her very last chance to get help for a burial for Tin Lun. There was no other way she could get help. She was at the mercy of Madam Kwan.

It was then that Siew Fen realised that Tin Lun had passed away. The flame of her anger was suddenly extinguished. What he'd done with his two shares of the Kwan estate was baffling! He must have squandered it all on women, gambling, and opium. All those properties and all the money from the settlement was gone within a few years. What a stupid fool, she thought!

Siew Fen was brought up a well-disciplined person. She considered what to do. Tin Lun after all was the Kwan family's elder son and heir. He was the children's father even though he never cared for or enquired after any of them for many years. She could see Yei Yee Tai was desperate and did not have the means to pay for his burial, or she would not come begging. Siew Fen thought she would never ever let herself lose face the way Yei Yee Tai had done by begging.

Siew Fen asked Luk-Por to go and fetch some tea and some dry towels for Yei Yee Tai. She told Yei Yee Tai to sit on the far side of the table where a concubine of less status should be. Luk-Por offered tea to Siew Fen first and then a smaller cup of tea for Yei Yee Tai.

Siew Fen said, "We have already settled the Kwan estate. By right, Master Kwan has no claim on anything from his children's share. However, since he was the Kwan family's elder son and heir, and he was the children's father, I will settle for a basic burial for Master Kwan."

Yei Yee Tai was grateful and relieved. She got down from where she was and kowtowed many times again to Siew Fen. Saying, "Thank you…. Thank you Madam Kwan. The Buddha will smile upon your gracious generosity. Good karma will fall upon your grace, Madam Kwan."

Siew Fen put a number of ten Tai-Yuan dollar bills into a white envelope called Gut-Yee (吉儀)[23] and handed it to Luk-Por to give it to Yei Yee Tai and dismissed her. Yei Yee Tai was grateful, and took leave from Madam Kwan with the Gut-Yee in her inner pocket. The two ladies never met again.

On the day of the funeral, Tin Lun's stepmothers and his siblings did not go to pay respect. Siew Fen would not allow her children to wear mourning attire for the passing of their father, and she would not wear mourning attire herself. She forbade the children to attend and to pay respect at their father's funeral.

Tin Lun had the most basic funeral. The Kwan family wealth was multibillions when Master Kwan returned to China. Nearly all of that wealth was gone within just one generation. The elder son and heir of this wealthy family ended up with a burial for poor commoners. There was no one there. None of his drinking friends attended his funeral, except Yei Yee Tai and Sam Yee Tai.

Was it karma? One never knew. One never could tell.

---

23 Gut-Yee 吉儀 was a white pocket used to give people attending a funeral. Inside this white envelope were money, a sweet and a white tissue paper. This was in contrast to the Lai-See 利是 which was a red pocket to give money at happy occasions e.g. New Year, birthdays, wedding and other happy events.

Part Two – Mee See the Teenager

A Near Miss, a Lucky Escape

Japan invaded China in 1931, occupying Manchuria. In 1937 the second wave of the Japanese invasion was launched with major attacks on Beijing, Shanghai, and Nanking. When the Japanese entered Nanking, the soldiers committed atrocities that shocked the world. Newspapers in China and around the world published reports of these atrocities.

The people in Canton were worried and they hoped the Japanese would not invade South China.

On 12th October, 1938, the Japanese landed at Bias Bay on the East Coast of Guangdong Province. As the East River district was so heavily fortified, the Cantonese hoped that it would be months before the Japanese would get anywhere near Canton. However, the news confirmed that the Japanese were advancing faster than expected. Canton was in a fever of fear. People began planning their escape to safe territories. Crowds were pouring out of the city. Rumours spread everywhere. The Governor of Kwangtung and the Mayor of Canton asked the International Red Cross to set up a Refugee Committee. The Mission Compound for foreigners issued consulate certificates in English and Chinese stating that it was British or other foreign territory. Some Chinese people asked for protection from the Japanese within these compounds.

Fierce fighting took place. Canton fell.

Stories of atrocities circulated and scared everyone. Japanese cruelty was well described in rumours which spread like wild fire amongst the citizens of Canton. The Japanese soldiers were looking for young men or strong teenage boys they called "Lai Fu (拉夫)[24]" to force them to work

---

[24] Lai Fu 拉夫, a term used at the time to describe the action of kidnapping young men to serve the Japanese soldiers as laborers behind the war or at war.

with the Japanese army to provide supplies or to fight in the front line. They searched for young girls they called "Far Koo Leung (花姑娘)[25]" to kidnap them back to their quarters, where unspeakable crimes were committed against innocent children. Looting, arson, and rape were everyday events. The Chinese were full of anger and hatred at the behaviour of the Japanese soldiers. Citizens from Canton avoided encounters with the Japanese soldiers and shunned everything associated with Japan.

Siew Fen did not know what to do with the family of nine members and the team of eight servants. To avoid trouble, the children stopped their schooling and were kept at home. They had to revise their lessons at home. Wing Yu and Wing Chung spent most of their time playing with model cars and marbles. Mee See, Ng Sook, Luk KuChar and Mee Jing practiced writing and spoke English using the notes they were given by the French nuns. They set homework for one another.

Siew Fen avoided going out. When she had to take the girls out, she painted their faces and hands with charcoal to make them look old and ugly. She made everyone stay away from the windows to avoid drawing attention that there were young men and girls in the house.

The Japanese had been systematically raiding the citizens' homes to pilfer and to pick up young men and young girls on the way. How could she protect all the children? Where could the children hide? Siew Fen went around the house to look for hiding places in case the Japanese soldiers arrived at the door. Down the stairs below the kitchen was a small cellar where the chef put all the raw meat, smoked sausages and other provisions to keep cool. The room was dark and colder than any other room in the house and it was filled with a constant aroma of smoked meat. Siew Fen walked in to assess the size of the room. It was not a pleasant place to be but she thought this would be an ideal place to hide.

---

[25] Far Koo Leung, 花姑娘 flower girl, referred to girls kidnapped by the Japanese soldiers as 'comfort women'.

To have an escape plan, it had to be well rehearsed so that everyone knew what to do. Siew Fen gathered the six children, Yee Ma, Sai Ma and all the servants including Ah-Din in the lounge room. Siew Fen explained clearly, "The Japanese are snatching young men and young girls from their homes. The atrocities that come from their exploits are horrendous. I don't want that to happen to us. We must be well-prepared in case they come into our home."

Wing Yu just reached his teens and he stood the tallest in the household. He felt strong and ready for a fight, "Ah Tai (亞大)[26], I can kick fast, and I can kick high. My legs are strong and solid. When a Ga-Tou (架頭)[27] comes in, I will kick him so hard, he will turn around and run off."

Yee Ma added, "Wing Yu is young and inexperienced. The Japanese will come in with guns and swords. Before you raise your feet, they will shoot you down. They won't blink an eyelid to kill at will. It might be better to hear what Ah Tai has to say. We must all learn what we need to do to be safe."

Siew Fen continued, "If the Japanese come in, I want each one of you to drop whatever you are doing, walk swiftly without running and without pushing. Walk down to the dark meat room below the ground floor kitchen. Go to the far corner and sit down. Don't utter a sound. Stay there with Sai Ma and wait for Yee Ma or me to come and fetch you."

Siew Fen looked at Wing Yu and Mee See and continued, "Wing Yu you are the elder brother, I want you to look after Wing Chung and Ng Sook. Mee See, I want you to look after Mee Jing and Luk KuChar. It is your responsibility to make sure they don't make a sound. If the Japanese hear any noise from any of you, they will find you. It will be horrendous.

---

[26] Ah Tai 亞大, The Kwan family refer to their supreme mother as Ah Tai 亞大. Siew Fen was called Ah Tai in respect of her hierarchy position in the Kwan household.
[27] Ga-Tou 架頭, A derogative name to refer to a Japanese because of the atrocities they caused over many years.

This is most important."

Siew Fen walked across to Sai Ma and said, "Sai Ma will go with you. Now I want everyone to listen to Sai Ma, no argument is allowed. Do you all understand?"

All six children nodded in agreement and answered together, "Understand Ah Tai."

Siew Fen turned to look at the servants and said, "I want you all to keep quiet about where the children are hiding. Don't show any sign to the Japanese to endanger the masters and misses. Just pretend that nothing and nobody is in the dark meat room and carry on with your daily chores. Understand?"

All the servants nodded and answered, "Right, Madam Kwan."

Siew Fen wanted everyone to practice a few times so that they would understand thoroughly what was expected of them. Everyone went off to return to their previous activities. Ah-Din went outside the iron-gate and knocked at the door with a wooden stick to create a loud noise to start the drill. Yee Ma, Sai Ma, Siew Fen, and the children practised hiding in the dark meat room below the ground floor kitchen. They practised a few times until the children were used to the drill. Each time, the children walked down to the dark meat room and sat at the far end quietly waiting for Yee Ma or Siew Fen to come and fetch them. The room smelt of smoky meat; it was cold, damp, and dark. It was rather an unpleasant place to be sitting, yet none of the children complained. They realised the gravity of the situation. Mee See held Mee Jing's hand to comfort her. The children practised so many times that they got used to the procedure. They followed the rules as though it was a game.

One fine day after the family finished their lunch, the boys were in the room playing chess. The girls were practising their English lessons. Siew Fen, Yee Ma, Sai Ma, and Luk-Por were sewing waist belts at the dining table. They had cloth material scattered all over the table and were in the middle of cutting out some sewing patterns. Suddenly there was the sound of knocking at the iron gate. They banged at the door as though they wanted to break through the iron gate.

The whole family was tense. Everyone looked at one another in fear.

Siew Fen looked calmly at Sai Ma and said quietly, "Sai Ma, go with the children to the dark meat room now. Yee Ma and I will deal with the rest."

As Siew Fen was talking, she handed a grey top to Yee Ma and put on another navy blue top. She smeared some charcoal onto Yee Ma's face and smudged some on her own face and forehead. Both ladies look decidedly ugly and much older than their age. The loose tops made them both look plump and unattractive. They messed up their hair to make themselves look even more undesirable.

Ah-Din shouted out as he walked towards the iron gate, "Coming... coming... who is it?" He went to open the door when the children and Sai Ma were well on the way to the meat room.

The Japanese looked impatient and scornful for being kept waiting outside the iron gate. They pushed open the door roughly as soon as Ah-Din released the catch. Without a word, four Japanese soldiers pushed Ah-Din over and marched over the threshold to get to the courtyard then to the front greeting room. They snatched a little rolled gold Buddha statue from the display cupboard and put it into their calico bag. They shouted some Japanese words to Siew Fen and Yee Ma and gestured for them to take them around every room.

Both Siew Fen and Yee Ma lowered their heads as they followed the soldiers. The Japanese soldiers entered one room at a time, they snatched several valuable pieces of decorative displays and some ornaments made of precious stones into their bags. They took things as though they were there for the taking.

Siew Fen was sick with anger in her stomach. She was very angry but she kept her calm composure without uttering a word. Yee Ma followed Siew Fen closely and in silence. Both were worried about the children who were hiding in the meat room below. They were hoping the children would not make any noise to expose their hiding place. Yee Ma's heart was pounding so hard that she could feel her forehead pulsating as she followed Siew Fen.

Siew Fen took the Japanese upstairs to search, hoping to divert their attention from the kitchen. It was a big house with many rooms. One soldier broke off from the rest and started to wander towards the stairs. Siew Fen dared not stop him from heading down the stairs. She was hoping he would not find the dark meat room below the kitchen. The soldier went through the kitchen and saw the kitchen maids preparing dinner. One was washing vegetables, and the other was plucking feathers from a chicken in the courtyard.

The soldier found a door leading to another room a few steps down from a corner of the kitchen. As he opened the door, a strong unpleasant smoked meat odor oozed out. He nearly chocked. It was too dark for him to see anything as his pupils had not adjusted to the darkness after looking at the maid in the bright sunlight.

Suddenly a whistle blew from above with a call coming from the upstairs landing. The inspection was complete. It was time for the soldiers to move on.

Ah-Din followed them out to the iron gate and shut it tightly after them. Siew Fen and Yee Ma took a deep breath of relief. Siew Fen went upstairs and stood by the closed curtain, peeping through the crack between the two-sided curtains. She saw the four soldiers meander out of Ching Wah Lane to the end and turn off to the left into Chin Ping Road and disappear.

Yee Ma and Siew Fen waited and waited to make sure they would not double back to revisit them before they went downstairs to fetch all the children and Sai Ma. Mee See and Mee Jing hung on to Siew Fen's navy blue loose top as tears streamed down their faces. They dared not make a sound but were holding tight to their mother's dress and would not let go. Wing Yu and Wing Chung were biting their lower lips standing really close to Siew Fen as if they wanted the security of being next to their mother. Yee Ma huddled up Luk KuChar who was crying and wiped the tears from her eyes. Sai Ma put Ng Sook on her lap and cuddled her son as tears streamed down her cheeks.

It was a close shave this time! They all felt fortunate for being able to survive such a dangerous encounter with the Japanese soldiers. Even though everyone was scared, they knew they were very lucky to avoid a horrendous tragedy. It was a lucky break this time. There was no telling when other soldiers would return. The next time the Japanese soldiers called, they might not be so fortunate.

During this time, a lot of Siew Fen's tenants either lost their jobs or ran off to the other villages or counties to escape Japanese atrocities. All of a sudden, there were only a few tenants around to pay rent. Money was tight. The reserves were running low as the family was living off their savings rather than on rental income. Siew Fen could not sell her jewellery as anyone with wealth had escaped. Everyone required cash at hand just in case they needed to escape from the Japanese occupied territories. There had been heavy gunfire in the distance. People were streaming out of the city of Canton. Those who could pack up and go had all packed up and left. There was a sense of urgency, and as time passed, the explosions seemed to be getting closer. There was panic on many faces and there were wild stampedes in various directions as people made for the country villages where they had relations or friends and where they thought they would be safe. Even the police were leaving and isolated bands of soldiers were marching off as well.

Siew Fen decided Canton was not a safe place while the Japanese occupation continued. It was time to escape to Xiqiao village.

Escape to Village Xiqiao from Canton

Yee Ma decided to leave Canton to go back to her parents at Yuen Long (元朗) Hong Kong with her adopted daughter Luk KuChar. It was sad to leave the Kwan family; however, Yee Ma decided it was time she left the Kwan family to return to her parents whom she hadn't seen for years. Sai Ma decided to follow Siew Fen to escape to Xiqiao with her son Ng Sook.

Siew Fen had to discharge the footmen and the rest of the servants, leaving minimal servants to travel with her to Xiqiao. At the ancestral home, there were precious paintings, silk screens, porcelain, and sets of fine bone china, lots of antiques in various display cabinets, jade trees, jade panels, gold embroidered wall hangings, and volumes of ancient scrolls that could not be taken. Most of the clothes and the children's toys had to stay. Ah-Din was left in Canton to look after the ancestral family home and all the other properties.

The ladies decided to sew long waist belts with a number of secured pockets where they could hide their jewellery, gold nuggets and the stacks of Tai-Yuans, the Chinese paper currency whilst travelling. Sai Ma, Luk-Por, and Sam-Mui all set to work sewing three long belts for the ladies to wrap around their waist securely. They circled the belt around their tiny waists a couple of times and buttoned them securely onto their inner garments. On top, they wore their grey and navy blue loose tops to hide the bulkiness of their waists. They all looked well-padded like peasants from the village to blend in with the common travelers.

It was time to say farewell as the ladies were going their separate ways. With tears in her eyes, Yee Ma held Siew Fen's hands and said, "I don't know how to thank you for fighting for our share of inheritance. I know for sure that if it was not for you, we would have been out of the Kwan family a long time ago with no property and no money to our name. We would have been beggars in the street. We are forever in your debt." Yee Ma put her hand on Siew Fen's shoulder and said, "You are a brave woman. You must call and visit my parents at Yuen Long when you visit

Hong Kong."

Siew Fen humbled by her mother-in-law's frankness replied, "I was just doing what was the right thing to do. Your share of the inheritance was justifiably yours. I can't stand by and watch injustice when I know I can help."

The ladies exchanged addresses and sadly but reluctantly bid farewell as they went their separate ways. Mee See and Luk KuChar silently wiped the tears from their eyes. They held hands until it was time to part.

Siew Fen took Sai Ma, Ng Sook, her four children, the servants Luk-Por and Sai-Mui, the cooks Sam-Chai and Sai-Chai to make their way to Xiqiao. It was dangerous going by land as Japanese soldiers occupied various camps en-route. Siew Fen took the long sea route to Xiqiao from Canton via a ship, changed to a boat, and then changed to a fishing junk to arrive at the jetty of Kun Shan village that Master Kwan built for the villagers some decades before. It took a total of three days and two nights to reach the jetty. They meandered down the village roads to reach the Kwan family summer residence.

Siew Fen opened the big gates to step over the threshold into the courtyard of their sanctuary. As she looked back at the five children and Sai Ma, they all looked tired and worn out after the long and uncomfortable journey. Sai Ma, who married into the Kwan family at fifteen, had long lost her youthful beauty. After all these years of uncertainty and worry, she looked tens of years older. For once Siew Fen welled up with tears as she looked at her surrounds. Siew Fen took a deep breath and secretly brushed off the tears with her sleeve so that none of the children and Sai Ma could see.

Decidedly, Siew Fen turned around and said to the group, "Good, we have arrived safely. This is our home from now on. Now, go find your room and clean up and put on a new change of clothes. We are having dinner at five then we will have an early night. We shall plan what to do in the morning."

As Siew Fen spoke, she gave Luk-Por a Tai-Yuan dollar and told her, "Take this to get some provisions. We want a chicken and some good food to thank our ancestors for arriving home safely."

Everyone went off to their own rooms to reassemble later for dinner.

Siew Fen was left on her own. She walked from the courtyard to the garden and sat on the flat marble stone by the rockery. Water streamed down the rockery making a peaceful dripping noise. She looked around deep in thought, "Now that we are safe in the village, what can we do to make a living? There are no more rents from the properties here to provide for our living expenses. Where can I sell the jewellery for cash? In this poor country village, who would have money to buy jewellery? Who would appreciate the value of this fine art? The cash that I have now will run out one day. Then where can I get the money to feed a family of seven with four servants?"

The afternoon sun angled down on the garden and reflected onto the fish pond. Some dark clouds moved to cover the sun leaving streaks of sunlight to peek through the shadows of the clouds. All of a sudden, Siew Fen doubted. Where was that decisive girl who always just knew what to do? Where was that brave girl who would stand up against any injustice? Where was that proud girl who would not compromise and who would fight until the end to win?

Siew Fen lost her confidence. How would she see through the year with all the family to feed? Since the Japanese occupation, the children had left school, their education had stagnated. Their previous visits to Xiqiao were different because they knew it was only for a summer break. However, this time, Siew Fen did not know for how long they needed to take refuge in the village. They would remain until the end of the Japanese occupation, or the Japanese cruelty ran out of steam. The future was out of her control.

She recalled her previous image. At five foot and a bit, she used to stand upright and dignified with her feet unbound. She had a striking

73

presence, in contrast to the obsequious demeanor expected from women of her time. Siew Fen looked down to see her reflection. Her face was dusty and tired. Her loose top made her look bulky and common. She was shocked to see what she had become at the end of this arduous, and tiresome journey. Siew Fen couldn't contain herself any longer. She put her face in her hands and started to weep quietly, not knowing how long she would keep weeping.

A gentle hand rested on Siew Fen's shoulder. Siew Fen raised her head to find Sai Ma standing closely by her side. She didn't know how long she had been standing there.

Sai Ma said, "Ah Tai, if it were not for you, all the Kwan children would be scattered. The Kwan family wealth would have been squandered with nothing left to take care of us. If it were not for you, my son and I would have been left to fend for ourselves and we would have become beggars in the street a long time ago." Sai Ma took a deep breath, and continued, "Because of you, we still have a number of properties in Canton even though we don't get much rent now, but we shall again one day when the Japanese occupation finishes. You have kept the family together. We are all grateful to you."

Siew Fen answered, "Even though we are here safe in the village, we have no properties and no rent to collect. We have no way to sell my jewellery. We don't know where the children can go to school in this village. The cash we have brought will run out in time. Both you and I have never worked to earn a wage in our lifetime. It is a pity the children are too young to send out to work to earn money. I have run out of ideas this time!"

Sai Ma said, "Come, dinner is ready. Let's have dinner and have a good rest after such a long journey. Tomorrow we may think of something. The servants will wait until you are ready."

It was Siew Fen's turn to have a good wash and to comb her hair. She put the long waist belt in the camphor chest in her bedroom and locked it with a padlock. She changed into a green silk top and trousers with silk thread floral embroidery. It felt good! She looked great!

Before dinner, the servants took trays of food to the family shrine. On the trays there were several cooked dishes, a couple of bowls of rice, and some rice wine in small wine glasses. There was a whole soya sauce chicken complete with the head on, a steamed fish, a vegetable dish, and soup in a tureen. They burned candles and incense at the family shrine to pay respect to the Kwan ancestors. Sai Ma and Ng Sook, being the eldest in the Kwan family rank, were first to bow and kowtow. Then Siew Fen took her place with each of her four children. She thanked the ancestors humbly for the blessing of giving the family a safe passage to return to the sanctuary of their summer home at Xiqiao. She pleaded with the ancestors to guide her. She did not know what she could do to earn a living to support the family of seven and four servants. They each burned red candles and incense before returning home for dinner.

The family surrounded the round table. There was soya sauce chicken, braised duck, steamed fish, green vegetable soup, and big bowls of steaming hot rice. The children laughed and joked as they helped themselves to the delicious meal after their long journey. The family enjoyed a hot and fulfilling dinner.

Siew Fen could not sleep even though she was exhausted after the journey. She sat on the same marble rock by the rockery beside the fish pond in the garden. There was little breeze around. The pond reflected moonlight, the water gently rippling outwards. Siew Fen looked up to see the moon as dark clouds were drifting to block the bright moonlight. She had no idea how to provide for the family.

A Life Line

The next village from Kun Shan village was a village named Lui Su (裏水) Village, There was a school called Lui Su Village School (裏水學館). All the children from the nearby villages of Xiqiao went there to learn to read and write. A scholar from Hong Kong had been running and teaching at this village school on his own for a number of years. He wanted to find a relief teacher so he could go home to his sick father in Hong Kong. He intended to go home for a month to sort out some family matters for his parents. In this poor farming and fishing village, where could he find a learned person who could take up this teaching post to relieve him? He heard that Madam Kwan from the neighboring Kun Shan village was an educated lady. The Lui Su teacher decided to pay her a visit.

The Lui Su teacher found Madam Kwan an articulate, well-educated lady. He was surprised to find that Madam Kwan, as a lady, had been educated in traditional literature, in history, and she had even read 'Sun Tzu the Art of War (孫子兵法)[28]', a text book of well-known war and combating strategies! She could write poetry, draw watercolour paintings, and write beautiful calligraphy. He couldn't help admire her many talents. He was hoping that, when he came back from Hong Kong, he could cultivate a friendship with Madam Kwan.

The Lui Su teacher asked Madam Kwan, "I wonder if you will kindly consider picking up the teaching post at my school at Lui Su Village. I need to go home to visit my sick father in Hong Kong. I hope Madam Kwan won't feel insulted to receive a teaching salary for your trouble."

Siew Fen was surprised and pleased. Never had she ever been praised for being educated. What she learned as a boy in combating and war strategy amazed the Lui Su teacher. She never had the chance to

---

[28] Sun Tzu the Art of War 孫子兵法 it was an ancient book on strategy and tactics in war, which remained to be the most important military treatise in Asia.

converse about these subjects at which she had once excelled. All her life, she had never needed to work, let alone earned a salary. The opportunity to earn a living as a teacher was a lifeline for Siew Fen just as she was feeling desperate. However, she had to keep her modesty. Keeping her composure, Siew Fen said, "I am not sure I can cope with the position as a teacher. I have never taught except to conduct lessons with my children at home. They had to give up schooling in Canton during the Japanese occupation."

The Lui Su teacher replied, "Oh Madam Kwan is too modest. With your learning experience, I have no doubt you can more than fulfill this teaching role at our simple village school. Would you like to come for a week to see how you would feel teaching before we decide if I could leave for Hong Kong?"

The Lui Su teacher paused and then continued, "Unfortunately, it takes a half day's travel on the river upstream to Lui Su village from here. But there is a little hut by the school where Madam Kwan can stay for weeks at a time." The Lui Su teacher then added, "Your children can all attend the same school. This is the only school around the nearby villages. This will save you the trouble of looking for a school for your children as well."

After watching Siew Fen conduct the classes, the Lui Su teacher was happy to leave the school in her capable hands. Siew Fen was surprised that she actually found teaching these village children easier than she first thought.

Siew Fen was employed as the new relief teacher. The Lui Su teacher promised to return in six weeks' time.

Siew Fen was glad there was a way to generate an income to feed the family. Siew Fen went home once every two weeks. She brought along three children each time so they could take turns to attend school as well. Sai Ma looked after the summer residence at Kun Shan village and the other children who stayed home when Siew Fen was away teaching.

On the day Siew Fen received her first salary package, she held the few ten Tai-Yuan dollar bills in her hands and was moved to tears, and then she burst out laughing loudly. She had seen very much more money than what she had in her hands. However, this was the very first Tai-Yuans dollar bills that Siew Fen ever earned. These few dollar bills gave her enormous confidence to do which she never thought possible. Now she had a job, and she knew she could make money to keep food on the table for the family.

Not knowing why her mother was crying and then laughing, Mee See joined in to cry and laugh with her. She attended her mother's school more often than the boys. Not wanting to disappoint her, she helped her mother wherever and whenever she could.

Once every two weeks, the children had to go with their mother to attend the school at Lui Su Village. Wing Yu saw it was a great opportunity for fun and games when their mother was away teaching. Wing Yu and Wing Chung spent time running around the village. They went fishing, caught tadpoles, kept frogs, and flew kites. When they were not at school with Siew Fen they spent little time studying. Sai Ma was happy as long as Wing Yu and Wing Chung came home for lunch and dinner and went to bed early. There was nothing happening at night in the village so the children all settled early to bed.

Wing Yu and Wing Chung were looking for more exciting things to do to occupy their leisure time. They started fighting crickets and playing marbles and card games with coins as stakes. It was a breeding ground for a gambling habit. As they didn't have pocket money, Wing Yu took a little jade Buddha from home to exchange for a small amount of coins which he used to gamble with the other neighborhood children. In time, they would steal coins that they found either from home or around the village. They picked up precious ornaments to exchange for coins to fund their gambling. The two brothers loved their freedom and often pretended to be unwell so that they could miss school. Gradually they cultivated the habit of stealing, gambling, and telling lies. Neither Siew Fen nor Sai Ma were aware of this.

As the teacher at the school, Siew Fen tried to instill into her children the principles that she held. She set them examples about being honest and being straight forward when dealing with people. She taught the children about exercising fair play and being a trustworthy person. Never in her wildest dreams did she think that her two boys were lying, stealing, and gambling while she was working to provide for the family.

A year passed by and the Lui Su teacher still did not come back. Siew Fen missed him and wondered if he had found a new life in Hong Kong and might not return to this poor and uninteresting village life. She continued teaching and was happy that her salary could be exchanged for food and provisions for the family. Life seemed to settle well in the village once again.

Village Xiqiao to Hong Kong

During the late 1930s when the Japanese occupied Canton, many city folks left Canton to settle in various cities to escape from the Japanese atrocities. Siew Fen's father Master Hui took Madam Hui, his concubines and their children to settle in Hong Kong. News arrived that Madam Hui was ill, and she would like to see her daughter and her grandchildren. Siew Fen was eager to travel with the family to Hong Kong to visit her sick mother. Siew Fen was now in the same predicament as the Lui Su teacher when she first met him more than a year ago.

Luck had it that the Lui Su teacher arrived unexpectedly at the village soon after the news arrived about Siew Fen's sick mother. Siew Fen was overjoyed to see him return. He apologised profusely for having been away for so long. Apparently his father had been very ill for some time and then his mother took ill as well. Being the only son, he found that he could not leave his parents. He also knew that the school was in Siew Fen's capable hands. Then, his mother passed away, shortly after his father died. At last, he sorted out their affairs and decided to come back to the Lui Su village to settle down. During the time that he was away, he missed Madam Kwan. He had all intentions that when he came back, he would cultivate his friendship with her.

Having waited over a year for the Lui Su teacher to return from Hong Kong now, Siew Fen had to leave for Hong Kong in a hurry. The Lui Su teacher and Siew Fen cordially bid farewell without expressing their thoughts for each other. Fate had it that the Lui Su teacher and Siew Fen would not have the opportunity to get together after all.

Sai Ma had not seen her family since she married into the Kwan family. In the meantime, her parents migrated to Singapore. Sai Ma decided it was time for her to go home to be with her parents.

Siew Fen was upset that Sai Ma was leaving for Singapore with no plan to return. Siew Fen felt sorry for Sai Ma being married at fifteen to her father-in-law. She had always looked out for Sai Ma even though she was lower in rank as the daughter-in-law. She took care of her when she was pregnant with Ng Sook when Master Kwan passed away. Siew Fen ensured that Sai Ma had a share of the inheritance to raise Ng Sook, the second son and heir of the Kwan family. They went through a lot of good times and bad times together over the years; however, it was time for them to go their separate ways.

Sai Ma said, "Singapore is like the other side of the world to Hong Kong! I don't know when we can meet again."

Siew Fen replied, "Yes, Singapore is so very far away. However, we have to follow our fate. It is your time to go home to your parents and my time to go home to mine as well. I do hope that we'll meet again one day."

Sai Ma and Siew Fen had a tearful farewell as they wished each other well and waved goodbye at the jetty. Sai Ma and Ng Sook climbed onto the ship that took them to Canton where they would catch the next connection to Singapore.

Life was full of contradictions! It would be comforting to see her parents after such a long time. However, it was such a pity that she could not stay to cultivate a friendship with the Lui Su teacher. He was the first man besides her father who showed her genuine consideration and kindness. He was a gentleman who appreciated her as a colleague and respected her as a fellow scholar. On the eve of leaving the village, Siew Fen was sitting on the same marble rock beside the fish pond. The air was still. The fish pond mirrored the reflection of the silver curve of the crescent moon as some grey clouds were drifting by. She was eager to go home to see her mother.   Once again, Siew Fen had to walk away from a settled life at the village into the unknown. She had no idea how things would pan out. All she knew was to move forward without being sure of what was in store for tomorrow.

The Disowned Son and Heir

It was a long and tiresome journey along the Pearl River from Xiqiao up to Canton, then down into Hong Kong. With the family of four children and four servants, Siew Fen finally arrived at Master Hui's home on Elgin Street (伊利近街) Hong Kong. It was the first time the children had visited Hong Kong. Unfortunately, Madam Hui passed away just before their arrival. Siew Fen and the children arrived just in time for the funeral of her mother.

When the Japanese occupied Canton, Master Hui was one of the first families to leave his Canton ancestral home with his supreme wife Madam Hui, second concubine Yee-Por and their son Sam Kufu, and his forth concubine Sai Por and their daughter Sai YeMa to set up residence in Hong Kong. Master Hui liquidated his property portfolio in Canton to re-establish himself in Hong Kong. When he arrived he purchased a number of properties in Hong Kong to provide a continuous income stream. Once established, Master Hui handed over the maintenance and management of the family to Madam Hui again. Madam Hui had firm control of all the family matters. The two concubines were never given the responsibility of running the Hui household. With Madam Hui's passing, Master Hui had lost his most capable and loyal financial controller.

Master Hui asked Siew Fen to stay on in Hong Kong to take care of the family and Siew Fen agreed to keep her father company and help him to manage the Hui household matters. Without his beloved wife, Master Hui lost the will to live. He took ill and passed away a year after Madam Hui. Siew Fen decided to stay on and continued to manage her father's estate.

At the time, the Hong Kong economy was stable and the rental income was able to cover all the family expenses. Siew Fen negotiated with each tenant to set a new rental lease agreement. She updated her mother's rental register to have a clear idea of the family's financial situation. She could see that the Hui family would be able to live comfortably with a significant surplus. She saved all the left over rental to buy gold nuggets. Nuggets by the ounce were small, easy to carry, and easy to liquidate in times of need. Siew Fen put all the Hui family savings into gold nuggets. She showed the stepmothers the rental register and tried to teach them how to balance the books. The stepmothers appreciated Siew Fen's effort, and both asked Siew Fen to continue handling the family's estate.

Sam Kufu was glad to have the teenage nephews Wing Yu and Wing Chung around. It was like having two bigger brothers to show him the games that boys played. Sai YeMa was overjoyed to have the older nieces Mee See and Mee Jing as companions. They were like her sisters playing dress-up with dolls. The younger children listened with eyes wide open as Wing Yu and Mee See related stories of village life, rice growing, festivities at harvesting, and fishing from the jetty at Xiqiao.

Once again the children settled into schools with Sam Kufu and Sai YeMa. Mee See and Mee Jing continued with their extra lessons in English as well as attending Chinese schools. Hong Kong, had been under British rule for years, so it was more cosmopolitan than Canton. The children enjoyed the rides on the ferries, the trams, and buses. The adults took the children to see movies at the cinema. The children saw their first Chinese street opera in the festive season. It was a new experience for the children after their secluded life in the village. Mee See and Mee Jing soon settled and enjoyed the city life in Hong Kong. They thought that living in Hong Kong was much better than life in the village.

Wing Yu and Wing Chung on the other hand hated Hong Kong. They missed the freedom to roam around doing nothing but playing and gambling with the other village boys all day. They did not have much pocket money and they found things unaffordable in the city. There were so many people living at the Hui grandmothers' house that they dare not steal anything even when they saw the opportunity. They had to find excuses to get out of the house to explore. Above all, Wing Yu and Wing Chung hated going to school. They hated doing homework after school. Worse still, there was the report card to prove that they didn't study for their examinations. They protested against having extra English lessons. They reckoned that those were for girls. They never settled in Hong Kong, and thought that living in Hong Kong was like a prison. Life was better in the village.

Wing Yu saw his mother had stacks of Tai-Yuan dollars. He wished he could use some of that money to buy a few of those luxuries he saw other youths had. Wing Yu planned how he could get some of the Tai-Yuans from his mother. Mother wanted the children to aspire and plan for a better future, and she always encouraged the children to think independently and to resolve problems.

Wing Yu told his mother, "Ah Tai, I'd like to earn a living doing some small business to supplement the income of the family. Can you support me to start such a business?"

Siew Fen was surprised and asked, "What business are you thinking of doing? How did you come up with such an idea?"

With confidence he spoke, "I have a plan to start selling small goods using a mobile trolley."

He repeated what the small businessman from the market had told him, "I can get goods at a cheaper price from wholesalers and sell them at a higher price to the public. Leave everything to me, let me organise everything."

Overjoyed even though she did not show it, Siew Fen thought that her teaching had finally influenced Wing Yu. She was comforted by the thought that, unlike his father Wing Yu was working to make something of himself instead of relying on the inheritance.

Siew Fen said to Wing Yu, "Here is a five Tai-Yuan bill to get you started. This is a lot of money. Take good care of it."

She was so excited that her eldest son was taking responsibility and aimed to make a living by starting a business. She was so proud of her son, who did not follow in his father's footsteps to lie and squander money. He was an entrepreneur in the making! Siew Fen had such great expectations of Wing Yu!

Wing Yu was ecstatic. He could not believe that it was so easy to cheat his mother. Rumour had it that his mother was an intelligent and smart lady. However, mother was so easily deceived. Wing Yu laughed loudly. He said to Wing Chung, "Come, have a look at this five Tai-Yuan dollar bill! Come, smell it... ng...ng... the smell of new money is on this note!! Let's enjoy ourselves and celebrate our new venture. There will be plenty where this comes from. Ah Tai will support our spending from now on. We don't need to steal for pocket money anymore."

Wing Chung was apprehensive and said, "Wow! I have never touched a five Tai-Yuan bill!! Let me have a good look at it. Are you going to do business with this money?"

Laughing even louder, Wing Yu replied, "No, what business are you talking about? That story is a bridge to get us over to the land of money, you silly!"

Wing Chung said, "Ah Tai always told us to be honest and uphold justice. You are scheming to swindle her of her money. She will not forgive us if she knows." Wing Chung took a deep breath and continued, "We all know what a bad temper Ah Tai has. Remember the time she was fighting with father until his nose bled? Why don't we get some stock and sell it at the market to make some money?"

Wing Yu said, "How would she know!? Unless you tell her! Hey, this is my money. I will decide how to spend it. Come on, I shall deal with Ah Tai if she asks any questions. Come on, let's go celebrating…. Are you coming or not?"

Wing Chung hesitated at first. However, it was good to be able to follow Wing Yu to the shops to buy marbles and other playthings, to eat at the little eateries, and to pay for bus and tram rides rather than walk home after an outing. After a little while, the two brothers were quite comfortable spending their pocket full of coins. Wing Chung forgot about Ah Tai's principle of honesty.

Siew Fen asked, "How did you lose all that money in business?"

Wing Yu didn't blink an eyelid and told his mother that all his goods were confiscated by the police during the incident when he could not escape from chow-qwiel (走鬼)[29] as he was trying to out run the police. Wing Yu lied to his mother about how he bought the stock from the wholesalers, how he sold it on a push-along trolley, how the police appeared from nowhere. Because he did not have a commercial license, the police told him that he was trading illegally. As a result, the police confiscated everything. There was nothing he could show from the five Tai-Yuan bill.

Siew Fen was skeptical about the story of chow-qwiel. However, she

---

[29] Chow-qwiel 走鬼, in Hong Kong all hawkers selling in the street required a commercial license to trade. Without one, all the goods could be confiscated by the police. Chow-qwiel described the action that hawkers ran with their goods to avoid being caught by the police.

kept her cool and listened quietly and analytically to what she was told.

Wing Yu asked his mother to support him once again. This time, he promised he would get the commercial license which would take more capital to restart the business again.

Siew Fen opened her purse and gave Wing Yu three five Tai-Yuan bills this time. She didn't want to ask any more questions. She thought that Wing Yu should have enough capital to buy the hawkers' license as well.

Wing Yu thanked his mother for her support and left to work on the next plan.

Wing Yu could hardly contain his glee when he found Wing Chung. Together they went out of the house into an eatery, waving the three Five-Tai-Yuan bills and giggling, "It is so easy to convince Ah Tai. She doesn't know the truth from lies! I wonder why everyone says how clever mother is!"

In those days, fifteen Tai-Yuan was a lot of money. Wing Chung was really worried, and said, "We had better not be found out! You have spent a lot of money with nothing to show for it! Dai Gor (大哥)[30] one day, we may be in big trouble."

Wing Yu answered, "Hey, you are so timid! I know exactly how to handle mother. Leave Ah Tai to me."

Wing Chung said, "We had better do some sort of business with this much money in your hands."

Wing Yu was proud of his ability to swindle money from his mother. He gambled on horses, went to the dance hall to pay for the dancing girls to keep him company. He learned to drink alcohol, and he even went to the brothel to try his luck with the lady escorts. He borrowed money from a loan shark to maintain his gambling and spending habits. Having

---

[30] Dai Gor 大哥 denoted big brother.

just turned seventeen, Wing Yu was worse than his father at the same age. At least his father could afford to gamble and squander. Wing Yu had no means to sustain the life style that he was living. As time passed by, Wing Chung was too scared to follow his brother into this new venture. He was too young to go to many places that Wing Yu frequented. He stopped following his brother but roamed around the street with the few coins that Wing Yu gave him as his share of the loot.

One day, Wing Yu came home. He bumped into Tuck-Soak the loan shark, who was just leaving. Tuck-Soak tipped his head to Wing Yu as he looked down on the floor and left quietly.

Siew Fen's face was ash grey and she looked serious. Her eyes carried the fire of anger that had not been seen for a long time. Wing Yu's heart beat faster. He knew then that something had gone very wrong. He turned around but could not find Wing Chung.

Siew Fen waited until Tuck-Soak had left. She could contain herself no longer. At the top of her voice, Siew Fen yelled, "This last month you borrowed thirty Tai-Yuan from Tuck-Soak the loan shark to gamble on horses. How do you explain yourself? I gave you a total of twenty Tai-Yuan to do business. Where are the goods you were selling? Where is the commercial license that you were talking about? "

Wing Yu looked up and tried to rescue the situation, "I borrowed money to add more stock."

Siew Fen's anger rose higher and higher as she continued, "Stop that lying. Stop right there!"

This commotion in the lounge room disturbed the rest of the household. Yee Por and Sam Kufu, Sai Por and Sai YeMa came rushing in, followed by Mee See, Wing Chung and Mee Jing. The servants stood outside the door waiting for their summons.

Siew Fen continued at the top of her voice, "I followed you last week. I saw you go to the dance hall. I saw you drinking at the bar and you visited a brothel. You didn't do any trading as you told me. Where is the money you borrowed? Where is the money I gave you to do business? Explain yourself."

Yee Por helped Wing Yu kneel down and say sorry to his mother. Sai Por ordered the servant to serve a pot of chamomile tea to calm Siew Fen.

Siew Fen got close to Wing Yu as he knelt down and with all her might, she slapped him on his left cheek and slapped him on the right cheek yelling, "The Kwan family does not have a deceitful son like you. "

Wing Yu put his hands on his cheeks which were painful and red. Each cheek had five bright finger marks. He rubbed his face to ease the pain and the heat that was steaming from the hard smack. He knew then it was useless to continue with the story of doing business. He looked at Wing Chung with hatred thinking, "It must have been Wing Chung's telling. I will personally deal with him when I get out of these accusations tonight."

Yee Por got the tea on a tray to give to Wing Yu so he could offer it to Siew Fen saying, "Now offer your mother this tea and tell her you're sorry."

To Siew Fen, Yee Por said, "Wing Yu is too young to know what is true and what is false. He may not be willfully cheating you."

Sai Por prompted Wing Yu by saying, "Wing Yu, quickly, say you are sorry to your mother and that you will not do it again."

Unfortunately, Wing Yu did not think that he was wrong. He wondered how his mother discovered the truth. He blamed Wing Chung for telling their mother. He was still thinking how to get out of this predicament and what other excuse he could use to change his story.

Siew Fen saw the expression in Wing Yu's eyes. She was disappointed, "Don't think that anybody has told me about you. I have been following you this week. I saw you with my own eyes and all the places where you went. Now what do you have to say for yourself?" Siew Fen continued, "Tuck-Soak came chasing me for the loans you incurred over the last three months. I had to settle your debt immediately. You schemed to cheat me with this elaborate plan of selling goods at street corners. I was hoping you would set a good example for your brother and sisters. I thought you were starting a business, earning an income. In fact you have been cheating money from me. You take me for a fool!"

Siew Fen was exhausted with rage. Yee Por and Sai Por were trying hard to calm her. They urged Wing Yu to admit to being wrong and to kowtow to his mother to apologise but to no avail. The children all kept quiet looking on. Wing Chung was looking at Wing Yu wanting to tell him that it was not him who told Ah Tai the truth. But Wing Yu retaliated with an angry look. Siew Fen was desperately disappointed when she saw the hatred in Wing Yu's eye as he looked at Wing Chung.

At last they all went into the dining room to have dinner quietly. Nobody uttered a word. Wing Yu never said he was sorry. He was sitting quietly at the far end of the table opposite his mother. He was contemplating how to punish Wing Chung for this incident.

It was another sleepless night. Siew Fen was hot and bothered. She twisted and turned in bed reliving every scene from the previous day when everything came to a disappointing halt. She got up and went to the garden for some fresh air. Sitting inside the pagoda, Siew Fen gazed into the fish pond. She saw the reflection of the moon in the still of the night. Now what should she do? How could she uphold the discipline of the household in the future? Where did Siew Fen go wrong with Wing Yu? Siew Fen reflected on the teaching of all her children. Wing Yu had committed all the vices that Siew Fen hated. He was only seventeen and he schemed to deceive. Wing Yu never admitted being wrong for what he had done, in spite of her angry interrogation. How could she maintain discipline for the rest of the children when Wing Yu openly rejected her teaching? Obviously he was not sorry for what he had done; he only regretted being found out.

A new moon appeared on the reflection of the fish pond as a couple of dark clouds moved away revealing the bright moon light. Siew Fen began to feel more confident about what she needed to do. It was not what she wanted to do; however, she was duty-bound to do what she must. This was to uphold discipline and the virtues of honesty, righteousness, and respect of the elders.

Early in the morning, Siew Fen assembled all the family members into the lounge room. Siew Fen was sitting with Yee Por and Sai Por on either side. Sam Kufu and Sai YeMa were standing close by their mothers. Mee See, Wing Chung and Mee Jing were standing close behind. Wing Chung had a black swollen eye on the left side. He also had a bruised forehead and a little cut on his neck. Everyone knew that it was Wing Yu's doing.

Wing Yu was quiet, standing on the opposite side of the round table.

The servants served tea to the adults at the table. Everyone was quiet in anticipation. One could have heard a pin drop!

Siew Fen sat upright and spoke quietly with a firm voice, "Wing Yu, you are the oldest of all the children. I was hoping that you would have set a good example to your younger brother and sisters. I never imagined that you would devise a plan to deceive me. You dared to cheat me not just once but again and again. I am thoroughly disappointed with you. You borrowed money, you drank alcohol, you sought dancing girls, and you went to brothels. You don't even acknowledge that you have done anything wrong. Instead, you blamed your brother and you assaulted him. This matter had nothing to do with your brother. It is entirely your fault. What do you have to say for yourself? "

Wing Yu was biting his lips. He looked at Wing Chung's black eye with anger. Wing Yu had nothing to say, but wished his mother would finish all her lectures soon, so that he could go back to his room to play with his games.

Siew Fen watched Wing Yu's closely and was once again disappointed.

She held out a big red Lai-See and put it on the table and said, "Inside this Lai-See, there is fifty Tai-Yuan. I give you this to find a living for yourself. Don't come home unless you have made something of yourself. I want you to pack your belongings now…. and leave." Siew Fen gestured for the servant to take the Lai-See to Wing Yu.

At once there was a great commotion in the lounge room. Yee Por and Sai Por both spoke to Siew Fen at the same time. They urged Siew Fen to think very carefully. Wing Yu was so young. Where could Wing Yu go? What could he do to earn a living?

Mee See, Wing Chung and Mee Jing started crying bitterly. They hung onto the corner of their mother's dress pleading, "Ah Tai, please don't send Dai Gor (大哥)[31] away. We promise we won't fight again. We will study hard. Please let Dai Gor stay." All three children were crying bitterly for their mother to spare Wing Yu.

Wing Yu was angry with his mother for counting out all his vices. He was still perplexed about how his mother knew of all those places he frequented. He didn't admit guilt nor did he say sorry to his mother. He didn't ask Yee Por or Sai Por to help him beg his mother for forgiveness. He quietly picked up the red Lai-See envelope and walked out of the lounge room to his room. He packed up and left quietly.

All of a sudden the lounge room only had the wails of the siblings.

Wing Yu left home that day and never returned. However, rumour had it that Wing Yu was caught and enlisted by the Japanese during the Japanese occupation in Hong Kong. It was also rumored that he died young as a result of not being able to endure the hard labour under the Japanese army.

This incident left a very deep impression on all the children. Mee See felt that their mother was too cruel, and so firm with her decisions. She could not understand why mother did not forgive Wing Yu and give him

---

[31]Dai Gor 大哥 was an endearing reference to the eldest brother.

another chance. However, she knew she would not dare disagree with Ah Tai. Wing Chung was secretly delighted that he did not follow Wing Yu and commit all those sins. He knew his mother was a strong woman of substance. He would not dare argue with her in future. Mee Jing on the other hand cried without stopping. She was the youngest and was Siew Fen's favourite child. From an early age Mee Jing found that her tears usually got her what she wanted. Siew Fen promised to get her a European doll with blue eyes and golden hair if she would stop crying and she did.

When Wing Yu left home, Mee See became the oldest of all the children. She took up the role of an elder to look after her brother and sister, Sam Kufu and Sai YeMa. She set a good example by being polite, honest, considerate, and protective of the young ones. The idea of Wing Yu doing business actually had merit. Mee See and Wing Chung re-assessed the old business plan and decided to proceed with selling goods door to door in the neighborhood. Mee Jing also wanted to follow her siblings to knock at the doors to sell goods. They bought stocks from wholesalers, but before they set out to push the goods from door to door, they worked out the profit margin to set the sale price. They carried bags of tooth paste, tooth brushes, combs, soap, little jars of face cream and hand cream, wrapping paper, envelopes and writing pads, etc. From the proceeds of the sale, they paid their mother back what they had borrowed to start the business. They kept the capital for the next round of trades before they shared the profit equally as their pocket money. After school and on the weekends they went from door to door to sell their wares. To their surprise, they managed to sell a number of goods in the neighborhood. In fact, many people were happy to purchase goods from Mee Jing because she had such a sweet smiling face when knocking at the doors. The three siblings were very happy to earn enough pocket money to share.

Mee See gathered some of their profits to purchase three tickets to invite the adults to see a picture at the cinema. Yee Por, Sai Por and Siew Fen were overjoyed that the children had saved up their pocket money to give them a treat. Siew Fen was comforted that the children had shown such consideration to the elders.

It had not been easy to keep discipline among the children without a male role model at home. It was comforting to watch the three children dividing their workload and sharing their profits. Siew Fen felt that she had done the correct thing in bringing up the children the way she did. She was also assured that she made the right decision in letting Wing Yu go. If Wing Yu learned the lesson and managed to make his living using the money she gave him, she would welcome him back to the family one day.

Little did the children know that what they learned in this trading exercise paved the way for their future vocation later in life. It furnished them with the knowledge for earning a living when they grew up.

Teenage Lover Ah Ku

The family settled well in Hong Kong. There was ample rental income to cover all their expenses and the children were earning their own pocket money. They studied hard at school and they were respectful to their elders. Life was orderly and life was good!! Now that life was settled, Siew Fen and the children went to Yuen Long to reconnect with Yee Ma and Luk KuChar.

Yuen Long was on the outskirts of the New Territories outside Kowloon. It was not very convenient to travel to Yuen Long in those days. Hence whenever Siew Fen and her children visited Yuen Long, they stayed for a few more days to experience the quiet country life. Yuen Long reminded them of the quiet village life at Xiqiao. The children ran in the vegetable farm, between the rice fields, and by the duck ponds. Mee See and Luk KuChar rekindled their long lost sisterhood. They had a good time together talking till all hours of the night. They shared their aspirations and divulged their dreams about what they would like to be when they grew up.

Luk KuChar had a cousin called Wong Nan Ku (黃立舉), Ah Ku (亞舉) for short. Ah Ku was a high achiever at school. He had just finished high school and took his scholarship examination to study medicine at Hong Kong University. His father was a poor fisherman and as such Ah Ku needed to win the scholarship or his father would not be able to pay the university fee for his education. Ah Ku found Mee See such a delightful girl. He tried to find every chance to be with Luk KuChar and Mee See. The three teenagers went up and down the village field catching tadpoles and went fishing in the duck ponds. They joked and talked all day and late into the night until it was time for Ah Ku to run home to bed. Ah Ku took every chance to be with Mee See. They enjoyed running in the rice fields and walking along the pathways between the fields.

Siew Fen saw the development of the two young teenagers, and she was not happy with what she saw. Ah Ku came from a poor fishing family. They had nothing to their name. Though he was hoping to study medicine at the university, it would be many years before he finished his degree as a specialist doctor. Siew Fen thought that it would be too long for Mee See to wait around for Ah Ku. Yuen Long was a long way from Hong Kong Island where they lived and the chance of them seeing each other was remote. On reflection, Siew Fen was not too concerned.

It was the spring festival, the lunar New Year in Hong Kong. Yee Por, Sai Por and Siew Fen took the children to the Shing Wong Temple (城王廟) to burn incense and candles to thank Buddha for the past prosperous year, and they made wishes for the New Year.

Siew Fen had a fortuneteller read Mee See's fortune. The fortuneteller predicted that Mee See would have a very hard life in her youth and would have to work very hard to earn a living. She would have heavy responsibilities and she would hardly make ends meet during her entire working life. However, in later years, her fortune would change. She was to meet her rescuer who would help her out of hardship. In her old age, she would enjoy some prosperous years. Siew Fen associated this prediction with the development of Mee See and Au Ku's friendship. If Mee See was to share a life with Ah Ku, she might have to spend a life in poverty with him. The fortuneteller must have given a timely warning for Mee See. Observing the budding friendship between Ah Ku and Mee See, Siew Fen was alarmed with the development. She had to look for a way to change Mee See's fortune.

Mee See was growing to be a pretty looking teenage girl. She stood at five foot four with the most beautiful complexion. She had large round eyes and long thick eye lashes. Siew Fen wondered if Mee See had picked up these characteristics from her half Incan father. Siew Fen decided that it was time for her to find a good family for Mee See to marry into so that she would be taken care of for the rest of her life. Besides, if Mee See were married early, she would avoid the misfortune of being caught by the Japanese as a 'flower girl.'

The Fung family

Master Fung Kin Chee (馮鏗池) and his family originally made their fortune in ship building in Nan Hoi Kou Kong (南海九江) in Southern China. He was the managing director of the Canton Chin Wah Steam Shipping Company (廣州市清華船務公司). Master Fung opted to retire in Canton when he reached forty years of age. He sold a large share of his business to his business partners and became a silent partner in the company. He used the proceeds of the sale to purchase a portfolio of properties in Canton to provide him with a stable income. His company continued to provide a level of passive income for Master Fung and he enjoyed a leisurely and peaceful life with his family after retirement.

Master Fung and Madam Fung adopted the only child of a poor cousin who lost his wife from tuberculosis. As this poor cousin was unable to cope with the new baby, they took him in and named him Chun Yun (振元) and treated him as their own son. Sadly, Madam Fung died at childbirth, leaving Chun Yun once again without a mother to take care of him. Master Fung remarried a lady from a well-to-do family called Ah Shui (亞水). Master Fung and Ah Shui treated Chun Yun as their own flesh and blood. Chun Yun had a happy childhood and he went to the best school. Later Ah Shui gave birth to a daughter called Wei Cheung (慧忠). The Fung family of four lived happily together in Canton.

Chun Yun was an exceptional scholar. He was educated in the best private school in Canton, learning both Chinese and English at high school. He studied economics with an honours degree at Canton University. On the wall in his bedroom, he displayed certificates, awards, ribbons, and trophies that indicated his scholastic achievement throughout his student days. His parents were proud of his achievements and often showed relatives and friends the ribbon-filled wall.

After graduation from the university, Chun Yun gained a position at the Jardin Financial Company which was a British company that had branches in Canton, Macao and Hong Kong. Chun Yun started as a senior credit clerk in the finance department. He suggested various new procedures to improve some of the processing methods used within the department. The result was an improved profit margin due to the reduction in error entries and streamlined processing cost.

At the time the company was expanding in the Far East and within a few years, he was promoted to be Assistant Manager in the department. Internally Chun Yun further improved the running of the department. Externally, Chun Yun instigated meetings with foreign customers to raise the company's profile and to generate more business. Having been educated in English, Chun Yun was able to communicate with these foreign customers at a personal level. The department increased the profit threefold after Chun Yun took over as Assistant Manager. Even the Managing Director noted the improvement in his division.

When the Japanese occupied Canton, a number of wealthy families in

Canton escaped to Hong Kong. Master Fung always liked Hong Kong more than Canton. It was a good excuse to set up an additional dwelling there. Master Fung took his family to establish a substantial residence in Hong Kong. Chun Yun requested a re-location to the Hong Kong branch, where he was going to implement the new procedures that he had established in Canton.

Siew Fen met with Ah-Shui and found that the Fung family also escaped to Hong Kong. They shared the same feeling of anger and hatred of the Japanese atrocities committed on innocent Chinese wherever they occupied. The two families resonated with each other over the Japanese invasion. The Fung family often invited Siew Fen and her children over for dinner.

At the time, Fung Chun Yun was in his late twenties. He was tall and good-looking with a serious guise that made him seem older than his age. He had just been relocated to Hong Kong as a Manager and Financial Controller of his division. While exuding confidence, Chun Yun was courteous and attentive to Siew Fen and her family.

Siew Fen thought, "Chun Yun is such an accomplished young man. He is well educated, has a good career, and must earn a good salary. He looks to have a bright future working at Jardin Financials. With a son-in-law like Chun Yun, Mee See's future could be assured." However, it was inappropriate for her to raise this matter with the Fung family.

On the morning of December 8, 1941 the Japanese launched an assault on Hong Kong. The British, Canadian and Indian army together with the Hong Kong volunteer defense forces resisted the advancing Japanese force. However, they were heavily outnumbered by the well-equipped and fearless Japanese army. After the fall of Wong Nai Chong Gap (黃泥涌峽), on the 25th of December, 1941, the British colonial officials, headed by Governor Mark Aitchison Young, officially surrendered at the Japanese headquarters.

At the time St Stephen's College was used as a hospital for the injured soldiers. Some drunken Japanese soldiers entered the hospital and shot two volunteer doctors. They then burst into the wards and bayoneted the wounded soldiers. The Japanese soldiers terrorised the local population by kidnapping and raping women, murdering many, and looting where they could. These Japanese atrocities were well reported in the newspaper.

After the St Stephen's College incident, Siew Fen heard that the Japanese were concentrating their advances on Hong Kong and other South East Asian territories and the Pacific. It might usher in a less vigorous attempt in Canton as the soldiers moved southwards. Siew Fen remembered with horror the time when the Japanese soldiers came into her ancestral home in Canton to search and rob with contempt. This residence in Hong Kong offered no place to hide. Siew Fen believed Hong Kong was not a safe place to settle anymore. Where could she escape with her young family? Recalling the close encounter with the Japanese soldiers, Siew Fen decided it might be safer to go home to Canton. However, Yee Por and Sai Por did not want to move as their financial base was in Hong Kong.

Return from Hong Kong to Canton

It was time to bid farewell to Yee Por and Sai Por. Siew Fen handed them the rental register and taught the two stepmothers how to manage their property portfolio and to use the rental income to support their living. She also handed over the gold nuggets that she saved using the excess rental income after she took over the management of their finances.

Yee Por and Sai Por were surprised to see the number of gold nuggets that Siew Fen had stashed away. They were very grateful to Siew Fen for being such a resourceful and honest stepdaughter.

Wing Chung and Mee Jing saw the gold nuggets. They picked them up and put them near their nose to sniff them. The nuggets looked like little flattened golden marbles that glistened in their eyes. They rolled them in their hands and wished they could have a few to keep.

Siew Fen gave the nuggets to the stepmothers and said, "These are not toys, children. Each gold nugget can be exchanged for money to feed the whole family for a month. Gold nuggets are best to keep for an emergency. They are better than any paper money, because their value rises in time of uncertainty when everything else loses value."

Siew Fen rolled them back into an old drawstring bag and continued, "You must hide them well because they can be stolen easily. Don't trust anyone with them."

Yee Por and Sai Por promised that they would look after the properties in the way that Siew Fen had taught them. They were grateful that Master Hui had left them a legacy that enabled them to live well and to pay for a good education for their children. Above all, they thanked Siew Fen for establishing a management strategy so that they could support themselves for their future.

Yee Por took a few gold nuggets from the old grey bag and put them in Siew Fen's hand and said, "Here, these three nuggets are for the children. Take them and spend them on whatever you see fit for the children."

Mee See had settled in Hong Kong and with her siblings, they had set up a little business earning good pocket money. In fact, they were just about to expand their little business to carry more stock items. Mee See did not want to go back to Canton. However, she felt helpless and was unable to disagree with her mother.

Siew Fen and the family visited Yee Ma and Luk KuChar at Yuen Long to bid them farewell. It seemed a short time since they last met again. Now there was another sudden departure, Siew Fen and the family were moving back to Canton from Hong Kong to escape the Japanese occupation for a second time. They each promised to visit again if circumstances allowed. Yee Ma decided to stay at Yuen Long with her daughter thinking that they would be safe enough from the Japanese in the village outside of the New Territories of Hong Kong.

Ah-Ku was disappointed as he was hoping to spend a lot more time with Mee See. He asked, "When will we meet again?"

Mee See replied, "Ah Tai told us yesterday that we are going home to Canton. She fears the Japanese atrocities may become wide spread in Hong Kong. In Canton we were hiding in a dark room under the kitchen when the Japanese soldiers came searching our house. Luckily they didn't find us hiding that time. Ah Tai says there is nowhere to hide in Grandma Hui's house. That's why she has decided it is time to go back to Canton."

Luk KuChar and Mee See were holding hands tightly with tears in their eyes. They promised that they would meet again one day no matter what happened.

The three teenagers were sitting quietly by the rice paddies, looking at the field of rice crops as the wind waved over the tall rice bushes. The rice plant had a main stem and a number of tillers. Each rice plant produced four or five tillers. Every tiller grew a flowering head or panicle, which produced the rice grains. As the grain began to mature near harvest time, the farmers 'locked up' the water on the bays, preventing any water run-off into the rice paddock. The soil then dried out in time for the harvest to commence.

As they gazed at this pasture of rice field, Ah Ku had so much he wanted to tell Mee See he loved her. He wanted to ask her to wait for him and to spend his life with her. However, the words would not come out in front of Luk KuChar. Mee See had tears in her eyes and was upset about having to leave Hong Kong against her will. But she could not tell if she was upset about leaving Luk KuChar or was heartbroken about leaving Ah Ku. Mee See was numb with sorrow. Finally they exchanged addresses and promised to write to each other hoping that one day they would meet again. Ah Ku affirmed that he would write very soon.

On the eve before the family departed, Siew Fen had doubts if she was doing the right thing going home to Canton. The family had settled very well in Hong Kong. Life was good in Hong Kong as the rental from Master Hui's estate was more than adequate for the family to live comfortably. There was no need for Siew Fen and her family to leave except for her fear of the Japanese atrocities. Siew Fen was sitting by the fish pond looking down at the reflection of the moon. Life was full of unexpected events. Once again Siew Fen had to move forward into the unknown. She did not know what was beyond tomorrow, but she felt that it was time to move on. She wished there was somebody she could confide in to make these major life decisions and to help shoulder the burden. There was no safe place under Japanese occupation. Under these circumstances, she just had to move on and be guided by her instincts.

With her three children, two servants and two cooks once again Siew Fen got ready to embark on the journey back to Canton. Mee See helped her mother to store all her jewellery, gold nuggets and cash into her long waist belt and covered them with the loose navy top. Mee See used the scissors to make a few holes in the oldest clothes that she and her siblings were going to wear. The servants washed these old clothes several times to make sure they looked genuinely well worn and the colour was faded. When the children all dressed in their well-worn clothes, they looked at each other laughing, thinking it was like a dress up game.

Siew Fen told the children, "This is not a game. We have to dress up so we can blend in with the common travelers on the public ferry and buses. Mee See you are the eldest, I want you to make sure Wing Chung and Mee Jing behave themselves and follow close to me without attracting people's attention. I shall rub charcoal on your face, and if we meet any Japanese, I want you to hold your heads down and keep quiet so as not to draw any attention. Let's hope we won't encounter any Japanese on the way home."

The party of eight set out on a ferry up the Pearl River to Canton. After an uneventful but tiring journey, the family arrived at the familiar iron-gate of their ancestral residence in Canton. Ah-Din opened the gate and was surprised to see the family at the door. He broke out with a broad smile on his face showing his uneven and tarnished teeth. He bowed to greet Madam Kwan and the family saying, "Madam Kwan, so happy you are home." Everyone was exhausted from travelling, but happy to arrive home. The servants went into their own quarters to settle once again and to prepare a good dinner for the family. The children went back to their rooms to clean up. They were so happy to see their long forgotten trucks, marbles, dolls, Chinese chess, and star checker game. They started to pull everything out from the toy boxes and relived the joyous games they used to play.

Wing Chung went to Wing Yu's toy box to pick out the favourites toys that he used to envy, thinking, "Ah Ha! All these are mine now!"

Siew Fen went into her own quarters and found everything was sparkling and clean. All her precious ornaments were exactly where she left them so many years ago. Siew Fen went into her bed chamber and saw her lovely red and gold embroidered silk quilt covers lying tidily on her bed. The beautiful bed drapes were still hanging around the bed frame, made of the finest dark Shun-Chee (酸枝) hardwood. She touched the bed covers and recalled all the finery that she had from her childhood.

Ah-Din was such a faithful servant, Siew Fen thought.

All of a sudden, she felt exhausted. The silk quilt looked luxurious. It felt soft and inviting. She lay down to caress that long forgotten smooth silk eiderdown with the fine golden thread embroidered patterns. She was surprised that she had never noticed how fine the stitches were on this beautiful red silk quilt cover. She ran her index finger along the smooth stitching of the golden phoenix. She had had this quilt since she was married into the Kwan family. It was one of the precious presents Madam Hui had given her daughter as part of her dowry. Siew Fen felt secure and stretched herself onto her comfortable bed in the ragged and dusty navy blue travelling suit that she had on for the last couple of days. Once again she enjoyed the luxury that she had known all her life. It was such a comfortable feeling. The next minute, she dozed off and was soon fast asleep.

All the servants knew Madam Kwan's discipline. Siew Fen always thanked the ancestors for her safe arrival each time she returned from travelling. As the servants had not seen Madam Kwan since her return, Mee See went into her mother's bed chamber to find her fast asleep on top of the beautiful red and golden silk eiderdown still in her old and shabby navy blue top and her dusty mud stained black trousers. She even had her dirty shoes on.

Mee See gently shook her mother's hand, "Ah Tai, it's time to wake up. Dinner is ready. Sam-Chai and Luk-Por have everything ready for us to pay our respects to the ancestors before dinner. "

Siew Fen woke up and saw Mee See all changed and clean. She was a beautiful daughter, Siew Fen thought, and said, "Oh, I dropped off after such a long and tiring journey. Let me clean up first. I'll come."

Mee See helped her mother take out the safety pins from her money belt before she left her to freshen up. Mee See told the servants to keep the food warm while waiting for Madam Kwan to come down when she was ready.

The Kwan family shrine was in a separate cottage near the fish pond in the garden. On a large red tray, the servants had a soya sauce chicken complete with the head and tail sitting on a plate, a whole steamed fish with ginger, shallots and a little oil and soya sauce, a plate of green vegetables, two tiny glasses of rose wine, and a couple of pairs of chop sticks. On a full-length table on the back wall, stood all the Kwan ancestral tablets according to their hierarchy. Towards the front of this table there were three ceramic urns each half filled with sand to take the candles and incense. Two coils of incense were burning continuously on top of the urns. On one side of the table, there were bundles of various sizes of red candles and incense sticks. Hanging from the ceiling were three separate dim red light bulbs emitting soft light in the family shrine.

This time, the Kwan family had only Siew Fen and her three children. Once again, the family took their turns to thank the ancestors for their safe return after years of being away. Siew Fen joined her hands together and bowed her head low before she went down on her knees to kowtow to show her gratitude for a safe return. She also sought guidance from the ancestors for the way to move forward, now that she was home safely with her family. The children each took their turn after their mother. Siew Fen and the children each burned a set of three incense sticks; put them into the urn, and let them burn with the smoke rising to the sky. The little family shrine was filled with smoke and the strong aroma of a mixture of candles and incense. Siew Fen finished the solemn ritual by pouring the small glasses of rose wine onto the floor as a gesture of yum-sing[32] (飲勝) bottoms-up with the ancestors. The children watched on patiently even though they were hungry and were ready for that delicious home cooked dinner in the security of their family home at last.

First Job in English

Even though a large delegation of Japanese soldiers moved southwards to Hong Kong and other South Eastern Asian countries, they still maintained some presence in Canton. Despite this, Siew Fen believed she made the right choice moving back Canton.

After all the interruptions to their schooling, the children decided not to go back to school in Canton. Mee See decided to look for a job to help Siew Fen with the living expenses. Wing Chung was happy not to go back to school too and decided to look for a job to earn his own pocket money. Mee Jing followed in her brother and sister's footsteps.

---

[32] yum-sing 飲勝, drink up, bottoms up, cheers with drinking companions.

As a result of moving around, people lost a lot of their possessions and most of their paperwork such as school examination results and birth certificates. Mee See was taller than most other girls of the same age at school. She was gentle and carried a lot of her mother's bearing and mannerisms. Mee See looked more mature than other girls her age. At sixteen, Mee See pretended to be three years older to apply for a number of clerical jobs. The fact that Mee See had been to high school and could speak and write English made her employable. She landed her first job at the Portuguese Consulate as a junior clerk. Her duties were to read the Chinese newspaper and other periodicals to find any articles that were written about Portugal and any Portuguese issues in the Far East which she subsequently translated into English. A Portuguese clerk's main duty was then to translate Mee See's writing into Portuguese. Together, they reported to the Portuguese Consulate officials in Canton. Mee See's first pay packet contained 250 Tai-Yuan bills, this was her pay for one month. Mee See jumped for joy and took all the money home to Siew Fen. She only kept enough for her own expenses and gave all the rest to her mother. From then on, she continued to let Ah Tai manage her earnings.

Their ancestral home was at Sharmeen, the wealthy side of town which was also near the area where many countries set up their Consulates. The Portuguese Consulate was only a short walk from Mee See's home. Even though she could go home for midday lunch, she took her lunch box to work so that she could work through her lunch hour.

Mee See was working well at the Portuguese Embassy. She learned about the news and current affairs of Canton and the rest of the country making good use of the two languages that she learned at school. She communicated in English with colleagues at work and was praised for her work by the officials at the Consulate. Mee See thanked her mother for sending her to learn English for all those years.

On the weekends, colleagues at work liked to go dancing at Wah Har Dancing Hall (華夏舞廳). Mee See was quick at learning the western style dances like the Waltz, Tango, Jive, Fox-trot, Rumba, and Samba. Although she only learned from various dance partners, she seemed to have the rhythm and movement of a professional dancer. In a very short time she became one of the most popular dance partners amongst her workmates. On most weekends, she was invited to dance parties at a number of popular dance halls in Canton.

Mee See continued to correspond with Ah Ku. It was decided that he would visit Canton and stay with Madam Kwan on the long summer holidays in the following year. When Ah Ku came to visit, he and Mee See planned to go around Canton sightseeing together. The two young lovers were developing a strong friendship despite the separation. Mee See was anticipating a future life together with Ah Ku when he qualified as a doctor.

Mee Jing was a pretty girl with a most infectious smile. She was quick witted and had a cheerful disposition. As the youngest sister and protected by the two elder siblings, Mee Jing was very confident. She had the ability to simplify problems and to resolve them step-by-step. Mee Jing was well aware that she was a capable girl. She was good looking, trim and nearly as tall as Mee See. Dressing like her sister, Mee Jing looked much older than her age. Mee Jing was popular with Mee See's Portuguese work colleagues because she was able to converse in English. Claiming to be a few years older so she could gain entrance to the dancing halls, she became quite a good dancer herself. With a good sense of humour, she mixed well with Mee See's friends and frequented the dance halls, café, swimming pools and cinemas on the weekends. Life was good for Mee Jing as she grew up.

Life, however, for Wing Chung was very different. Not having a male role model at home throughout his childhood had taken a toll on Wing Chung's confidence. Wing Chung missed his elder brother Wing Yu, the siblings' leader. Wing Yu always knew what to do and how to get around problems. Wing Chung seemed to lack ideas and needed to follow someone's example. He was at a loss most of time when confronted with problems. Fortunately he had Mee See and Mee Jing to confide in whenever he needed to make a decision.

Wing Chung was not comfortable working in an office like Mee See, because he never benefited from the few years of high school that he attended. He was never comfortable talking in front of a group of people. He chose to listen quietly to people's discussions. He liked the idea of going door-to-door trading so he did not have to approach people to find a job. He would rather deal with the public one at a time.

Mee Jing suggested that Wing Chung and she should seek work by approaching the fruit shop near the wholesaler from whom they purchased their small good supplies. Mee Jing innocently approached the fruit shop owner and asked if there was a job for two eager helping hands. Wing Chung managed to get a part time job stacking fruits and Mee Jing worked part time as a sales girl. They earned their pocket money working three days a week. For the rest of the week, they sold small goods door to door as they did in Hong Kong. Each month they took enough pocket money for themselves and they kept the excess as capital for more stock in their business.

Siew Fen revisited the properties she owned in Canton and once again got new paying tenants. Even though she could not command the same level of rental as she had before the Japanese occupation, it was an adequate income that managed to keep the family expenses with a little spare cash for saving. With the three children working and new rental from the properties, Siew Fen once again re-established a healthy income stream. Life was good in Canton once again.

PHOTOGRAPHS – EARLY 1900s

Mee See in her late teens

Outside the ancestral home in Canton
Wing Yu, Siew Fen, Wing Chung & Mee See

Mee See's first job as an English
interpreter at Portuguese Embassy in Canton

Mee See's best friend Ah Lin

Part Three – Arranged Marriage

Chun Yun

Siew Fen meet Master Fung by chance near Sharmeen, where they lived. She found out that he also brought his family back to Canton soon after the Japanese occupied Hong Kong. The Fung family was living just a couple of streets away from the Kwan ancestral home. The two families had a happy reunion. They concurred on how they abhorred the Japanese invasion and how much it had upset their families. They both exchanged news of the children since leaving Hong Kong. Siew Fen heard that Fung Chun Yun was promoted once again to be the Financial Controller of the Canton branch of his company. Wei Cheung the younger sister was at high school and wanted to continue her studies at a university overseas.

Siew Fen complimented, "Wei Cheung has always been a clever girl. Chun Yun is such an accomplished young man. You must have the Buddha smiling upon your family. Ah, I am really happy for you and Master Fung."

Ah Shui was eager to find out how the Kwan children were.

Siew Fen told Ah Shui, "Mee See has a job working for the Portuguese Embassy as a junior clerk interpreter. She interprets Chinese news into English text for another Portuguese clerk to translate from English to Portuguese. They report to the Consulate official about news and articles written about the Portuguese government." Siew Fen stopped and then continued, "The younger brother and sister are still too young to think of a career for now. They fill in time doing some trading to earn some pocket money in the meantime."

Master Fung was very impressed and said, "Mee See is very intelligent. You can see it from her bright eyes. Such a young girl and working at the Portuguese Embassy and using English as an interpreter! I am very impressed indeed!"

Siew Fen smiled and said modestly, "She was lucky to get this job. I am sure she is struggling to do her job or other work mates must have helped her along."

Master Fung affirmed, "Oh Madam Kwan is too humble. Mee See must be very good with her English or they wouldn't keep her. I couldn't see many men holding down a job like hers. She is clever in my book."

Ah Shui was Master Fung's second wife. Whenever Mee See met Ah Shui, she always addressed her as Madam Fung instead of her correct title, Fung Yee Tai (馮姨太) meaning Fung family's second madam. Ah Shui was very happy that Mee See always showed her due respect referring to her as the wife supreme.

The two families met often for dinner and went on outings together.

Since Chun Yun was promoted as the Financial Controller of his division, he was viewed as one of the up and coming young executives for career advancement in the Jardin's Financials Canton Branch.

Ah Shui said to Master Fung, "Chun Yun is such a successful young man. He has always been our pride and joy. He is now in his late twenties, it is time he married and settled down with a family. Surely you want to have some grandsons around to carry your name."

Master Fung smiled and answered, "You just know what is on my mind. However, I have never heard Chun Yun talk about going out with girls. Madam Kwan's elder daughter is such a beauty and a clever girl. She must be very capable to be working at the Portuguese Embassy. I like her a lot."

Ah Shui smiled broadly and continued, "I already know you are very keen on Madam Kwan's elder daughter. Nowadays, the young people talk about 'chee ye lun oi (自由戀愛)³³' finding their own partners. We don't use Mui-Yan-Por anymore these days. Let me talk to Madam Kwan. We should give the young people a chance to get to know each other. Just leave this to me."

Ah Shui came to visit Madam Kwan, and said, "Madam Kwan, our Master Fung thinks the world of your Mee See. We would like to invite your family over to have dinner with us to celebrate Chun Yun's promotion."

When they were in Hong Kong, Siew Fen was already keen on Chun Yun as an ideal son-in-law. She accepted the invitation with glee and complimented, "Congratulations to young Master Fung. I can see that he is a very capable man. He is so young and yet so accomplished. I am really happy for you and Master Fung."

Ah Shui saw Madam Kwan was full of praise for Chun Yun and added, "I am hoping to give Chun Yun and Mee See more chances to be together. By the way I hope your Miss Mee See has not been spoken for."

Siew Fen remembered Mee See had got on very well with Ah Ku in Yuen Long Hong Kong. She also knew that Mee See was talking about Ah Ku coming to Canton to visit them on the next summer holiday break. The images of Ah Ku and Fung Chun Yun appeared in her mind side by side. Ah Ku was a poor student. His father came from a poor fishing village. Chun Yun always wore the best suits and held an important and well-paid job in a major financial company. There was no comparison between the two men. She pushed Ah Ku's image to the back of her mind and decided Chun Yun was a much better match for Mee See.

Siew Fen quickly answered, "Mee See is going on seventeen. On the weekends she goes out with her work colleagues to ice skating, swimming and dancing. She gets on well with everyone at work, but she

---

³³ Chee ye lun oi (自由戀愛) Young people wanted to find their own marriage partner, instead of using the ancient method of engaging the service of a matchmaker to find a marriage partner.

does not have anyone in particular whom she goes out with in Canton."

Ah Shui was so happy to hear that Mee See was available and said, "Master Fung admires your Mee See. He can't stop talking about her being a good companion for Chun Yun. He thinks Mee See is young and accomplished. Holding down an English interpreter's job is very impressive indeed."

Encouraged by his parents, Chun Yun and sister, Wei Cheung, took the Kwan siblings out to the cinema, ice skating and went swimming together. He discovered Mee See had a good sense of humour. She seemed to know a lot about news and current affairs. She was much more mature and aware of the world than most young girls her age. Chun Yun admired Mee See and wanted to have a closer friendship with her, but he did not know how to approach the subject with her.

Chun Yun decided to speak to Ah Shui about Mee See.

Ah Shui asked, "Then what are you waiting for? You are not young now. It is time to get settled with a nice girl. Madam Kwan's daughter is such a capable girl, good looking and well educated. She is intelligent and has such good manners. She is a rare find."

Chun Yun felt uneasy and told his mother he did not know how to approach this matter.

Ah Shui laughed and said, "Here you are! A manager of your division and you can't tell a girl that you want her to be your wife? Ayarh! Leave this to Madam Kwan and me. Your father will be very pleased with you. He likes Madam Kwan's eldest daughter a lot."

Chun Yun said, "I am very grateful."

Ah Shui was overjoyed. She could not wait to call on Madam Kwan to ask for Mee See's hand. The ladies sat together at Madam Kwan's drawing room. In the middle of the room there was a black Shun-Chee round occasional table top with a round white marble-insert. The servant served up some Tit Kuen Yum (鐵觀音)[34], placing the tray on this table. After a few casual polite interchanges, Ah Shui approached Madam Kwan and gently said, "I have a mission today at the request of Chun Yun. I cannot fail my son or Master Fung. The reason I come today is to ask Madam Kwan for Mee See's hand in marriage for Chun Yun."

Siew Fen had dreamt of this day ever since the two families met again in Canton. However, she had to hold her decorum and be reserved so as not to show her eagerness. She knew that Chun Yun was interested in Mee See, but she could not rush to give chase for her daughter. Siew Fen thought, "This is such a good chance to settle Mee See's future and to finish her childish dreams about Ah Ku. Chun Yun would give Mee See a good living for the rest of her life. If Mee See was married, there would be one less worry about her being caught as a 'flower girl' by the ruthless Japanese soldiers."

Siew Fen was deep in her own thoughts and Ah Shui was getting a little worried as she hadn't got a response from Madam Kwan. Ah Shui added, "I do hope our Chun Yun is good enough for Madam Kwan's precious eldest daughter."

Siew Fen gathered herself quickly. With a broad smile, she responded, "This is too good to be true! We are honoured to be matched with Master Fung's family. Although our Kwan family had been one of the known families in Canton, since Master Kwan passed on we had to sell up to escape to our summer residence at the village Xiqiao and then to Hong Kong. We only have some furniture and some jewellery for Mee See as a dowry for her marriage. I am afraid we may not be a good match to the wealthy Master Fung's family. That's why I hesitated."

Ah Shui added, "My mission is to talk you into giving your Mee See to marry our Chun Yun. For a long time, our Lau Yau has admired her as being capable and well disciplined. Our Chun Yun aspires to have Mee See's hand in marriage. They have given me this mission to persuade

---

[34] Tit Kuen Yum 鐵觀音 a quality tea reserved for honoured guests

Madam Kwan today. Madam Kwan is too modest. All I need today is for Madam Kwan to agree." Ah Shui drank another sip of the lovely tea and continued, "Nowadays, very few people talk about a sizeable dowry. Let us look after everything for the wedding. Of course once Madam Kwan's eldest daughter becomes our young Madam Fung, she would not need her position at the Embassy. In fact as the young Madam Fung, she would never need to work."

The two ladies drank to a happy match. They looked forward to a closer relationship in the future. As it was the first time in a long while that the two families have had a happy event in their household, they began to discuss the wedding plans. Ah Shui wanted everything befitting the Fung family's standing in Canton society. Since both Mee See and Chun Yun worked in European establishments with European department heads and European colleagues, the parents decided to opt for an East and West combined wedding ceremony. They would have a daytime European marriage ceremony at the church with a white satin and lace wedding dress and formal tuxedo. In the afternoon, they would follow the Chinese traditional wedding banquet with the proper tea ceremony. At night they had invited guests for over 100 tables for the wedding banquet at the most famous Smiling Buddha (佛笑樓) restaurant.

The two mothers were so happy about this union. They talked for hours about how they could prepare for this significant festivity for the two households. Siew Fen forgot that she had not asked Mee See if she was happy with the arrangement. Siew Fen thought, "This is such a good match! I am sure that Mee See cannot do any better. One day she will realise this is for her own good."

It was decided that Mee Jing and Wei Cheung would be the flower girls. Wing Chung was to be the best man.

Ah Shui went home very happy with her mission accomplished. The Fung family started the preparations for this major occasion. Everyone was excited, anticipating a happy and successful event.

Mee See had been working at the Portuguese Embassy for nearly a year, and she was quite settled in her role as a junior interpreter making full use of the English language that she perfected every day. Being hardworking and a quick learner, she executed her duty with accuracy and diligence. As time passed, Mee See gained confidence in her role at the office. She had made lots of friends inside and outside of the Embassy. Life was good.

Siew Fen told Mee See the Fung family thought a lot of her. Madam Fung expressed her son's wish of asking for her hand in marriage. Master and Madam Fung were hoping to have a daughter-in-law like Mee See.

Mee See only had Ah Ku in her heart. They were planning a future together. When Ah Ku finished medicine, she would be in her twenties. That would be just right because it would give her a few more years to continue her career. Mee See was looking forward to spending time with Ah Ku next summer break from the university. How could she break her promise and let Ah Ku down? Besides, Chun Yun was more than ten years older than Mee See. She was surprised to hear of his admiration for her. The reason that she went out with Chun Yun was to please Madam Fung and her mother. Mee See liked him, but was far from viewing him as someone she would want to spend the rest of her life with.

Mee See was astonished and said, "Ah Tai, this is such a surprise! I am too young to think of marriage. I am not ready for marriage now."

Siew Fen could not take no for an answer, because she had already promised Mee See to the Fung family. She would lose face to go back on her words. If the Fung family heard about it, they would be very upset, and it would affect their impression of Mee See.

Siew Fen was frustrated, raising her voice; she slammed the table and said, "Not marrying! That is not up to you!"

It was the very first time in Mee See's life that her mother was angry with her. Mee See was a little threatened and she did not want to upset her mother and explained quietly, "I was not saying I won't want to marry ever. Just that it is not the right time now. It was so hard to get into a good vocation. I am working so well at the Portuguese Embassy. Our life is settled in Canton. I was hoping to work for another six or seven years to gain some experience in work and in life before I thought about getting married."

Siew Fen returned, "In six or seven years' time, you will be twenty-three, twenty-four years old! You can't expect to be married and be the supreme wife by then. At that age you may be lucky to be somebody's concubine, or some rich man's Yee Tai Tai. Don't ever dream about being the supreme wife at that age."

Mee See recalled her mother's marriage history. Both mother and father came from such wealthy families. Unfortunately, they could never see eye to eye. They even fought over the family inheritance in the law courts for seven years. Then her mother had to be a school teacher to earn a living to support the family at the village. Mother's wealthy match ended in despair.

Siew Fen reiterated, "How can I make you understand that I am only thinking about your own good? This is your chance for a good husband. The Fungs are wealthy. Chun Yun is so well educated. He has such a good job and a bright future. How can I make you see that this sort of chance doesn't come every day? The Fungs are so fond of you. They would be so good to you!"

Siew Fen continued, "The Fung family thinks so much of you, in particular Master Fung. He has picked you as the supreme wife of his only son and heir. You will be the young Madam Fung. It is hard to find a family of good repute these days. Most good and wealthy families have left Canton since the Japanese occupation. If you don't marry Chun Yun, where will you find an eligible family and such an accomplished young man? I also fear the Japanese might pick you up as a 'flower girl' which would be horrendous."

Siew Fen was exasperated and angry that she was unable to convince Mee See to see her point of view. She continued firmly, "Fung Chun Yun will not wait for you for six or seven years. He will find someone else before then. If you don't take up this opportunity, you will regret it one day. I really don't know what else you want from life?"

Mee See told her mother "My real age is only seventeen, even though I lied about being twenty at work. I have hardly started my working life! I know you are planning for my future." Mee See wanted to tell her mother the truth that she promised to wait for Ah Ku to finish medicine. As mother was so angry at the time, she dared not speak about Ah Ku.

As though she could hear Mee See's thoughts, Siew Fen continued, "If you want to wait for Ah Ku to finish medicine, he might want to study further after his university degree. You may plan to wait for him for six, seven, ten or twelve years. How can you be sure that he will still want you at the end? By then, you would have wasted your youth waiting around for nothing."

Mee See considered what her mother was saying. It made sense that waiting for Ah Ku might not work in the long run. Tears started to flow down her cheeks, and she slumped on the chair feeling absolutely helpless and hopeless about continuing the fight against her mother's reasons.

Siew Fen was getting desperate, she insisted, "This is such a good marriage, can't you see everything is working for your good future? If you don't want to marry, do you want to work for the rest of your life? If you do, go to work then don't consider coming home to see me anymore. Don't ever tell me about your problems anymore."

Mee See remembered how determined mother was when she sent Wing Yu away for cheating so many years ago. She knew that her mother had already decided on the match with the Fung family. It would be futile to fight against her mother, unless she was prepared to leave home.

Mee See was considering how she could tell Ah Ku. She really would like to talk to him in person, but there was no way she could leave Canton to find him in Yuen Long. Mee See was desperately unhappy, she felt she had lost control of her destiny. She wrote a letter to Ah Ku and explained to him that mother had arranged a marriage for her. She could not see herself rebelling against her mother's wishes. She told Ah Ku to find another more deserving girl as his companion. She wished him well and she knew he would be successful in his studies. Mee See did not have the courage to send the letter. She kept Ah Ku deep in her heart.

Mee See sat by the fish pond, leaning against the pagoda. As the moon light reflected on the mirror of water in the pond and the dark clouds were moving to cover the moon, leaving shards of light emitting between the clouds, Mee See wished she could see Ah Ku and talk to him. She gazed at the distant moon. It was a new change that was forced upon her. She did not know what the future would hold. She knew that her mother would choose the best for her.

To save money, Siew Fen was going to do a lot of the wedding preparations herself. She was going to cash in some of her gold nuggets to buy nice clothes for Mee See. The Kwan family must not lose face by a measly dowry. Mee See must have sets of fine clothes and matching shoes. Siew Fen gave Mee See some pieces of the best jewels from her own collection. Sam-Chai was chosen to follow Mee See to the Fung family as her own personal servant.

Master and Madam Fung had thought of everything for the wedding. They brought over everything that was needed for the bride's family. They sent over a tailor and a shoemaker to measure the whole family for all the outfits that were needed for the wedding. Home decorators came over to consult with Mee See about her favourite colour scheme so they could redecorate the living quarters where the newlyweds would reside in the Fung's walled estate.

Mee See was measured for the white satin and lace-wedding gown for the church ceremony. She was also measured for the Chinese red silk wedding Qipao suit that had golden phoenix embroidery for the traditional tea ceremony and the Chinese wedding banquet. Then there were also several sets of Qipao and the going away outfit. Shoemakers came to measure for a number of matching leather shoes and handbags.

Mee Jing was measured for a beautiful pink flower girl dress with matching shoes. They even added a little matching jacket for the evening. Wing Chung was measured for a new three-piece suit as the best man. It was Wing Chung's very first European suit. Even Siew Fen, the mother-of-the-bride, was measured for several silk Qipao with matching shoes and handbags for the joyous occasion.

Master Fung and Ah Shui would spare no expense for Chun Yun's wedding. They were extremely generous to the bride's family. It was a reflection of how much Master Fung thought of Mee See. The Fung family was doing everything to make Mee See feel welcome.

Siew Fen recalled how she was taught by her mother and other elders before she was married into the Kwan family. After all these years, it was her turn to teach her daughter how to behave as a daughter-in-law in a wealthy and traditional family to show that she had the discipline and knew her place. She would not shame her parents by behaving inappropriately. Siew Fen was busy teaching Mee See how to behave as the supreme wife of a wealthy household. Mee See was preoccupied with the preparation for the wedding. She learned how to walk in her lovely Qipao to show her best image without flaunting her fineries. She was taught how to behave and to respect her father and mother-in-law and how to care for her husband. She was taught how to treat the servants in her husband's household.

Mee See began to be convinced that her mother was right in planning her life to marry into a good household. She rewrote her letter to Ah Ku. This time, she was more rational about the whole situation and explained her mother's arrangement for her to marry into the Fung family. Mee See posted the letter and felt better afterwards. Soon her sadness for Ah Ku was replaced with all the activities for the grand occasion.

At last the wedding day arrived. There was the European wedding in the morning at the local church. Ah Shui employed assistants to help with the make-up and to take care of all the dresses to be worn by the bride, the bridesmaids and the mother-of-the-bride during the day. The assistants also looked after the hairstyles and make-up for the ladies in the bride's family. Mee See wore a white satin and lace-wedding gown with a matching pair of white satin beaded high heel shoes. She had a new hair-do that complemented the headdress and the long white veil that draped elegantly behind her. With professional make-up, she was so surprised to see the attractive image in the full-length mirror. She turned left and right and tried walking forward as though she was walking down the aisle. She was amazed at her transformation! She looked so mature that she could not believe that the beautiful image in the mirror was the same seventeen-year-old Mee See. Finally, Mee See was grateful that her mother had insisted on her getting married.

The young people, in particular, enjoyed the church wedding. After the couple exchanged vows and the wedding rings, they signed the marriage certificate that was witnessed by Master Fung and Mee See's boss at the Portuguese Consulate, who also gave the bride away. It was a refreshing change to have part of the ceremony in English for the benefit of a number of Chun Yun's senior Branch managers, the many Portuguese Consulate officers, and Mee See's work colleagues.

Siew Fen exclaimed, "How times have changed. We didn't need a piece of paper to say that we were married in our days."

Mee Jing and Wei Cheung wore pink lace dresses with long deep red sashes that tied in a bow at the back that showed off their tiny waists. They had the most engaging smiles and were admired for their youthful beauty. Many girls came over to touch their beautiful dresses, and wished they too had dresses like them.

Wing Chung stood upright in his smart and well fitted mid grey three-piece suit. He wore a deep red bow tie that matched the colour of the bridesmaids' sash. He never felt so handsome. It was good to dress up smartly, he thought. He kept checking the wedding rings in his pocket all morning in case he lost them. He was so relieved after handing them over to the priest during the ceremony.

Chun Yun was in a dark grey three-piece suit with a deep red bow tie and a deep red rose in his buttonhole. He stood at five-feet-ten looking more handsome than usual. He was so happy that this was the big day he had been waiting for. He kept peeping at Mee See and saw her long eyelashes and relaxed demeanor, her undisturbed free spirit at such an occasion being the center of attention of so many people. She could still carry her smile and responded to all the well wishes from the guests she knew and also from guests she had never met. Her pale face with a little highlight on her cheeks made her looked stunningly beautiful.

The newlyweds stood together and looked such a handsome couple. Many pictures were taken. The photographer organised the family to stand together in different poses with the newlyweds. All the young people wanted to pose with the beautiful new bride.

After the wedding at the church, the assistant helped Mee See into her Chinese red silk wedding suit. It was red silk with golden thread embroidery of a dragon and a phoenix on the top with a matching long skirt with tassels on the bottom edge. The assistant replaced her long wedding veil and headdress with a bright red silk rose on a line of diamonds clipped to one side of her hair. The assistant and Sam-Chai helped Mee See every time she had to get down on her knees to kowtow to the elders of both families. Sam-Chai helped to collect and put away all the Lai-See given by the elders and by each well-wisher.

All the foreign friends witnessed a very different wedding as many had never been to a traditional Chinese wedding before. They were intrigued by the tea ceremony with all its colour, sight and sounds being played out in front of their eyes. In the middle of the alcove of the restaurant, there were two wide Shun-Chee chairs with red and gold back and seat cushions embroidered with the words, "Double Happiness (囍)". In front of the two chairs there were two thick red and gold cushion stools. This was where the newlyweds would kneel to pay their respects to the elders of the two families according to their rank in the family hierarchy. Sam-Chai and the assistant had prepared a number of tea cups and saucers ready for this occasion. They put a dry red prune into the tea cup before pouring in the tea and set them aside on the saucers.

The Master of Ceremonies (MC) invited Master and Madam Fung to be seated to receive the newlyweds. Chun Yun and Mee See, supported by Sam-Chai and the assistant, moved forward in front of Master and Madam Fung. The couple bowed low to show respect and got down on their knees on the stools in front of Chun Yun's parents. Sam-Chai and the assistant helped Mee See with her skirt making sure it did not get caught in her beaded red satin high heel shoes. The MC recited poems in a singsong tune finishing with counting - one kowtow, two kowtow and three kowtow as the young couple kowtowed at each command. With a broad smile the senior Fungs took a sip of the tea then handed it back to the assistant. They each took out a big red Lai-See for the newlyweds, who received with two hands and bowed deeply to express their gratitude for their blessings. All the while the MC continued chanting poems to bestow blessings on the newlyweds. Sam-Chai helped to put away the Lai-Sees that the newlyweds were given. Madam Fung leaned forward with an elaborate heavy gold necklace to put on Mee See's neck. That was followed by a thick matching heavy gold bangle which was secured on her wrist. She bowed deeply to thank Madam Fung for her generous wedding gift. Master and Madam Fung then slowly stood up and walked to the side as the MC called out for the next elders in rank to come forward to receive the newlyweds. All the aunties and uncles on the Fung side of the family took their places before Siew Fen took her place from the Kwan side of the family. Siew Fen chose the heaviest set of her gold chain and bracelet to give to Mee

See.

At the end of the tea ceremony, Mee See had several gold necklaces draped around her neck plus many sets of bangles on both wrists. For the first time Mee See was in possession of all that sparkling jewellery. Sam-Chai and the assistant helped Mee See change into the next outfit for the wedding banquet. Mee See was relieved of all the weighty jewellery. Sam-Chai locked it away with all the Lai-See in a chest provided by the restaurant for them to take home at the end of the banquet. Mee See only wore the set of jewellery from Madam Fung as a mark of respect for her mother-in-law.

There were a hundred tables of guests attending the Fung/Kwan wedding banquet. Besides the family and relatives from both families, the guests included officials and colleagues from the Portuguese Embassy, English managing directors, other senior managers, and work colleagues from Chun Yun's Financial Company. Many owners from well-known ship building companies and many of Master Fung's business associates came to help Master Fung celebrate the occasion of his only son and heir's marriage.

There were many courses at the wedding banquet. The MC sang out in poetic rhyme as each dish was brought to the head table. Then it was time for the newlyweds to go around to each table to drink with the guests to thank them for their gifts and to show appreciation for their attendance at this joyous union of the two families. There were many more Lai-See given to Mee See from the guests at each table. Sam-Chai helped put them all away. It took a long time to visit all one hundred tables.

Mee See changed several times during the day and the evening. The MC did a superb job coordinating all the activities to make sure the day went smoothly with lots of music and activities. There was a live band playing modern music. It was a wedding mixed with Eastern and Western traditions. All Mee See's friends from the Embassy were very impressed with her wedding. They saw the extent of the luxury displayed unashamedly. The ladies' jewellery sparkled on their necks, on their ears, around their wrists, and on their fingers. The standard of the banquet and the decorations of the whole ceremony displayed the wealth of the Fung family. It was a long, tiring, but joyous day full of good wishes.

Siew Fen was laughing and smiling all night. She reflected on her own wedding so many years ago. She was satisfied that Mee See's wedding was also such a huge event with so many guests. This wedding even had a number of English guests from Chun Yun's firm and a number of Portuguese Embassy officials from Mee See's work place. In fact, she admitted that Mee See's wedding was even more luxurious than her own. She was comforted that she had done her duty and married Mee See to the right family. She was sure Chun Yun would give Mee See the living that was appropriate for the Kwan's eldest daughter.

She was proud of the fact that she had discharged her responsibility as a good mother.

Ah Ku's Misery

Inside the church and outside, in the church yard, was full of gaiety. There were bustling movements with happy laughter, jokes, and lively conversation. Everyone was having such a good time.

However, opposite the Church, the mood was different.

Ah Ku was hiding behind a tree, watching the wedding progress from outside the church. He dared not get closer as he was not invited. Mee See did not have the heart to send him an invitation knowing it might cause him grief. Ah Ku received Mee See's letter explaining to him why she had to obey Madam Kwan and marry into the Fung family. In the letter she wished him success in his studies. It was fate that she could not wait for him to qualify as a doctor. She wanted him to find another girl to share his success. She ended the letter wishing him happiness with another girl who would be more deserving to share his life.

Ah Ku was broken-hearted. He read the letter again and again and he could feel the helpless and hopeless situation that Mee See was in. He came from Yuen-Long to Hong Kong to catch a ship to go to Canton. He just wanted to see Mee See one last time before the wedding. He was hoping to persuade her to run off with him. He called at Madam Kwan's house and found that he had arrived on Mee See's wedding day! The wedding party had already left for the church. He still wanted to see Mee See one last time to talk to her. He was sure that Mee See would talk to him if she saw him or knew that he was there. At least he wanted her to be aware that he was present.

There were so many people surrounding the church yard. Ah Ku thought it would be hopeless trying to talk to the bride. But he still wished she might be able to see him across the street. He would settle for Mee See knowing that he had come all the way to see her.

The crowd screamed and hands clapped as the newlyweds walked from the side door of the church. Mee See was in a beautiful satin and white lace-wedding gown. She was carrying a bunch of flowers with deep pink long flowing ribbons. She placed her long veil on her arm so she could walk without tripping over it. She was absolutely adorable. The groom was tall and he looked handsome in a well-tailored dark grey three-piece suit. He was supporting the bride as they stood where the photographer had organised to take photos with relatives and friends. The shy young bride was leaning against the groom for protection as they were walking on the undulating grass by the church yard.

Ah Ku was green with envy. The feeling of jealousy rose in Ah Ku's heart as he saw the groom holding hands with the bride. Everything blurred as tears welled up in his eyes. He swallowed hard to hold back those tears. He would not let them run down his face.

Several girls rushed to surround the newlyweds. They teased the bride jokingly. They were laughing merrily. A number of foreigners came up to shake hands with the groom and then the bride. Mee Jing and Wei Cheung with a number of other girls were throwing lucky rice, paper flowers, and coloured ribbons at the new couple. Church bells were ringing. A choir was singing hymns. Laughter and light-hearted conversation surrounded the smiling newlyweds. The bride looked happy and shy as she was assisted into a silver stretched limousine that was decorated with white satin drapes over the seats and the floor. The groom sat next to the bride, after he made sure that Mee See was comfortable in her seat. The car drove off followed by no less than thirty other cars.

The church yard lost all that commotion and returned to peace and quiet. Ah Ku was leaning against the fence opposite the church sobbing bitterly and quietly. No one took any notice of his presence. He was heartbroken, he was defeated. However, he did not hold a grudge against Mee See. He knew that Mee See did not want to give him up, she simply had no choice. He did not resent Madam Kwan either. How could he resent a mother who wanted the best for her precious daughter? He looked down on himself. He was too poor. His family was no match in any shape or form to the groom's family. Madam Kwan came from a very wealthy family. He would not be able to give Mee See the lifestyle which she was accustomed to. If the wedding was for him today, he could not see himself as the groom. He could not afford such extravagance. Everything he saw today was lavish and luxurious. He would not know where to start to provide such comfort for Mee See. He only blamed the fact that he was born under wrong circumstances. He was not meant to be with Mee See.

Suddenly Ah Ku felt peaceful and calm. He thought, "Well Mee See is married and has a husband now. The friendship between us comes to an end. I should be happy for her. I am simply too poor. How could I support her? This groom looks like such a good match for her. Even if I could somehow get between them, I can't see Mee See giving him up for me." At that moment, Ah Ku decided he would study harder in medicine. He wanted to be the best medical doctor in his field. He would not disappoint his father. He could see the many lines and the sun-beaten expression on his father's face as a result of the years of exposure to the harsh weather; fishing for a living. His hands were leathery and rough from a lifetime of heavy manual work. Even though Ah Ku had won a scholarship for his schooling, it was still lots of hard work for his father to earn enough money to send him to the university.

He was determined he would not fail his father. He also decided he would never fall in love, ever again.

Happily Married

At the time, Macao (澳門) and Hong Kong were the two special administrative regions of the People's Republic of China. Macao was on the western side of the Pearl River Delta[35] across from Hong Kong which was to the east, bordering Guangdong province to the north and facing the South China Sea to the east and south. Hong Kong was a British Colony; Macao was a Portuguese colony. They were the first and last European colonies in China. Portuguese traders first settled in Macao in the 16th century and subsequently administered the region until the handover on 20th December 1999.

As a Portuguese colony, Macao had a strong Portuguese influence. Many buildings were influenced by Portuguese architecture. Chun Yun's company had a small branch office in the colony and during the year, Chun Yun had to inspect the business in Macao a number of times.

Chun Yun and Mee See went on a two-week honeymoon to Macao. Mee See had never been there before. The newlyweds had a fabulous time during their honeymoon. Chun Yun took Mee See sightseeing to many of the tourist attractions including St Paul's Cathedral, the A-Ma Temple, the New Garden skating rink, the Casino Lisbon, and the Smiling Buddha (佛笑樓) seafood restaurant. Chun Yun was most attentive to his beautiful young wife. Everything went smoothly and was agreeable. Mee See enjoyed all the attractions of Macao. Secretly, Mee See was happy that she followed her mother's advice to marry Chun Yun. Their

---

[35] Pearl River Delta, see Diagram of Locations (Not to scale) on page 13.

honeymoon was a fabulous way to begin a new life together.

Before they left Macao, Chun Yun took Mee See to the Central Entertainment Complex Casino (中央賭塲). Mee See didn't know that a gambling house was a tourist attraction. She had some reservations about going into a gambling house. Mother had always warned against gambling and she remembered her elder brother, Wing Yu was disowned because of he was deceitful and his gambling habit.

However, Mee See did not want to spoil the fun of their honeymoon by refusing to go gambling. She justified the fact that she only went there to please her husband. Chun Yun bought a whole lot of gambling chips and gave Mee See half of them to play at the various gaming tables. It looked as though Chun Yun was pretty good at this. Chun Yun introduced Mee See to a number of gambling games like Tai-Sai (大細), Fan-Tan (番攤) and Pai-Gow (牌九). They were all ancient traditional games that wagered at the Casino. It must have been beginner's luck. Mee See won several times on the roll of the dice. They doubled their chips in a very short time. The couple ended a very happy honeymoon with big wins at the Casino. Mee See realised for the first time that chips at the casino were a substitute for money.

After Mee See was married, she lived at Master Fung's ancestral home at Po Yuen Road (寶源路). Master Fung and Madam Fung treated Mee See as if she was their daughter. Mee See brought her own maid Sam-Chai as her personal servant. Ah Shui took control of the Fung family household. Chun Yun had contributed to Ah Shui housekeeping money since he started working. He gave Ah Shui an additional allowance to cover the expenses now that he was married.

Mee See had to resign from her work at the Portuguese Embassy as the Fung family would lose face if the young Madam Fung had to work and earn a living. Chun Yun also gave Mee See an allowance which was more than she used to earn. Living with the Fung family, Mee See very seldom needed to spend her allowance. She remembered her mother's teaching and used the money to buy gold nuggets by the ounce as soon as she had saved enough money. Mee See was very grateful that Chun Yun also gave additional allowance for her mother.

Chun Yun took Mee See along when he had to travel to Macao and Hong Kong to inspect business until the children arrived. She always brought home exquisite presents for the in-laws. The senior Fungs thought Mee See was such a respectful daughter-in-law and Wei Cheung thought her such a thoughtful sister-in-law. She was kind and courteous to all the servants and footmen. Often she would rather send her own servant to do her errands without troubling the Fung family servants. She was well thought of by all the servants as well.

Chun Yun continued to take Wing Chung and Mee Jing out with Mee See picnicking and to the movie cinemas. The siblings thought Chun Yun was such a generous brother-in-law.

Mee See was happily married. After four years they had three children. As a mark of respect to Master Fung, all the children were named by Master Fung. The elder son was named Kai Ming (鉅明), the second, a daughter, was named Yau Mui (友梅) and the third, a son, and was named Kai Chung (鉅忠). As was the tradition with wealthy families, the young madam of the family would not need to feed nor care for the babies. Madam Fung employed a Sup-Ma (濕媽) and a Kon-Ma (乾媽) to take care of each baby until they were toddlers. Mee See's personal maid Sam-Chai supervised all the servants to make sure they took good care of the young Fung family. The three children brought much joy to the household. Master Fung and Madam Fung loved their grandchildren, in particular the sons that carried the Fung's name. These four years were the best years of Mee See's life.

Siew Fen was comforted that her son-in-law was so generous to her. It showed how much he loved her daughter. She believed that she might have changed Mee See's fate by stopping the relationship with Ah Ku and finding her the right marriage. It affirmed Siew Fen's belief that one could control one's fate by changing the circumstances when opportunities presented themselves.

Mee Jing's Match

Near where Mee Jing and Wing Chung worked at the market fruit shop was Tuck-Yick Sauce Manufacturer's 　(得益醬油) main shop. This shop was the main distributor of all the products from their village factory at Sheck Kai (石岐) Village near Canton. This factory produced all the major lines of sauces; soya sauce, oyster sauce, sesame sauce, chili sauce, Hoi Sin sauce, and fish sauce just to name a few. These were ingredients that were used in all Asian restaurants, and they were basic cooking ingredients for each household.

The owner Master Tam Dai Yeur (譚大爺) and Tam Dai Leun (譚大娘) made their fortune from humble beginnings. The Tams worked as laborers at the sauce factory. When the Japanese occupied Canton in 1938, there was looting of several Tuck Yick shops. The boss of Tuck Yick Sauce Manufacturer decided to cut his losses and sold all the shops in Canton and the factory at Sheck Kai. The Tams managed to buy the factory at below cost price and continued producing all the sauces that they had done all their life. Dai Yeur carried the products to Canton to supply the restaurants and distributors. It was hard work to push the trolley to deliver their products to the city from the village. However the profit was well worth the effort. They also added new product lines under the well-known banner of Tuck Yick Sauce Manufacturer. Over the years, they built up the business and established a Tuck-Yick Sauce Manufacturer shop in Canton. The Tams supplied the Japanese soldier camps with free sauces in exchange for their protection. The Tams managed to expand their business and traded in peace. The Tuck Yick Sauce Manufacturer business grew and they started opening distribution branches in Macao, Hong Kong, and Hainan.

The Tams started their family late in life. They had one son and heir, Tam Kin Wah (譚健華). Kin Wah attended the best high school in Canton but there was no plan for him to do further study. It was the parents' expectation for him to take over the business as the older generation retired. At twenty-one, Kin Wah spent his time at the main shop in Canton to learn the family's business when he met Mee Jing and Wing Chung.

Kin Wah was attracted to Mee Jing for her beautiful complexion and her cheerful and jolly approach to life. He befriended Wing Chung to have more excuses to see Mee Jing. The three young people often went to the cinema. Kin Wah often walked them to their home before he went home to dinner.

It so happened that the Tuck Yick Sauce Manufacturer's shop needed a cashier. At the time Mee Jing was only sixteen years old. Kin Wah persuaded his father to give Mee Jing a chance working as a cashier. Mee Jing was smart and could apply what she learned quickly. When she was selling household products from door to door with her sister and brother, she saw her sister log all the products, sale price and profit margin in a list. In a very short time, she learned to note the products and trade transactions in the register, in particular the bulk buyers from the chain restaurants. Kin Wah often stayed on to help Mee Jing finish the register.

The senior Tams were surprised at Mee Jing's ability to work systematically. Kin Wah was the only hope they had of handing over the business that they had created through hard work. They were intrigued by this young new cashier who had the power of making their son stay at work late before coming home to dinner. They were impressed that their son was, at last, interested in working at the business.

Tai Luen decided to go to work at the Tuck Yick Sauce Manufacturer shop to get to know this young cashier who enticed her son to work diligently at the shop. She found Mee Jing a cheerful girl who made the customers feel at ease in the shop. She helped with their selection and showed them what other sauces would go well with their selection. Mee Jing was quick and accurate with the abacus. Most girls her age did not have this calculating skill. Although they were a new found wealthy family, they wanted to make sure their son's choice of partner came from a family of good repute.

Wanting to know more about Mee Jing's background, Madam Tam enquired, "Mee Jing, you are so clever and quick in learning our business. Your parents must be very proud of you."

Mee Jing was naïve. Without thinking she answered, "I was born in Canton Sai Kwan Hospital[36](西關醫院). My father died when I was young. I only have a mother at home. We live at Fung Yuen North Street our ancestral home. My sister married a few years ago. She lives a couple of streets from us at Po Yuen Road. There is only mother and my elder brother living at home now."

Sharmeen, Po Yuen Road, and Fung Yuen North Street were streets located on the wealthy side of Canton. Tai Luen imagined that Mee Jing must have come from a wealthy family. Tai Luen added, "I hear that people living at Fung Yuen North Street are all wealthy families. All the houses over there are garden mansions. They are unlike the ancient walled Chinese style houses in which we live. Your home must be very modern and very spacious."

Mee Jing smiled and answered, "Our ancestral home has two stories. Each level has four lounge rooms and seven bedrooms. We have the usual garden with a fish pond and several other cottages within the walled iron-gate. It is a very plain building really for that area. May be one day, we will invite you and Master Tam over to have dinner with us."

Mee Jing went home and told Siew Fen, "Madam Tam is interested in the house we live in. I have invited her and Master Tam to come over

---

[36] Canton Sai Kwan Hospital 西關醫院 was a well-known private hospital. Only the wealthy families could afford to seek treatment from this hospital.

and have dinner with us one day."

Siew Fen told her daughter, "I don't know Master and Madam Tam. I have no reason to invite them to dinner. If they had manners, they would not accept your invitation either." Siew Fen was trying to instill in Mee Jing the manners of a traditional family.

Tears streamed down her face, she was angry with her mother for not agreeing with her request, "I have already told Madam Tam we would invite them for dinner. I will lose face if you will not invite them. You have always taught me to keep my promise. Now you will not support me. How can I face them again?"

Being the youngest, Mee Jing was Siew Fen's favourite child. She often made use of this advantage to get her way. She knew that Kin Wah was interested in her and she wanted the two parents to meet.

Mee Jing added, "Why don't you come to the shop to buy some cooking ingredients. You would then meet Madam Tam. She only comes to the shop on Monday afternoons. There are many new sauces that we don't have at home."

Siew Fen always had chefs and cooks to work in her kitchen since her birth. She didn't need to look at her kitchen, let alone to check for cooking ingredients. She had never gone to the market or shopped for her own food provisions. As Kin Wah was the only son and heir of Tuck Yick Sauce Manufacturer, a well-known brand in Canton, he would one day inherit the family fortune and he looked an eligible son-in-law. Siew Fen decided she had better get to know the Tam family in case they wanted to be associated with the Kwan family. It was worth a journey to go with her servants and cooks to see what new sauces the servants might need for the kitchen.

Siew Fen stopped Mee Jing's crying saying, "All right, all right, Ah-Din will come with us when I take Sai-Mui and Luk-Por to shop at the Sauce Manufacturer next Monday afternoon."

It was the beginning of Madam Kwan's association with Master and Madam Tam. They became good friends and soon after they became good in-laws.

The Tam family wedding was a huge event for their only son and heir. The parents decided that Mee Jing and Kin Wah would have a traditional wedding. Mee Jing had the traditional red silk wedding outfit that included gold embroidery with a dragon and a phoenix on the top and was matched with a full-length skirt. Mee Jing wore a red silk rose on one side of her hair and her ears had two sparkling diamond and pearl drops with a matching necklace, which was one of Siew Fen's prized possessions.

The wedding was held at the Smiling Buddha seafood restaurant where many of the wealthy families had their wedding banquets. They had over seventy tables entertaining a lot of the Tam family business associates and restaurant owners who were Master Tam's valued and faithful customers.

As with Mee See, Siew Fen wanted to teach Mee Jing how to behave as the supreme wife in a wealthy household. However, Mee Jing had more confidence than Mee See and said, "Ah Tai, it is a new world these days. Nobody cares about traditional family rules nowadays. I know what to do with my parents-in-law when the time comes." Siew Fen had to accept that Mee Jing always had a mind of her own. She was different from Mee See who was always more obedient. At least Mee Jing was married into a well-off family. Her future was assured, Siew Fen thought.

At the wedding banquet, Siew Fen laughed and smiled all night. She reflected on her own wedding so many years ago and recalled Mee See's huge wedding reception. She was satisfied that Mee Jing's wedding was also a huge event. There were a number of major restaurant owners as honoured guests from the Tuck Yick Sauce Manufacturer. She was comforted that she had done her duty and married Mee Jing to the right family. She was proud of the fact that she had discharged her responsibility as a good mother.

Wing Chung's Match

Since the sisters were married, there was only Wing Chung and Siew Fen living at the big ancestral house and the family became very quiet. Siew Fen continued to rent out the top level to generate some income to supplement living expenses. Mee See continued to give Siew Fen money from Chun Yun to help to support the family. Since Mee Jing was married, she no longer contributed to the family. Wing Chung paid a small part of his keep from working at the fruit store and his door-to-door trading business. As Japanese occupation continued, the rental coming from the other ancestral properties was not high. At least they were occupied and generated some income and most importantly, the tenants prevented the homeless vagrants from moving in to occupy her premises. Siew Fen now only had Luk-Por, the cook Sai-Mui and the old faithful butler Ah-Din as her servants. Even though it was not the opulent living she once enjoyed, Siew Fen continued to live comfortably.

Life was always a struggle for Wing Chung. He never worked hard at school, hence never benefitted from his years of education at one of the best high schools in Canton. He always blamed his brother for taking him out of school to play games in the street; hence, he failed his studies. However, it was lucky that he never got the gambling habit that plagued his elder brother. He learned from his brother's lesson and did not dare to do wrong deeds. However, it also inhibited him from exploring other living skills. He would not try anything new. He dared not make a decision in case it was the wrong decision. Wing Chung had to earn a living as a labourer. He only had enough money to buy a trolley and fitted it out himself with shelves to display his wares. He sold toothbrushes, toothpaste, soap tablets, talcum powder and other small household goods. He put everything he could sell onto his trolley. Underneath, he carried a fold-up stool for himself. On the days he did not work at the fruit shop, he took the trolley near the railway station, the ferry crossing, or the corners of main roads. He set up his trolley, pulled out the folding stool, and sold all sorts of small goods to passers-by.

Wing Chung met Yee Hong (綺紅) who was also working at the fruit store as a stacker. She lived with her parents who worked in the factory. She only finished primary school for she had to work to earn her keep. Born with a little red mark near the right bridge of her nose, she was very conscious of this unsightly mark and tended to hold her face towards the right side hoping people would not notice it. Yee Hong felt inferior because of this mark. Being self-conscious, she whispered her answers and would not raise her head to attract attention. She usually waited until people had made the decision and followed the crowd. Wing Chung found Yee Hong quiet and unassuming, unlike his sisters who were opinionated and decisive. They laughed and joked loudly that he never could get a word in. His suggestions were ignored by his younger sister who always had a better idea and a stronger collaborator in the elder sister. Yee Hong was a refreshing change. He often helped her lift heavier boxes onto the lorry. He found her a good listener.

He told Yee Hong, "All my life, all I wanted was to start a small business selling home products to the public. I come from a multibillion family. We were wealthy, we were powerful, and we were influential in Canton at one time. My father used to have several streets of properties. I want to do some small retail business, yet there is no money for me to get started." Wing Chung gave a big sigh and added, "My life is such bad luck, but I still have a vision to do some small business. I like to confide in you."

Yee Hong had never had anybody ask for her opinion, let alone to confide in her about their future plans. She was grateful that Wing Chung discussed his plans for his future. Wing Chung was attracted by Yee Hong's quiet and gentle manner. He had long forgotten the red mark near the right bridge of her nose. They both worked together on Wing Chung's plan and together decided what to sell at what profit margin. When the fruit shop was not busy, the two young people pushed the trolley to do business at various busy locations together. Wing Chung carried an extra folding chair for Yee Hong so that she could sit down with him during the day to rest her weary feet.

Wing Chung already wanted Yee Hong for his wife. However, when he considered his two sisters' prosperous wedding ceremonies, he was disheartened. How on earth could he afford a wedding of that enormity for Yee Hong? It would be a long time before he could save for a wedding of any style. Although Wing Chung did not have enough money to hold a wedding ceremony, they often talked about their future life together. Yee Hong's parents already knew that it was only a matter of time before the two would be getting married. Yee Hong told Wing Chung that she did not need a huge wedding ceremony. All she wanted was for them to work together and live a stable life building a happy family together.

Wing Chung reflected on the Kwan family history and came to the conclusion that because his parents fought over the family estate, they had wasted so much money over the years. He regretted that all that wealth was then divided, ending with so little left. As the only son and heir of the Kwan family, he had nothing to his name. Wing Chung felt very hard done by by his mother.

Wing Chung brought up the subject with his mother and said, "I want to get married to Yee Hong. If I had my share of the inheritance, I could buy a corner shop to do business with Yee Hong."

Siew Fen was surprised that Wing Chung had actually asked for his share of the inheritance. She was angry that he was eyeing the last asset they had to maintain a reasonable life style and said, "If you had gone out and got a decent job, we would not have to count on the monthly rental money for our living."

Wing Chung was getting angry because he had bottled up a lot of resentment over the years and bellowed, "Talk about the rental. In fact some of the rental should be my share of the inheritance. You have always held the family finances." Wing Chung had a temper that he seldom showed. He slammed the table with his hand and yelled, "I am the most unlucky person in the Kwan family. My grandfather had billions of Tai-Yuan when he came from South America. Within one generation, here I am, the only son and heir and I can't even have money to get married." Wing Chung pointed his index finger at Siew Fen and continued, "If you did not waste all that money fighting father in the law court, we would not be in this position right now. I am so unlucky because of you." He was getting more agitated as he dwelt on his bad luck, he demanded, "Where is my share of the Kwan family inheritance?"

Siew Fen then realised that although Wing Chung had been quiet at home, he held many grudges inside. He was too young to understand the reasons for the court case and the way the Kwan family assets had to be divided according to the court order at the time. From the sound of his words, he had no intention of looking after Siew Fen if he got anything from the family inheritance. What would Siew Fen live on if Wing Chung was to take the properties? He had never considered the need to cater for his mother because she always seemed to have the means to survive all sorts of difficulties. It was such a long time ago and too complicated to explain in detail the circumstances behind the family feud. Besides she could see that Wing Chung was not prepared to listen. Siew Fen decided to let Wing Chung think whatever he wanted about the past. She also decided to look at the market to sell the properties to give him a share to help with his wedding and some money to start a new business.

With the Japanese occupation and China in turmoil, it was not the right time to sell properties. Siew Fen found herself in an unenviable position when she had to liquidate all the properties at this undesirable time. This situation rekindled an ancient proverb that says 'Chun Son Jai, Butt Chee Kuen Son Chin (親生仔, 不似近身錢)[37]', meaning even having a

---

[37] Chun Son Jai, Butt Chee Kuen Son Chin 親生仔, 不似近身錢 even your son being your next of kin, would not be as secured as the money being next to your skin,

son being the next of kin, would not be as secure as the money being next to your skin. She suddenly appreciated the depth of this wise axiom. It was such a true motto in her life!

After much thought, Siew Fen said, "I shall attempt to sell the properties and give you a share to help with starting a business and to get married. But I can't promise when I can settle the sales because with the Japanese occupation, now is not the right time to sell."

Mother and son finished their unpleasant exchange. Siew Fen did not need to give explanation of her action. She never mentioned it to the girls because she was certain she had chosen the correct path all along.

Compulsive Gambling

When Mee See was pregnant with her fourth child, she noticed something was not quite right with Chun Yun. He came home and stayed quietly in the study room of their suite. He lost interest in playing with the children and was impatient with things in general. Mee See tried to keep things quiet for her husband and often sent Sam-Chai to take the children to the park to have an ice cream or to play in the big garden downstairs to keep them away from Chun Yun. Mee See was quietly alarmed. Having seen so many wives in the Kwan and the Hui's household and her own father with other women very early in his marriage, she dreaded the same misfortune might fall on her. She was worried that Chun Yun had another woman. Nothing was worse than the fear of the unknown, and she could not talk to the in-laws and dared not discuss the matter with her husband.

Using an excuse that her mother was unwell, Mee See, heavily pregnant, took the three children, their servants, and Sam-Chai to visit her mother. Siew Fen saw the very pregnant Mee See arrive, and could see something was not right. Siew Fen sent the servants to take the children to play while mother and daughter could have a good talk. She brewed a pot of hot Tit Kuen Yum (鐵觀音) tea, sat down and talked.

Reasoning with Mee See, Siew Fen said, "How do you know Chun Yun has another woman? You cannot accuse him unless you have proof!"

Mee See thought for a while, sipped her tea, and then responded, "No, Chun Yun comes home every night after work. We have dinner with Lau Yai and Lai Lai[38](老爺和奶奶). Then he would sit quietly in the study as though he is pre-occupied with something important." Mee See wiped a tear from her eyes and added, "He has lost interest in the children. He has lost interest in all household matters, and he even has lost interest in me when I wanted to discuss the choice of the children's kindergarten."

Siew Fen analytically looked at the picture presented to her. She took another drink from her tea and said, "Chun Yun goes to work all day. If he comes home straight away for dinner like you say, and stays home afterwards, when does he have time for another woman? If he stays home and contemplates quietly, he may have problems at work that he wants to resolve. Why don't you ask him directly instead of suspecting? Don't start putting shadows in your mind. It wastes your time worrying. It ruins your relationship unnecessarily."

Mee See thought her mother was so wise and reasonable and started to blame herself for being so unfair about suspecting her husband. She felt a lot more settled and decided to ask him directly what was troubling him.

Siew Fen followed with some more wise words of advice, "I can see Chun Yun does care a lot for you and for the family. But as a woman, living in a male dominated society, you must protect yourself and your children. If a man changes or he finds another women, you are best to let him go. But you must have as much money saved up as you can without telling him. The money that you stashed away will be your saving grace one day." Siew Fen paused and continued, "Whatever money you have saved will be useful for raising your children one day."

---

[38] Lau Yai and Lai Lai 老爺和奶奶 a respectful way to refer to the two in-laws.

Not long after Mee See visited her mother, one evening Chun Yun came home while Kai Ming was playing with a car, "Broom broom… look pa pa, look at my car."

Chun Yun raised his voice, "Don't disturb me." He suddenly took the car from Kai Ming and threw it to the side of the study.

Kai Ming was scared and started crying. Mee See picked up Kai Chung, held Yau Mui's hand, and told Kai Ming to follow her down the stairs for Sam-Chai to take care of the three children. Mee See went back to the study to confront Chun Yun, "Why do you have such a bad temper? You scared the children and you frightened me as well. What is the matter with you lately? Do you have another woman?" Mee See had been waiting for a long time to ask these questions.

Chun Yun quickly denied, "No! Where did you get that silly idea? I only have you in my heart. There is nobody in the world for me except you." Chum Yun sat down with his hand supporting his chin, the other rubbing his forehead deep in his troubled thoughts again.

Mee See was relieved. She waited patiently for an explanation.

Chun Yun's face was pale. Then he uttered quietly and said, "Lately, I have had such bad luck. Every time I play the game, I lose. Once I even needed a friend to lend me the money to buy the ferry ticket home from Macao."

Mee See quietly released a breath of silence, thinking, "Thank goodness it is not a woman." Then Mee See asked calmly, "Well, how much did you lose?" Mee See never thought gambling could lose a lot of money drawing from her first experience at the Macao Casino.

Chun Yun hesitated, and then mumbled, "Three thousand Tai-Yuan."

Over the last few years, Chun Yun's company was making a good profit. The business expanded from Canton, Macao, Hong Kong to Singapore and Hainan. Chun Yun's division was the financial center for all the additional branches with the annual figure increased by three-fold. Two years ago when his division had to submit their year-end financials, there was an unexplained excess of several thousand of Tai-Yuan. The division was working overtime till 3 o'clock in the morning and still could not balance the ledger to meet the deadline. Chun Yun created a division ledger and a journal for the excess thousands of Tai-Yuan so as to balance the books. Years passed by and nobody knew or cared about this special ledger.

Chun Yun was at the Macao branch to inspect the business again. He took the money from this ledger and used it as company expenses for the trip. He chanced a visit to the Central Casino to fill in some time waiting for his boat trip back to Canton. Luck had it that he doubled his money. Chun Yun bought a red leather handbag and shared with his dear wife the winnings. Mee See imagined that Chun Yun got an extra bonus from his company, and he never told her it was his gambling windfall.

From then on, Chun Yun used this ledger to feed his gambling habit. He would journal the company's income into this ledger every so often as though it was legitimate company expenses. Over the last two years Chun Yun had used about ten thousand Tai-Yuan in losing bets. He kept trying to win back what he lost. However, the more desperate he was, the more he lost.

Recently the head office had a directive to all the divisions that every department was to go through an auditing procedure within six months to streamline processing to improve productivity. Every division manager was directed to cooperate with the auditors. If Chun Yun was found out, his job would be in jeopardy and his name dishonoured. His only option was to repay the ten thousand Tai-Yuan before the auditor arrived at his division. Where could he come up with ten thousand Tai-Yuans in such a short time? He regretted ever setting foot in the Central Casino.

Mee See exclaimed, "Three thousand Tai-Yuan! How did you lose so much money? You must have gone to the Central Casino each time you inspected the business at Macao!" Mee See thought things over and continued, "Oh, you must not tell Lau Yai and Lai Lai as they have such high expectations of you. They would be so very disappointed if they knew you had been gambling."

Not knowing how serious the matter was, Mee See continued, "Oh well, you have already lost the money. You will have to work hard to save up again. One thing is for sure, you must promise me you will not gamble again."

Chun Yun was remorseful and said, "I deeply regret what I have done. This money is from the company. Recently the main office gave a directive to audit every division and this shortfall will appear in auditing. They will soon find out I have taken the money."

Mee See suddenly realised the gravity of the matter. She could not help sobbing quietly because she did not want the rest of the household to know what was happening. She said, "Oh that is embezzlement! You have stolen the company's money and lost it by gambling. You will be locked up in jail." As Mee See spoke, she hung on to Chun Yun as though he was going to be caught and be thrown into jail immediately.

Chun Yun cuddled his dear wife. Deeply sorry, he said, "I am so very sorry, so very sorry. I thought my fortune would change. I was hoping to win back the money I lost. You have seen me double my winnings before!" Taking a deep breath, he continued, "I promised myself, that I would not gamble again, if I could win back what I lost. I am getting really desperate."

Mee See could not sleep all night. She twisted and turned trying to think of the ways that she could help her husband. She could hardly wait until the next morning to see her mother. She brought with her everything of value that she had saved since marrying into the Fung family.

After Mee See told her mother everything about Chun Yun's crisis, Siew Fen said, "Chun Yun must stop gambling. Many people suffer family break up because of gambling. I have seen some men even sell their wife and children to fund their gambling habit. When did Chun Yun start gambling? One does not just have a gambling problem all of a sudden. As a wife, it is your duty to remind him and steer him away from such a bad habit."

Mee See put all her savings and jewellery box on the table and said, "Over the last years, Chun Yun often gave me stacks of money. I have saved most of the money in gold nuggets. As each child was born, he came home with a diamond ring as a gift. Here, I wonder if these are enough to cash in for three thousand Tai-Yuans. I want him to put back the money so he won't be found out when the auditors arrive."

Siew Fen was comforted that Mee See had listened to her teachings and now she had the means of helping her husband.

Mother and daughter went down town to Siew Fen's jewelers. They cashed in all the nuggets on the value of the gold according to the daily gold price. Mee See only needed to cash in one of her diamond rings. They could only sell the ring at the value of the diamond, but lost the value of the gold that mounted the ring. It was hard for Mee See to decide which one to sell as they all had different designs. They all sparkled brilliantly, and each had a sentimental history behind it.

Siew Fen told Mee See, "Money and possessions are there for us to use. When it is time to use them for good purposes, we should be decisive and use them well." Ah Tai was so right about everything, Mee See thought. She was glad she had her mother there to guide her. Mee See had exactly three thousand Tai-Yuan. They took the money home in high spirits thinking they had saved Chun Yun from public disgrace and salvaged his career.

Chun Yun was speechless and surprised to take the pile of Tai-Yuan. Mee See had the most charming smile on her face and said, "Yes, there are three thousand Tai-Yuan there, exactly! We counted. Yes, this is for you to pay back the company all you owe."

Chun Yun swallowed and said, "Where did you find this money?"

Mee See was naïve and spoke earnestly, "These Tai-Yuan came from you. I listened to Ah Tai and have been saving all the spare money for an emergency. Unfortunately, I had to cash in the diamond ring you gave me when Kai Chung was born to make up the amount. Now, let's use it to settle your debt to the company." Mee See added, "But you must promise me. You will not gamble anymore."

Chun Yun was holding the stack of Tai-Yuan in his hands. He couldn't help but give Mee See several kisses on her cheek, saying, "I promise when we get through this crisis, I will not gamble any more. I will repay you and there will be more diamond rings to come."

That night, Mee See was able to sleep very well and had a sweet dream thinking all the trouble would be blown over very soon. Chun Yun watched Mee See fast asleep in bed, heavily pregnant with their fourth child which was due shortly. Her face was peaceful with a smile at the corner of her mouth. Her long, thick and curly eye lashes rested peacefully on her flawless cheek. He was lucky to have such a wonderful wife who was only concerned for his welfare.

Soon Mee See was admitted to hospital to wait for her fourth child, due any day. The Fung family was joyous in anticipation of the new baby's arrival. All the children were waiting impatiently to have Mummy home with their new baby.

Chun Yun kept counting the pile of Tai-Yuan notes, which was not enough to resolve the problem he had. Next month the auditing process commenced. There was no telling when auditors would arrive at his division. There was such an urgency to get things right prior to their arrival. How could he make up for the other seven thousand Tai-Yuans? However, if he took the money to wager, there might be a chance that he could win back what he lost. All he needed was to double the money twice and he could rescue the entire situation. Then, he would stop gambling. It was the best opportunity to go to Macao as Mee See was in hospital. He would have won all the money before the baby was home.

Chun Yun arrived at the Central Casino. He changed two thousand Tai-Yuan into chips and kept the last thousand inside his inner pocket. If he won enough, he might not even need to touch the last thousand Tai-Yuans. Agitated, Chun Yun was feeling somewhat disconcerted. He had been to the Central Casino a hundred times over these last few years. However, there was so much at stake this time! He could feel his heart beating hard inside his chest and on his head pulsating. His hands were sweaty. He took his handkerchief to wipe the sweat from his forehead and rubbed it on his hot and sweaty hands. But before he could settle on a chair at the Dai Sai table, he felt he could not concentrate. He was unable to hear what was being called out, and he could hardly breathe. He turned around and walked out into the street to get some fresh air.

It was the first time Chun Yun was so nervous at the casino. He took another deep breathe just outside the casino. Then he walked back inside straight to the Tai-Sai table and sat down. The table attendant, Ah Lin (亞玲) smiled from ear to ear saying, "Ayarh! Young Master Fung, I saw you walking out just now. I thought you were not coming back anymore! I haven't seen you for so long, is it your wife won't let you come to the Casino?"

Ah Lin had been working at the Central Casino for the past two years. She was petite, about four feet ten inches and skinny. She had a pair of large round eyes and the most attractive dimples on her face. She was good at striking a pleasant conversation to create a relaxed atmosphere for her customers. He often gave her big tips because she could make him feel comfortable at the table, and he enjoyed her company while wagering. Chun Yun started to joke with Ah Lin which helped him relax. Ah Lin sensed something was different with the young Master Fung as he was unlike the usual carefree self-confident customer that he had been for years. She ordered a Ginseng tea for Chun Yun to calm his nerves.

That was a long night. It was 2:00am when Chun Yun lost the entire lot of Tai-Yuan, including the last thousand that he kept in his inner pocket. All he had now was enough money for the boat ticket and taxi fare home. Ah Lin had long stopped her pleasant comments. She looked serious and was feeling sorry for every Tai-Yuan that Chun Yun lost. Finally she slowly swiped the last few chips down the hatch for the last time.

He got home, he crept into his bed chamber and rolled over as he dropped off to sleep exhausted. He dreamt of the judges sentencing him to jail; the reporters were busy writing down the case about his shameful deed to report to the public; the policemen were pointing at him laughing and ready with handcuffs to take him to serve his sentence. Chun Yun woke up disoriented to find himself alone in his bed soaking in a cold sweat.

Chun Yun was so pre-occupied with his crisis, he was not aware that his fourth son had been born that night. Master Fung said, "Man must be trustworthy. Let's name the new baby - Kai Son (鉅信)[39]."

At last, Chun Yun had to tell Mee See what had happened with the three thousand Tai-Yuan. Mee See cried until there were no more tears and her voice was hoarse. It was fortunate that Mee See had a Sup-Ma and a Kon-Ma to take care of baby Kai Son, and other servants were looking after the children. Mee See was unable to do anything but drift into a depressed motionless state. She was desperate not knowing what the future would hold. Mee See asked Chun Yun angrily, "You have now wasted all my savings in gambling. What other plan do you have? How are you going to get us all out of this crisis? Where else could you get another three thousand Tai-Yuans to pay back the debt to the company?"

Chun Yun then explained to his wife, "In fact, the debt is more than ten thousand Tai-Yuans!" Chun Yun rubbed his forehead trying to convince his wife, "I thought that I might as well take the money to the casino to

---

[39] Kai Son 鉅信 'Son' rhymed with the Chinese word 'trust'.

throw everything in to wager for a better return. Never in my wildest dreams did I think that I could lose all the money in one night!" Chun Yun put his hand on Mee See's shoulder and continued, "I do apologise. I am deeply sorry. It is my stupid fault. I should not have gambled the way I did."

Mee See shook off Chun Yun's hand from her shoulder. She nearly threw up at the thought of ten thousand Tai-Yuans. She was so frustrated that she hit her fist into the pillow a number of times with all her might. She wanted to scream at the top of her voice to vent her desperation. But she had to keep her voice down so as not to alarm the rest of the household. Mee See continued in a controlled voice, "When this incident is revealed, everyone will know from the newspaper! How can you face Master and Madam Fung, my mother, our relatives, and your work colleagues? Where else can you work in Canton? We will lose face with all our relatives and friends. How can we continue to live here?"

Mee See started another round of sobbing. She had run out of ideas on how to resolve this predicament. She needed to go home to talk with Ah Tai, who always knew what to do in a crisis. If Chun Yun was in jail, who would support her and her four children from then on? What about the children's education? Mee See sat on the rock next to the fish pond in their immaculate garden. She was staring in the distance aimlessly. The moon light reflected onto the fish pond. She looked up to see the moon above. Everything she saw was out of focus as tears welled up in her eyes once again. It was only a few weeks ago when life was sweet with the expectation of her fourth child. What had gone wrong all of a sudden? She was ashamed of her beloved husband. How could they avoid the impending disaster? Suddenly she realised she really had no control of her future!

'Three Evils', ' Five Evils' Anti-Corruption

Siew Fen and her family lived through the turmoil of the Chinese Civil War between the years 1927 to 1950. The civil war was a struggle between the Kuomintang (KMT 國民黨) the governing party of the Republic of China (ROC 中華文國) and the Communist Party of China (CPC 中國共產黨) for control of China. Eventually it led to the division of the country into two Chinas, the Republic of China (ROC) in Taiwan and People's Republic of China (PRC 中國的人民共和國) on the mainland.

By the end of the Sino-Japanese War in 1945, the balance of power in China's civil war had shifted in favour of the Communists. After the fall of the capital Nanjing (南京) in April 1949, the People's Liberation Army from CPC was pursuing remnants of KMT forces southwards in southern China. The KMT Nationalist Government under the acting President Li Zongren relocated to Canton. The Communist forces entered the city on October 14, 1949; this led the KMT Nationalists to blow up the Haizhu Bridge which was a major link across the Pearl River. The acting President left for New York. Fierce street battles between the soldiers of both camps occurred. Major hostilities ended in 1949, when the Communists won the civil war and established the People's Republic of China in the Mainland China. The KMT-led Republic of China Nationalists set up the Nationalist government and relocated their capital to Taipei in Taiwan.

Following the end of the Civil war and the establishment of the People's Republic of China, a movement was launched at the end of 1951 called the 'Three Evils (三反)' and 'Five Evils (五反)' campaign. The movement against the 'Three Evils' was the struggle against corruption, waste, and bureaucracy among the personnel of government departments and state enterprises. The movement against the 'Five Evils' was the struggle against bribery, tax evasion, theft of state property, cheating in government contracts, and the stealing of economic information among owners of private industrial ventures and commercial enterprises.

The State Council announced a number of provisions for dealing with corruption, waste, and overcoming bureaucratic errors. They adopted a punishing corruption policy to eradicate the country of the 'Three Evils' and 'Five Evils'. The struggle against corruption included people from all walks of life. They wanted to detect, expose, and punish those involved. The guilty were dismissed from office, criticised, re-educated, punished or sentenced to prison to be reformed through hard labour. The objective was to reform the entire bourgeoisie to obey the laws and decrees of the state. The state would attempt to recover their economic losses through the payment of evaded taxes, restitution, fines, and confiscation of property. The worst among the bourgeoisie were shot.

This struggle was given wide publicity. Horrendous news spread from the Northern provinces that many descendants of wealthy families were prosecuted. The state demanded that they repay what they were supposed to owe in unpaid tax. Some descendants were shot because they were accused of hiding the state's property and not surrendering what was due to the state. People in Canton were feeling unsettled as this struggle against corruption was advancing from the Northern capitals to the Southern provinces. Those who could, went overseas to Hainan, Singapore, Macao or Hong Kong or even to America, Canada and Europe.

Siew Fen's father Master Hui was a high court judge in Peking. Siew Fen's father-in-law, Master Kwan was a wealthy merchant retired from South America to Canton. Both had accumulated much wealth in their lifetime and they were well-known, big landowners and had powerful connections in Canton. They would both be classified as bourgeois and would have been subject to investigation if they were alive. However, rumour had it that the investigation went beyond the first generation. There had been prosecution of the descendants of descendants to recuperate what was meant to have been 'lost' by the state in unpaid taxes.

The Hui family had already sold up and moved to Hong Kong, a British Colony. Master Kwan's family fortune had dwindled since he passed away. Siew Fen still held a few of the Kwan ancestral properties to provide rental to support her living. Siew Fen was worried what would become of her since she was the descendant of two such wealthy families. These families were known for their wealth and their previous decadent way of life. However, she no longer possessed that sort of wealth. How could she extricate herself from such accusations? Canton was not a safe haven for Siew Fen. But where could she escape to?

As Wing Chung wanted to get married and was complaining that he had missed out on the family's fortune, Siew Fen decided to cash in all the properties she had in Canton. She planned to give Wing Chung a share to help him start a business for his livelihood. Canton was in a flux of instability. People who had money had left. The people who were left were officials or workers who still had jobs. Siew Fen decided she had to accept whatever the market would pay before the Communist prosecution movement hit her household.

After the sale, she negotiated to pay rent to stay on at the ancestral property where she had been living most of her married life. This would give her time to decide what to do with herself. Siew Fen gave half of the proceeds to Wing Chung after the sale. That was his share of the family fortune. Wing Chung and Yee Hong got married. Wing Chung rented half a shop near the factory a couple of streets from Yee Hong's parents. Wing Chung did not invite Siew Fen to live with him and Yee Hong. Siew Fen had to contemplate her future alone this time.

Following Mee See

Siew Fen was all by herself with her three life-long servants living in this now rented huge ancestral house of four lounge rooms and seven bedrooms plus servants' quarters. Siew Fen called in a well-known antique dealer friend to assess the entire stock of the collection. She was going to choose several favourite items and keep as a remembrance of her roots. However, it was hard to carry any of these items if she needed to escape inconspicuously in a hurry. At last Siew Fen decided it was not the time for sentimentality about material items and let the antique dealer remove everything and accepted the cash in exchange. She knew that she would have gotten more money for her entire collection in better times. However, she stopped calculating and put all the cash in her inside pocket. Canton was still in turmoil and she could see the value of money would further fluctuate until stability returned. She exchanged her cash for gold nuggets for easy storage but left enough cash for daily living.

Siew Fen walked around the house and saw all the walls were empty except for the dust marks where the wall hangings had been. All the display cabinets were empty. The fine lace Jade panels had disappeared from her favourite drawing room. Most of the antique Shun-Chee furniture, the side tables, and the corner tables for the Ming Vases and Qing porcelain urns were all gone. Every room was empty of all the finery that made it a Kwan family home. Siew Fen could not help feeling a great loss. Emptiness surrounded her as she sat by the fire place on the raised step and buried her face in her fine silk handkerchief, crying softly.

It was at that very moment, Mee See walked in.

Because of the birth of her new baby and her preoccupation with Chun Yun's crisis, Mee See had not visited her mother for a while and had no idea of her mother's recent decision to sell all her properties in preparation to leave Canton. This time Mee See came home to confide with her mother about Chun Yun's crisis. Ah-Din quietly opened the iron-gate with his eyes down cast and he had a serious look on his face.

Mee See walked in and saw everywhere was empty. Where had all the paintings and wall hangings gone? Where were all the fine displays in the cabinets? Where were the replica jade musical instruments and the fine porcelains, the vases and the jade panels? She was shocked to see her mother wiping tears from her eyes.

Mee See asked Siew Fen urgently, "What has happened? Were there thieves in the house? Were we robbed?"

Luk-Por brewed a fresh pot of Tit-Kuan-Yum tea. She also served a couple of hot face flannels on a fine bone china tray.

Siew Fen refreshed herself with the face flannel, sipped her tea and replied, "No there were no thieves. I have sold everything including the rest of the properties. Wing Chung needed money to start a business. I shared with him the proceeds of the sale of all the properties."

Mee See said in amazement, "Oh no Ah Tai! You even sold this ancestral home? But why?" Mee See was eager to hear the reasons.

Siew Fen continued, "Rumour has it that the descendants of large land owners and wealthy families were being prosecuted by the Communists. Demands were made of the descendants to repay the tax that their families were meant to have owed the state. Your Kon Kon (公公)[40] and Ya Ya (爺爺)[41] were big land owners and extremely wealthy when they were alive. Being a descendant, I don't know what sort of treatment I would get in this movement to clean up the 'Three Evils' and 'Five Evils' as the people's struggle against corruption."

Mee See reasoned, "But you don't have all the wealth now. Besides it was a long time ago that our Kon Kon and Ya Ya were wealthy and powerful."

Siew Fen said, "I know. But horrendous rumours from the Northern provinces have spread all over Canton. Many descendants are in prison for hiding assets. The descendants are accused of not handing over money the parents and grandparents were meant to have owed the state in back taxes. Besides, Wing Chung needed money to get married,

---

[40] Kon Kon 公公 grandfather on the mother's side.
[41] Ya Ya 爺爺 grandfather on the father's side.

and he wanted to start his business. I decided it was time to move on, I want to escape the instability in Canton. So I sold everything, so that I can leave discreetly and travel light."

However, Siew Fen did not mention the impertinent disagreement that Wing Chung had with her about his inheritance. She concluded, "We have lived in this ancestral home for so many years. All the antiques were handpicked from both the Hui and the Kwan family. Suddenly it dawned on me what a lovely home we have to leave behind." Siew Fen recollected, "Don't worry about me, I'll get over it."

Siew Fen then realised Mee See looked preoccupied. She saw Mee See's sunken eyes and dark rings around those eyes as though she had not slept for days. Siew Fen asked, "Whatever is the matter with you? You must look after yourself. You have just had a new baby. It is no time to rush around. Did Madam Fung instruct the servants to make sure you are taken care of after childbirth? Did you have plenty of ginger vinegar (薑醋) and ginger rice (薑飯) [42]?"

Tears welled in Mee See's eyes. Mee See took the other wet face flannel to freshen her face. She took a fresh cup of tea, a deep breath and said, "Ah Tai, this time I really don't know what to do. The truth is Chun Yun didn't just embezzle three thousand Tai-Yuan; it was ten thousand in total! While I was in the hospital, he took the three thousand Tai-Yuan I gave him to Macao hoping to win back the money to put into the company account before the auditors arrive next month. Of course, he lost the entire amount!"

Siew Fen kept silent listening intently to Mee See.

Mee See could not help sobbing into her wet face flannel. She took a deep breath and continued, "I have run out of ideas how we can get out of this crisis. Chun Yun is completely immobilised by the thought of being exposed. He is unable to think straight now." Mee See caught her

---

[42] Ginger vinegar 薑醋 and ginger rice 薑飯 were two of the essential foods for ladies who has given birth during the first month. It was meant to help to recuperate.

breath and said, "When the news of his embezzlement comes out, Chun Yun will surely lose his position in the company. We will lose face. We cannot live in Canton anymore. We must leave Canton before Chun Yun is caught. But then where will we go? What can we do? I can't sleep. All these questions go round and round my head."

Siew Fen suddenly realised the gravity of the entire matter.

Mother and daughter discussed what they could do to help Chun Yun from being caught so that he could go somewhere else to start afresh. With his education, his knowledge, and work experience, both mother and daughter thought that provided he would give up gambling, he should be able to build a new life for his young family. Macao was the place of choice because the company only had a very small branch there. Macao was under Portuguese administration. Siew Fen would be safe as it was also outside the jurisdiction of the "Three Evils" and "Five Evils" movement.

Mee See worked with many Portuguese at the Embassy. She had always found them friendly and helpful. Chun Yun would be lying low for a little while, then regather himself to find a new career in Macao. Both Chun Yun and Mee See had English as a second language. That should give them an edge when looking for a job in Portuguese Macao.

Siew Fen said, "I will use my money to help the family set up a new home somewhere. I will also help to look after the children while you and Chun Yun work to re-establish a new career." Siew Fen took a deep breath and added, "I regret forcing you to marry Chun Yun. This is a way I can make up to you. "

Mee See said, "Oh, I have never blamed you Ah Tai. Besides Chun Yun has been a model husband until these last few months. You only wanted the best for me. I will be very grateful if you will live with us and help us. You always have the best solution for problems."

Siew Fen lived with Mee See's family for the rest of her life.

Part Four – Macao

Escape to Macao

Mee See and her mother set to work on an escape plan to Macao. They required proper migration papers to move to Macao to work. Mee See used the envelope and the company stationery from Chun Yun's branch office in Macao to write herself an employment letter, stating she was required to be in charge of the typing pool. She was to report to work on a certain day at the office. With this employment letter Mee See sought the help from the chief official at the Portuguese consulate to apply for migration to Macao. The consulate official still remembered her wedding celebration. It was such an unforgettable mixture of Chinese and European wedding ceremony. He also remembered what a diligent and good worker Mee See was when working under his direction. Without much investigation, he signed the entrance application papers for the family. He even teased Mee See that he would visit them in Macao once they settled. Mee See was very lucky that the official did not check the details that were presented in her letter. Mee See was very brave to forge her employment papers.

Once the migration paper was signed, Siew Fen, Mee See and Chun Yun met to plan the departure. They had to cover all aspects. The plan was for the family of seven to slip away without a trace from all friends and relatives. Siew Fen cashed some of her gold nuggets to fund the expedition.

Chun Yun told his mother-in-law, "Ah Tai, without your help, I am destined to go to jail. I will never forget you. When I get a new job, I will repay you and Mee See."

Siew Fen told Chun Yun, "You really must give up gambling. If you don't give up gambling, it is useless promising anything now. I saw many cases when I was in Peking with my father, the people who didn't give up gambling could never turn over a new leaf no matter what new opportunity was in front of them."

Chun Yun told Siew Fen and Mee See, "I will listen to what you say. I will cut off my fingers if I ever gamble again." He meant every word he said at the time.

To avoid the Fung family noticing, Mee See packed four small sized cases with the children's essentials for Chun Yun to take over to Siew Fen's house at various times. One of the suitcases contained all of Mee See's important documents, the marriage certificate, everyone's identity cards, each child's birth certificate and most importantly, the migration documents required for entry into Macao. Mee See had to leave all of Chun Yun's qualifications and work records, in case they were used for proof of who he was and where he used to work. It was the intention that he would lay low for a while, before changing his identity to start fresh in Macao.

Mee See found an excuse to discharge the Sup-Ma and Kon-Ma. Kai Son was fed with milk powder formula instead of breast-milk from the Sup-Ma.

Siew Fen had to discharge all her servants. She gave Ah-Din thirty Tai-Yuan and thanked him for having stood by her all her life. She gave Luk-Por the servant and Sai-Chai each twenty Tai-Yuans. All her servants had served her since she was a toddler. She could not tell them where she was going and the servants knew not to ask. She could not disclose anything except to thank them for serving her faithfully all her life. They were more like family than servants after all those years together. Siew Fen saw them off with sadness in her heart.

On Saturday morning, after the family had a hearty breakfast with Master and Madam Fung, Mee See told the servants to change the children into their best clothes as Young Master Fung wanted to take the children to the park, then they had a dinner engagement and would not be home till late. Mee See told her mother-in-law that they would be late. They should not worry or wait up for them.

The two older children ran and skipped to the iron gate with their father following close by with a soft bag for the children's jackets, a ball, and a few toys. They turned around smiling waving, "Bye bye Ma Ma[43]. Bye bye Ya Ya[44]." Mee See held Kai Chung's little hand with the new baby in her other hand and followed Chun Yun out the door.

Madam Fung called out, "Have you got jackets for the children? Don't let them catch cold, the weather is so changeable these days."

Mee See stopped, turned around and said with a gentle smile, "I have brought jackets for the children. Please don't worry. They will be fine."

The whole family gathered at Siew Fen's home. They had to leave in such a hurry and in such secrecy that Chun Yun could not think of a way to let Master and Madam Fung know how much he appreciated their love and for providing him with a lovely home and the best education. He just wished that one day he would have a chance to tell them he wanted to repay them for all the kindness that they had bestowed on him and his family. Chun Yun had written a letter to express all his appreciation to Master and Madam Fung. However, he hadn't the courage to leave it on the desk in his quarters nor did he dare post it to them. He was remorseful and wished he had never continued gambling once he was on a losing streak.

Mee See kept Chun Yun's letter for Master and Madam Fung and hoped one day there would be the chance to see them again to explain it all. However, she could imagine the shock the family would have when they found out they had taken off and disappeared without a trace. They definitely would be very angry. Mee See wondered if there was ever a chance they would meet again.

Siew Fen and Mee See wrapped around their tiny waists the calico belts with all their jewellery, gold nuggets and several stacks of Tai-Yuan divided inside several secret pockets. They pinned them well onto their

---

[43] Ma Ma 嫲嫲 grandmother on the father's side.
[44] Ya Ya 爺爺 grandfather on the father's side.

inner garments. Mee See put on her loose pregnant top which served the purpose. Siew Fen once again put on her navy blue loose top for travelling. They both looked quite full figured. The loose tops protected all the money they carried to start yet another new life in another new land.

The family of seven started their journey from Siew Fen's home. Chun Yun took two of the bigger suitcases with Kai Ming hanging on to the handle of one. Mee See held baby Kai Son in one hand while Kai Chung held the other hand following Chun Yun. Siew Fen took the two last suitcases while Yau Mui walked by her, copying brother Kai Ming, hanging on to the handle of one of the suitcases.

The family took the ferry from Canton to Macao. Kai Ming said, "Are we at the park yet? I want to go on the swing. I want an ice cream."

Mee See took the time to review all her paper work. She reexamined her curriculum vitae and read again the letter of employment that she had written herself. She memorised the job title and the date and place where she was to commence work with Chun Yun's company in Macao. Once again, she reassembled all the entrance application forms with the Portuguese consulate signature and the water insignia of the official's approval of the whole family. Mee See couldn't help but feel it was such good luck that her official friend at the Portuguese Consulate never bothered to ring up to validate the facts. She wished that she actually had a job in Macao instead of this bogus claim.

The entrance to Macao was the very last hurdle for the safe refuge in a foreign jurisdiction to start anew. The fate of the family of seven was on Mee See's shoulders. She turned around and saw her mother, the children and Chun Yun. All of a sudden, Mee See no longer felt hopeless or sad about having to leave everything behind in Canton. Living in Canton was a life of security, luxury, and a life of plenty. She no longer felt ashamed or inadequate, waiting for impending disaster. In fact, she was filled with self-confidence. This journey to Macao would give them a chance for a new life. All she needed was for Chun Yun and herself to work together to build a new home for her mother and the children. From that day on, Mee See was no longer indecisive. She had to take responsibility to rebuild a family for her children and for her mother.

The ferry arrived at the Macao wharf. Mee See put all the documents inside a black leather portfolio briefcase that Chun Yun used for work. She took a deep breath, stood upright, and walked into the migration officer, where she slowly and methodically gave the documents for the officer to examine. The officer looked at Mee See, tilted his head to look at the family of seven, smiled and said "Good. You have just arrived at the right time for dinner. Once you get out of the door here, turn left to the bus stop. This bus will take you to the city center, there you will find restaurants and hotels." As he was talking and smiling, the officer put a red ink insignia over each entrance permit. Then he ran over each logo with a blotting paper roller. He handed all the papers back to Mee See, who placed them in the black portfolio briefcase. The family happily nodded their heads and thanked the officer as they moved on towards the exit door.

It was unbelievable that it was that easy to pass the final hurdle of their entrance to Macao. Siew Fen picked up Kai Son and held the hand of young Kai Chung. Mee See took the two smaller suitcases with Yau Mui hanging on her mother's arm. Chun Yun carried the two bigger suitcases with Kai Ming hanging onto his father's arm. They walked out of the migration office and entered Macao safely.

Mee See turned around and looked at the Macao wharf behind them. The sun was setting slowly in the west. Golden rays were sparkling on the shimmering Pearl River. The glittering light waved up and down on the water below as though it was beckoning this family that had just arrived. It was signifying a brand new start with a new chance in life. With Siew Fen looking after the children, Mee See and Chun Yun could work hard to recreate a new family. Mee See was full of new hopes.

Near the ferry wharf, the family found a third rate hotel in which to stay temporarily. From then on, Mee See took care of the provisions for the family whilst Chun Yun laid low until he reestablished a new identity to find a new vocation. The four children followed their grandmother, who looked after their needs making sure they were cared for and well disciplined.

Chun Yun was quiet. He had his head held low. He was glad that he had avoided being disgraced in Canton. He was full of regrets. As a brilliant scholar, he was a young executive with potential of a brilliant career. Here in Macao, he had no certificate to prove his ability or what he had achieved. How was he to find a vocation to feed this family of seven? He had no confidence to seek a good job without his academic certificates. Chun Yun had no idea where to start in Macao.

Siew Fen was comforted that Mee See had grown up and was responsible in finding solutions for the family. Her bravery in getting the whole family through the migration application process had convinced Siew Fen that she could plan with an eye for detail to ensure everything worked well. Siew Fen was remorseful and wanted to make up for marrying Mee See to Chun Yun.

Mee See was only twenty-two.

The family was living on Siew Fen's savings. They knew that they had to earn a living soon, otherwise they would use up the money that Siew Fen had brought with her. First of all, they needed to find alternative accommodation to settle into a routine and to reduce the hotel bill. They were hoping that Chun Yun, being the head of the family, would take up the role and find a solution. Chun Yun got up early each day and left the hotel. He came home in the evening at dusk, ate dinner with the family quietly, then went into his bedroom and dropped off to sleep.

Siew Fen was unhappy with her son-in-law's lack of initiative in dealing with the situation. She asked, "Where does Chun Yun go every day? We have been here for weeks now. What plans does he have for the family? We cannot stay in the hotel indefinitely. Have you asked him where he goes every day? Has he been looking for a job? " Siew Fen paused and continued "You have already got us all here safely. He should have a plan for the family."

Mee See knew that her mother's words were right. She also felt that Chun Yun had lost his energy since arriving in Macao. Agreeing with her mother, Mee See said, "Chun Yun never mentions about moving into a more permanent living arrangement. He hasn't talked about finding a job to bring in an income to support the family. Ah Tai, I really have no idea how to motivate him to move forward."

Siew Fen suggested, "Chun Yun is the head of the family. You should ask him directly what plans he has for the family. I just hope he is not gambling again after he has already ruined his career." Siew Fen added, "You should talk to him openly about what plans he has. If he does not have any idea, then you have to step in to take charge and make decisions. There is no time to waste. Staying in the hotel is so expensive. We cannot go on indefinitely."

Mee See decided to follow Chun Yun to see where he went every day. Sure enough, her mother was right. Chun Yun went into the Central Casino. He spent the day there around the Dai-Sai and Pai-Gow table. He changed hundreds of Macanese Pataca for chips to gamble. Mee See wondered where Chun Yun had got the money to gamble. Mee See left Chun Yun at the casino and went home to discuss the situation with her mother. Mee See opened her drawer and found one of her diamond rings and a 24ct gold chain had disappeared. Mee See wrapped all the remaining jewellery and cash and handed it to Siew Fen to store in her mother's room. She was incensed. This time, she no longer felt disappointed or sad for Chun Yun for losing his career. She was ready to confront him when he returned home in the evening. She was going to demand that he stop gambling and stealing from the family. She wanted him to take responsibility as head of the family. Mee See rehearsed the accusations in her mind a number of times. She was prepared for a big argument.

Mee See confronted Chun Yun, "Why are you gambling again after you promised you'd give up betting. You even told mother you would rather cut off your fingers if you ever gambled again! What do you have to say for yourself now?"

Chun Yun could see his desperate wife was trembling with frustration. He answered quietly, "I am hoping to make a living winning back the thousands that I lost in the Casino. I only gamble for you, for the family." Chun Yun held his head low as he listened quietly to everything Mee See had to say. He admitted that he was wrong. He swore that he would give up gambling and promised that he would look for a job to support the family and that he would not steal again. After agreeing to everything, he went straight to the bedroom, climbed under his blankets and went to sleep soundly.

Mee See stood there alone absolutely frustrated. She knew very well that he did not mean one word he had promised. Both Siew Fen and Mee See were very disappointed with Chun Yun, yet they did not know what else to do with him. Without waiting any longer, they took some gold nuggets to exchange for currency to rent a basic two bedroom flat for everyone.

Casino Rescue

Mee See went into the Central Casino by herself. She couldn't help but feel a little apprehensive. She plucked up her courage to walk to the Dai-Sai table where Chun Yun was the other day. Mee See gathered all her nerve to smile and chat with the same girl who looked after the Dai-Sai table. She said courteously, "How are you? How is business today?"

Ah Lin, smiling warmly answered, "Usually we are not so busy midweek. I don't think I have seen you here before. I see that you haven't any chips yet." Ah Lin was very friendly. She made Mee See feel less intimidated in this new environment and continued, "We are two girls short in this area. That's why there is nobody to relieve me at lunch time. Come, let me lock up the till box and shut down the table. Then I will take you to change some chips."

Ah Lin smiled and ushered Mee See on. She was a petite girl a lot shorter than Mee See. She was thin and well proportioned. She wore a mid-length bob with a butterfly hair clip to hold back a long fringe on one side. With a pair of bright round eyes, she had the sweetest dimples and a very pleasant smile on her face. Ah Lin was young, vibrant and friendly.

Mee See did not want to refuse Ah Lin's kindness. She followed Ah Lin as they left her table, and said, "In fact...I am not here to gamble. I wanted..." Mee See hesitated. She did not know how to express the reason why she had come to the Central Casino.

Ah Lin was a smart girl. She was sharp in picking up on people's body language. She could see that Mee See was not a customer in the casino. Two years ago, Ah Lin walked into the Central Casino to ask for a job and she still remembered she felt sick in her stomach with nerves, as she slowly walked into this big hall of gambling tables. She saw that Mee See was hesitant and nervous and thought that she must have come to look for a job too. Ah Lin thought Mee See was attractive and resembled a movie star she'd seen in the cinema. She liked her calm composure and gentle demeanor and couldn't help wanting to assist Mee See.

Ah Lin said, "You are in luck. We are two people short at the Dai-Sai table. It is lunch time. This is the best time to find Ah-Puck Kin-Lee[45](經

理)." Ah Lin took Mee See to the office to meet Ah-Puck the manager.

Ah-Puck was a medium height, middle-aged married man. He had been the manager at the Central Entertainment Complex for the past ten years. He was known to be fair but firm with his staff at the complex that housed two restaurants, the casino, and a night club. The complex provided visitors with a complete package of tourist excursions. Many visitors were foreigners from Hong Kong or local Portuguese ex-pats. While the tourists stayed at the Central Hotel, they took advantage of

---

[45] Kin-Lee 經理 , manager.

all the extra facilities because they were convenient. Ah-Puck was taken aback as Mee See walked in quietly behind Ah Lin. He thought that she was attractive and there was an air about her that was unlike the other girls he employed at the casino. He found Mee See gentle, softly spoken and well mannered. Her bright eyes showed that she was intelligent. He wondered if she was suited for work in the casino, she might attract more customers to the Dai-Sai tables.

Ah-Puck decided to give Mee See a chance and said, "You are in luck. We are two girls down at the Dai-Sai tables. Can you start work tomorrow?" Turning to Ah Lin, he continued, "Ah Lin will show you the casino routine. You will learn from her. I will give you a trial for a month. You will earn 100 Macanese Pataca during the trial period. Then it is 150 Macanese Pataca a month. Go, collect you uniform and I'll see you tomorrow."

Ah Lin and Mee See both thanked Ah-Puck for his kindness. Ah Lin said, "I guarantee Mee See will do well at the Dai-Sai and the Pai Kow tables."

Mee See took the uniform with her as she walked out of the Casino in a daze. It was like having a dream, a wonderful dream!

When Mee See passed by the market, she picked up some fresh roast pork and a soya sauce chicken to take home to their little apartment. The family was overjoyed to celebrate Mee See's first job in Macao. The wages were not high, but according to Ah Lin, there was the potential of lot of tips if she was friendly and helpful with the customers. Ah Lin said often the tips were more than the monthly wage. The family was very happy that Mee See was starting work in the morning and would be bringing home an income in the future. For the first time in three months, the family were laughing and joking heartily at the dinner table. It was the first time the children had had fresh roast pork and soya sauce chicken in a long time. It was tasty, like having the exquisite suckling pig back home in Canton. The children saw their mother and grandmother were in such a joyous mood, they too joked and chuckled louder with much boisterous laughter.

Chun Yun was very surprised that Mee See could get employment at the Central Casino. She had never had any experience in casinos. How could she persuade the manager to trust that she could do the work? Chun Yun was puzzled said, "You are clever! How on earth did you find this job?"

Mee See dared not tell the truth. She went to the Central Casino to find the manager to beg him not to let Chun Yun gamble any more. She was going to tell the manager that he had a wife, a mother, and four children to support. He did not have a job and he could not afford gambling money that he did not have. On reflection, she realised how naïve she was to pose such a ridiculous request. The casino would not worry about a customer losing all their money. In fact the more customers lose, the better it was for the casino's profit. She recognised how silly she was to have gone to the Central Casino. However, it was fate that she met Ah Lin who misunderstood her intention and got her a job to fill one of the vacancies. If it was not for Ah Lin, she would never have dreamt of a job at the casino!

Mee See explained to Chun Yun, "A few years back you took me to the Central Casino to gamble. I remember the girls who were dealing behind the tables. Two girls have just left and they were looking to fill those vacancies. Ah Lin took me to see their manager Ah-Puck and he was willing to give me a trial for a month starting tomorrow." Mee See thought and added quickly, "Perhaps I can ask Ah-Puck if there is a good position in their accounting department. They may have work for you too Chun Yun. Would you like me to ask around for you as well once I settle there?"

Chun Yun did not ask any more about the job. As Mee See was working at the Central Casino, he would have to find another casino so as not to bump into his wife.

Siew Fen did not know the real reason for Mee See going to the Central Casino. She was so proud of her daughter, who was so brave and decisive. From now on, there would be income to support the family.

Siew Fen looked at Chun Yun and once again felt that she had made the worst choice in life to have picked Chun Yun as Mee See's husband. At least Chun Yun could not gamble at the Central Casino anymore.

Mee See worked at the Central Casino on the seventh floor of the Central Entertainment Complex. She and Ah-Lin became the best of friends. Mee See learned fast and was able to follow the many rules in each betting game. She was quick in calculating the winning or losing chips at each table. She had a good sense of humour which helped to relax her customers who sometimes did let their losing streak get the better of them. Each night Mee See wrapped her tips in a big handkerchief to take home to her mother for housekeeping. These tips made up the short fall of their very low base wages whilst mother was looking after the children, she could settle to work at her job.

New Living Skill

The whole family moved from the very tiny temporary two-bedroom apartment to Fook Lun Sun Kai (福隆新街) near the Central Casino so that it would be convenient for Mee See to go to work. This was a ground floor dwelling with one lounge room, two bedrooms, a kitchen connected with a small dining room, a toilet, and bathroom. Siew Fen cashed in a few gold nuggets to setup a simple household with just the basic essentials for cooking.

The couple occupied one bedroom with a basic double bed, a chest of drawers and a wooden bedside table. It was half the size of Mee See's drawing room in her bedroom suite at Master Fung's ancestral home in Canton. The children occupied the other bedroom with Ah Tai. Kai Son slept in a wooden cot in one corner and the three children shared the same bed with their grandmother. They had a chest of drawers for their clothes with the top drawer locked up with a padlock; this was where Ah Tai put all the family's valuables. Ah Tai got all the basic equipment and ingredients to furnish the kitchen, which was one recess corner of the lounge room. The kitchen was a new domain for Ah Tai who never cooked or boiled the kettle for tea until now. Unlike their Canton garden residence, the toilet was a hole in the ground with two raised steps on either sides. The children soon learned to balance themselves over the toilet. A bucket of water was poured over the hole in the ground when necessary. There was an aroma in the toilet that encouraged everyone to shut the door when not using the facility.

The landlord Mr. Chan lived upstairs.

The little children were growing and settled well into their new life being cared for by their grandmother while their mother went to work to support the family. During the day, Siew Fen carried Kai Son on her back with a cloth sling that tied in the front leaving her hands free to take the hands of Yau Mui and Kai Chung while Kai Ming, being the eldest, walked by grandmother and helped to carry the shopping bags. The children called grandmother 'Ah Tai', which was the respectful name for the supreme wife in the Kwan family. That name stayed with the family for the rest of their lives.

Faced with the new challenges of caring for the children and cooking for the family of seven, at forty-one, Siew Fen set her heart to learn some new living skills. She had to learn to change nappies, mix baby food, washing and ironing. Siew Fen now had to learn to cook rice, to gut fish, to pluck the feathers of a chicken, mince the meat by chopping, and to cook dinner every day. Furthermore, Siew Fen learned to sweep the floor and to dust the furniture to keep the home tidy and clean. After a while, she found that it was not hard work doing these household chores. She even found a new culinary interest and enjoyed cooking.

Mee See worked at the casino from late morning till all hours past midnight. She slept till mid-morning to get ready for another work day. On the weekends the casino got busier and her work hours got longer. Mee See had little time to check with Chun Yun about his job hunting. They saw little of each other as he left home in the morning when Mee See was still asleep. When Mee See came home in the middle of the night, everyone was fast asleep.

Mother and daughter usually caught up mid-morning, chatting over their new experiences. The children sat around playing quietly as they listened to the adults' conversation. They seemed to accept the fact that Daddy was out all day, Mummy went to work on the night shift, and Ah Tai looked after them. They never complained that Mummy was not around for most of the day and night.

Siew Fen told Mee See, "It has been more than half a year now. Chun Yun still has shown no signs of trying to get himself into some sort of employment. I don't know what to do with him."

Mee See defending her husband said, "Chun Yun was an executive and division manager. It is very hard for him to come from such a position to look for lowly work. Without his qualification certificates, he has to start from the bottom again. I can understand that it must be very hard for him to accept. Let's give him a little more time. I hope he will be responsible and support the family again soon."

Siew Fen always spoke her mind. Being a disciplinarian, she had always been direct and to the point, "I think Chun Yun is an irresponsible man. How can he live on his wife's earnings? He sees you working day and night. How can he let you work like this and sit every night at the dining table and eat the food bought with the money from your hard work? He has no self-respect. Don't give him any more excuses." Siew Fen taking a deep breath continued, "You and I come from a wealthy family where we never needed to lift a finger to do any chores around the house. Both you and I are doing our best, learning new skills to cope with this changed situation. You don't need to defend the indefensible anymore. We both know Chun Yun has not done his fair share for the family."

Mother and daughter left the topic unresolved.

With the extra tips from work, Mee See just made enough money to support the family. Being a good financial controller. Siew Fen shopped wisely and looked out for nutritious, tasty and inexpensive food to conserve the family budget. Life was peaceful and stable for a time.

Parted in Despair

Mee See took ill with cholera. She was running a high temperature and had to stay in bed so she took a few days off work. Siew Fen used a straw to dip into powder antibiotics called penicillin to blow into the white spots that appeared at the back of Mee See's throat. Siew Fen administered the medicine three times a day for several days. It took a few days before Mee See recovered and was ready to go back to work. There was no income during the time that she was ill, so they had to rely on Siew Fen's savings that she had brought from Canton.

Mee See took one of her diamond rings to exchange for the cash to settle all the bills. After paying the doctor, she put the left over money inside her pillow so that she could pay the rent and give Siew Fen the food money in the morning. To Mee See's distress, the money disappeared from her pillow the following day. On questioning, Chun Yun admitted that he borrowed it and hoped he could raise more money to support the family. Having just recovered from her illness, she simply did not have the strength to raise the issue with Chun Yun anymore. Chun Yun was quiet and admitted that he was wrong. His eyes had lost the sparkle they once had back in Canton. Mee See found that everything that had any value had disappeared. She knew in her heart that Chun Yun had taken them to the pawn shop to exchange for money to gamble again. Her wedding ring, her gold watch, all disappeared when she washed her hands or went to sleep. Chun Yun once woke her up as he was attempting to unhook the gold chain she was wearing while sleeping. Mee See thought, "How can you stop a thief in our own home?" Mother and daughter were at the end of their tether. They had long stopped asking Chun Yun where he went, or if he had tried looking for a job.

One late morning, Mee See was getting ready for work when Mr. Chan, the landlord, called in to say hello. He had been waiting for an opportunity to catch Mee See at home. Mr. Chan politely said, "Fung

Dai So (馮大嫂)[46], Master Fung asked me for a loan of two hundred fifty Macanese Pataca. He told me that when you got your pay from the casino, he would pay me back. It was over a month ago. Master Fung still has not paid me back. I wish Fung Dai So would forgive me for asking, but could you help by settling this loan please."

It was such a surprise that Mee See did not know how to respond to Mr. Chan. She hesitated and quickly replied, "Oh Master Fung must have forgotten to tell me about this. I definitely will pay you back this loan."

Siew Fen and Mee See went through their purses and the drawers to gather all the money they had in the house, including a one hundred Macanese Pataca which was saved as next month's rental. Mee See gave the money to Mr. Chan apologising, "I am so very sorry Master Fung has owed you all this money for so long. Please do me a favour Mr. Chan. Please don't lend any more money to Master Fung, no matter how urgent or whatever reason he gives in the future. I shall not be able to repay his debts anymore."

Mr. Chan took the money and put it into his inner pocket. He smiled politely and said, "We have a good landlord and tenant relationship. You Fung Dai So always pay your rent before it is due. I never need to concern myself with your rental. As Fung Dai So also works in such a big organisation as the Central Casino, I was sure Master Fung would not run off with his loan. However I will listen to Fung Dai So's advice, and I promise that I will not advance anymore loans in the future."

Chun Yun came home for dinner and was surprised to see Mee See home too. Siew Fen took all the children to her bedroom early to read them stories and have an early night.

Mee See had been suppressing her anger all day. She waited until the children and Siew Fen retired to their room. She held her temper then calmly spoke to Chun Yun, "Mr. Chan asked me to pay back your debt of

---

[46] Fung Dai So 馮大嫂 was a polite greeting to Mee See as Mrs Fung.

two hundred fifty Macanese Pataca. When did you borrow that sort of money?"

Chun Yun held his head low and admitted, "Last month."

Mee See could not hold her anguish any longer. She raised her voice and said, "What did you do with all that money? You told Mr. Chan you could repay your debt when I was paid!"

Chun Yun swallowed and responded slowly, "I thought I could win back some money. What bad luck!"

Mee See had had enough. She took their marriage certificate and tore it right down the middle. She doubled the paper and tore it down the middle. She doubled that up and tore it once again, and again and again until she could not tear it any smaller. She threw the marriage certificate into the air. Small bits of paper flew in the air like snowflakes floating down slowly, landing on Chun Yun's head, face, the table, chairs, and all over the floor. Mee See was in despair. She looked at Chun Yun hopelessly. She was determined and told Chun Yun firmly, "From this day on, we are no longer married. I have endured enough. Here are two gold nuggets. This is your suitcase with all your clothes. You leave here immediately. I don't want to see you ever again in this life. You go now."

As Mee See was talking, she pushed the gold nuggets into Chun Yun's hand. She opened the door, threw the suitcase out and pushed him out the door. She closed the door immediately and pulled down the shutter to lock up securely. She closed all the windows and pulled the window drapes together. She went back to her room and sank on top of her bed. She was absolutely exhausted. Mee See was still fuming with anger, and her hands were trembling. She sobbed quietly so that she would not disturb her mother and the children in the next room. The children did not know that it was the last time they would see their father.

The events of these last few months flashed back in her mind. They stole away to Macao leaving no forwarding address to anyone, not even a note for her only sister and brother to avoid Chun Yun being found. Mee See realised that he was never going to change and they would not be building a happy home together. All that sacrifice was for nothing. In the end, she had to let Chun Yun go. There was no one she could rely on to provide for the family. As the children grew older, there would be the school fees to consider. How was she going to meet the needs of this family? All of a sudden, Mee See felt insecure not knowing how she could save this family from destitution. In the darkness Mee See lay on her bed as tears streamed down sideways. Through a tiny opening in the curtains, she could see a crescent moon rising in the pitch dark sky. She did not know when her trial would be over. She longed for the feeling of being at peace and at ease again!

Concierge for Foreigners

The Central Entertainment Complex was a high class establishment that included a Chinese restaurant, a Portuguese restaurant, a Casino and a Night Club with live music. Adjacent to this complex was the Central Hotel, a high class hotel belonging to the same owner. Ah-Puck was the General Manager of the entertainment complex and another General Manager ran the hotel side of the business.

Macao was the only city in the surrounding country territory that had legalised gaming facilities. Many visitors from nearby Hong Kong, Singapore, Canton, and other provinces from China came to Macao to gamble. Hence the Central Casino was a well-known place of interest in many foreigners' sightseeing itinerary. Many foreigners and local Portuguese came to the Casino to try their luck on various wagering games.

On many occasions, Mee See used English to converse with foreigners and showed them how to place bets on various games and explained the payout rate on wins. Usually foreign customers were surprised to find this Chinese attendant could converse in English. They all left Mee See with large tips as they departed. Another group of foreigners arrived on the seventh floor; they hesitated as they got onto the gaming hall. They arrived at Mee See's table looking somewhat perplexed. Obviously they were new to this game. With a most welcoming smile, Mee See talked to them in English, "Good afternoon. Can I help you?"

One English gentleman was surprised and exclaimed, "Oh, so you speak English! Splendid! We come from Hong Kong. How do you play this game?"

There were twelve or thirteen tall, blond, fair-skinned foreigners standing in front of Mee See's Dai Sai table. They were happy and eager to place a bet to try their luck. Mee See walked from behind her table and stood amongst the tall and jolly customers. She raised her voice so they could all hear her explain how to play the game. With imperfect English, she explained the gaming rules and the payout principles. Some of the happy customers were trying to understand the gaming rules; others were eager to change their money into chips to begin wagering. Mee See helped them change their money and showed them the way they could participate in the joyous game. She managed to get all thirteen foreigners settled and they enjoyed playing for the first time the ancient Chinese game called Dai-Sai. The English customers were very generous. They gave Mee See fifty Hong Kong dollars as well as their left over chips.

Ah-Puck was walking the floor just at that moment and watched how Mee See handled all these foreigners with such ease. She actually made them enjoy staying and played this game for over two hours. He was surprised to hear Mee See conversing in English. Ah-Puck was amazed and thought, "Where did this Chinese girl learn to speak such English? Her imperfection in English somewhat added attraction to these foreigners who laughed and tried to correct her grammar and syntax while learning the rules of the game."

When the foreigners came to the Central Casino, they usually watched. Not knowing how to participate in the game and not having anyone around to show them the rules of the game, they tended to stay for a little while and then walk away without gambling.

Mee See noticed that Ah-Puck was standing in a corner watching her as the English customers were leaving her table. She didn't know how long Ah-Puck had been watching her movements. Ah-Puck walked towards Mee See and asked her to see him in his office before she went home. She regretted she had spoken English and had been so demonstrative with the foreigners. She was remorseful for having joked and laughed so much with the customers. She packed away her tips in case she had to surrender all her tip-takings to the company. Her inferiority complex kicked in. She thought she should have kept her place, behind the table and accepted bets without demonstrating how the game was played. She was worried that if she lost her job at the casino, she would not know where she could find another job to support the family. Thoughts went round and round her head for the rest of the afternoon until it was time to see Ah-Puck. She was ready to beg and promise him that she would not speak English and would not be so eager to serve foreigners again. Mee See took several deep breaths outside the office door and knocked.

Ah-Puck who was sitting at his desk, drinking a cup of tea, said, "I didn't know that you spoke English."

Mee See was agitated and said nervously, "When I was studying in high school in Canton, my mother sent my sister and me to a private school to study English. We studied English for quite a few years. In Canton, my first job was at the Portuguese Embassy as a Chinese and English translator. I used to converse with my work colleagues in English as I didn't know Portuguese and they couldn't speak Chinese."

That afternoon was the first time Ah-Puck had witnessed Mee See's operation with a group of foreigners. She was at ease with the number of foreign customers who towered over her at her table. She was able to control the situation and entertain these customers by showing them how to play the game. Now he knew that she had a high school education as well as having studied English, he realised that he never had such a well-educated game attendant before. Most attendants had hardly finished primary school and many could not even write their own names. They signed their names using their thumb prints. Ah-Puck couldn't help but admire Mee See.

With a friendly smile, Ah-Puck told Mee See, "From tomorrow onwards, you don't have to be a games attendant behind a Dai-Sai table anymore."

Mee See covered her mouth, as tears welled up in her eyes. Her long eye lashes sparkled with teardrops. She thought that she had been dismissed. She stood there motionless as though she was waiting for an execution.

Ah-Puck continued, "I want you to start working as the Central Casino's English speaking hostess. In future, you only look after foreigners. Any foreigners arriving in the Casino will be under your care. I saw you operate today and I liked what I saw. I want you to do exactly the same with every foreign customer. You are relieved of your Dai-Sai table duty from now on. You will have a pay rise of fifty Macanese Pataca each month, plus, you can keep all your tips. I know foreigners give very good tips."

Mee See's tears streamed down with relief, "Thank you Ah-Puck Kin-Lee. Thank you very much."

Mee See left the office in a happy daze as she absorbed the good news on the way home. Mee See specially went to the market to buy a fresh roast duck to take home for dinner. When Mummy came home with special roast food, the children knew it was good news. They could even smell the beautiful aroma that came from the package that Mummy brought home. The children jumped up and down surrounding Mummy when Ah Tai served up the roast duck, a steamed fish, and hot bowls of rice. It was the first time the children were introduced to the delicious aroma of fresh roast duck and they all enjoyed the taste. The whole family sat round the dining table joking and laughing. They couldn't wait to hear Mummy's good news. Mee See related everything that had happened during the day describing with laughing gestures some of the foreigner's mannerisms. The children all laughed at Mummy's funny description. Mee See finished by breaking the news that she had a pay rise of fifty Macanese Pataca.

Mee See thanked Siew Fen, "I have to thank you for sending us to study English. At the time we never knew how useful it was to have another language. This skill opened a new door for me when I worked at the Portuguese Embassy. Now I have the opportunity for a promotion. I shall only be looking after foreigners in the future. They give good tips and often leave all their left over chips to save changing them back into Macanese Pataca which they would still have to change back into their own currency."

Life was steady and happy in this new found home. Siew Fen said, "Macao has given us the chance of a new life. I am sure if Mee Jing and Wing Chung hear about your achievement, they will be very happy for you too."

Mee See knew that her mother missed Mee Jing and Wing Chung at times and said, "Chun Yun is no longer a family member now. I don't know where he has gone. I also don't care what happens to him anymore. Now we can tell our relatives and friends where we are. It is time to re-establish contact and let them know we have settled well in Macao."

Mee See wrote a letter to Mee Jing and Wing Chung. Soon there after the siblings re-established contact and corresponded with Mee See often. Siew Fen also wrote to her stepmothers at the Hui family in Hong Kong to let them know about her news.

Mee See had kept the letter that Chun Yun had written for Master and Madam Fung, but she never felt that she could send it. She opened the letter and read it again. Mee See wrote another letter to Master and Madam Fung. She wanted to let them know the family had settled well in Macao and their grandchildren were doing well. She thanked them for all their kindness to her and the children. Mee See also explained that she had separated with Chun Yun without explaining the reason why. But she lost the courage to mail it after all. She kept the two letters together and hoped that one day she would have the chance to see them again to give them the letters in person.

Mee See started her new role as the hostess for foreigners at the Casino. Many tourists came for a short trip to Macao as part of a side trip en-route from Hong Kong. Macao, with its casino, became a place of interest for many foreign visitors from America, England, Germany, and France, as well as many local Portuguese. The Central Casino became more popular because they had an English speaking hostess dedicated to look after foreigners. Many customers were delighted with the introduction to a new form of entertainment which brought a lot of laughter and happiness irrespective if they won or lost. They often left Mee See all their chips without cashing them in before leaving. At the end of every shift, she continued to wrap all the tips in a scarf to take home to her mother. After living expenses, Siew Fen exchanged Mee See's money for gold nuggets to stash away for emergency. Mee See felt settled and secure. Mother and daughter were happy with life in Macao.

Ah Lin

Ah Lin was happy to show Mee See the procedures and the gaming rules of the various types of games. Mee See was willing to listen carefully before she acted and tried to reason and asked sensible questions. With a good sense of humour and a quick mind for numbers, Mee See also had a wide vocabulary and often used words that Ah Lin had never heard before. As Ah Lin was a few years younger, she called Mee See her dear big sister, Mee See Chair (美思姐). Ah Lin had seen Mee See speaking English with the foreign customers many times before she was promoted and liked the way Mee See conducted herself. She admired Mee See from a distance and often subconsciously emulated her speech and her gestures.

Ah Lin lived with her sister Lyn Gar Chair (蓮家姐) who was a widow for many years with a four-year-old daughter named Lai-King (麗琼). The two sisters used to work in a cigarette factory in Macao. Ah Lin did not like being a factory hand. When the neighbour told her that they had a vacancy at work, Ah Lin plucked up her courage and went to the Central Casino with her neighbour and got a job as a game attendant.

Ah Lin, and Lyn Gar Chair invited Mee See's family home for dinner to celebrate Mee See's promotion. Mee See's two eldest children were around the same age as Lai King and they played happily together. By now Siew Fen had become a competent cook and brought along a number of her special dishes for everyone to enjoy. She cooked steamed scrambled eggs with fish intestines, braised chicken with chestnut, and stuffed fish with minced pork and mushrooms. These were the dishes her cooks used to excel in Canton.

After they had a scrumptious dinner and drank to Mee See's promotion, Mee See said to Ah Lin, "If you like, I can teach you how to speak English. One day we can both be the hostesses for all the foreign customers."

Ah Lin's eyes lit up with glee, "That would be fantastic! But … I didn't even finish primary school, I am not educated like you, Mee See Chair?"

Mee See re-assured Ah Lin, "I never finished high school either. But working as a hostess at the casino, you really don't need to write in English. All you need is to be willing to speak in English and not be afraid of using the wrong words and you can always learn the correct terminology afterwards." Mee See took a drink of her Chinese tea and continued, "I haven't written in English for many years. I am afraid I would have problems writing a good English passage now. First of all let me teach you some everyday conversation. My sister Mee Jing and I used to do that when we were at school. When you have learned enough vocabulary, you can practice talking to the foreign customers. I shall be around to help if you get stuck for words."

Lyn Gar Chair was embarrassed that Ah Lin had little education and said, "Our parents passed away when we were young and Lai-King's father also passed on so early. Otherwise we could have let Ah Lin continue with her schooling."

Siew Fen comforted Lyn Gar Chair and said, "Don't worry. I believe that in this world, how wealthy we are; how much food we eat, how well we dress, and what education we are meant to have are all written in our fate. Let Mee See teach you to converse in English. It may give you another skill for a better future. Mee Jing and Wing Chung are coming to Macao soon. When they come, Mee Jing and you will be able to practice English together."

Mee See said laughingly, "An old Chinese saying goes like this, 'Sum Koi Nu Yan Yut Koi Hu (三個女人一個山墟)' meaning three women talking at the same time is as noisy as a village market! When we three talk together in English, it will be as noisy as a foreign village market without travelling abroad!" With that, all the adults had a hearty giggle. The children followed the adults and laughed out loudly together.

Ah Lin and Mee See worked at speaking in English whenever they had the chance. Six months later, Ah Lin joined Mee See as the other English speaking hostess for the foreign visitors. The Central Casino was getting well-known among tourist groups because they had dedicated English speaking hostesses to take the tourists around to show them how to wager on various games that were offered. As Ah Lin was able to communicate in English she became more popular among the local Portuguese who frequented the Central Casino. She had many suitors from the local Portuguese community who took her out to the cinema, swimming, picnics and ice skating.

PHOTOGRAPHS – CANTON / MACAO

Kai Ming and Yau Mui at Fung's ancestral home

Siew Fen & children in Macao

Kai Ming, Kai Chung, Siew Fen, Kai Son & Yau Mui

Mee See & Ah Lin

Part Five – Seven Days Three Roles

Letter from Macao

At last, Mee Jing and Wing Chung received a letter from Mee See with a postage stamp from Macao. They realised Mee See and her family had gone to Macao with their mother. Wing Chung told Mee Jing, "When mother sold the ancestral properties in Canton, we didn't know where she had gone. Mee See Chair and her family also disappeared without a trace. Maybe Chun Yun had a promotion and became really wealthy. He might not want to associate with us poor relatives anymore."

Mee Jing was more analytical. She thought it through and said, "As Ah Tai was a descendant from a wealthy merchant and powerful judicial family, she sold all the ancestral homes and discharged all the servants to avoid being summoned for questioning from the 'Three Evils' and 'Five Evils' movement. She had to lay low to wait until the movement blew over. Ah Tai always had a good reason for her decisions."

Wing Chung did not make a comment. He still begrudged the fact that Siew Fen was holding the family inheritance. He did not want to talk about his argument with their mother over his share of the inheritance. Wing Chung responded, "Macao is a Portuguese colony. That's why Ah Tai finds it safer there."

Mee Jing continued to read and said "Oh, why hasn't she mentioned Chun Yun in this letter?"

Wing Chung took the letter and examined the three pages and Chun Yun was not mentioned in the letter. Wing Chung then added, "Ng…very strange indeed! Mee See Chair hasn't mentioned him at all. I wonder if he's dead and Mee See Chair is too sad to talk about him."

Mee Jing said, "Good reasoning! Look here… Mee See Chair said she was working at a casino as a hostess. If Chun Yun was around, he would not allow Mee See Chair to work such a low class chore! Poor Mee See Chair must be supporting the family!"

Wing Chung added, "Ah Tai would not be able to find a job. At her age, what can she do? Besides she was used to the good life and good food. She would not be much help for Mee See Chair."

Mee Jing defended mother, "Chung Kor[47](中哥), you have always been unfair to Ah Tai. Mother was brought up in a wealthy family; she should have a life of luxury. That was her good fortune being born to such wealth. Please don't be unfair to mother. Let's answer Mee See Chair's letter."

From then on, the family corresponded frequently. Soon it was Siew Fen's birthday. Mee Jing got her in-law's permission to visit her mother in Macao while the servants took care of the boys. Mee Jing suggested that Wing Chung should come as well to celebrate their mother's birthday and to visit their long lost sister.

The siblings took a ferry from Canton to Macao to spend a few days with the family. A lot had happened in each of their lives since they had last met. The family was eager to meet again. Mee Jing hugged their mother while holding Mee See Chair's hand. The three women burst into tears. Even Wing Chung wiped his eyes with a handkerchief. The three children followed them and burst out howling. All of a sudden, the entire family was in the depth of sorrow. Siew Fen looked around and saw the children were pulling the corner of Mee See's dress and sobbing. It was lucky that little Kai Son was asleep in his cot. Siew Fen used the wide sleeve of her top to wipe her tears and said, "Look, we frightened the children. Come let's freshen up. Mee See will brew some tea. We have so much to catch up."

Mee See dried her tears and began to make a pot of Jasmine tea. Siew Fen gave a face flannel to Mee Jing and Wing Chung. She used a third

---

[47] Chung Kor 中哥 was a respectful way to address Mee Jing's elder brother.

one to dry the tears and wipe the children's' faces. Siew Fen gave Yau Mui the doll from Mee Jing and the toy truck from Wing Chung to the boys and told the children to go and play quietly. The children were accustomed to playing quietly without fighting. They knew that if they misbehaved, Por Por (婆婆)[48] would take the toys back. The children thanked Yee Yee (姨姨)[49] and Kou Fu (舅父)[50] politely before they took their toys into their bedroom to play quietly.

The freshly brewed tea filled the little room with fresh Jasmine flagrance. It reminded them of years gone by when they were sitting in their huge drawing room with all the finery at their ancestral home. Now they faced this simple combined lounge and dining room with a small kitchen on the side.

Siew Fen began, "I don't know where to start. So many things have happened over the last few years that have changed our lives forever. It was like a very bad dream. I have done the wrong thing to marry Mee See to Chun Yun. I regret ever doing that. Now Mee See has to carry this heavy burden. I will feel guilty the rest of my life."

Ah Tai always had the confidence to do the right thing. She was methodical and decisive and she always knew what should be done. It was unlike her to admit defeat. It came as a surprise that she admitted that she was wrong and apologised. Mee Jing and Wing Chung had never heard mother so humble. They did not know how to respond. Mee See realised how remorseful mother had been.

Mee Jing could not wait any longer and asked, "Where is Chun Yun now?"

Mee See explained, "I threw him out. I tore up our wedding certificate, we are no longer married. I don't know where he has gone and I don't

---

[48] Por Por 婆婆 grandmother from the mother side.
[49] Yee Yee 姨姨 aunty from the mother side.
[50] Kou Fu 舅父 uncle from the mother side.

care either."

Wing Chung asked, "Why did you leave him? Tearing up your marriage certificate[51] is such a final step."

Mee Jing said, "When I married Kin Wah, you were still living as the young Madam Fung. Chun Yun had such high education and a senior position at work. The Fung family were much wealthier than our Tam family. Why did you suddenly disappear without a trace? Even old Master and Madam Fung couldn't tell us where you were."

Looking at Wing Chung, Mee Jing continued, "Cheung Kor (中哥)[52] thought that Chun Yun must have been very successful and earned so much money that he would not want to know us anymore. But I thought differently. I thought that it must be something unexpected for you to disappear. Leaving Canton was a huge sacrifice!"

Mee See took a deep breath, collected herself and began to relay the events of the last few years. It brought back a lot of frustration, anger and sadness as Mee See told her siblings Chun Yun's exploits over the last couple of years, finishing with, "The last straw was when he borrowed money from the landlord leaving me to settle his debt. He had to go because I couldn't get him to give up his gambling habit."

Mee See continued, "Then by chance I got a job at the casino. Once again it was by chance that they found out I could converse in English and gave me a promotion." Mee See was calmer and more collected when she talked about work at the casino. She felt a lot more confident about the future. Taking another deep breath she said, "I have wanted to write to you for a long time. Let's keep in close contact and take care of each other."

Siew Fen added, "If I had not insisted on Mee See marrying Chun Yun,

---

[51] Tearing up the marriage certificate to Mee See was the way to destroy the evidence of their marriage.

[52] Chung Kor 中哥 respectful way to address an elder brother Wing Chung.

she would not have married this compulsive gambler."

Mee See put her hand on her mother's and said softly, "Don't regret it anymore. I have never blamed you. At the time, Chun Yun had very good potential. We all thought he would have a bright future. Nobody knew he had this compulsion for gambling. Don't look back and regret any more Ah Tai. At least Chun Yun was always faithful. The great pity was that he could not shake off his gambling habit."

Siew Fen added, "Good job Buddha is kind to you. Now you have a stable job to support this family. You are really capable."

Mee Jing added, "Our Mee See Chair has always been outstanding. She always set a good example ever since we were little." Listening to Mee See's misfortune, she couldn't help but feel sorry for her sister, and said, "Mee See Chair's fate was like a nightmare. It was a good job you made the decision to chase Chun Yun out of your life. If a man is useless, you should leave him early and not waste your youth on him."

Mee See replied, "I always thought he would reform. If he had stopped gambling, he would have had a chance to re-build his career, after all he had a university education. I just couldn't understand why he couldn't change this bad habit. But now we are finished. I want to bring up the children the best way I can and fulfill my duty as a good mother. That's all."

Mee Jing said, "If it was me, I would give the children back to the Fung family. Let them educate their flesh and blood. They have money, influence and they can afford to send them to the best schools and support them even to the university. How are you going to find the money to send them to school?"

Mee See said, "Mee Jing, now that you have two children, would you give your children to your in-laws, walk out, and never see your children again?"

Mee Jing responded immediately and firmly, "I am not being

complacent, if Kin Wah and I split up, I would definitely give the children to the Tam family."

Mee See commented, "You are very hard-hearted! How could you bear to leave the children?"

Mee Jing added, "Then what are your plans for the future?"

Mee See replied, "My wages are not high, but I do get a lot of tips, which very often is double what I earn in wages. Ah Tai helps me to save what is left every month for the children's schooling. Well, I don't know what will happen tomorrow. I just take one day at a time and do what I have to do to survive! … Don't we all?"

Mee Jing's Marriage Break Up

When enquired about her life in Canton, Mee Jing calmly replied, "Frankly, I think Kin Wah has another home overseas."

Siew Fen, Mee See, and Wing Chung were astonished with such a revelation. It was even more of a surprise that Mee Jing seemed to be emotionless about the news. She showed no sadness, no disquiet and no apprehension.

Siew Fen asked, "How do you come to this conclusion? Don't be presumptuous. What proof do you have to accuse him?"

Mee Jing was composed and replied quietly, "The business simply prospered everywhere with new branches in a number of South East Asian countries. Kin Wah has changed. He uses the excuse of inspecting businesses to stay away from home for six months at a time. He treats me like a housekeeper. All he wants is for me to take care of the boys and bring them up. I only hear about his movements through my in-laws.

Siew Fen asked, "Did you ask him directly why he is not happy with you?"

Mee Jing said, "Yes, he did not deny it when I asked him if he has another woman. Now seeing Mee See Chair is independent and raising a family of six, I have decided to leave Kin Wah. I don't want to waste my youth on him anymore."

Mee See said, "You have to think carefully before you throw away the security of being at the Tam household. You will have a heavy responsibility raising the children on your own and living a lonely existence!"

Wing Chung was listening quietly. He wondered how Mee Jing could live outside of the Tam family and asked, "What are you going to do for living if you leave the Tam family? Can you find a job in Canton?"

Full of confidence Mee Jing said, "Look at Mee See Chair. She can raise enough money to feed and keep her family of six. If I worked hard at any job, surely I can earn enough to keep myself. There is an old saying, 'Lin Sick Hoi May Yook, Butt Sick Sout May Fan (寧食開眉粥，不吃愁眉飯)[53], I would rather eat congee happily, than devour a feast in misery."

From that point, Mee Jing was more determined to find an opportunity to leave Kin Wah. She was planning to come to Macao to build a new life for herself. She would need sponsorship to enter Macao. She was sure that Mee See Chair would act as guarantor for her when the time came. However, it was not the time to talk about her plans yet.

Wing Chung's Failure

Wing Chung was not going to tell the sisters about the quarrel he had with mother over the inheritance. He was also hoping that Siew Fen would not mention it to his sisters.

Siew Fen also did not want to mention the squabble she had with her son over what was left of the Kwan family fortune. She would rather

---

[53] Lin Sick Hoi May Yook, Butt Sick Sout May Fan 寧食開眉粥，不吃愁眉飯 meaning one would rather be happy poor, than to be rich but miserable.

forget about the whole sorry affair and move on with life. She was settled now. She was happy living with Mee See and caring for the four grandchildren.

Wing Chung always had an inferiority complex. He felt that he was not good enough compared to his siblings. He was not going to tell them that his business was not viable and that Yee Hong had to work in the factory to make ends meet. Telling the truth would be an act of losing face! Wing Chung said, "I only have half a shop. Business is fine. We don't need two people working at the shop. Yee Hong is bored at home, she decided to go to work in the local plastic flower factory for pocket money. She took holidays from the factory to work in the shop so I could come to celebrate Ah Tai's birthday."

Wing Chung gave a parcel to Siew Fen and said, "This is for your birthday Ah Tai." Inside the bag there were tooth brushes, tooth paste, bars of soap, face flannels and a bottle of eau de cologne that were from Wing Chung's shop.

Mee Jing put a red soft woolen wrap over Siew Fen's shoulder and said, "Ah Tai this should keep you warm on cold winter nights. Have a happy birthday. "

Siew Fen held in her hands the bag of goodies from Wing Chung, and touching the soft wool shawl on her shoulder, and she felt comforted to have her children surrounding her at last. She said, "I often dreamt of meeting with you all together. Today, my dream has come true. Let's try my cooking tonight."

Siew Fen had taken up cooking as a leisure pursuit instead of as a duty to feed the family. When she went to the market, she talked to those servants who were shopping for provisions to prepare dinner for their mistresses. She learned from these cooks a number of dishes that her chefs used to excel at. Siew Fen found that she too could cook like her chefs. This night she cooked a number of the family's favourite dishes including braised duck with taro, stuffed fish with mushroom and ham, soya sauce chicken with star anise, and steamed eggs with tofu and dried shrimps.

Mee Jing and Wing Chung looked surprised when they saw the dishes come from the little kitchen. Mee Jing exclaimed, "Ayarh, when did you learn to cook Ah Tai! These are Sam-Chai's signature dishes! You never stepped through the kitchen door if I remember rightly. You didn't even know how to boil water."

Siew Fen, beaming with happiness said, "Ma Say Lok Da Hun (馬死落地行)[54]. We have to cook when there is no chef around! Actually cooking is not that difficult. It is just trial and error. Come! Let's eat before the food gets cold!" Siew Fen was comforted to see the family share a hearty meal together. They were joking and laughing over stories from their youth. Looking back, Siew Fen was sure she was correct in fighting and winning the Kwan's settlement from her husband so she could afford to support Mee See, Mee Jing and Wing Chung and bring them up the best way she could. Siew Fen felt she had done her duty as a good mother, now a good grandmother.

Exodus to Macao

Mee Jing went home and put into action her plan to leave her husband. Every day when she tended to the boys, she felt a sense of being beaten because she had to give up the boys to leave Kin Wah. She could not help but feel the loss of her children already. She knew that when she left, she would leave the children, the security and the family that she helped to build over the years. She did not know when they would discuss the separation, she was hoping for a peaceful conversation with Kin Wah to work on a settlement so he could help her with money to start a new life.

Since marrying into the Tam family, Mee Jing had been saving all the left

---

[54] Ma Say Lok Da Hun 馬死落地行 when the horse died, one had to climb down from the horse back and start walking.

over housekeeping money. Kin Wah also gave her more money to care for the boys. Mee Jing had very little expenses except for the children's clothes and the occasional outings. Ever since she suspected Kin Wah had another family overseas, Mee Jing became more cautious with her spending. She had saved a lot of cash and gold nuggets over the years. In her little drawstring bag she had over thirty nuggets each weighing an ounce. She was grateful for her mother's teaching. Mee Jing put her savings away quietly and regained her confidence.

Mee Jing asked Mee See to sponsor her to migrate to Macao. Mee See knew a number of the Portuguese consulate officials who often came to the Central Casino. As a guarantor, she gave them Mee Jing's application papers and soon afterwards Mee Jing's application was approved.

Kin Wah came home from overseas and he brought with him toy cars for the boys and presents for everyone except Mee Jing. He was embarrassed, as he had literally forgotten about his wife when he was selecting presents for everyone in the family. He explained, "So sorry I was very busy in Singapore this trip. I didn't get a chance to get you a present. Here, take this money and buy yourself something nice the next time you go out."

He put a few hundred Tai-Yuan on the table.

Sadness welled up inside as Mee Jing kept her calm composure. She knew very well that Kin Wah had completely forgotten about her while he was away. She wished she could pick up the hundred Tai-Yuan bills and tear them into bits and throw them in his face to vent her anger. However, Mee Jing needed every single Tai-Yuan she could get for her departure. She might as well tolerate this treatment for a little longer. Mee Jing swallowed her pride, got up slowly to pick up the hundred Tai-Yuan bills from the table and quietly put them inside her pockets. Using all her might to calm her voice, she whispered softly, "Good."

Never in Kin Wah's imagination could he visualise the hatred that was in

Mee Jing's heart. Kin Wah was naïve to think that Mee Jing would look after the children and provide the motherly love for his children whilst he travelled out of the country to earn a good living for the family.

Kin Wah said to Mee Jing, "Next month I want to move the family from Singapore to Canton and they will live in the Tam estate. I will organise for you to relocate into another brick cottage beyond the garden. You will have a younger sister here to look after, respect and serve you."

This news hit Mee Jing hard. She mustered all her self-control to keep herself on the chair. She held her hands together so they would not shake. She was dealt such an unfair blow; the news was repulsive to her. She thought it was useless to protest. There was no point in bringing up the subject of separation now. She decided to keep quiet. Mee Jing held down her voice and said, "As you wish."

Kin Wah was surprised that there was no sign of protest from her. The next moment, he turned away from her and took the children to the park with their new cars.

Mee Jing was at the point of throwing up as Kin Wah disappeared from the door. She was overwhelmed with jealousy. She was furious that she was evicted from her home where she had lived ever since she married. She knew then there was nothing for her in the Tam family. She would not submit herself to the insult of moving out of her home for Kin Wah's new wife. She packed up a simple suitcase and took all her savings with a few clothes and left in the middle of the night without leaving a note.

Mee Jing was only twenty-three at the time.

Mee Jing took the last ferry to Macao to live with Mee See. She looked out from the ferry window onto the simmering Pearl River as the ferry moved down the river. In the far horizon, the moon was rising, signalling a new beginning. Mee Jing put her hand inside her inner pocket. She could feel the nuggets rolling inside the old grey bag in her hand. She felt numb as tears rolled down her cheeks like pearls from a broken string. It was heart-rending, but it was her choice. She was without her children and without her husband. However, she was not remorseful. She had freedom now. She had no idea what tomorrow would bring.

Mee Ying was grateful to have her sister and mother around to give her the support she needed at this point in her life. On Mee See's recommendation, she went to the Central Entertainment Complex to look for a job. Ah-Puck said, "Unfortunately we do not have a vacancy in our gaming division."

Mee Jing smiled gently and added in earnest, "I come from Canton and am living with Mee See Chair. I really want to be independent so I won't be a burden to my sister. The Central Entertainment Complex is such a big organisation. If there are other vacancies, I am sure I will be able to learn the work. I promise I will not disappoint you. I am only looking for an opportunity to start if Ah-Puck Kin-Lee would give me a chance."

Ah-Puck saw Mee Jing was young and pretty. She had a delightful smile. Looking at her fine hands and thin fingers, she was not used to hard physical work. But he did not know what she would think of his job offer. He stated, "On the fifth level we have the Grape Vine Night Club which is a dance hall with live music each night. We need a full time hostess at the Grape Vine Night Club. On the fourth level we have a European restaurant which serves Portuguese and European cuisine. We need two part-time waitresses. But these are temporary vacancies only."

In her teens, Mee Jing followed her sister in Canton to learn how to dance. She was delighted that what she had learned in those days now came in handy in earning a wage. With a broad smile on her face Mee Jing quickly said, "Oh when I was in my teens, I always went with Mee See Chair to the Canton Wah Har Dance Hall to go dancing in the afternoon. I can do ballroom dancing like the Fox Trot, Jive, the Waltz, Samba, and the Rumba. But I have not been a hostess at a dance hall before. What is the duty of a hostess?"

Ah-Puck was surprised to hear that the two sisters knew ballroom dancing as well, and enquired, "Do both you and your sister dance? Do you speak English as well?"

Mee Jing didn't even stop to think and said, "Yes, both my sister and I studied English at a private college when we attended high school in Canton. But I must admit I have not used English for a number of years. But if I practice with Mee See Chair, I am sure English will come back to me."

It was not easy to find a hostess to work at the night club. Ah-Puck was overjoyed to hear that both sisters could dance and could converse in English as well. He decided to use Mee Jing. He also thought he might be able to use Mee See to help should they need an extra hostess to work in the night club area.

Ah-Puck said, "Good. Let me take you to meet Yuen-Yee (婉兒) on the fifth level. You will learn from her. Since you know how to speak English, you can also look after the foreigners who come to the night club. Your monthly wage will be two hundred Macanese Palaca. The trial employment is for one month and the wage is one hundred fifty Macanese Palaca. You have to wear a Chinese Chong Sam to work. Yuen-Yee will show you what to do. You will start work next Monday."

Mee Jing was very happy and said, "Thank you Ah-Puck Kin-Lee, thank you. Would the tailor be able to sew one in such short notice? Also, how much does a tailor charge in Macao?"

Ah-Puck stood up, handed over a fifty Macanese Palaca bill and said, "This is the first fifty for you to get the things ready for work on Monday." As Ah-Puck was talking, he took Mee Jing to the fifth level to leave her with Yuen-Yee. She looked after Mee Jing to get her ready for work.

Yuen-Yee was a little taller than Mee Jing. She had a sweet smile and was friendly and helpful. Mee Jing followed Yuen-Yee to get everything that she needed. From that moment on, Yuen-Yee and Mee Jing became the best of friends.

At dinner time, Mee Jing couldn't wait to tell Siew Fen and Mee See Chair what had happened during the day. She showed them everything she had bought ready for work. Mee Jing said, "Today Ah-Puck gave me a job to start work next Monday. I got fifty Macanese Palaca advance on my wages as well."

Siew Fen asked, "What sort of job gives an advance? I have never heard of any job like that!"

Mee Jing smiled and answered, "The night club needs a hostess. When we were in Canton, we learned how to dance at the Wah Har Dance Hall. I remember all the dances that we learned. Ah-Puck asked me if Mee See Chair could dance as well. He also asked if I can speak English."

Mee See explained, "Ah-Puck gave you the position of hostess on level five to be a dancing girl."

Mee Jing said, "Yes, I know. Yuen-Yee has already told me what this job is about. The duty of a hostess is to be the dancing partner for customers who come in without a partner. Often customers come in to the night club to celebrate their business success or to talk business. The hostess will make thing easy for these customers by ordering drinks or food for them. If the customers want to talk and tell jokes, we keep them company. If they want to dance, we dance with them. The aim is to entertain the customers to make their stay at the night club an enjoyable one. I am paid two hundred a month, but one hundred fifty during the first month when I am on trial. He gave me fifty today to have my dress made and to get new shoes and a little hand bag for work."

Siew Fen said, "Dancing customers may have other ideas. You may want to think carefully before you accept the job."

Mee Jing thought it over and said, "I don't need to think anymore. I have this job that pays me so well. I won't be a burden to Mee See

Chair. How can I let this opportunity pass me by?" Mee Jing turned to talk to her mother, "I need a job and Ah-Puck is willing to employ me. Yuen-Yee has already told me the duties of a dancing hostess. She will keep an eye on me. It is a good wage for a single girl like me. It really does not matter whether I shall be a hostess or a dancing girl. At least I have a paying job now."

Mee Jing told Mee See, "Now I have an income, I want to start paying for my keep. I also want to share half of Ah Tai's living expenses. That is only fair."

Mee See said, "I should take care of Ah Tai because she is taking care of all the children. Otherwise, it would be very hard for me to settle in a job."

Siew Fen said, "If your boys come over as well, I can look after them too."

Mee Jing was very firm with her answer, "I never intended to take my boys with me. They are the Tam's offsprings. The Tam family has all the money to support them and give them the best education. Master and Madam Tam love their grandsons. My boys will not be ill-treated by anyone in that family."

Breakout to Macao

Wing Chung took the ferry home to Canton. He was depressed as he began to realise that his business was not viable. He decided to walk around the location to see how he could improve trade and to increase the passing traffic. To his horror, he found the council was building a road round the corner. Workmen had blocked off the traffic that used to turn into the road where he had his shop. No wonder there was less and less traffic coming down the road and subsequently less and less people walking by his shop. It would be months before the council would finish this work. Wing Chung conferred with Yee Hong and decided to close the business to cut their losses. Wing Chung wondered what he could do to earn a living.

Yee Hong suggested, "I hear the plastic flower factory needs extra hands. Why don't I ask the foreman if there is a vacancy in our area? With our wages joined together and without the outgoings for the shop, we should be able to live comfortably. You can always start another business afterwards."

Wing Chung held Yee Hong's hand. They were rough with blotches and scratch marks and her nails were short and stained with dirt. Yee Hong used to have such soft, white hands with fine fingertips. Her hands were her best feature. Wing Chung realising it was the price Yee Hong paid to support the business, "I am useless!' said Wing Chung, "I am so sorry I can't afford to provide a good living for you. I don't know when I can repay you."

Yee Hong comforted her husband, "We share the good times as well as the bad. There is no repaying to talk about. Let us face the facts, we both need to get a job and earn wages to make a new start."

Wing Chung was grateful his wife always seemed to have a reasonable approach to his problems.

Regretfully, Wing Chung and Yee Hong closed the business at the shop. They moved all the stock home for their own use. Each day the couple walked down the road to work at the plastic flowers factory. Together, they each brought a three-tiered tin container to take the left-over food from the previous night for lunch. It was good to be relieved of the pressure of running a business that never turned a profit. Without the shop, they enjoyed free time on the weekends and the couple walked hand in hand in the park. On pay day they even shared the luxury of a meal eating at the street hawkers. It was carefree and they shared some happy times.

Wing Chung had a carefree childhood. As he often skipped classes and did not put any effort to learning scholastic skills throughout his school years. Except for a brief period when Wing Chung was employed as a part time stacker at the fruit shop, he had never worked in full employment under a superior's direction. For most of his working life, he was his own boss. He was not equipped with the skills of getting on with workmates or following instructions. Wing Chung was not used to taking orders. He became angry when things did not work as he wanted.

At the flower factory there was a procedure to follow and a schedule to meet delivery deadlines. Workers were not given autonomy. After working at the assembly line for a short while, there was friction between Wing Chung and the foreman. Yee Hong knew Wing Chung had a temper that he sometimes could not control. She was worried that his work at the factory may not last if he could not follow the foreman's instructions.

At one disagreement Wing Chung repudiated and yelled, "You are always finding fault with me and getting an excuse to tell me off. I have had enough. You do it the way you want it. I won't!" As he yelled back at the foreman, Wing Chung picked up his tin lunch box and went to find Yee Hong. The two resigned together, leaving immediately. All of a sudden they both found themselves out of work losing two incomes at the same time. In the heat of the moment, Wing Chung's temper overwhelmed him. There was no time for him to consider where they could find the next employment. Unfortunately Wing Chung was not regretful. He was furious and could not see reason as he stormed home with Yee Hong.

As Yee Hong walked behind Wing Chung with her head held low, she knew that this incident would have happened sooner or later. She deeply regretted that she failed to talk to Wing Chung about keeping check on his temper. She wished that she could have stayed to keep earning, even if Wing Chung wanted to leave. It was too late for anything now.

Wing Chung said, "Why don't we go to Macao? We have my mother and sister there to look after us."

Wing Chung asked Mee See to help sponsor them to migrate to Macao. He did not tell Mee See about the incident at the factory. He only mentioned that the shop business was affected by the council road construction. He had decided to close the shop and take the money to try his luck in Macao.

Once again, Mee See used her contact with the Portuguese consulate officials to get approval for her brother and sister-in-law to migrate to Macao. To prepare for Wing Chung and Yee Hong's arrival, Mee See's family moved into a premise with three bedrooms at May Kee Kai (美姬

街) near the well-known Happy Buddha seafood restaurant.

It had a better environment than their previous residence and was also near the Central Hotel and Entertainment Complex for the girls to get to work conveniently. With increased rental and two additional adults to support, Mee See felt the extra pressure. She was hoping that Wing Chung and Yee Hong would not take a long time to find jobs so they could support themselves and pay some of the rent to lighten her load.

Mee Jing could see that it was a heavy load for Mee See as she often saw Mee See would skip lunch to save the lunch money for the family. She decided to contribute the rental and food bill to support Ah Tai and brother Wing Chung and let Mee See look after the children and Yee Hong. Mee See accepted Mee Jing's assistance and said, "I appreciate your help. But we must tell Wing Chung and Yee Hong so they know that you have helped them to settle here as well." Mee See added, "There has been business expansions in Macao. It should not be difficult to find work in Macao. I think they will take a couple of months to settle, but as soon as Wing Chung and Yee Hong find a job, they will be able to support themselves."

Mee Jing continued, "We won't need to tell them who is supporting them. They must know that only you and I have the income to support them."

Siew Fen added, "I really feel good that you sisters are so kind to your brother. It is good to have the family living together once again."

Wing Chung and Yee Hong settled into the routine in Macao at Mee See's home and felt secure and happy. Yee Hong was happy to find a job washing dishes in the kitchen of the restaurant on the fifth level of the Central complex with a monthly wage higher than what she was earning at the plastic flower factory in Canton.

It was not as easy for Wing Chung to find a job. He did not want to work in a factory anymore in case he met another foreman like the one at the factory in Canton. He did not want to work in the kitchen either because he didn't know what to do in a kitchen. He wanted to re-start the same hawker business that he had before. He was delighted to find that he didn't need a licence to trade as a hawker in Macao. It was possible for him to do the same trade on a mobile trolley. However he needed money to start a business even though it was a small concern. He had depleted his inheritance while waiting for the entrance application. He was considering on approaching Mee Jing to lend him some money.

Yee Hong said, "I can see money is important to Mee Jing. You can tell by the way she counts her money. If you ask her for money and she won't lend it to you, it would be very embarrassing to remain under the same roof. We don't know how much she could afford to lend you."

Wing Chung said, "I see her bringing home a stack of money every night. Maybe she doesn't even know how much money she has. If I quietly borrow some money from her, when I make a profit from trading, I can repay her."

Yee Hong was alarmed and said firmly, "Oh you mean to steal her money? Money means so much to Mee Jing. She would know exactly how much she has for sure. If you are discovered, we would no longer be able to stay here. No, Wing Chung you must stop thinking about stealing from her, you promise me!"

Wing Chung mumbled, "All right then."

Yee Hong knew that Wing Chung still had a temper that was uncontrollable and she often tried to smooth things over to avoid confrontation. Wing Chung did not have the ability to systematically analyse a situation. He often jumped to the wrong conclusion and could not express himself coherently. He maintained that as the only son of the family, he didn't get a fair share of the inheritance. He attributed his business failure to not having a big share of the inheritance because of his mother. Wing Chung began to get jealous and was angry with Mee Jing. He did not know how much money she had stashed away. However, he still blamed her for having a lot of money, and that she should be considerate to her poor brother and help him start his business. He did not blame Mee See because she allowed Yee Hong and him to stay for free. Mee See had a hard life, he thought.

Thieving

Wing Chung saw Mee Jing count out a number of dollar bills for Siew Fen for house-keeping. She gave money to Mee See for her share of the rental, and she took the rest into her bedroom to put away. He did not know that Mee Jing was supporting his living. He thought Mee See was supporting the couple as they were staying with the family. Yee Hong kept her wages and gave Wing Chung pocket money so he had spending money to look for an opportunity for their future.

One afternoon Siew Fen went to the market with the children. Yee Hong and Mee See had gone to work together mid-morning. Mee Jing was running late, she rushed out of the door forgetting to lock the suitcase under the bed and left the padlock and the key on her pillow.

Wing Chung saw the unlocked suitcase under the bed, where Mee Jing kept her savings. He walked by the sisters' room and stood at the door a number of times looking at the unlocked suitcase under the bed.

Wing Chung looked at his watch. Time was moving. He had to look in the suitcase and put everything back before Ah Tai came home with the children. It was an old and battered suitcase. Wing Chung opened it thinking, "You would not imagine anything of significance to be found in this silly old suitcase." To his surprise, there were stacks of notes everywhere. There were piles of hundred, fifty, twenty and ten bills, and loose ones all rolled up tidily with rubber bands. There might have been hundreds of Macanese Palaca. It was much more than Wing Chung had imagined. Wing Chung put back the notes carefully, making sure the suitcase looked like how he found it.

As he was closing the suitcase, Wing Chung saw a side pocket with an old grey drawstring bag. It was like the bags he used to have for his marbles when he was a boy. He opened to find many gold nuggets. Each had the signage of 'one ounce' to indicating its weight. He counted. There were more than thirty shiny gold nuggets; they could not all fit in the palm of his hand. Wing Chung thought, "Where on earth did Mee Jing get all this gold? She must have stolen it from the Tam family." Wing Chung rolled the nuggets back into the drawstring bag. One nugget rolled down under the bed. He picked up the last one and rolled it up and down in his palm. The gold nugget shimmered. He could not bring himself to put it back into the bag.

Wing Chung considered the situation. If he had a gold nugget, he would be able to start his business again. He could then be independent and would not be a burden to Mee See Chair anymore. Above all, Mee Jing should share some of her riches with her siblings. It was not good for anyone to have too much stashed away. He decided to keep the last gold nugget and carefully put it inside his pocket, then he put back the drawstring bag, closed the suitcase and pushed it under the bed, leaving the padlock and the key on the pillow. Wing Chung walked out of Mee Jing's room, took a deep breath pretending nothing had happened that afternoon.

When Mee Jing arrived home she went to her room. She screeched loudly, "Who has been in my room? Someone has been in my suitcase."

Siew Fen, Mee See, and Yee Hong all went into the sisters' room to find what had happened. There was a big commotion as all the ladies were talking at the same time.

Siew Fen said, "You always lock your suitcase. Nobody knows what you have inside the suitcase. Nobody knows where you keep your key either."

Mee Jing said, "I was late for work today. I rushed out without locking the suitcase. The padlock and the key are still on my pillow. I left them there this morning."

Mee See said, "Let me see. Your suitcase, the padlock, and the key are all here in the room. If somebody came to rob us, they would have taken your suitcase and everything."

Yee Hong was standing at the side quietly. She dared not make a noise.

Mee Jing said, "I have lost one gold nugget."

Siew Fen replied, trying to reason with everybody, "Did you count incorrectly? It is so easy to make a wrong count because they are so small. If anybody came to rob us, they would have stolen everything. They would not be so stupid to just take one of your gold nuggets. You must have miscounted."

Mee Jing was very sure and confirmed, "It can't be. I count them every single day. I am missing one nugget, but all my notes are intact. I always know exactly what I have in this suitcase. Who came here today? Who was at home today?"

Mee See said, "Ah Tai went to the market today with the children. Yee Hong and I went to work mid-morning. You and Wing Chung were here as we left to go to work. After you left for work, Wing Chung was here alone."

Everyone looked around and found Wing Chung was missing. The four ladies went out into the lounge room to find him. Four pairs of eye were staring at Wing Chung looking for an answer. He looked uncomfortable with his eyes downcast. He dared not meet anyone's gaze. Yee Hong knew that it was Wing Chung who had taken the nugget.

Mee Jing asked Wing Chung directly, "Chung Kor, can you explain this?" Mee Jing was not accusing Wing Chung. As he was the only one in the house all day, she was hoping he would have a reasonable explanation. Perhaps he could help to find the nugget.

Unfortunately Wing Chung thought he was being accused. He thought that Mee Jing should have offered him help and shared her good fortune with her poor relatives. One person should not have so much money.

Wing Chung said, "You have so much money and so many nuggets. It should be all right for you to lose one nugget!"

Immediately everyone knew that Wing Chung had stolen the nugget. The four ladies were disgusted with his attitude.

Mee See had to speak her mind, "It does not matter how much Mee Jing has. You have no right to steal from her. If she wants to share her fortune, it is up to her to do so. Come on Wing Chung, give the nugget back to Mee Jing and we can forget the whole sorry saga. Mee Jing works very hard to accumulate her savings. How can you say that it is alright for her to lose a gold nugget?"

Wing Chung was getting agitated. Without thinking what he was saying, he spoke, "Mee Jing is only a dancing girl. She dances with whoever pays for her. I don't know where her money comes from. How can she have so many nuggets? Maybe she stole them from the Tam family!"

Mee Jing realised that her brother was thinking lowly of her because of her work. Greatly disappointed, she retaliated, "Those nuggets are Kin Wah's conscience money. He gave me excess housekeeping over the years to keep me quiet because he was having an affair. I saved everything he gave me for an emergency. He thought he could give me more money to appease his guilty conscience." Mee Jing took another breath to strike back, "That's right, I am a dancing girl. I get paid by dancing with whoever pays for my company. I work for my money honestly. I have a clear conscience. I am not a thief. I will never take anything that does not belong to me. I would rather go and earn my living than to burden people. I will not disgrace myself with such a lowly act as stealing from the people who feed me."

Mee Jing deliberately provoked her brother about his situation.

Wing Chung was furious. He had never taken kindly to criticism. He raised his hand to strike Mee Jing. Yee Hong saw it coming and swiftly moved between them and got hold of his arm mid way. She used her body to protect Mee Jing. At the same time she spoke loudly for the first time at Wing Chung, "Wing Chung, you must not strike anyone. Sit down! We can talk this over. Everything has a solution!"

Siew Fen told Wing Chung, "My family doesn't accept anyone who steals. Give back Mee Jing's nugget right now!"

On Siew Fen's command, Wing Chung's anger multiplied as the thought of his ill fortune came back to haunt him. He became even more agitated and slammed his hand on the table, pointed his finger at Siew Fen and yelled, "It is all your fault. You fought father in the court for seven years. How much money have you wasted? I should have so much inheritance being the only son in the Kwan family. This is all your fault!"

Unexpectedly, Wing Chung stepped forward and swung his hand towards Siew Fen. None of the ladies expect such a move from him and all rushed to Siew Fen's aid. Siew Fen was pushed, lost her balance and fell on the floor. Mee See, Mee Jing, and Yee Hong all helped her up.

With anger and disappointment, Siew Fen cursed, "You dare hit your own mother. You will never be a rich man, ever!"

Mee See never knew Wing Chung had such a temper. He had shown that he was an unreasonable person with an uncontrolled temper. Now he also showed that he was a thief with a violent nature. They could not cope with someone like Wing Chung in the family even if he was their long lost brother. His behaviour was unacceptable. Mee See was disappointed and said, "Wing Chung, you can no longer stay here. I think you and Yee Hong should move out."

Mee Jing added, "I want you to give back the nugget before you leave. You are bad. How can you hit your own mother! You are not my brother anymore!"

Wing Chung had no remorse. He was too angry to see any sense. They packed their cases to leave immediately. With one hand he checked his pocket to make sure he still had the nugget. He regretted that he was found out so soon and wished he had taken a few more. The couple left on the ferry for Hong Kong to build a new life together.

Siew Fen wondered where she had gone wrong raising Wing Yu and Wing Chung. She didn't have an answer.

Financial Hurdles

The family moved to Ngai Lin Fon (雅蓮房), a two-bedroom apartment to save rent. With lower rental and two adults less to feed, Mee See breathed a sigh of relief. It was a heavy drain supporting the family of five adults and four children even with Mee Jing's help. Life settled again after a while.

The children were growing up. The next hurdle for Mee See was the children's education. With four children going to school, Mee See had to find a lot of money for their school fees. She was worried with the income that she was bringing in. She knew she could not afford to send all the children to school at once. But she did not want them to miss out on an education. Once school started, it would be many years before they finished their high school education. She dared not even think of schooling after high school.

Mee See discussed the children's education with her mother and sister, "The children are growing up quickly. When all four go to school at the same time, the school fees will be horrendous. I have to find some way of earning more money to save up. It will be too late to wait until the time they start school."

Mee Jing suggested, "I don't understand why you don't hand the children back to the Fung family. Master Fung only has a daughter. He hasn't a son to carry the Fung name. Your children are the Fung family's direct descendants. You should hand them back to them. They will not mistreat your children."

Mee See said, "The older generation will 'chun nam hang nui(重男輕女)[55]', I worry that Yau Mui may be discriminated against. She may be treated unfairly. I would hate to think what would become of her."

Mee Jing said, "There is an easy solution. Just give the three boys back to the Fung family but keep Yau Mui with you. Then you only have one child to provide for. Let them support and educate the boys. With only Yau Mui, you will have a much lighter load. Life will be a lot easier for you!"

Siew Fen added, "If you can, it is better not to split the children. To separate them all of a sudden is a very hard thing to do!"

The adults looked over to see the four children playing five star checkers at the little blue plastic table and chair set. Young Kai Son was kneeling on the chair to reach the table and leaning against Kai Ming to join in the fun. They were laughing and joking about the game. Kai Son was too young to understand the rules of the game, yet he followed the elders laughing heartily. Looking at the four children, Mee See said, "I cannot split them up to send them away to anyone."

Mee Jing said, "The Fung family is wealthy. Your children will be able to enjoy the life style that the Fungs can provide. Have you thought that

---

[55] chun nam hang nui[55] 重男輕女 in that generation, the family elders value boys higher than girls. There were many privileges for boys that were not extended to girls.

you might have deprived them of life's opportunities by not living with the Fung family? Besides, you will have to work so hard to provide for them for the rest of your life. I can see it is already such an effort. I just feel sorry for you!"

Mee See seeing the sense of Mee Jing's analysis replied, "I can understand everything you say. I have thought of this matter many times, believe me! However, every time I look at the children, I simply can't do it. I have decided to keep them and raise them the best way I can. I am thinking how to generate more income and how to reduce expenses to set money aside for the school fees."

Mee Jing accepted her sister's wish and said, "I admire your decision. If you want to keep all the children, then you have to prepare to have a life of hard work with little leisure. However, be prepared that when they grow up, there is no guarantee that they will be good to you and take care of you when you are old. I don't want you to be disappointed and have regrets, when your youth is spent and if they are not kind to you."

Mee See turned around and gazed at the children. They were still laughing and playing the checkers game. She replied, "If they don't reward me when they grow up, it is up to their conscience. I know in myself that I have done my best for them."

Mee Jing said, "This is what I can't understand about you."

Mee See wanted to give the children the best education that she could afford. Her plan was to provide the best education for Kai Ming, hoping that he would look after his younger brothers and sister once he was established.

Siew Fen, touched by Mee See's attitude, said, "I admire your strong will in deciding to keep all the children together. I took all of you to escape the turmoil of the Japanese war in your childhood. But then, I had money, gold nuggets, and jewellery, above all, I had a number of properties and rental income to support the family. You have nothing to your name, and you still have the dream of bringing up all the children together and by yourself. I shall always look after the children so you can concentrate on working to bring in the money to support us all."

Mee Jing looked at her sister who was so determined in spite of all the odds. She thought for a while and suggested, "Let me take care of Ah Tai and I shall pay half of the rental from now on. That should, in a small way, help with the expenses."

Mee See was grateful and accepted her sister's generosity.

When Mee See was at school, the family had to move around from city to village and from school to school to avoid Japanese atrocities. It affected her education, and as a result, she did not finish high school even though she was a high achiever. Mee See wanted a stable environment for her children's education. She selected Tuk Ming Primary School (德明小學), a school that offered both primary and high school education without having to change schools. She used the money that Siew Fen helped to put away for Kai Ming's school fees.

It was a big event in Mee See's household when Kai Ming started school. Siew Fen helped Kai Ming put on his uniform. He had a white shirt, dark blue shorts, and white bobby socks with a pair of white rubber soled lace up shoes. He looked smart! Yau Mui wanted to follow brother to his school as well. She could not wait for the time when she started school. Siew Fen took lunch to the school and the brothers and sister sat by watching Kai Ming eat his lunch. The siblings admired their eldest brother and wished it was their turn to go to school.

A year passed and it was Yau Mui's turn to start school. She was looking forward to the day she could walk hand in hand with Kai Ming into the school that she knew so well. Mee See counted the money she had been saving all year and was worried that she could not make the two lots of school fees when school started. Yau Mui was imitating Kai Ming with books and a school bag pretending to go to school. The children played school games with Kai Ming after school. She did not want to disappoint Yau Mui and delay her school enrolment. She dared not think of Kai Chung's school fee the following year and Kai Son the year after. The years passed so quickly! The immediate problem of trying to find Yau Mui's school fees was overwhelming. Tears fell down her cheeks as she was looking towards the future. She did not know how she could manage the rest of her life.

It was the day before the start of the new term. Mee See could not find enough money for the two children's school fees. She buried her pride and the shame of being a worker at the casino and went to see the Principal, Lee Shei Ying (李雪英校長), the head mistress of Tuk Ming Primary School. Mee See was honest and spoke of her desire to bring up the children and provide them with the best education she could afford. She did not wish Yau Mui to delay starting school because the money she saved was not enough to pay for the school fees. Mee See pleaded for assistance so that the children would not miss out on schooling in their formative years.

Principal Lee was a kind head mistress. She could see Mee See was an educated person who was articulate and wanted the best for her children. She decided that Kai Ming would continue on full school fees. Yau Mui would start with a half fee. Kai Chung would start with a half fee the following year and Kai Son would be free of charge when he commenced school the year after. Mee See could not believe it when Principal Lee explained the provision that the school had extended to her family. Without her granting such a generous allowance, it would have been impossible for the children to commence school at the age when they were ready.

Mee See and Principal Lee became good friends for life. The children continued their education in Tuk Ming Primary School (德明小學) and then high school. Thanks to Principal Lee, the children were never without schooling as a result of the inability to pay their school fees.

Siew Fen demanded the children work hard at their school work. Each day she took food for them at lunch time. She walked the children to school and picked them up afterwards and watched them do their homework after school. It was instilled into them that they must work hard so they would not waste their mother's hard earned money for their education. The children were indoctrinated to be grateful for Principal Lee's generosity by scoring high marks in their school work. There was much pressure on the children to achieve high grades even at such a tender age. They were aware of the fact that they did not have to pay full fees to attend school. This made them more diligent with their school work and they believed that they had to do well at school to justify the generosity that was extended to the family.

When Mee Jing started to work as a hostess at the Grape Vine Night Club and manager Ah-Puck learned that Mee See was a competent dancer as well, he often requested for Mee See to help in the night club when they were short of hostesses. Mee See was happy to oblige as she could earn extra money for working the extra shifts.

Mee See discussed with her mother and sister, "As the children grow older, there will be more expense. I am planning to ask Ah-Puck if I can continue to work five days at the casino plus two extra days at the night club. The night club pays better than the casino. I can save everything I earn from the night club for school fees."

Siew Fen said, "You have to look after your health. Working seven days and nights at these irregular hours is not healthy for you. Long term sleep deprivation may ruin your health, besides aging you quickly. Think carefully before you commit yourself."

Mee See replied, "Yes I am well aware of this. But I need to earn more for the extra expenses that are coming. Let me work at this rate for a little while to accumulate some savings first. Once I have some money as a buffer, I can always ease off."

Ah-Puck was happy to employ Mee See for the two extra days at the night club.

Business Plan

Mee See remembered that she had for a short while, taught people how to dance at the Wah Har Dancing Hall (華夏舞廳) in Canton. Mee See told Ah-Puck, "I have thought of an idea for the Night Club to increase business and make more profit."

Ah-Puck was intrigued that Mee See could converse at a level that was unheard of amongst all the dancing girls or the gaming attendants. He was interested and wondered what it was all about, and said, "Go ahead and tell me. You and your sister always surprise me with unexpected revelations."

Mee See took a deep breath and continued, "A number of customers have already asked us to teach them to dance the popular European dances like the Waltz, the Tango, Jive, Fox-Trot, the Rumba, Samba and Cha Cha. These dances are very popular in the bigger cities like Canton, Shanghai, and Hong Kong. Macao has not yet caught up with this latest fad. There is nowhere for people to learn these new dances. They would pay to learn if there was a place for them to go. During the tea dance and evening night club time, it is not appropriate to teach these new steps."

Ah-Puck was listening with interest "Our Grape Vine opens at 4pm to 8pm for tea dance and from 8pm to midnight for evening dance. We open from 4pm each day."

Mee See in agreement said, "Yes, but from lunch time to 4pm, there are four hours where we can make use of the dance hall to conduct dancing lessons." Mee See paused, then continued, "If we open the club at 12 midday to 4pm for dancing lessons, we will add four more hours of trading. The customers can come to learn to dance. We can charge according to the difficulty and complexity of each dance. It would be a new line of business for the company to attract more customers. The bar and restaurant will have additional business as people will need food and drink while they are here. As people learn new dances, they might come to practice the new steps that they have learned with our hostesses at tea dance or at the night club. The follow on effect will increase business at the Centre."

Ah-Puck suddenly realised the potential of such a proposal. He was delighted with the idea. He could already see the increased trade as a result of more activities generated for the company. However he asked, "Who can take charge of this new venture? How do we start?"

Mee See hadn't thought that Ah-Puck would accept the proposal so readily. Mee See collected herself and suggested to Ah-Puck, "As this is a new line of business, it will need someone senior, an executive, like yourself, to champion its success. The people selected to work in the dancing class need to be mobilised. They need to start work prior to 12 midday. Ah-Chow (亞周) the music chief on the gramophone would need to be there to organise the music suitable for the dancing lessons. Yuen-Yee the senior dance hostess should be the chief in charge of this new facility."

She paused and continued, "A few years back in Canton, I assisted a teacher at a dancing school. Under Yuen-Yee's direction, if she wants, I am happy to be one of her assistant teachers. Mee Jing will be good at teaching as well as she is such a competent dancer. …" Mee See took another pause and said, "There is only one matter. Mee Jing and I are already scheduled to work in our own areas during the day and night. If we are to join Yuen-Yee to provide dancing lessons, it will mean our working hours will be extended."

Ah-Puck agreed, "Let me talk to Yuen-Yee and give her this new idea. If the company needs you and Mee Jing to work the extra hours, there will be the extra pay accordingly."

Ah-Puck could not believe how methodically Mee See was able to articulate this proposal. He could see that this would be workable, because they would be making use of the premises and other un-utilised resources to generate more income. Why did he not think of it before? Ah-Puck couldn't help admiring Mee See as she walked out of his office and closed the door behind her gently.

Before the Grape Vine Dancing School started, the chief dancer Yuen-Yee, Ah-Chow, the music chief, Mee See and Mee Jing, the dance assistants, worked on the teaching program. When Ah Lin heard about the new facility, she also joined the team as a dance assistant. They marked the floor with white chalk to show the foot prints in dance order and stepped through the routine. Yuen-Yee thanked Mee See for passing on her teaching experience to them. They put the dancing steps in a journal and selected the music for each dance for Ah-Chow to play. They referred to this journal for each dance using the same procedure and with the same gramophone music. This way each assistant had the same teaching method to avoid confusion to the customers.

The Grape Vine Night Club now opened its doors from 12 midday to 4pm as a dancing school. Every hour they taught one type of dance. As a result of the dancing lessons, the four dance teachers became very popular. They had many customers demanding their company.

Mee See and Mee Jing greatly increased their monthly wage. Every week they had extra income from the dancing lessons and many students left them with tips at the end of the lesson. They had many followers in the night club because their names as dance teachers were broadcast everywhere in the Hotel and Entertainment Complex. Many night club customers left them bigger tips at the night club when they could manage to secure the company of these special teachers at their table.

Life was good again as there was additional income to support the family. It felt good to have a little left-over to put away for an emergency. It was well worth the hard work and the additional work hours.

Mee See came home tired but happy and said, "Since the dancing lessons started, the Central Entertainment Complex has more business.

Many gentlemen and surprisingly many ladies come to learn how to dance. I didn't think that there were so many people interested in learning European dances."

Mee Jing described to Siew Fen how the dancing lessons worked, "We only teach about four people how to dance each hour. They can be men or women. If the customer is a gentleman, I take the lady's part. If the customer is a lady, I take the gentleman's part. Usually the gentlemen give us more tips. Many even bring presents for us." As she was talking, Mee Jing took the Macanese Pataca notes and counted a number of them to give to Siew Fen for housekeeping and rental. She also paid for Siew Fen's keep.

Siew Fen took Mee See's handkerchief and looked at the Macanese Pataca notes. Among the many notes, there were several brand new notes that did not have a crease on them. She sniffed the bank notes. They had a very strong aroma of camphor, and the whole room was filled with the strong smell. Siew Fen smiled broadly as she handed the pile of new bank notes to Mee See and Mee Jing, "Ayarh! Smell this! These bank notes are permeated with strong camphor. I am sure this person must have stashed his money in the bottom of his camphor chest. The poor guy was saving his money. But he thinks it is worth spending it on your dancing lessons! He he he!"

Mother and daughters all rolled around laughing as they passed these bank notes around to sniff. They each had a good laugh admiring these unblemished and fragrant bank notes.

Mee Jing, showing a present to Siew Fen and Mee See, exclaimed, "Oh look Ah Tai, this is French Perfume, this must cost a lot of money! I have never used it before. Come smell it! The gentleman who gave me this is Mr. Hong[56](熊先生). Fancy calling himself a wild bear! How strange! I bet he uses a fictitious name. Maybe he does not want anyone to know he comes to find dancing girls. Ha ha ha!"

---

[56] Hong 熊 the word Hong was the same word in Chinese as a wild bear.

Siew Fen said, "Since you have lost weight after arriving in Macao, you are so beautiful and you look so trim. Being a single girl, I am sure you will have many chances to meet someone and get married."

Mee Jing answered, "Ah Tai, I know what to do. Now that I am independent, I am not going to consider getting married unless I find a man who is an ideal 10 out of 10! What is the hurry?"

Mee See told their mother, "Mee Jing has a lot of suitors at the night club. She is ever so popular! Many customers request for her to sit at their table. They try to book her each night early so they can have her company for the night. It is just a matter of time for Mee Jing to spot Mr. Right."

Mee See showing a new pair of dancing shoes to mother, said, "Ah Tai, look at these glittering dancing shoes, and they are the right size as well. A customer brought them in today. No wonder he commented about my hands and feet being trim and narrow. He asked for my shoe size jokingly. That must be the reason so he could get me this pair of shoes. He is ever so kind."

Siew Fen said, "Working at the Central Entertainment Complex, you have the chance to meet many gentlemen. Both of you are such beauties. There must be a chance to meet the right gentlemen for marriage."

Mee See answered, "It would be easy for Mee Jing being so attractive and being single with no complications. I have four children. Who would choose my family of six? I have decided to concentrate on raising the children and providing the best for them. We sell dances only. All I care about is to make enough money to build our future."

Usually when the customers arrived at the night club at the fifth level, Yuen-Yee, the senior hostess would greet them and find them a seat at a table. If the customer knew which hostess they desired as their companion, they would request for her by name, or else Yuen-Yee would suggest a hostess to keep them company. The bar waiter would take orders for drinks and food from one of the two restaurants on level four. The hostess would keep the customer company and converse on various topics or as their dance partner. As many customers came to the night club to conduct business, the hostess would make sure they had an environment that was conducive for conversation. The aim of a hostess was to entertain and to make sure the customers had a pleasant experience at the night club. Each hostess was available at certain times during the night. When the time was up, she moved to the table of the next customer who had purchased her time slot. Some established customers would buy several hours of her time so she would stay for the hours. The customers usually gave her tips quietly as extra appreciation for being attentive and making their evening pleasant and enjoyable.

Mee See soon became accustomed to making conversation with customers and was able to respond to jokes and laugher with ease. She took three changes of clothes and shoes every day to work for the different roles during the day. Her daily routine would start with working at the casino on the seventh level where she wore her casino uniform and low-heeled shoes for comfort. As a hostess for foreign customers at the casino she would be very busy entertaining a number of tourist groups at a time. At midday she changed into a casual outfit with some plain dancing shoes to teach dancing at the Grape Vine night club. From 4pm to 8pm, she would go back to the casino depending if there were foreign customers. From 8pm onwards, Mee See dressed in her Chinese Qipao and dancing shoes to work as a hostess at the night club. As Mee See entertained many customers during the day, there were multiple tips from various customers. Therefore the take home tips each night could be sizeable.

Mee Jing and Mr. Hong

Mr. Hong (熊先生) and Mr. Chan (陳先生) were successful entrepreneurs, staying at the Central Hotel on business from Hong Kong. Mr. Hong was the owner and Managing Director of the Ching Wah Cinema chain. Mr. Chan was the owner and Managing Director of the Lee Gardens Entertainment Centre. They came to Macao to purchase the Sun Wah cinema chain as a joint venture. Purchasing the cinema chain in Macao would improve their film distribution and expand their market base into this Portuguese colony. It was a resounding success. Both business partners were very happy that they managed to complete the transaction. They would be taking ownership in the very near future and could soon start the film distribution channel to Macao. Both men intended to stay the night in Macao and return to Hong Kong the following morning. They celebrated their partnership in the restaurant where they drank to their success and enjoyed a satisfying and scrumptious dinner. After they had conducted their business, the two bosses relaxed and enjoyed the rest of the business trip.

Mr. Chan had lost his wife a long time ago and he never remarried. He channeled his energy into building his business. He specialised in buying entertainment complexes, show grounds and stage premises. He was cautious, serious and meticulous in his approach to work. As a result, he had been alone for many years and enjoyed a peaceful and calm environment. Mr. Hong had a wife and children in Hong Kong. He was a very successful business man, specialised in buying cinema chains and entertainment complexes. He lived a happy family life. He was sociable and he liked the night life. In his younger days, he was an accomplished dancer. After a few drinks at dinner they wanted to find some entertainment to celebrate the success of this trip.

Mr. Hong said, "The night is still young and we can't sleep this early. Would you like to go to the casino on the seventh level? Or would you rather go to the night club on the fifth level? Let's check out this entertainment complex."

Mr. Chan responded quietly, "I have no interest in gambling. Let's go to the night club and have a few drinks to celebrate the success of our partnership."

Yuen-Yee had a pleasant smile as she greeted the two bosses and welcomed them to a front table half way from the stage where the band was playing and where they had a good view of the dance floor. As she ushered them to the chairs, she gestured to the bar captain and said softly, "I have never seen you here before. What can I get you gentlemen to drink?"

They exchanged pleasantries as they ordered a bottle of the best Brandy. The band was playing some melodious music, and when their eyes got used to the dim light of the night club, they saw a couple of guests were starting to dance. The music was mellow and the light was soft and gentle. The atmosphere was soothing and a little up-beat. It made people relax and forget about the daily grind, worries, and stress. Everyone had a smile on their face. Yuen-Yee could see that they were new-comers to the night club scene. They obviously did not know the practice of the night club, remarked, "Would you like to have a couple of ladies to keep you company at your table?"

Mr. Hong said, "Yes, that would be good. We leave this in your capable hands."

Mr. Chan noticed Yuen-Yee as soon as he entered the night club. She looked trim, refined, and was soft-spoken. He thought that she had a certain quality that seemed flawless. He asked, "Don't trouble yourself. Can you keep us company?"

Yuen-Yee was flattered. She smiled sweetly into Mr. Chan's eyes and answered, "I am so honoured. Let me find Mee Jing to keep you company. Mee Jing is our top hostess. She is very much in demand. I can't promise that we can both stay for the night. We both have previous bookings. Usually we are very busy on Fridays, Saturdays and Sundays, but leave it to me. I'll see what I can do." She politely took leave to fetch Mee Jing as the bar captain arrived with the Brandy.

Mr. Hong found Mee Jing a pleasant girl. She was young and beautiful and had such an attractive smile. He used to like dancing with his wife before the children arrived and he was keen to rekindle his dancing skills again. It was such a pity that he didn't ask Mee Jing to dance before she moved on to another table. Mee Jing apologised time and again that she had to move on. Mr. Hong watched her nimbly walk across to another table. He watched her dance a couple of times, she was light on her feet as she danced around the floor. He watched her joking and laughing in the distance and was mesmerised by Mee Jing. He found her most fascinating and would have liked Mee Jing to come back to their table. However, she was booked for the rest of the night. Each time she passed by, she made a point of stopping by and chatting with him, apologising and wishing she could be entertaining him instead.

Mee Jing smiled and said jokingly, "Next time you can book me early so I can look after you, Mr. Hong." 'Hong' rhymed with the Chinese word for a wild bear. She thought that Mr. Hong could not be his real name. She was assuming he was using a fictitious name to avoid being known.

Yuen-Yee returned several times during the night. The two bosses wanted to get to know the girls better, however, they had scheduled to return to Hong Kong in the morning and regretted they could not stay another day.

Mr. Hong was a sociable man, who had several concubines at various times outside of his marital home in Hong Kong. He was highly competitive, decisive, and had an eye for the best and the rarest. He usually managed to get what he sets his eyes on because he was tenacious and would not give up until he could possess it as one of his collections. Mr. Hong was a good dancer in his younger days, but it was a pity that his wife was not interested in dancing after starting a family. She had got rather plump after she had the children. As she was not used to socialising in public, Mr. Hong didn't take her to any company functions. When he met Mee Jing, he could not help taking another look at her youthful composure. She had such a tiny waist. She was agile, lively and walked with a spring in her footstep. It was obvious that she was a polished dancer. Mee Jing was an ideal dance partner. Mr. Hong thought it was time he rekindled his dancing technique, so he decided to stay an extra day to get to know Mee Jing better.

Mr. Chan teased Mr. Hong for being infatuated with Mee Jing. He left to go back to Hong Kong on his own.

Mr. Hong saw the advertisement for dancing lessons in the afternoon. He thought it would be a good idea to have a few lessons to refresh his dancing technique. After all, he had nothing else to do to pass the time. He bought an expensive bottle of French perfume for Mee Jing. At midday he was waiting at the night club with the others who came for the lessons. At last he saw Mee Jing arrive in her casual outfit as a dancing instructor. She was bright and cheery as she greeted him with her infectious smile. She was just as attractive in day light, Mr. Hong thought. It was worth the stay.

Mee Jing was young and energetic in her approach to teaching. She was precise and accurate with her tempo. Mr. Hong revived that long lost youthful enthusiasm for dancing. Being with Mee Jing brought back his vitality. He suddenly found himself laughing and reliving a carefree approach to life. He reminded himself that there was plenty of life beyond forty.

Mr. Hong decided he wanted Mee Jing to be his companion all afternoon. He purchased all of Mee Jing's available hours for the night at the Grape Vine Night Club. He had not been so relaxed and carefree for a very long time. He stayed until the last dance with Mee Jing. He took Mee Jing home in a taxi before he came back to his hotel alone. It was well past two o'clock in the morning when he went to bed. He was too excited to sleep. He felt a little silly about being infatuated by such a young lady at this time of his life. He was a little uncomfortable because he had a family in Hong Kong, however, his rationale was that if he did not tell his wife and children, then nobody would be hurt. Mr. Hong decided he would return to Macao to find Mee Jing again, soon. He was so glad that he had opted to stay for the extra day.

Mee Jing took the French perfume home. She told her mother and sister the story about Mr. Hong, the wild bear.

Soon after that, Mr. Hong returned and bought all of Mee Jing's hours to take her out to dinner. This time, he had a big diamond ring to give her at dinner.

Mee Jing was very happy and surprised to see the solitaire sparkling under the light at the restaurant. She smiled broadly and commented playfully, "Oh! What a big diamond sitting on such an exquisite setting? Are you kidding me or not!"

Mr. Hong told Mee Jing frankly, "The very first time I saw you, I already wanted to tell you. I don't want you to work at the night club anymore. Let me look after you. "

Mee Jing said, "I have a mother to take care of. I go to work to support my mother. How can I not work at the night club?"

Mr. Hong said, "That is simple! I want to buy a block of flats for you in Macao. Your mother and you can move into your own flat. You can rent out the other levels and keep the rent. Also I shall give you a monthly allowance. The only condition is you must not work anymore. I can't bear anyone dancing with you and I won't allow anyone to dance with you anymore."

Mee Jing took Mr. Hong's sleeves and burst out laughing, "Someone is jealous! I never thought you cared!"

Mr. Hong had a smile in the corner of his mouth. He knew he was winning at last.

Mee Jing wanted to ask Mr. Hong that if she accepted his wish, what position she would have in his household. It looked like he was not going to forsake his wife in Hong Kong. He was going to establish a second home in Macao. She realised that it would be unwise to raise such a question. She looked at the huge solitaire that gave out such a shimmering glare on her thin and refined ring finger. There would be a block of flats in her name and she could also keep the rent and she would also have a generous allowance. The only condition was that she should leave the night club. Mee Jing thought, "Hooray! This is a good settlement!" Mee Jing wanted to agree immediately. However, Mee Jing was a wise girl. She wanted Mr. Hong to wait and worry about the answer.

She was turning her new diamond ring round and round her finger. She hesitated and looked up at Mr. Hong with a gentle smile. She knew Mr. Hong thought her smile mesmerising and attractive. Mee Jing said in a soft voice, "I must go home and ask my mother and my sister first."

Mr. Hong was eager for an answer. He proposed, "For now, you can continue to live in Macao. When the opportunity is right, I want you to join me in Hong Kong. Then I shall settle your mother in Hong Kong with you as well. You can rely on me from now on. I promise to look after your mother as well."

By the time Mee Jing got home, it was well after midnight. She was too excited to sleep. However, she remained quiet so she did not wake Mee See Chair who was fast asleep on the other single bed. She waited until morning when her mother and Mee See Chair started to stir. Mee Jing jumped out of bed to tell them the good news. She showed them the new diamond on her finger.

Mee Jing said, "Look! This ring is from Mr. Hong. He is going to buy a block of flats in my name in Macao. He said we can all move into the flat while I can rent out the others floors and I keep the rent. On top of that, he will give me a generous monthly allowance." She was so excited.

Mee See looked at the diamond ring. She was very happy for Mee Jing, "Wow! That is a substantial diamond on your finger. I am so very happy for you. Mr. Hong must think a lot of you. From now on, you won't need to work all hours of the night. You have a pillar to support you."

Siew Fen couldn't help asking, "Fact of the matter is ... What will your rank be in the hierarchy of Mr. Hong's household?"

Mee Jing replied, "He did not mention what rank or position I will have. In fact he never mentioned his household to me. I know he has a wife and children in Hong Kong. That's his business. He has to sort that out by himself. I will continue to live in Macao." Mee Jing took a deep breath and continued, "I don't care about rank or position, as long as I have a block of flats in my name. I will collect my own rent and have a generous allowance. Who cares what position I am in his household?"

Siew Fen thought how the situation had turned around. Mee Jing was broken-hearted because she had lost her husband's love when he established a separate home with another woman as a concubine; hence, she left her family home and children with her in-laws to be independent. Now Mee Jing was the concubine. Mr. Hong's wife would feel the same disappointment and be broken-hearted about losing her husband's love. Siew Fen wondered if Mee Jing was aware of how the situation had turned around for her. However, she saw Mee Jing was so excited about her good fortune, she decided not to discuss this matter.

Mr. Hong bought a block of flats with three floors on Fong Son Tong Gai (風順堂街) in Mee Jing's name. Mee Jing, Siew Fen, Mee See, and the children moved into the third level. They divided the top level into a front and back flat with the bathroom, toilet, and kitchen in the middle. Mee Jing chose to live in the front, leaving the back for Siew Fen, Mee See, and the children. The middle level and ground floor were rented to two separate families. Mee See and the children lived there rent free.

Mr. Hong came to Macao very often. He also took Mee Jing with him on business to South East Asia where he introduced her to his business associates as his personal secretary.

Mee See was happy for Mee Jing finding her future with Mr. Hong. She was grateful for Mee Jing's generosity. Siew Fen helped save all of Mee See's rental money for Kai Chung's school fees. Mee See focused on getting on with work. She had a firm belief that one day when the children grew older, life would be easier for her.

PHOTOGRAPHS – MEE SEE'S SIBLINGS

Mee See's brother Wing Chung

Mee See & younger sister Mee Jing

Mee Jing, Luk KuChar, Siew Fen & Mee See

Part Six – Felo

Felo from Portugal

Macao was a Portuguese colony so many government management positions were filled by Portuguese officials who had been seconded

from Portugal to work in Macao on multiple-year contracts. They often brought their wives and family, hence, there was a community of Portuguese nationals living in Macao. They were given subsidies for rental, membership to the Portuguese clubs, and a servants allowance to help the family settle in this Far East colony. As a result, many Portuguese expats were living on the rich side of town. They were neighbours to the local rich and wealthy merchants and senior government officials.

Felo was a good looking 28 year old, of medium height, blue eyed and a head of curly hair. He was seconded on a three-year contract from Lisbon as the Deputy Post Master General in Macao. Felo only had a father at home, he came to Macao on his own. The Deputy Post Master General role was a promotion. He planned to return to Lisbon and continue his career with the Portuguese Post and Communication when his term ended. To celebrate the arrival of a number of Portuguese work colleagues, the Portuguese Post Master General, James, took a group of these expats to the Central Entertaining Complex to introduce them to this new environment where they would be living for the next few years. He wanted to entertain the new-comers with Chinese cuisine, the gaming hall and the night club, to dance and listen to some live European music.

James told his young colleagues, "These Asian beauties are absolutely stunning. It is such a pleasure to be in their company. You will find them very different from the beauties back home."

James found the manager, Ah-Puck and said, "My friends have just come from Lisbon to start working in Macao. I told them they must come to your establishment to experience what you have to offer." With his arm on Ah-Puck's shoulder, James continued, "We would like to start with some very good Chinese food. Then we will try our luck in the casino. To finish, we will go to the night club for a dance and a night cap. I want my friends to have a great time to start their new venture in Macao."

Ah-Puck nodded and turned to catch the eyes of some of the young people, beaming as he answered in English, "Good, you have come to the right place to have a good time. Leave it to me."

After a Chinese banquet with beer and wine, everyone was happy and cheerful. For nearly everyone, it was their first experience in Asian food, and they thought the Chinese food was delicious. After dinner, Ah-Puck took the guests to the casino and handed them over to Mee See and Ah Lin.

Mee See and Ah Lin saw the group enter with Ah-Puck. Mee See came forward with a broad smile and greeted them, "Good evening, let me help you." She explained the rules and the game of Dai Sai, which was one of the simplest games. The young people were cheerful and merry after a satisfying and interesting Chinese meal. Mee See raised her voice a little so they could hear her explanation. With imperfect English, she explained the gaming rules and the payout principles. Some of the happy customers tried to understand the rules, whilst others were eager to change their money into chips to begin gambling. Ah Lin assisted by helping them change their money and explained how to use the unit of chips to play this game.

The girls placed the group at two tables so they could give them more individual attention. Soon the young Portuguese were settled and enjoyed this ancient Chinese game. Some were laughing, others were choosing what number to bet on, others were cheering on the side, and some others were holding their chips and did not place a bet. Some won, some lost, and some kept guessing what the next lucky number would be. Everyone agreed that it was a delightful game and that they would definitely return. They were sure that they would have much better luck the next time around.

Felo and the other officials were surprised to see these two attractive attendants who could speak fairly good English. While they made some grammatical mistakes explaining the rules of the games, neither of them minded being corrected and laughed happily as they repeated the sentences correctly. Felo thought Mee See was such an attractive girl. He kept watching her movements and was quite taken by her charm.

Later in the evening, the group moved onto the fifth level at the Grape Vine Night Club. The senior hostess came to meet them and seated them at four tables. Since Mee Jing had left the night club, Mee See and Ah Lin were the hostesses responsible for looking after foreigners. The girls each dressed for their night shift and changed into a beautiful Qipao and black high heel shoes for dancing. They applied face power and painted a layer of light rouge on their cheeks and a matching soft red lipstick.

Both girls looked stunning in their Qipao, compared with the uniform of the Casino. They entered the dimly lit dance floor and walked with a smile towards the tables where the groups of young Portuguese were seated. They took another look at these attractive hostesses and suddenly recognised Mee See and Ah Lin were the same helpful Casino attendants they had just met. The girls helped them order drinks and snacks for each table and told the bar attendants to pay special attention to them. As it was the first time these guests were at the night club, Mee See suggested, "This is one of the top bands in Macao. They also can play the latest music. How about we introduce a few hostesses to keep you company? They will be most happy to be your dance partner as well." Mee See told the senior hostess to find two hostesses for each table. Ah Lin and Mee See would circulate to assist the hostesses by translating for them.

The group of young people were happy chatting and laughing in this relaxing atmosphere. James spoke for the group, "A great idea indeed, let's enjoy ourselves tonight."

The Grape Vine Night Club had a soothing atmosphere. The lighting was seductive, the band was playing the latest music, and a few couples were dancing. They were surprised to hear familiar music that they played at home. A few guests got up to dance. The hostesses were beautiful and they were all very good dancers. The guests chatted and enjoyed themselves and for a while, they forgot they were thousands of miles away from home.

Felo's eyes never left Mee See for the entire night. He was attracted to her the minute he set eyes on her in the casino. He was amused to hear her imperfect English, and how she tried to correct the words when she was told the right pronunciation. He was surprised to see her again at the night club. He tried to find an opportunity to sit next to her and talk to her but she was busy with the other hostesses helping to translate at other tables. It was the first time he had been in the Far East and the first time he had met Chinese ladies dressed in Qipao. He simply thought Mee See was the most attractive of them all. She was slim and well-proportioned and she danced in perfect tempo. Felo tried to ask Mee See to dance, but he was so polite that he was left behind while others went in front of him.

Everyone had a good time at the Central Entertaining Complex. All the young people had a happy induction to Macao. They all agreed that it was a very pleasant place to be working even though it was thousands of miles away from their hometown.

Although Felo did not get much of a chance to be with Mee See on the night, he could not get her out of his mind. Felo could not settle but kept recalling the evening when he had met Mee See. A few lonely weeks went by. Using gambling as an excuse one Saturday night, Felo found a couple of his colleagues to visit the Central Complex. His aim was to go to the casino and the night club to find Mee See. It seemed like hours before they had finished eating and drinking at the restaurant.

Mee See smiled as she met Felo and his work colleagues coming through the door of the seventh level into the casino. She shook Felo's hand saying, "Oh Felo, long time no see! Let me see… it was three weeks ago when you and your colleagues came to the Central Complex. At that time, you had only just arrived from Lisbon. I remember there were many of you in the group. How have you been?"

Felo was overjoyed. Not only did Mee See remember his name, but she even remembered that it was three weeks ago when he was last there. She also remembered that he had come from Lisbon. Felo was so glad that he had plucked up enough courage to come and find her. He and his friends stayed at the casino and played several games at the Dai-Sai table until they went to the night club. This time, Felo got the chance to sit with Mee See. They talked, they laughed, and they found they had the same interests in many things. Felo got close enough to see Mee See's long, thick eye lashes and her flawless skin. Under the dim light, Felo thought Mee See was indescribably beautiful. It was a pity that Mee See was such a popular girl that she had to leave Felo's table a few times during the night. While she was away, the other hostesses kept Felo and his friends company, which Felo didn't care too much for. He then realised that if he wanted Mee See to stay at his table, he had to pre-book her hours so she could stay as his companion for the night.

From then on, Felo began coming to the night club by himself. He often bought an entire night so Mee See could be by his side. He even paid the extra levy to take her out of the night club to dine at exclusive restaurants and to see a movie at the cinema. Felo saw a lot of Mee See.

Despised as a Dance Hostess

When James invited Felo home for his birthday celebration, he suggested, "Would you like to bring your girlfriend to the party?"

Felo was a little embarrassed, smiled and answered, "Where would I get a girlfriend?"

Even though Felo was in denial he had already decided that Mee See was his ideal companion. He decided to take Mee See to his boss's birthday party.

Mee See had an inferiority complex and didn't think that she was good enough for Felo and his friends. As the young Madam Fung, Mee See had been to big functions in Hong Kong and Canton. However, her position was so different now. She was working at low-paying jobs serving customers instead of being a respected young Madam from the wealthy Fung household and the wife of an executive of a British finance company.

Mee See declined the invitation and said, "I am afraid that I only work as a hostess at the Central. I don't know if I am good enough to attend your boss's party."

However Felo would not hear of her excuses and insisted she come along, saying, "James and the other work colleagues have all met you before. I am only a Post Office employee. You are my very good friend, and my friends will accept you as you are."

On the night, Felo drove his car to collect Mee See from her home at Fong Son Tong Gai. Felo waited downstairs patiently for her. It was the very first time she had been invited on a date since coming to Macao. Mee See started getting ready early and wore a newly tailored pink Chinese Qipao and a pair of black high heel shoes. She lightly powdered her face, used a little rouge and some red lipstick. She carried a small beaded clutch bag and wore a black shimmering woolen shawl. She decided she must look good and not lose face in front of all the foreigners she would meet that night. Mee See stood in front of the mirror and was happy with what she saw. She looked elegant.

Siew Fen was overjoyed that Mee See had been invited to Felo's boss's party. She was hovering around helping her to dress and shining her shoes. She said, "This is the first time you have been on a date. I am very happy for you."

Mee See was happy that Felo was such a gentleman. He was handsome with deep blue eyes that were like the blue sky on a bright sunny day. He had that European frank and forthright approach that was most attractive to Mee See. He had never married, he had no vice that she could observe, he had a good profession and above all he cared deeply for her.

Mee See was nervous and said to Siew Fen, "He is only taking me to his boss's birthday party. Please don't read more than what meets the eye. We are only friends."

Siew Fen was watching from the upstairs window as Felo arrived at their door. He patiently rang the bell. He wore a red rose bud in his lapel. He brought a fresh red rose to pin on Mee See's Qipao. He helped Mee See into her seat before walking to the driver's seat. Siew Fen felt comforted as she watched the car drive away. She was satisfied with how things were moving and that Felo had never married. She burned incense to Buddha and prayed that Mee See and Felo would have a good future together.

James' home was a new style garden residence. The Kwan ancestral home was many times larger than James' residence. Even Master Fung's family home was quite a few times bigger than this residence. This residence had been decorated in a modern fashion with a touch of European style and all the fittings were well coordinated.

There were more than twenty guests at the party, all Portuguese. Only Mee See, the servants and the cooks were Chinese. James introduced her to his wife and a number of female guests. Mee See was comfortable conversing in English with the other guests.

Music was playing and two couples got up and danced. Felo nodded his head and took Mee See's hand to lead her to the dance floor. He whispered quietly in her ear, "You are the most attractive girl here. My friends are all jealous of me!"

Mee See smiled. She knew she looked most attractive when she smiled. "I hope you are not kidding me. Please wait a little while. I shall be back." Mee See was contented. Thank goodness that he insisted she come as his partner. She was glad to be there.

In the bathroom, Mee See met the three guests whom she had been talking to earlier. One lady asked Mee See, "How much did Felo pay to get you out for this performance?" The other two ladies coldly looked at Mee See eying her up from head to toe and snarled as they walked out.

All of a sudden, this cruel interaction had brought Mee See back to reality. It was as if a bucket of cold water had woken her from her sweet dream. Mee See locked herself in the toilet. She leaned against the toilet door and didn't know what to do. She regretted coming to the party. The ladies exposed what people were thinking about her, and how she was working for a living. Mee See lost the confidence that she had just a few moments ago. Mee See did not have the courage to face anyone. All the people must think how lowly she was. But she could not hide there all night. Felo did not know what had happened, he might misunderstand her.

She took a deep breath and found her strength. She was brought up in a wealthy family, she was the young Madam Fung and she had a high school education. Although she was working as a hostess, she had never sold her body or her soul. She worked hard to raise a family of four children and there was nothing to hide or feel ashamed about.

Mee See held her head high. She stood upright and opened the bathroom door. She saw her reflection in the full length mirror, and she knew she was a beautiful woman and she had style. The three ladies were jealous of her, they wanted to put her down to spoil her friendship with Felo. She must not let them succeed. Mee See took a deep breath to collect herself. She saw the three ladies again as she walked out of the bathroom and nodded her head to greet them. They looked at Mee See, but they dared not meet her eyes and walked away.

Felo was waiting for Mee See outside the bathroom and wondered why she had taken so long. He saw the three ladies ignore her without returning her greetings. He imagined the ladies must have had a few words with her. Felo asked, "Is everything ok? Is anything the matter?"

Mee See quietly swallowed, turned away and blinked her eye-lashes to clear her eyes. She was trying hard to hold back her tears. She turned around, looked into Felo's deep blue eyes and said gently, "Nothing is the matter. It was all a little misunderstanding."

Felo was intuitive. He knew that the ladies had given Mee See a hard time. They must have tried to embarrass her. How unkind these ladies must had been to Mee See, he thought. He was more attentive to her for the rest of the night.

Filo's Marriage Proposal

Felo decided that he would look after Mee See and not leave her vulnerable by making sure such incidents would not happen again. Felo began to spend more time at the casino and at the night club after work just to be with her. He took Mee See to all the gatherings and special functions for the Portuguese expats. All Felo's friends accepted Mee See as his girlfriend. As Felo got to know Mee See more, she told him about her four children and her mother at home.

Felo said, "Oh that's why you are never free on the weekend for trips with me. It is a heavy responsibility to raise four children!" Felo paused and continued, "Mee See why don't you move in with me? I can help to take care of your children and your mother. Let your mother and the children continue to stay in Mee Jing's flat. I am very selfish. I want to be with you all the time. When I am at work during the day, you can visit them. This way you will have more time with your children and mother as well."

As Felo spoke, he put a number of hundred dollar bills into Mee See's hand for the month's expenses. He insisted she take them home to consider his proposal. Felo's plan was to take Mee See home to Lisbon when his contract finished in a couple of years' time. He would continue to send money to Macao for Mee See's mother to keep supporting the children. However it was too early to mention these details.

Felo said, "I want to take you home to Lisbon. Will you marry me? My father said that it would be such an honour for him to conduct our wedding ceremony. I know my father will like you very much. Would you like to talk it over with your mother? I know that we will be very happy together."

Mee See knew that Felo would bring up the subject of marriage sooner or later. She was overjoyed that he accepted her family and her mother and was willing to support them. He had given her a lot of money, which was more than she could make working all those hours. She was very happy with this new development.

Mee See took Felo's money home to talk to Mee Jing and her mother, "Felo asked me to move in with him. He wants me to leave work at the Central Entertainment Complex now, and then follow him to Lisbon to be married when his contract finishes. He wants to support Ah Tai and the children. Here, this is the money he insisted I take home for this month."

Mee Jing was surprised but very happy for her sister, "Felo is so generous! He is so good to you to take on your children and Ah Tai. Mr. Hong is paying for Ah Tai's living. Now Felo is paying for Ah Tai's living. Ah Tai you can eat twice as much from now on!"

The three ladies laughed and joked together till tears rolled down their eyes. The future looked secure. Their prospect looked bright.

Siew Fen recalled, "The night when Felo came to take you to his boss's birthday party, I already could tell that he truly cared for you. Thank Buddha for changing your fate. From now on, you won't need to work all hours of the night! When are you going to Lisbon?"

Mee Jing said, "When you move to Felo's you will have more time to be with the children. You have always worked seven days and have little time with the children. Even though you raise the money to support them, it is Ah Tai who takes care of your children really. Moving to Felo's will make little difference to the children."

Mee See said, "How can I tell the children I am moving out? They may not be old enough to understand."

Siew Fen said, "The children seldom know if you are home or not. They are used to seeing you at odd times. They have never asked for you because I am always around. I suggest you leave it be."

Mee See agreed, "You are both right. When I move out, Felo doesn't want me to work anymore. In fact I will have more time to come home to see you during the day. I have only to get back to his place before he arrives home from work. We haven't talked about when we will go to Lisbon. But I think it will be when his contract finishes here, in two years' time."

Siew Fen still had her traditional thinking, commented, "It is good that he wants to marry you. I am really happy for you. There are no more hard struggles from now on."

Mee Jing added, "If he will support you and the family, why should Mee See Chair worry if she is married to Felo or not!?"

Felo and Mee See were happy for Siew Fen selecting a date to celebrate their engagement. They invited many friends and relatives for a banquet at the Happy Buddha (佛笑樓) to mark this special date when they made their commitment to each other. Siew Fen, Mee Jing, Ah Lin, Ah-Puck, Lyn Gar Chair and a few close friends at Mee See's work were invited. Felo's boss and a number of his close colleagues and their families attended this joyous occasion as well. After that Mee See moved into Felo's residence.

Mee See was quietly happy with her change of fortune. She deeply appreciated Felo's love for her. She wanted to be a good wife and to take very good care of him. She would now have more time for her children. She wanted to make up for the time she was not around for them.

Soon afterwards, Ah Lin and Joseph, another Portuguese national, moved in together. Ah Lin also resigned. At the time all the girls at the Grape Vine Night Club were envious of both Mee See and Ah Lin. Quite a few girls were having English speaking lessons from them. They looked at the two girls as their role models and wished the same good fortune would befall them. They hoped to meet some foreigner who would rescue them from having to work as dancing girls.

The Central Entertainment Complex was a big organisation, they often had staff movements as the employees moved on to different work. However, it was not such an easy task to replace two ladies like Mee See and Ah Lin at the same time, as they were both casino hostesses for the foreigners and dancing instructors and hostesses at the night club. Ah-Puck found two suitable ladies, and Mee See and Ah Lin promised to teach the new girls to be competent before they left work.

Ah-Puck told his two favourite girls, "Many customers say how much they enjoyed coming here because of your service. Remember that if you need to return to work for whatever reason, you will be most welcome!"

Grateful to Ah-Puck for giving her the job in the first place Mee See said, "I really thank you for giving me the opportunity to work at the casino. Without that break, I really don't know where I could have started earning a living to raise my children! I am forever in your debt." She was ready to marry Felo and be his wife for the rest of her life. With a plan to go to Lisbon, it would be most unlikely that she would ever want to come back to work at the Central Entertainment Complex again!

Ah Lin laughed heartily and said, "Thank you for looking after me for all these years Ah-Puck Kin-Lee. Once we have taught the new girls to take over from us, you won't ever need us anymore!"

Felo's Missee

Felo's servant Ying-Chai (英姐) used to work at James' household and learned Portuguese family traditions and cuisine. Ying-Chai knew how to look after Felo according to his living habits and his routine. Felo also had a chauffeur, Duck-Soak (得叔) who drove him to work during the week and took Ying-Chai to the market, the dry cleaners, and other errands for Felo. They both took Sundays off and returned at 6 o'clock in the evening ready for a new week. During the weekends, Felo liked to drive the car to picnic spots outside the city. He also enjoyed giving dinner parties and entertaining friends at home. He instructed both servants to address Mee See as "Missee", the mistress of the house, and they must look after her when he was at work.

Mee See was used to having a number of servants before. She had always been polite, fair, and courteous to her servants. She treated Ying-Chai and Duck-Soak with the same courtesy and consideration that she did with her previous servants. Soon, she won the hearts of her new servants. Mee See was willing to learn from Ying-Chai the Portuguese way of life. She had never worked in a kitchen in her life, however, she asked Ying-Chai to teach her some Portuguese cuisine. She invited Mee Jing and Ah Lin to learn from Ying-Chai how to prepare some special Portuguese cuisine like Portuguese Chicken, Bolo De Bacalhau (fish cakes), and Arroz Gordo (Portuguese rice jumbo). Every so often, Mee See chose to personally cook for Felo the dishes that she learned.

After Duck-Soak took Felo to work at the Post Office in town he came home to see what Mee See and Ying-Chai had planned for the day. Before midday Duck-Soak would finish all the household errands with Ying-Chai, then he would take Mee See home to her mother. She often took home Portuguese food for the family to enjoy. During school holidays Mee See took the children and her mother to the seaside. Mee See taught Kai Ming and Kai Chung how to swim while Siew Fen, Yau

Mui, and little Kai Son watched on. The children learned to call their mother 'Mummy', which they called Mee See the rest of her life. Yau Mui loved to hang onto Mee See's hand and lean against her arm enjoying Mummy's sweet smelling perfume. In the afternoon, Duck-Soak took the children and Siew Fen home before returning to Felo's residence with Mee See.

It was the very first time the family had a chance to enjoy the beach and had so much time during the day with Mummy since coming to Macao. There was also a car to deliver them to various places. Mee See no longer needed to worry about the living expenses or forth-coming school fees. She lived a life of leisure and happiness. When the children were at school, she took Siew Fen to a tea house to treat her to Yum Cha (飲茶)[57] with her favourite dim sums to thank Siew Fen for all those years of caring for the children. With Duck-Soak to drive the family around during the day, the family rekindled the lifestyle that they enjoyed all those years ago in Canton.

Felo always made sure that she was happy and that the money for the family was plentiful, so she didn't need to worry. Knowing that Felo enjoyed entertaining at home, Mee See often suggested house parties to invite Felo's favourite friends over, where she did the cooking herself with Ying-Chai 's assistance.

Felo and Mee See lived in a stylish one-storey garden residence. There were three bedrooms, a spacious lounge room, a separate study, and a large dining room next to the servants' quarter. He had employed a designer to co-ordinate the decoration. There was a dark brown leather suite with soft golden scatter cushions, matching drapes to frame the large picture windows, and an air conditioner to keep the temperature even throughout the year.

Living at this residence was comfortable.

---

[57] Yum Cha 飲茶 a tradition scrumptious luncheon at a tea house restaurant where hundreds of varieties of dim sum and little dishes were served.

Mee See sat on the huge brown leather settee alone. She often wished she could bring her mother and the children over to enjoy all this luxury. Mee See visualised her life with Felo, her mother and the children in Europe one day. However, Mee See knew that she could not bring the children over at the moment as Felo wanted to be with her alone and would not allow anyone to intrude on the close relationship he enjoyed with her. Mee See decided that it was not the right time to raise the subject of moving the children and her mother over just yet. Each day Felo was eager to come home from work to relay to her the stories from work, as well as jokes and funny incidents that he encountered during the day. He found that she was good at problem-solving and was able to give an objective perspective. Felo admired her intelligence, which he didn't know before.

Mee See took Ah Lin to the Portuguese Club for a buffet lunch. The head waiter addressed Mee See warmly and seated the ladies at a window seat overlooking a well-manicured golf course. It so happened that the three ladies that Mee See had met at James' birthday party also came in after them. Mee See remembered well the exchange at the party and was ready to stand her ground and to retaliate. She raised her shoulders and sat upright and decided not to let them disgrace her in the way they did at the party. Mee See was well-prepared as they walked to their table.

One lady put her hands on Mee See's shoulder, smiled and said, "What a pleasant surprise to see you here Mee See! This club house is well-known for the best buffet lunch in town."

Another lady got closer and agreed, "You must try the famous Portuguese egg tart here. It is the best!"

Their unexpected pleasantry was such a surprise that, for a split second Mee See hesitated. Collecting herself, she quickly responded, "Oh yes, you are so right. This club is famous for its buffet. Felo and I have been here a few times before. Meet my dear friend Ah Lin. I want her to try the buffet as well."

Ah Lin nodded her head, smiled broadly and said, "Well, we must leave room for these well-known Portuguese egg tarts."

The three ladies commented as they left the table, "We are sure you won't be disappointed!"

Mee See's engagement to Felo had changed her status in their society and gained her people's acceptance. However she could not forget the snarls and the nasty looks on their faces. Even though the ladies had changed and were polite to Ah Lin, Mee See would not accept them as her true friends.

Coming from a poor family, Ah Lin had never experienced how wealthy people lived. This day at the Portuguese Club House, sitting shoulder-to-shoulder with all the foreigners whom she used to serve was such an uplifting experience. They were the only two Chinese guests among the Portuguese nationals. Ah Lin was in seventh heaven looking at the affluent environment surrounding her.

Smiling from ear to ear, Ah Lin said, "Wow, this is such an expensive place, with crisp white table cloth and all silver servers. I have never been anywhere with so many rich people around. There is so much food piled up like little mountains on many tables, and we can have as much as we can eat! This lunch must be so expensive!"

Mee See knew that Ah Lin had never ventured to such a luxurious dining place, nor had she tried the buffet luncheon. Now that she had the capacity to give Ah Lin a special treat at the clubhouse, to celebrate their special friendship, Mee See explained, "The Clubhouse usually has a lot of subsidies from various sources. That's why club members enjoy many discounted facilities. Felo has given me a membership card, so I can use the facilities at will. Let's celebrate our happy future together!"

They clinked their glasses of ice water to toast each other's health and good fortune.

Ah Lin said, "We are being chauffeured in a nice car. Now we have met such friendly European ladies. Mee See Chair, you are living it up and you have such style!"

Until the family escaped to Macao, Mee See was accustomed to the level of comfort well above what she experienced at Felo's residence. It was too much to explain to Ah Lin that Mee See decided to keep quiet about her lifestyle prior to meeting her. However, she must warn Ah Lin what the ladies could be like so that she would be on her guard. Mee See spoke in Chinese quietly to relay what had happened in the bathroom with the three ladies at James' party.

Ah Lin was angry for Mee See, and exclaimed, "How can you treat this incident as a passing event without retaliating when you saw them today! If it was me, I would have shown my displeasure. I would have given them a few choice words and told them to get lost. You have Felo now. You don't need their friendship!"

Mee See explained to Ah Lin, "Whatever we do, we have to consider the consequences. Granted, I don't need them for my social standing. But I don't know where their husbands work, nor do I know if their husbands' positions could affect Felo's professional standing." She took another drink from her glass and continued, "Besides, even though Felo and I are engaged, we are not married yet. If Felo returns to Lisbon without me, everything I enjoy today will disappear. I don't really have a secure position. Obviously today our situation is much better than when we worked at the casino!"

Ah Lin admired Mee See's reasoning, "Mee See Chair, that's the reason why I always admire your decisions! You are wise. You can always consider far and wide. I really have to learn from you."

Mummy Across the Street

Yau Mui and Kai Ming were playing hide and seek in the streets near the main road opposite the GPO. In front of the GPO, Yau Mui saw Mummy with a few foreigners. She had a deep red Qipao with an embroidered silver beaded phoenix spreading from the left shoulder to the right side of her hip. She had on a pair of matching deep red beaded satin sling-back high heel shoes. Mummy looked stunning.

Yau Mui's immediate reaction was to run across the road yelling, "Mummy, Mummy." Then she saw the group of finely dressed foreign ladies and gentlemen with bow-ties standing around having a cheery conversation with Mummy. There was a good-looking foreign gentleman in dark blue suit, his hand was supporting Mummy's arm and he stood close by her side. Yau Mui froze and hesitated, she had another look to establish that the fine lady was definitely her Mummy. Looking down at herself, she saw her old hand-me-down navy dungaree with the off white rubber sole shoes that had holes where her toes stuck through. It was a contrast with the finery that Mummy was wearing, she dared not approach.

At that moment, Kai Ming spotted Mummy as well. With a finger to his lips, Kai Ming gestured to Yau Mui to keep quiet and moved Yau Mui backwards to hide behind the bus stop shelter in case Mummy was aware of their presence. The children watched as the adults moved into the GPO gradually and Mummy disappeared. The children dared not mention this incident to Mummy the next time she came to take them for their outing. In fact they never talked about it, not even among themselves.

Life is Unpredictable

A happy eighteen months passed by. One afternoon Ah Lin arrived at Mee See and Felo's home unexpectedly. Mee See could see that she had been crying for a long time. Her eyes were puffy and red. She had lost her usual bright eyes and pleasant smile.

Mee See held her hand and inquired, "Oh my gosh! Whatever has happened?"

Ah Lin took the warm face flannel that Mee See offered and covered her eyes, sobbing as she said, "Somebody came knocking at the door today looking for Jose. It was his wife. She had just arrived from Lisbon. She was such an ugly fat woman!" Ah Lin started to cry more bitterly.

Mee See asked, "What did Jose have to say about the whole matter?"

Ah Lin was angry and upset. She replied, "The fat woman is his wife. No wonder he never mentioned his family in Lisbon! Come to think of it, he never told me that he wanted to return to Lisbon. In fact he never mentioned getting married to me! It really is my fault! I just assumed that he was not married; he chased me as though he was a free man! All I knew was that he was fun to be with, he cared for me and was willing to support Lyn Gar Chair and Lai King as well." Ah Lin took another deep breath and continued, "He said he didn't want to go back to Lisbon. His wife was very angry with him. She was going to strike me. Jose held her back. He protected me; otherwise, she would have pushed me over. She was fierce and very strong."

Mee See told Ying-Chai to prepare one of the guest rooms for Ah Lin and comforted her, "You stay here and have a good rest. There is bound to be a solution in the morning. I shall explain to Felo when he comes home."

Ah Lin cried until her voice was choking, "How can I sleep tonight, or any other night! I hate Jose. I hate Jose's fat wife. I don't know how to tell my sister about this? Oh, how can I face anybody? I have lost face!"

She was grateful for Mee See and Felo's kindness. She was absolutely exhausted after the ordeal. She dropped off to sleep unchanged on the top bed cover.

Felo was sorry for Ah Lin when Mee See told him what had happened, and said, "I didn't know that Jose was married. Let her stay here for as long as she needs. If she needs my help, please don't hesitate to let me know."

Mee See was quietly elated that Felo was single, kind and considerate!!

Jose tried to get his wife to return to Lisbon. But she insisted that she wanted to stay in Macao. As a consequence, Ah Lin moved out of his residence. He gave Ah Lin several hundred Macanese Pataca, insisting she take them. Ah Lin knew that it would be the last time he supported her living. What was she going to do? Where could she find money to support herself and her sister's family? Without Jose, she had to find a job, and soon!

Ah Lin considered her options with Mee See, the reality hit them both that there was no alternative but to go to the Central Entertainment Complex and plead with Ah-Puck for her old job again. Mee See felt sorry for Ah Lin. She had to swallow her pride to move back with her sister. It was embarrassing but she simply had to pluck up the courage to ask Ah-Puck if she could work at the Central Entertainment Complex again. Ah Lin explained that she was not aware that Jose was married, and that his wife was fierce and unforgiving. Ah-Puck was sorry for her and was happy to offer her old job. All her colleagues sympathised with her ordeal and were more considerate to Ah Lin.

Two years slipped by swiftly as Felo and Mee See had the best time of their lives living together. They lived like newlyweds. A telegram arrived for Felo from Lisbon to confirm that his term in Macao would finish soon, and he would be promoted to Post Master General on his return to Lisbon. Felo was excited and rushed home to show Mee See the telegram and said, "Look at this telegram! Here, it says I will be promoted. I have always wanted to be a Post Master General. Life is meaningful because I have you by my side."

They decided to take the sea journey to Portugal in two months. James held a party to celebrate Felo's promotion and to thank him for his good work for the last three years. James told Mee See, "You will like Lisbon. It is such a beautiful city. It is open and spacious. Felo, you must take Mee See to see the other cities nearby as well."

Felo, smiling with one hand around Mee See's waist and the other hand holding a glass of Mateus Rose, told James, "Cheers, I will return home two weeks earlier so I can take Mee See around Lisbon before I start work."

All the ladies wished Mee See well for her journey to Lisbon and repeated, "We are very envious that you are going to Lisbon! We must keep in touch!" Mee See was very happy as she had been anticipating this trip for a long time. It would be a reality in a short few weeks!

All evening, Mee See thought that she must talk to Felo about her desire for her mother and the children to come to Lisbon as well. She regretted that she hadn't discussed this matter with him earlier. The children and her mother did not have passports. Now they only had a few weeks to get all the proper paperwork for them. She thought she must get that happening soon.

Felo continued to announce, "When we return to Lisbon, my father will be waiting to meet Mee See. He will conduct our wedding as soon as we get home." Turning to Mee See, Felo whispered, "I want to be with you for the rest of my life."

Mee See was happy that Felo repeated his wish to get married. She replied, "I, too, will love to meet your father. I know you will enjoy your new role at the Post Office." Mee See quietly reflected that she would not wear a European white lace wedding gown again. She would rather wear her Chinese Qipao in white with pearl and silver sequins or her red

Chinese Qipao with gold Phoenix embroidery.

Felo cared deeply for Mee See and did not want her to be worried about her children and mother when she went to Lisbon with him. He proposed, "When we go to Lisbon, I will continue to send money to your mother to support her and the children. They will be able to continue their schooling. Will you talk to your mother and tell her not to worry because you are leaving Macao."

Mee See was quietly alarmed to hear that Felo did not consider taking the family. She probed gently, "Would it be possible for mother and the children to come with us?"

Felo was a frank and straight forward person. It had never entered his mind that anyone would come between the two of them. He was a little shocked at her request. He spoke what was on his mind without holding back, "I have not prepared for your mother and children to migrate to Lisbon as well. We always said that we would get married in Lisbon as soon as my contract expired. Your mother always looked after the children living in Macao. I have not considered taking them to Lisbon."

This was the very first time the lovers had a major disagreement about what they wanted from each other. Mee See needed to talk to her mother and Mee Jing to resolve this major problem. Time was passing and they did not have long to find a solution that would work for all parties. Suddenly it dawned on her that she and Felo had a different idea of their future life together. He obviously had never considered her children as part of his family. He provided the money to support the family so that she could be free to be his companion. Mee See regretted that she had been so happy being Felo's companion that she never considered this fact. No wonder he had never invited her mother or the children to their home for dinner. She suddenly realised that he had never met them. This fact was suddenly clear to her. How could she convince him to accept the children and her mother as a part of her life?

When Siew Fen and Mee Jing saw Mee See's facial expression, they asked urgently, "Whatever has gone wrong? We thought Felo had a promotion and things were going fabulously for you two."

Mee See said, "I always thought that mother and the children would be coming to Lisbon. However, Felo's idea is to go to Lisbon with me alone, leaving Ah Tai and the children in Macao. He is happy to continue supporting them in Macao."

Mee Jing analysed the situation and didn't think it was such an issue, so she said, "This should not be such a problem! The only thing is that Felo should send a little more money to Ah Tai so that she can save for an emergency. If there was any delay, you wouldn't want Ah Tai to run short and be worried."

Mee See said, "But I cannot come back easily to visit Ah Tai and the children from Lisbon. How can I bear to leave them here and go off to the other side of the world?"

Mee Jing said, "Gar Chair[58](家姐), you have to leave them if you want to marry Felo. You might even have more children with him. There will be complications having your new children together with the four you already have! It is by far better to let Ah Tai continue to look after the children while you start a new life. All you need to do is send more money to Ah Tai. What do you think Ah Tai?"

This time Siew Fen dared not make a comment one way or another. Felo had been Mee See's rescuer. Over the last two years, she had lived a life of leisure, and the family was living a secure life with no worries. The children were able to see their mother more often. It was the first time they had enjoyed having Mummy around in their waking hours since arriving in Macao. It was all thanks to Felo for making this possible, but there was no guarantee that Felo would continue to support the family when Mee See went with him to Lisbon. Siew Fen could feel the dilemma and would not tell Mee See what to do this time. However, if

---

58 Gar chair 家姐 respectful way to address one's elder sister.

Mee See didn't go to Lisbon with Felo, that spelt the end of their relationship! It would mean that she would have to go back to work, like Ah Lin. The idea was untenable! Siew Fen didn't know what to say. She remained silent.

Mee See was in a quandary. She wanted the children and her mother to come to Lisbon with her. She could not understand why Felo didn't love her enough to allow her to bring the family with her. Felo, on the other hand, believed that if Mee See had the children and her mother with her, their marriage wouldn't be complete. He couldn't understand why she wouldn't come with him on her own since she had always had her children cared for by her mother. They worked hard to find a solution, and they both could understand each other's standpoint. Time was passing. The lovers had pondered about the pros and cons but still could not find a solution to satisfy each other's needs.

At last they decided that Felo would go home alone. They didn't sleep a wink all night. Both Felo and Mee See could not bear to part from each other. They had such a perfect relationship and never had a cross word between them, yet they could not see a way to compromise. What had gone wrong with their expectations? Whose fault was it? They knew that when they parted they would never be together again!

Mee See took Felo to the wharf to say farewell. He held her hand tightly. Not a word was uttered. The ship was blowing the final horn. The sailors urged Felo to climb up the gangway so that he would not miss the boat. At last Felo gave Mee See a long final hug, put a thick white envelope into her hand, turned around, and jumped onto the gangway without looking back. He stood quietly at the top of the railing looking down at her. She was standing quietly at the wharf, looking up at him.

There were bright-coloured balloons, ribbons, and streamers flying in the air, farewell songs broadcasting with horns, trumpets, whistles blowing, and people shouting their last well wishes. The two lovers gazed at each other silently. The ship retreated in the distance. It became smaller and smaller until it was only a tiny spec on the horizon, then it disappeared. Their relationship was finished. There was nothing they could salvage.

Mee See was numb with pain and sadness in her heart. There was emptiness all around her. At that moment she lost all confidence to continue. She had to start thinking about making a living once again. Now she had to face her fate alone in Macao and the responsibility for a family of six again. She gazed at the ocean. The moon rose on the horizon signifying a new beginning. Mee See could not stop her tears from dropping onto her cheeks. A feeling of insecurity crept in, now she had lost Felo forever. She couldn't help feeling a little regretful.

Mee See moved back to Mee Jing's house, to live with Ah Tai and the children in the rear of the third level flat. When the four children saw Mummy at home, they jumped up and down with joy. It was the very first time for a long time that they had seen Mummy every day and night! The children surrounded her and wanted her attention. Kai Ming wanted Mummy to look at his teachers' marks on his homework. Kai Son, the youngest, climbed onto her lap and sat there quietly with his thumb in his mouth. Kai Chung followed his brother and wanted Mummy to help with his homework. All Yau-Mui wanted to do was to snuggle closely to Mummy with a broad smile on her face. For a while Mee See enjoyed being home with the children and Ah Tai all day and night without having to watch the clock to plan for her departure. She thought it was worth the sacrifice to be with the children and her mother.

In the white envelope, Felo had given her money to settle his rent and to discharge Ying-Chai and Duck-Soak. There were nearly a thousand Macanese Pataca left. Mee See gave it all to Siew Fen for living expenses until she could find work again. At first, Mee See did not intend to go back to work at the Central Entertainment Complex to avoid questions from her colleagues. It was embarrassing after the grand plan for marriage and the journey to Lisbon. Mee See tried finding work in the department stores but the wages were so low that she couldn't afford the school fees after paying their living expenses. She also tried looking for work in the factories. However, there was no work for her because the factory foreman could see that she was not used to the labour of a factory hand.

Ah Lin and Mee See discussed her options, "Mee See Chair, Ah-Puck always thought highly of you. I am sure he would welcome you and give you another chance." Having gone through a broken relationship, Ah Lin felt the same desperation and loss that Mee See was feeling. She hoped that Mee See would, like herself, put away her pride and go back to the Central Entertainment Complex. She was sure all the workmates would extend their sympathy to Mee See's bad fortune like they did with hers. Things would blow over in time.

Mee Jing enquired, "I do feel sorry for you! What plans do you have for the future?"

Siew Fen, sympathising with Mee See answered, "Mee See has already tried looking for work as a shop assistant. She even tried to be a factory hand. But where do you find work that pays as well and with such good tips as at the Casino and Night Club?"

Mee Jing said sadly, "Looks like you have to follow in Ah Lin's footsteps and go back to the Central Entertainment Complex!"

Mee See took a deep breath and said quietly, "That's right." She continued, "There is an old saying 'Ho Ma Bud Sick Wu Tau Cho[59] (好馬不食回頭草)', but now I have to 'Ma Say Lok Dai Hung [60](馬死落地行)'. I have to ask Ah-Puck to take me back. I want to work in the Night Club more nights because the money is better there and with better tips."

---

[59] Ho Ma Bud Sick Wu Tau Cho 好馬不食回頭草 a Cantonese idiom translated as a good horse would not graze on past pastures, meaning one would not go back to one's old ground once moved on to a better pasture.
[60] Ma Say Lok Dai Hung 馬死落地行 a Cantonese idiom translated as when the horse died one had to get down to walk meaning one had to do what one need to do when one had nothing to lean on anymore.

There were rumours that the couple had had a big fight, and Felo departed angrily for Lisbon alone leaving Mee See behind. Mee See had always closely guarded her private life. She had never told Ah-Puck about her wealthy background nor did she intend on explaining to anyone the reasons why they separated. Ah-Puck couldn't help but feel very sorry for her. He thought badly about Felo without knowing the details. He always felt that she had a different style that was unlike the other girls he employed. Ah-Puck respected her and did not ask further. Although she had worked at his establishment for many years, she had never lost that special gentle and noble manner. She could articulate thoughts with words that other girls did not have in their vocabulary. He had a hunch that Mee See came from a well-off family even though she didn't mention her family background.

Ah-Puck didn't even hesitate and said, "Come back to work next Monday."

Mee See's silence about her relationship with Felo caused more rumours at the Central Entertainment Complex. Some rumour was that Felo had never intended to marry Mee See. He had cheated her all the time. They reckoned that gweilos[61] (鬼佬) were never trustworthy. These gweilos would sweet talk you and then they would dump you in the gutter. They only used you when it suited them. They recalled Ah Lin's recent experience with Jose, and now it was the kind and gentle Mee See's turn. Mee See buried her pride and went back to work as an assistant dance teacher, a hostess at the casino looking after foreigners, and as a dance hostess at the Grape Vine Night Club. She did not talk to anyone at work about her predicament. She never uttered an unkind word about Felo either.

---

[61] Gweilo 鬼佬 Chinese slang for a European male, at one time a derogatory or vulgar term referring to a European man as a pale face ghost or devil.

PHOTOGRAPHS – FELO AND CHILDREN IN MACAO

Felo (centre) & Mee See in Macao

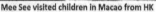

Mee See visited children in Macao from HK

Kai Chung, Kai Ming, Kai Son stayed in Macao

Part Seven – Fate's Turnaround

Hong Kong Connection

A large group of foreigners arrived at the Central Casino. With a most attractive smile, Mee See greeted and introduced them to various betting games. As usual, she was clear and concise when explaining how to place the bets. There was a petite and beautiful Chinese lady in this group of tourists and Mee See introduced herself to her.

The Chinese lady answered in English, "Yes, I speak Cantonese and Shanghainese. I am Doris (多利是). This is my husband Bob Hughes. We have come to Macao with our friends who are visiting from England. We heard that the Macao Central Entertainment Complex was a place that we must not miss."

Doris was happy to meet another English speaking Chinese lady. Mee See showed Doris and her friends the facilities on the other levels. Doris was particularly interested in the dancing lessons. She had always wanted Bob and herself to learn dancing. Mee See encouraged her and her lady friends to learn some of the latest European dances while the gentlemen were gambling at the casino. Doris and her friends took up the suggestion. Everyone was entertained doing activities that they enjoyed. It was a resoundingly successful weekend trip to Macao. Doris decided they would organise another trip to Macao when they had another opportunity. They liked staying at the Central Hotel in the Complex because it had access to all the entertainment that suited their itinerary.

From then on Doris and her husband went to Macao many times. They always took various groups of sea captains, chief officers, and chief engineers from visiting warships that anchored in Hong Kong Harbour. Doris became good friends with Mee See and Ah Lin. She would like to

255

employ them to work at her bar, Hollywood Bar (荷里活酒吧), in Hong Kong as she was always on the lookout for prospective hostesses who could speak English well. Wages in Hong Kong were much higher than in Macao and the tips were better when good service was provided. Hostesses could make nearly double money working less hours in Hong Kong, leaving more time for leisure. Doris suggested that Mee See could work in Hong Kong whilst her mother could continue to look after the children in Macao. As Hong Kong was only a few hours on the ferry from Macao, she could always go home to visit the children and her mother on her days off.

It was fortunate that her present wages were adequate to support the family. However, Mee See knew that when all the children went to high school, she would find it hard again to meet the additional expenses. For now Mee See could not entertain the idea of leaving her children unless there were no other options.

Mee Jing had always wanted to move to Hong Kong because life in Macao was boring without Mr. Hong. She was worried that Mr. Hong might meet someone new if she was not around him often. Mee Jing's plan was to try to fall pregnant as soon as possible. She wanted to bear a son by Mr. Hong so she could strengthen her position. A son would definitely secure a share of Mr. Hong's wealth. Every time Mr. Hong came to Macao, she created a perfect family atmosphere. He loved home cooking and Mee Jing became an exceptional cook of Chinese and Portuguese cuisine. Mr. Hong loved dancing and Mee Jing was an ideal dance partner. She was also a good listener, Mr. Hong loved to tell her his business dealings and he often took her to business functions. Mee Jing succeeded as an ideal companion for Mr. Hong.

Happily, Mee Jing told her mother and sister about her impending move, "Mr. Hong bought me another apartment in Causeway Bay. He wants me to move to Hong Kong next week. He also welcomed Ah Tai to come and stay with us." Mee Jing continued to explain, "The apartment in Hong Kong is in my name too, so his wife can't find out."

Mee See smiled and said, "You always have your feet firmly on the ground Mee Jing. I am really happy for you. What's more, you have helped me a lot and I am grateful to you."

Mee Jing answered, "Gar Chair, I will always remember that you had given me a new start here."

Siew Fen, comforted that the two sisters were caring for each other, and said, "Ayarh, why are you so courteous to each other? You are sisters! I want to stay in Macao to continue looking after the children. What would you like me do with the property here?"

Mee Jing said, "Ah Tai, I won't sell this because this is my base, just in case things don't work out in Hong Kong. You can help to rent this out and save the rents for me to pick up when I come back to visit you."

Soon after, Mee Jing moved to Hong Kong. Mee See's family occupied the entire third floor rent free. Ah Tai and Mee See moved into the back room, each on a single bed. It was a lovely change for Ah Tai, she could have a good night sleep without the children's disturbance. The four children occupied the front room sleeping on a bed made up of flat planks supported by two wide benches. The wooden board was hard and they made a squeaky noise as the children rolled over. Two children slept facing the head of the bed and the other two facing the foot of the bed. They soon learned to sleep quietly so as not to move the boards and make the bench collapse. The children thought it was a luxury that they had their own room without being chastised by Ah Tai during the night. The second front room became the lounge and dining room combined, leaving a larger area for the kitchen by the toilet in the middle of the flat just next to the staircase. It was a treat to bathe in the kitchen area in a bigger iron tub. Siew Fen added several kettles of boiled water to make sure the water was luke-warm. The children took their turns to bathe using the same water. They were allowed to wash their hair only when they were the last one on the bath roster.

Siew Fen continued to rent out the lower two floors and accumulated gold nuggets for Mee Jing.

Ah Lin's Calamity

Every girl in the night club had a dream that she would meet a wealthy and kind gentleman who would rescue her from having to earn a living. The sisters knew that many Chinese men had a low opinion about hostess servicing at the night club or casino. They and their male friends were happy to be entertained by these girls, but they would not befriend dance hostesses or casino attendants. However, foreigners were less concerned about the girls' background. Mee See and Ah Lin were the special hostesses of choice whenever foreigners arrived at the Entertainment Complex. Many sisters envied their ability to communicate in English and asked to be taught English during the day. Mee See and Ah Lin started an informal class during the day for a number of sisters.

Sadly, Lyn Gar Chair passed away. Ah Lin did not have money for her funeral.

Mee See and Siew Fen counted their money from the savings for the children's next term school fees. Mee See told Ah Lin, "Take this money first. It is urgent for Lyn Gar Chair to rest in peace. The children's school fees are not due until next term, in the New Year. We'll sort something out by then."

Ah Lin took the money and added what she had saved. It was still not enough for the funeral parlour owner, who would not conduct the funeral until the full amount was paid.

They met at the coffee shop in the casino to discuss what they could do to raise more money. Mee See said quietly, "The only person with money to lend is Mee Jing. We are in such a hurry, how can we go to Hong Kong to ask for help? Maybe we can borrow from money lenders. That may be our only option." Ah Lin had already begun to cry.

Just at that moment, Doris walked into the coffee shop with a broad smile on her face. She came to buy coffee and cake for her husband and their friends. Doris could sense something was wrong with the girls and walked across to their table and sat down quietly, enquiring, "Whatever is the matter?"

Ah Lin wiped her tears as she explained, "My sister passed away. We are discussing how we can gather our savings to let her rest in peace."

Doris had seen much hardship in her younger days. She could see by their expression that they needed urgent help and asked earnestly, "We are good friends. Tell me how I can help."

Mee See added, "We have put our savings together but we still don't have enough money to pay for the funeral. We plan to seek help from money lenders."

Doris said, "Don't be so silly! Money lenders charge you a lot of interest. You'd better not to touch those loan sharks. How much money are you talking about?"

Ah Lin said, "Mee See Chair has already given me the children's school fees. I am still short by two hundred Macanese Pataca."

Doris counted two hundred and fifty Macanese Patacas to Ah Lin and said, "Take this money for your sister's funeral, and let her rest in peace."

Ah Lin and Mee See promised to repay Doris' generosity. Lyn Gar Chair was given a proper funeral.

Hong Kong Solution

It was the end of another school term. Soon it was time to pay the next term's school fees. Kai Ming was already in high school at Tuck Ming Middle School (德明中學). Yau Mui was in year six, Kai Chung was in year five and Kai Son was in year four in Tuck Ming Primary School (德明小學). It was time that Mee See offered the older children an English education. Yau Mui smiled and jumped at the chance of moving into an English school. She promised Mummy that she would study hard and not waste a good opportunity to study English. Yau Mui was accepted at the Macao Sacred Heart Canossian College (澳門聖心英文書院), a Catholic School run by the Canossian nuns. The school fee was more expensive than the Chinese School. The first term's school fee was two hundred Macanese Patacas plus the special school uniform, shoes, and school blazer. It was an expensive beginning of the new school year. Mee See was secretly pleased that Kai Ming didn't want to change schools. The high school fee was already higher than the primary school. She knew there was no way she could work more hours at the Central Entertainment Complex. She would have to find a way to make up the short fall somehow.

The only option she had was to accept Doris's offer to work in Hong Kong. There, she was told, she could earn twice as much which would resolve her shortfall in expenses. Mee See took a deep sigh as she looked out at the dark sky. She couldn't help recalling that she refused Felo's hand in marriage and gave up a life of security and leisure because she did not want to leave her children and her mother in Macao. Now she still had to leave them to go to work in Hong Kong. Once again, her life lost equilibrium. What was life like as a hostess in Hong Kong? She couldn't help but feel anxious and insecure. She did not know how she was going to survive the rest of her life.

The two good friends decided to move to Hong Kong to look for a better opportunity. Since her sister had passed away, Ah Lin has no reason to remain in Macao. The fact that she could earn double the money in Hong Kong was an incentive to move. She could then repay Mee See and Doris the money for her sister's funeral.

Siew Fen enquired, "Is Doris trustworthy? This time if Hong Kong doesn't work out, there may be no return. You had better consider carefully before you resign from your secure work here!"

Ah Lin added, "It was Doris who paid the shortfall for the funeral. If I could earn over six hundred dollars a month, I could pay her loan from my wages each month. At the same time, I can start paying back the children's school fees to Mee See Chair."

Mee See said, "With us both working together in Hong Kong, we can look out for each other. If I have six or seven hundred dollars to send home, it will be enough to support the children, and you and I don't have to work seven days and may even have two days off to rest."

It was decided that it was best if Lai King, Ah Lin's niece was cared for by Siew Fen whilst Ah Lin settled in Hong Kong. She could have the children's company and they could do homework together. Ah Lin would send money to support Lai King every month when Mee See Chair sent her money.

Siew Fen comforted them both, "It is only a few hours boat trip between Hong Kong and Macao. You can come back whenever you like."

Mee See smiled and said, "The boat fare is not cheap. I may be able to come home every two or three months only."

Siew Fen couldn't help but feel a sense of loss for Mee See. She had missed a fine opportunity for an ideal husband in Felo. Now, just a few months later, she still had to leave the children behind to head to Hong Kong to work.

The girls went to Ah-Puck to resign together. This time it was a lot easier because Mee See had been teaching a number of sisters how to converse in English. They were happy to fill the vacant positions. Ah-Puck was philosophical about the situation. He wished the girls good luck in their new venture. They parted happily with good wishes for one another.

The Hollywood Bar

Doris was very happy that both Mee See and Ah Lin decided to work in Hong Kong in her establishment. She knew that she had picked two very good hostesses to work for her.

Hong Kong was a British colony with a deep sea port for many warships. Many countries conducted their air and marine military exercises in the Pacific Ocean. Warships from Britain, America, Holland, France, and other countries stopped in Hong Kong for a recreational break from their exercises. When they were in Hong Kong, they conducted maintenance on their warships and gathered supplies ready for the next leg of their sea journey. Except for the duty maintenance staff, the rest of the ships' personnel stayed ashore to take leave in Hong Kong for a few days and then regrouped for their scheduled departure.

HMS Tamar was a Royal British base station with dry dock facilities that was located between Wan Chai and Causeway Bay on Hong Kong Island. Many warships docked at HMS Tamar where maintenance and refurbishment were done.

When the warships docked, hundreds of naval officers landed on the shore of Hong Kong. They congregated near where they docked. The areas near Wan Chai, Causeway Bay, Hennessy Road, Central, Nathan Road, and Tsim Sha Tsui were filled with sailors. Western eateries, Chinese restaurants, night clubs, bars, shopping centers, and the Chinese Emporium were full of visitors searching for entertainment and goods to take home. These men, who had been at sea for some time were ready to purchase electrical goods, leather goods, artifacts, silk embroidery, and souvenirs to take home. They were willing to spend money to enjoy themselves and seek entertainment and companionship before leaving again. Many sailors had visited Hong Kong a number of times and they often returned to visit the shops and friends they had met on previous trips.

Doris's Hollywood Bar was right at the junction of Wan Chai and

Causeway Bay. It was one of the busiest places on the seafront. When the warships arrived, the Hollywood Bar would be packed with customers on leave from their ships. Many sailors enjoyed their short freedom from the regimented mariner's routine, but some could not handle their alcohol and became rough and noisy. The Hollywood Bar had extra protection as the boss, Bob Hughes, was one of the Chief Police Inspectors in the Royal Hong Kong Police Force. Any drunken or noisy incidents were resolved swiftly. The Hollywood Bar and the surrounding area was known as the safest area for entertainment. It was well-known as a high class drinking house frequented by the ship captains and masters, high ranking officers, and engineers.

The hostesses (sisters) working in the Hollywood Bar were all handpicked by Doris. The sisters were not only the most beautiful Chinese girls, they were all well-spoken and fluent in English. They knew how to serve customers, how to dance, and enough about Hong Kong to suggest places of interest for tourists. They were very popular with all these high ranking men who found friendship with these Asian beauties and brought them home as wives and life companions. Hence, Doris had to continue recruiting to replace the hostesses at her establishment.

At the Hollywood Bar, Doris and Bob Hughes also conducted a program called, 'Macao Casino two day trip' since gambling was illegal in Hong Kong. Bob Hughes and Doris conducted tours to Macao for entertainment. They stayed at the Central Hotel where they could enjoy Portuguese cuisine, gambling or dancing at the night club. It was a very popular tourist destination for the higher ranked naval officers who only had a short stay in Hong Kong.

Many of Bob Hughes' police friends also frequented the Hollywood Bar to drink. They would while away a balmy evening under the warm bright neon lights by the seafront in Wan chai overlooking the lovely view of Kowloon Tsim Sha Tsui. Many British expats were drawn to join Bob Hughes and his wife at the bar for drinks and to listen to music and dance. They were a popular couple, and the Hollywood Bar was a well-known place for both local expats and foreign visitors.

Payroll

Doris had a profit sharing system to reward her sisters. Every day they were given a new yellow card to record all the customers they served during their shift, including their food and drink plus the length of time they were away with each customer. Every morning Doris's brother Chan Choy would calculate the wages for each sister before the day's work began.

Mee See saw Chan Choy's method was cumbersome and confusing. There were many disputes about wage discrepancies. Mee See could draw similarities with the way her siblings shared their profits from their trading experience. She sat with Chan Choy at the front desk and set the profit sharing principles for each sale item. She calculated wages based on the data from the yellow cards using the same method. This system provided accurate wages for each sister in less time than Chan Choy used to take.

Mee See was then asked to come to work earlier each day to calculate the pay for each sister before they started work for the day. Doris paid Mee See additional wages for doing the payroll.

Mee See and Ah Lin rented a room with two single beds in Causeway Bay. They each put their earnings into a glass jar and at the end of the first month, they counted their earnings. There was just less than one thousand dollars! They were both overwhelmed with the money they had earned in just one month. Doris's estimate was spot on! The two good friends went to celebrate this good result at a wonton noodle (雲吞麵)[62] shop near Causeway Bay. It had been such a wise move to work in Hong Kong!

Ah Lin was beaming, and said, "I never imagined I would be able to earn this much money!"

---

[62] Won Ton noodle 雲吞麵 a small dumpling made with a thin flour sheet wrapped with minced pork, prawn and chopped vegetable cooked in clear broth served with noodles.

Mee See, lamented quietly and said, "This money is not easy to come by. We have sacrificed a lot to get this result. But… it is well worth the effort."

Mee See deducted the money needed for rent and her own spending and sent the rest to Siew Fen. She knew that Ah Tai would save everything for school fees and other expenses. It was the first time in her earning life that Mee See had earned more than she expected to spend. Mee See began to regain her long lost confidence. For once she felt she was in control of her life. She knew that money was not everything. But with that extra money as a buffer, it gave her security. It had been such a long time since Mee See had had such a good sleep. She felt that she could cope with life from now on.

Gradually Mee See settled into her working life in the Hollywood Bar and she got to know more about Doris' background. Doris was born into a very poor family in Shanghai, she was sold to a brothel at ten, before she finished primary school. Doris grew up in the brothel. As a teenager, she escaped from the harsh conditions and hid in a cargo train south bound for Hong Kong. She ended up at the Hollywood Bar in the kitchen washing dishes. She was determined to learn spoken English by talking to the sisters and the customers. In time, she became a hostess at the bar.

Bob Hughes was seconded to Hong Kong as a Chief Police Inspector in the Royal Hong Kong Police Force. He frequented the Hollywood Bar to drink with his colleagues, to listen to the jukebox and talk about old times in the Mother Country. Bob Hughes sympathised with Doris's life in Shanghai and decided to rescue her from her ill fortune. He bought the Hollywood Bar and presented it to Doris as a wedding present. He used his influence as a Chief Police Inspector to ensure the area where the Bar was situated was safe and secure. In time the location surrounding the bar was known to be the safest entertainment area where higher ranking foreigners congregated.

Doris's clientele of high ranking executives was provided with high quality services in every way. The hostesses, whom she called her sisters, were handpicked. The price for service at the Hollywood Bar was slightly higher than the other bars in the area, which served as selection criteria for the better clientele who were prepared to pay more for better quality service.

Doris didn't forget her background and she made sure the sisters would not have the same ill-fortune as her. Her principle in conducting her business was to do to other sisters what she would like done to herself. She encouraged the sisters to be healthy and to have a happy disposition. Each sister had at least one day off a week to recoup and to prepare for the new week. One day a month, the bar closed for a big day outing that she organised and paid for. They would have picnics on the beach, visit restaurants in the New Territories, or play Mah Jong [63](麻雀) by the seaside. This once a month outing let the sisters relax and enjoy each other's company. Doris paid the sisters well and had a share-profit bonus scheme. Doris also enjoyed being a match maker. A number of sisters had met their life companion at the Hollywood Bar. It was a big event when a sister from the bar was married and the sisters were grateful for the genuine concern that Doris had for them. She continued to fill the positions as the sisters left when they married and moved overseas with their foreign husbands. They all thought that Doris was a good boss.

Although Mee See had never told Doris that she had come from a very wealthy family, Doris could tell that she was from a good family. Mee See had a clear analytical mind and was always suggesting good ideas. From the easy way that Mee See resolved the complicated formula of calculating the sisters' wages, Doris knew that she had the highest education of all the sisters. She was good at solving complex problems, yet she did not think much about her ability. Doris admired Mee See's unique ability.

---

[63] Mah Jong 麻雀 a game played with three or four people, similar to the Western card game Rummy. Mahjong was a game of skill, strategy and calculation involving a certain degree of chance.

Mee See went back to Macao only once every two or three months. It was such a happy occasion to spend a couple of days with the children, in particular when Mee Jing and Ah Lin went together as well.

Reconnecting with Old Pals

Mee See had the old address book with all her relatives' contact details from the village Xiqiao, Canton, Macao and Hong Kong. It was time to re-establish her Hong Kong contacts.

Mee See wanted to find Yee Ma and her daughter, Luk KuChar in Yuen Long, outside of Kowloon[64]. Even though Luk KuChar was ranked her parental auntie in the hierarchy of the Chinese family, they were about the same age and had been the best of friends. Sadly, they parted in their teens because of the Japanese occupation and her family had to leave Hong Kong to live in Canton. Life had changed so much that Mee See wondered what would happen if they met again. Mee See also thought of her first love Wong Nan Ku (黃立舉, Ah Ku 亞舉 for short).

Mee See had not seen him since that sorrowful day when they parted in Yuen Long. When she had to marry Fung Chun Yun as arranged by her mother, Mee See wrote to Ah Ku explaining the circumstances. She didn't hear from him and wondered what had happened to him after all those years.

The neighbours at the old address of Yuen Long told Mee See that Yee Ma had passed away some years ago. However Yee Ma's daughter, Luk KuChar, was now living in Yuen Long Farm Yard, The Third Street, in the sixth house. Much had changed in Yuen Long. The rice paddies and the fish ponds gave way to low rise apartment blocks. Mee See didn't recognise the roads anymore. However, she was determined to find this dear old friend. Eventually, she came to the house. She saw a lady with sun glasses and a broad brimmed sun hat holding a basket of roses in one gloved hand and a pair of secateurs in the other, she was cutting

---

[64] Kowloon - an urban area in Hong Kong comprising the Kowloon Peninsular and the New Territory.

roses to put in her basket.

Mee See's heart skipped a beat. Excitedly she called out, "Luk KuChar!"

The lady turned slowly, stood up, and removed her sun hat and sunglasses. She looked at Mee See. Suddenly she dropped the basket and ran between the hedges with her hands wide open. She was vivacious and called out, "Mee See!"

They both ran forward for a hearty hug. They were so excited and surprised to see each other after all these years. They had so much to say, but they didn't know where to begin. Mee See was overwhelmed with emotion, and tears rushed down her cheeks.

Luk KuChar, holding Mee See's hand said, "What a silly girl, don't cry. Let's come inside first."

After they settled with a pot of tea, Luk KuChar said, "My mother was always grateful for Ah Tai's fair and just treatment of all the Kwan children. She always mentioned Ah Tai was an exceptional wife supreme who fought for seven years in court to get a share of inheritance for my mother, so she had the means to support our living."

Yee Ma always had a weak heart. Luk KuChar left school after the third year of high school to find a job as a shop assistant to help maintain their living as the inheritance had run out. At that time, Luk KuChar's husband, Luk Ku Chenng (六姑丈), a well to do merchant, who lost his wife a long time ago, was looking for a wife from a family of good background. He was hoping to have a son to continue his family name. Yee Ma persuaded Luk KuChar to marry Luk Ku Chenng, who promised to look after Yee Ma with the medical bills for her heart ailment and provide them with a good living.

Luk Ku Chenng came home in the afternoon. He was well over half a century old and he looked every bit his age. His hair and even his eyebrows were all silver. He greeted Mee See with a warm and friendly smile. It was obvious that he cared a lot for Luk KuChar. He told Mee

See, "We live in Gloucester Rd in Causeway Bay. We often come to our country cottage at Yuen Long for the weekend. We do have spare rooms in both residence, so you are most welcome to stay with us whenever you come to the country."

Luk KuChar asked, "Where do you live in Hong Kong? Now that you are here, we must meet more often! How is Ah Tai? Do you have children yet?"

Mee See saw that Luk Ku Chenng was quite well-off. She could not bring herself to tell them she was working as a hostess serving sailors at the Hollywood Bar. She kept quiet about her working location and answered, "My husband and I separated a long time ago, leaving three sons and a daughter with me. Ah Tai look after the four children who are studying in Macao while I work in Hong Kong. I work at a friend's shop looking after the wages and business transactions, and send money home to Macao for the family."

Luk KuChar replied, "When Ah Tai and the children come to Hong Kong for a holiday, they must visit us. We have spare rooms for them." Luk KuChar paused and continued, "Unfortunately, we are not blessed with any children! We would love to see your children when they are on school holidays. In fact, you could let your daughter stay with us during the school holidays."

Mee See promised to visit them the next time the children came for a holiday.

Since marrying the mature Luk Ku Chenng, Luk KuChar had followed his mature approach to life. There was only a year between Mee See and Luk KuChar, but Luk KuChar looked at least ten years Mee See's senior.

Mee See wanted news about Ah Ku. However, she was embarrassed to ask about him directly and said, "Many years ago, I remember we had a great time running along the rice paddies and fishing at the ponds in Yuen Long. How time has passed!"

Luk KuChar remembered when they were teenagers. She said, "Those were the days when we had no worries and not a care in the world! Oh yes, remember Ah Ku, my first cousin? At the time I thought he was really keen on you! I thought he was planning a future with you." Luk KuChar continued, "He had a scholarship for the university and his medical fellowship. He is now a doctor at the Royal Elizabeth Hospital as the Chief Medical Officer in Psychiatry. He is a well-known specialist in Hong Kong. He is well respected by his peers here and overseas."

Mee See added, "Wow, how successful! Do you see him much these days?"

Luk KuChar said, "Since his father passed away, he seldom comes to Yuen Long. He is such a successful and well-known doctor. Sometimes I see his picture in the newspaper. I have read in the gossip columns that he is not married and doesn't have a female companion. The girl who gets him one day will be most lucky! Unfortunately, I haven't kept in touch with him for a long time."

The long lost friends were happy to reconnect again after so many years. They exchanged telephone numbers and promised they would meet again soon.

Mee See was happy to hear that Ah Ku had been successful in his career. She was somewhat at a loss because they did, at one time, have a plan to build a future together. Fate had it that she was not able to wait for him. It was such a pity!

Reconnecting with Senior Fungs

Mee See saw Master Fung Kin Chee's (馮鏗池) Hong Kong address in her address book. It was time to look them up. Mee See didn't have the courage to post the letter that Chun Yun wrote for the senior Fungs. She took with her the letter hoping she could hand-deliver it. It was very bad to have left Master and Madam Fung without an explanation! But at the time, it was impossible to utter a word to anyone.

Many times on her days off, Mee See walked alone outside the gate of Master Fung's address. She could not pluck up the courage to ring the doorbell. However, she knew that there were people living in the house. This day, she was outside the gate as it gradually opened in front of her. A black chauffeur-driven car drove slowly through the gate. Mee See saw Master and Madam Fung in the rear seat. They were looking in her direction. The car went down the road. Mee See could feel her heart beating fast. The car stopped, and reversed to where she was standing.

Master Fung got out of the car, walked to her, and said, "Da So[65] (大嫂), please come, do come in."

They went into Master Fung's ancestral home. Mee See struggled to hold back the tears as she handed Chun Yun's letter to Master Fung.

When the young family disappeared without a note, Master and Madam Fung were worried. They went to Siew Fen's ancestral home to look for the young family and discovered that she had already sold it and left Canton. Master Fung imagined Siew Fen was leaving town to avoid the 'Three Evils' and 'Five Evils' campaign as they expected Siew Fen had the need to go overseas to avoid questions about her family's wealth and position. However, they were perplexed with the reasons for Chun Yun's disappearance.

As Chun Yun's letter didn't explain the reason why he had to leave in such a hurry, Master Fung was still no wiser about the reason why he took his family away so suddenly from such a seemingly happy family. It was also just after Mee See had given birth to her fourth son. She would not have had a chance to recuperate from this birth at the time.

Surprisingly Chun Yun's company had never chased after him. Mee See was perplexed why Chun Yun's company didn't chase for the missing money. According to Master Fung, the enquiries were all friendly. It did not sound as though anything untoward had happened to Chun Yun's

---

[65] Da So 大嫂 a respectful way to address the supreme wife of the first son and heir.

account. She decided not to mention the embezzlement and did not disclose his gambling habit. However, she must give Master Fung a good reason for Chun Yun's leaving. She definitely could not tell them about the type of work she was doing in Hong Kong.

Mee See swallowed and explained slowly while she considered her explanation convincingly, "In those years, Chun Yun's company was prosperous. His department was handling transactions in the billions. During the year-end financial totals, his department had a substantial amount of discrepancies. There was no way he could balance the books. Hence, he decided to move to Macao for a new opportunity to expand his horizon."

Master Fung was a well-experienced managing director himself. He nodded his head and said, "Chun Yun was being silly. He should have talked to me. Having discrepancies in a year-end financial is a normal occurrence in a company of that size. They have many branches over the country. There is always a way to explain the accounting variance. Where is he now? With his degree and his experience, he must be doing extremely well in Macao. Why isn't he here to visit me as well?"

Mee See swallowed another time and decided not to tell of Chun Yun's gambling habits and replied quietly, "We separated in Macao many years ago. I don't know where he is now. The four children are with me. Thank goodness for my mother. She looks after the children while I work to support the family."

Madam Fung said, "The children must be grown now. Wei Cheung is in fifth year in high school. She wanted to go to a university overseas to study law."

Mee See smiled and answered, "Wei Cheung was always a capable scholar. I am sure you are very proud of her achievements. Kai Ming is already in his first year at high school. Yau Mui is studying English at Macao Sacred Heart School. Kai Chung and Kai Son have been in primary school for a few years already."

Master Fung said, "I have always said you were incredibly capable. With four children at school and Yau Mui studying English as well. Chun Yun was so silly. He did not know to treasure the good luck he had."

Mee See knew that Master Fung was wondering how she could support the family of six with all of the children attending school. She explained, "I work at a friend's shop looking after the workers' wages and transactions, and send money to Macao to look after everyone there."

Mee See promised to take the children to visit Master and Madam Fung in the next school holidays when they came to Hong Kong. They exchanged telephone numbers and promised to meet again soon. Mee See avoided giving them her address and place of work. Mee See was glad to deliver Chun Yun's letter. However, she knew that Master Fung realised the real reason was because he had embezzled the company's money.

PHOTOGRAPHS - HONG KONG

Mee See, Chan Choy worked on payroll

Doris & Bob Huges
Owner of Hollywood Bar

Mee See & Ah Lin shared a room in HK

Mee See, 'sisters' worked at Hollywood bar

Doris took 'sister' to the beach

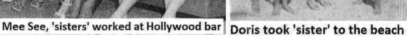

Part Eight – Nervous Breakdown

Depression

When Mee See heard that Chun Yun's company had not chased after him for the missing money, she realised that Chun Yun should have told Master Fung about his predicament, she was sure that his father would have helped him to resolve this problem. In fact, there would have been no reason for them to leave everything they had in Canton and escape to Macao. Considering all the past events, Mee See felt that she had wasted her life for the wrong reasons. What she had gone through over these years was a nightmare! What a waste of her youth! However, as it transpired, there was nothing she could do now but to continue this struggle with no foreseeable end date.

Mee See wished she could talk with her mother. However, Macao seemed to be so far away and she could not leave work to visit her mother just yet. Mee See hoped to talk with Mee Jing, but she was happily preparing herself for a month's trip to Singapore with Mr. Hong. She simply did not have time for her sister. Ah Lin was Mee See's bosom buddy. However, she had never disclosed her background so it was too difficult to tell Ah-Lin about all of the events that had transpired. Mee See didn't know who to tell or where to start revealing her life story.

The thought of Felo flashed back to her. She couldn't help but feel a sense of sadness and loss. She had wasted all the kindness and love that Felo had bestowed on her. She declined his offer of marriage because she did not want to be separated from her children. Now she still had to be away from her children! Looking back, it was such a waste of Felo's affection. She knew that they were both true to each other, yet at the time, they both could not see a way to compromise.

One morning, after waking, looking in the mirror Mee See could see a couple of fine lines near her eyes. This gave her a big shock. She felt time had passed by too quickly. She knew that she could not do the same work when she gets older. Suddenly the shadow of insecurity returned. She hoped she could have someone to rescue her from this predicament. But where could one find such an opportunity?

She was intrigued to hear that Ah Ku was still not married. She wondered why he was still single. This news rekindled Mee See's sentiments at their farewell. It was such a heartrending experience. She still could feel the hurt in her heart that she had to forsake Ah Ku as Ah Tai told her in no uncertain terms that she must forget about him to marry the better prospect - Fung Chun Yun. The rest was history. After so many years, she was different from that teenage Mee See that Ah Ku knew. She thought he might be disappointed with her if he knew the situation she was in now. Mee See couldn't help but feel worthless, inferior, and ashamed of herself. She was not good enough for Ah Ku anymore. She would avoid him if she met him again, she decided. Life was not a rehearsal! It was too late to meet him again now!

She repeated to herself once again that if it was not because of supporting the family, she would not have been a casino attendant, a night club dancing girl, and now a bar hostess. Every night she had to wear a beautiful smile to keep customers happy, to drink and to dance till all hours of the morning. She needed to reassure herself that her motivation was to provide the children with the best opportunity she could give by any means that were at her disposal. She looked around and felt trapped in such a hopeless and helpless whirlpool that kept pulling her down. What did the future hold? Who could rescue her from this situation? She looked at the glass jar where she put all her earnings to send home for living expenses. She knew the family in Macao was waiting for a full jar of money to continue living.

Suddenly, the pressure of life overwhelmed her, and she doubted that she could overcome all these challenges. She was tired of struggling, tired of working, and was tired of waking to find another trial with each daybreak.

There were subtle changes in Mee See's behaviour. She was easily startled. She seemed to be preoccupied all of the time and whispered to herself quietly. She lost the sparkles in her eyes. A couple of times, she was unaware of her surroundings, and she was nearly run down by passing traffic if Ah Lin had not stopped her in time. Suddenly, Ah Lin could see something was wrong, Mee See seemed to have lost some balance in her thinking, and she was not the same sharp-thinking and quick decision maker that Ah Lin used to admire.

Ah Lin went to Doris immediately, "Mee See Chair is in trouble! Lately, she seemed to be nervous about everything around her. She is not the same quick-thinking and good-humoured person. She doesn't seem to be as decisive as she was before. She mumbles to herself at times. Doris, I am worried about her."

Doris asked, "When did this start?"

Ah Lin answered, "Ever since she started visiting relatives in Hong Kong. She has deep thoughts. She stares into thin air and is pre-occupied. She would have walked into oncoming traffic if I hadn't stop her."

Doris listened with empathy, and said, "I think Mee See is hiding a lot of unhappy life experiences. Even though she never let on to anyone, she has many unresolved problems. As time passes, all these unresolved issues may affect her equilibrium. I am worried she may get ill as a result of working too hard. She may have a nervous breakdown."

Ah Lin knew that Doris was right and agreed with her analysis, said, "What can be done to help her? Should we tell her mother?"

Doris answered, "There is no need to tell her mother. It will only cause alarm as she isn't in a position to do anything to help. Also she needs to be in Macao to take care of Mee See's family. We will need to find a good psychologist to look after her straight away."

Ah Lin said, "Psychologists are very expensive. Where can she find that sort of money? We have a glass jar where we put our earnings. At the end of the month, Mee See Chair sends nearly all the money to support her family." Ah Lin, taking a deep breath continued, "I still owe Mee See Chair the children's school fees that she lent for my sister's funeral. As I have just finished paying my debt to the company, I can start paying Mee See back. But that will not be enough for her expenses in Macao. Now we have to find more money for the doctors."

Doris appreciated the difficulties of the situation and said, "Now let me give her one month wages in advance so she won't need to worry and can concentrate on getting better."

Doris continued, "She needs to see a doctor immediately to start her treatment. I have heard of a doctor named Wong Nan Ku. He is the head psychiatric doctor at Royal Queen Elizabeth Hospital. It is a public hospital, so there is no charge except for special medicine at a subsidised price. As it is a free service, there are many people who see the doctors every day. For now, let her stay at home to recuperate. She can't work in this condition. Wait and see what the doctor says after she has been to see him."

Ah Lin was touched by Doris' kindness and tears welled up in her eyes. She said, "You have always been so considerate to us sisters. Thank you for helping Mee See Chair. I just hope the doctor will be able to help her. I feel really sorry for her!"

Ah Lin took the month's wages from Doris to put into the glass jar. Mee See saw the glass jar was full of money, smiled broadly and said, "Good, I have earned so much money this month! How wonderful!"

Ah Lin didn't explain as she didn't think that Mee See would have the mental capacity to understand.

Mee See regressed to the gentle days of her childhood. She behaved like an obedient child. She would eat when food was on the table. When she was told to go to bed, she curled up and slept like a good girl. Ah Lin settled her in bed and told her not to go out before leaving for work each day. She found that she could trust her to stay indoors until she came home to check on her during the day. Ah Lin was worried. She didn't know how this illness would progress. She had no idea how to take care of Mee See.

The following day, before seven o'clock, Ah Lin took Mee See to the Royal Queen Elizabeth Hospital psychiatry outpatient clinic and waited to be seen by the doctor. They were prepared for a long wait as there was a long line of people. It was lucky that her condition did not affect her gentle temperament. She stayed put when Ah Lin told her to sit and wait patiently.

Help Behind the Scenes

Wong Nan Ku (黃立擧 Ah Ku) had a successful career. He was one of the senior medical officers at the Royal Queen Elizabeth Hospital Department of Psychiatry. He was also a consultant specialist doctor at several hospitals. Ah Ku wanted to be a doctor ever since he was a child. As his father was unable to afford the school fees, he won a scholarship during his student years until he qualified as a medical practitioner in Psychiatry. Sadly, when he was appointed as one of the senior medical officers, his father passed away. He was most regretful that his father was not able to enjoy the rest of his life in comfort now that he was able to provide for him. He rebuilt the Wong family shrine and placed his father's plaque as a remembrance. He put two placards inside the shrine with the inscription of a famous Chinese saying, '樹欲靜時風不息, 子欲養時親不在'[66] to express his remorse at not being able to share his success with his father.

Ah Ku always remembered Mee See. He often thought of those Yuen Long days when they were teenagers. Ah Ku reread many times the well-worn letters that Mee See had sent him, in particular the very last

---

[66] 樹欲靜時風不息, 子欲養時親不在 Trees have no peace as wild winds won't stop blowing; sons have plenty to offer but parents are no longer around to accept. – meaning it was too late to serve the parents after they had passed away.

one, which had cello tape over the creases. In the letter, Mee See explained how fate controlled her life. She told him that she could no longer keep her promise to wait for him to finish his studies. Unbeknown to Mee See, the last time Ah Ku saw Mee See was on her wedding day. He plucked up his courage to travel to Canton to find Mee See hoping to persuade her to elope with him to Yuen Long. Unfortunately, he arrived on Mee See's wedding day. He was hiding in the trees across the road hoping to have a few words with her, but Mee See was not aware that he was there. Ah Ku felt inferior as he saw the handsome groom leading Mee See into the wedding car to drive off to start their new life.

He buried his thoughts of Mee See in his heart. As the years went by, she became his virtual idol. Since his father had passed away, Ah Ku had become even more reclusive. He channeled all his energy into studying and building a career. He scored high distinctions in his studies and received a number of commendations from the School of Psychiatry and the medical society. His entire life was spent to serve patients with mental health problems. He often did not charge his patients when he found they had financial hardship. As a result, he was recognised as one of the most successful and kindest doctors in the hospitals where he practised.

Dr. Wong Nan Ku arrived at work really early on this particular morning. He didn't know why but he had a restless night and decided he might as well come to work early. His assistant got Dr. Wong a fresh pot of his favourite tea and brought in some early breakfast along with the pile of patient cards. This morning he decided to do the patient cards himself because he was so early. Dr. Wong sipped his cup of hot Chrysanthemum tea. The fresh strong aroma permeated the still air in his office. Casually flicking through the stack of patient cards, he suddenly saw the name Kwan Mee See (關美思) on a new patient card. There was no previous medical note. The referral diagnosis was 'possible nervous breakdown'.

Behind the curtains of the examination cubicle, through the crack where two curtains met, Dr. Wong peeped into the waiting room. He recognised Mee See the minute he set his eyes on her as she sat in the line of patients. She still wore that calm composure. She was still so attractive. She sat straight against the back of her chair. She was the fifth patient on the waiting list.

Over the last decade, Dr. Wong had seen thousands of patients with potential nervous breakdown. He had examined countless patients and knew exactly what to do for them. There had been so many times that he actually dreamt of meeting Mee See again. Yet now, Mee See was waiting for him to heal her. For once, Ah Ku didn't know what to do. If she wasn't his patient, he would have rushed out to rekindle that long suppressed friendship. However, as Dr. Wong, he decided he could not reveal his presence. For Mee See's sake, he needed to know her condition to formulate a treatment regime. When she regained good health, he would reveal the fact that he had been treating her. It would give him a chance to get to know what had happened to her over the years.

Dr. Wong found his senior assistant Dr. Sal Chee (秀枝), gave her Mee See's card, and said, "I want you to see this patient first and give her special attention. I want you to personally take charge of her and give her preferential treatment. You will report on her progress to me every day, but I don't want her to know of my involvement at all."

Mee See came to see Dr. Sal Chee every week. Ah Lin came in to each consulting session and learnt of her background, upbringing, and life history prior to their meeting at the casino. Ah Lin felt sorry for Mee See and respected her even more. Mee See's illness did not change. Every time, when she took the medication home, she pushed it into her bedside drawer and went to sleep.

All the doctors were perplexed as to why she did not respond to the prescribed treatment.

Dr. Sal Chee told Ah Lin, "We are very surprised that Mee See doesn't seem to be responding to the treatments we have prescribed. She should have started to improve by now. Do you know if Mee See is taking the medication? "

Ah Lin suddenly realised and said, "Oh dear, I have not seen her taking the tablets. When we get home, I settle her and go to work. I come home to check on her a few times during the day and night, and she is always sleeping calmly in the same way I left her. I haven't asked her about the medication. How very careless I have been!"

Dr. Sal Chee said, "I hope you understand, if she doesn't get better or respond to the medication, we may have to admit her to the Ching Shaun Mental Hospital (青山精神病院) for more invasive treatment. Of course, if the medicine works well, then it will not be necessary to admit her to the mental institution at all."

Dr. Wong (Ah Ku) was behind Mee See's treatment regime. He prescribed the treatments he thought were best for her. From Dr. Sal Chee's notes he learned all that had happened to her since they parted. He decided that this time, he was not going to let her leave him again. It took a lot of self-control not to reveal his identity to her each time she came for consultation. Ah Ku saw that her condition was weak and fragile. It would do her a disservice to break his cover. But when he saw there was no progress, he was afraid that going to Ching Shaun Mental Hospital for more intense treatment might have to be the last resort. Ah Ku really didn't want to send Mee See there, but he might not have any other option.

Ah Lin went home and searched the bedroom and found the untouched medication bottles in the bedside drawer. Mee See had not taken one tablet from the Royal Queen Elizabeth Hospital. She was curled up like a contented child in bed with the blanket tucked right under her chin, fast asleep.

Ah Lin's was shaking because she was so disappointed. She raised her voice as she shook Mee See's shoulder to wake her, "Wake up, Mee See Chair, you wake up! Look at all these bottles of tablets! This medicine will make you better and cure your illness. Why didn't you listen to the doctors? Why did you hide these tablets? You haven't taken one tablet to help yourself get better! You have wasted all my efforts to help you! You have wasted Doris's kindness!"

Mee See awoke abruptly due to Ah Lin's screaming and scolding. She opened her eyes and looked around. It was as though she had just been dragged out of a stupor. She shook her head trying to clear the cloud in her head. She looked at Ah Lin and said, "Alright then, I will take the tablets. Don't be cross with me!"

Ah Lin had never before raised her voice to Mee See. She was desperate because she saw Mee See was not improving. Ah Lin told her firmly, "From now on, I am coming home to see you take the tablets three times a day!"

Ah Lin was very worried. What would happen if Mee See didn't get better? The doctors would send her to the Mental Hospital. How long would she need to stay in the hospital? How long could Doris extend her kindness to accommodate Mee See's sickness? What about all the people in Macao that were waiting for her monthly support? What about the children's school fees? Ah Lin dared not continue to think!

That night, Ah Lin could not sleep. She tossed in her bed and saw Mee See fast asleep. She was completely oblivious to the consequences if she did not get better and go back to work. Ah Lin had never prayed before. She closed her eyes and concentrated really hard. Her inner voice was calling out, "Please let Mee See Char come to her senses. Please make her better. She cannot go to the Ching Shaun Mental Hospital. Somebody, please help her!"

From then on, Ah Lin came home from the Hollywood Bar three times a day to give Mee See her tablets according to Dr. Sal Chee's instructions. They went to the hospital twice a week, very early in the morning. Dr.

Sal Chee would see Mee See before any other patient. She was given all the medication without cost. It saved a lot of time waiting in line for services. It was all free of charge. Ah Lin was grateful for this special treatment for Mee See, as she was not aware of the other forces at play.

Dr. Wong took Dr. Sal Chee's notes home to read through carefully. He evaluated the response to the prescribed treatment and adjusted the dosage accordingly. He realised that Mee See had been hiding her emotions for a long time. The pressures of life were too overwhelming. This caused her nervous breakdown. It would take a long time for her to reconnect with her inner strength. She had to gather her own strength to recuperate. He instructed Dr. Sal Chee to continue managing and monitoring Mee See's progress. She was not to know about his involvement.

With Ah Lin's tender care and proper medication, Mee See gradually improved and wanted to know what had happened. Ah Lin related all of the events since she took ill. Mee See then realised that she had been ill for over a month and a half. She would have been admitted to Ching Shaun Mental Hospital if her condition had not improved. She was deeply grateful to Ah Lin and knew that it was her help that made her better. Mee See thanked Doris for all her support. Doris told her that she should completely recover before she went back to work. Mee See was recovering well. Before returning to work, she went to Macao to see her mother and children. She told Siew Fen about her nervous breakdown. She was told by Dr. Sal Chee that even though she was better, it would still take a long time to regain her equilibrium. In fact she had to change her lifestyle and outlook in life to ease the pressure which she had bottled up over the years. She told Siew Fen that she was within a week of being admitted to Ching Shaun Mental Hospital.

Siew Fen was alarmed and said, "From now on, you must have a different attitude and give yourself time to rest and recuperate. You have done more than any mother could have done for her children."

Mee See said, "It was the pressure of life and the fear that I could not fulfill my duty that affected me and caused a chemical imbalance. I had special medication to settle my nerves. When I calmed down, I returned to clear thinking." Taking a deep breath and a sip of tea, she continued, "I owe my well-being to a lot of people. And there is always you, helping me with the children; otherwise, I would not know how I could cope."

Siew Fen said, "For the children's sake, you must look after yourself. Now for once in your life, you must put yourself first. The children have me here."

Mee See had a new perspective on life and decided to work five days a week leaving two days for entertainment with friends and with the long lost relatives. She had spare time to relax and she gave herself a budget for recreation. When Doris organised the outing with the sisters, Mee See volunteered to prepare the food or book a venue, or help to plan the itinerary. She went back to calculate the wages. This made her feel that she was fully recovered.

Mee See went home to Macao more often to be with the children. She even invited Luk KuChar, Sai YeMa and Mee Jing to Macao to visit Siew Fen. Gradually Mee See regained her confidence, and was ready to return to work. Focusing on everyday life again, she regained her sense of humour. All the sisters welcomed her return. They surrounded her and wished her well. The sisters collected money to put in a Lai-See as a present to celebrate Mee See's full recovery.

Mental illness had a certain stigma with some of the sisters, who doubted if Mee See had truly recovered. They watched to see if they could find any trace of behaviour that they should report to Doris or to Ah Lin. Some sisters had good intentions to make sure Mee See could get help early if her illness relapsed. Other sisters over reacted and spread rumours about Mee See's behaviour, which caused some barriers with her.

When Mee See came back from Macao, after visiting her mother, she returned to Doris the month's loan that she lent her when she first took ill.

Doris was surprised and said, "Where did you find the month's wages in such a short time? You know you can pay me back later or you can even deduct it from your wages over time."

Mee See smiled and said, "Since working for you, I have been sending every last dollar to my mother to put away for a rainy day. She told me she nearly has all the children's school fees for next year already. That's why we are in a position to pay back this loan. Ah Tai insisted I must pay you back now!"

Doris put the money into her handbag without counting. She admired Mee See's and her mother's honesty and integrity.

Mee See continued consultation at the hospital once a fortnight, then once every three weeks. She had no idea it was Ah Ku who had treated her through his assistant. Ah Ku was looking forward to the time when he could uncover himself and re-establish contact with Mee See. However it was not the right time just yet.

Part Nine – New Beginning

Bob Sayers from London

Bob Hughes and Doris often entertained a number of British expats at home. They had Bob Sayers and a number of other British expats who had just joined the Royal Police Reserve Force as voluntary police officers. The couple simply wanted to make them feel at home while they served in the Far East away from their homeland.

Bob Sayers was born in London. He joined the Royal British Navy in his early teens, which enabled him to travel far and wide, visiting all the countries of the Commonwealth. Bob studied mechanical engineering and graduated as a Chief Engineer on the ship he served. Bob and his wife Hannah lived in Portsmouth where they had a son David. Unfortunately Hannah passed away leaving their three year old son David in the care of Bob's parent who lived in the East End of London. Bob was captivated by Hong Kong Harbour and was attracted to Asian culture. He retired from the British Royal Navy and took a Chief Engineer position at HMS Tamar. Bob had settled in Hong Kong for a couple of years. He was interested in law and order and civil security so he joined the volunteer police force as a part-time Police Inspector. There he made a number of friends who were also seconded to Hong Kong from England. Bob became good friends with Bob Hughes.

Bob told Doris and Bob Hughes about his son David in London. He thought David would be an excellent playmate for the couple's two-year-old son Bobby.

Doris said to Bob jokingly, "We have to find you a good wife in Hong Kong. You need someone kind and good to look after you and to take care of your son."

With one hand on Doris's shoulder and the other holding his Sam Miguel beer Bob Hughes said, "I strongly recommend you find a Chinese beauty. They know how to make life comfortable for you. They are so considerate!"

Bob smiled and said, "That would be wonderful. However I have found it hard to find the right companion. Every Chinese girl I have met here is a beauty, but none of them can converse in English. How will it work if there is no communication?"

Doris told Bob, "I have just the right person. She is honest. She is attractive and she is such a gentle soul. Not only can she speak the language but she was educated in high school. She is considerate and she will make you an ideal companion."

Soon after, Bob Hughes invited a group of expats from the police force to the Hollywood Bar for a weekend gathering and entertainment. He especially introduced Mee See, Ah Lin, Julie, and the others to his police inspector friends. The group had drinks, listened to music, danced, and ordered food from a restaurant next door. Everyone had a great time. Bob had an eye for beauty and he thought Mee See was very attractive.

The group had a discussion about how could the Mother Country gauge the feelings of the colonial subjects when they were so far apart in culture and in distance. Mee See joined in the discussion drawing on her experience of working at the Portuguese embassy. She simply stated how the embassy officials could source local interpreters to capture the current thinking of the local people on a range of topics. Bob found she articulated well about how to bridge the cultural gap and was impressed with her depth of the conversation.

Mee See had a pleasing manner. She did not join the other girls giggling and exaggerating emotions to attract attention. Mee See moved slower than the other girls who jumped ahead to get there first. Yet she got there with style and grace. Bob felt it was such a pleasure being around her.

Bob came to seek her company very often. Bob would buy Mee See's time to take her to the movies, sailing and fishing. He even took her to inspect HMS Tamar where he worked. He took Mee See to the police social club activities that were offered to senior police officers and introduced her to his friends as his girlfriend.

Mee See could see that Bob was really interested in her. She discussed Bob's friendship with Ah Lin.

Ah Lin said, "The first time that Bob Hughes brought him to Hollywood, I already could see that he had chosen you. He hung around you and listened to every word you said. I am really happy for you."

Since Felo had left Macao, Mee See still felt the heartache when she recalled being at the wharf bidding Felo farewell. The reason for their separation was that he could not accept Mee See's four children as a part of the family. If Bob wanted to bring up the matter of marriage, she would not know what to do. Mee See really did not want to miss this opportunity again. She had to prepare herself before Bob raised the matter.

She said, "Mee Jing advised me many years ago not to admit that I have so many children. She suggested I admit to having a daughter only. That would be more acceptable to men. But how do I hide the three boys? The truth has to come out one day."

Ah Lin responded, "Mee Jing's suggestion is reasonable, but your situation now is different from Felo's time. Bob wants to settle here in Hong Kong. Your children are studying in Macao, which is so near to Hong Kong. It is very easy for you to go home to see the children. This is such an ideal situation. Mee See Chair, Bob is such a good person. Don't miss this chance."

At the Hollywood Bar, every sister was hoping to find a companion who would rescue her from the work that she was doing. Julie was introduced to Bob at the same time Mee See was. Being a gentleman, Bob was courteous to every girl at the bar. Julie believed that if she had a chance to be with Bob, she could snatch him away from Mee See. At last Julie cornered Bob and told Bob that Mee See had a mental illness and that she was still seeing a 'mental doctor'. Julie implied that Mee See would be too unstable emotionally to be able to take care of Bob. Bob smiled kindly at Julie while she was telling him about Mee See. When Mee See turned up, Bob politely took leave from Julie. As he took Mee See by the hand to the Police Social Club Annual Ball, Julie stared at their backs with jealousy and envy. She was hoping now that Bob knew of Mee See's mental condition, he would turn around to find her instead.

The Police Social Club ran various welfare evenings for all police members including their voluntary members during the year. Once a year, they had a grand ball to celebrate another year of success. At the celebration, there were awards recognising many who had excelled in the past twelve months. It was also a gathering for club members to thank all the officials for their support and hard work in organising all the activities for the club members throughout the year. Most police members brought their spouses along to enjoy a gala night of entertainment, dinner and dance. The seating arrangement was organised in tables according to rank and service locations. Bob was sitting at Bob Hughes's table along with other district commissioners, police inspectors, and other senior voluntary officers.

The hall was decorated with yellow, blue, silver, red and green paper streamers. Each pillar and pole was hung with multicolour balloons and sparkling paper cuts. The entire police club was looking the best for this occasion. Everyone wore a broad smile on their face greeting each other as though they were long lost friends. It was such a happy occasion for one and all. Bob took Mee See to mingle with various groups of friends from different divisions. She felt comfortable chatting with the English ladies who had been living in Hong Kong longer than she had. Mee See was an expert in small talk at such parties.

Bob Hughes and Doris watched quietly as Mee See and Bob mingled around their friends. They nodded their heads and agreed that Bob and Mee See looked like an ideal couple.

As another round of music started, Peter, a young inspector working in Bob Hughes' division came to chat with Mee See and asked her for the next dance.

She stood up slowly, turned around and half apologised to Bob, "Please wait a little. I shall be back presently."

Peter led Mee See by the arm to the dance floor. Bob Hughes, Doris and Bob watched as the two dancers descended onto the dance floor. It was more than a year since Mee See had last danced at the Grape Vine Night Club in Macao. She listened to the beat of the music and followed Peter's lead. Her dancing technique had never left her. In a very short time she got back to the swing of the rhythm of the dance. She was trim and she was attractive. Bob was a little jealous as he watched Peter dancing so well with her. He regretted not asking Mee See to dance before she was snatched by Peter.

Bob Hughes smiled at Bob and said, "Mee See is such an attractive girl. If you don't watch out, you may miss out, old fellow!!"

Bob asked in a casual way to investigate if Julie was telling the truth, "I am well aware of that. I really do like her a lot. I heard that she had been unwell lately?"

Doris added immediately, "That's right, Mee See has a very heavy responsibility to support her family. She went to the doctor to help her to resolve a number of personal issues. She is honest and trustworthy which is a very good quality. Who has been telling you gossip about Mee See? You can ask her yourself. I am sure she will tell you about it too."

Bob smiled and replied, "I overheard it only. I will talk with Mee See to see how I can help her. I want to take care of her."

Bob Hughes had his arm around Doris's tiny waist. With his eyes on Peter and Mee See dancing around the dance floor, he spoke to Bob,

"Very good. Let's drink one for you two! Let's 'yum sing (飲勝)[67]! We wish you two lots of happiness! Don't delay!"

Bob was a patient person. After several dances Peter walked Mee See back to her seat. Bob said to Peter jokingly, "Thank you so much for entertaining my girlfriend."

Peter quickly apologised quietly, "Oh! Forgive me! I did not know Mee See was yours. I just thought she was Doris's good friend. Please accept my apology."

Marriage Proposal

The police club annual dinner and dance ball drew to a close. Everyone had a great time and farewelled each other after the successful conclusion of another year of club activities.

Bob suggested to Mee See, "It is such a balmy night. Let's go to the Peak to look at the beautiful lights in Victoria Harbour, then, I shall take you home."

Mee See was tired. However she thought it would not take long to see the harbour view and said, "That will be nice!"

Bob drove his car to Victoria Peak (老襯亭). They looked at the bright lights of Victoria Harbour, Central and Tsim Sha Tsui in Kowloon, with Wan chai and Causeway Bay to the right. Blocks of apartments along the hillside shone brightly in the night. Hong Kong was such a beautiful city. Mee See was so busy working that she never had the chance to come to the Peak at night to feast on the bright city sight. She was happy to see such a magnificent view. The soft wind was blowing. Her tiredness was blown away as they walked around the Peak. Bob suggested they head for the Peak Cafe to have a night cap.

---

[67] Yum Sing 飲勝 an expression to drink up, usually meaning bottoms up.

Bob helped Mee See into a comfortable chair at a table with the best harbour view. He ordered a hot milky Horlick for her and a black coffee, no sugar, for himself. They had just had a full dinner with all the trimmings and a delicious dessert at the annual ball. She was far from being hungry or thirsty.

Bob said to her, "Mee See marry me. Let me look after you. Let me protect you."

Mee See knew that Bob was very interested in her. However it was a surprise to hear him proposing. Suddenly, she didn't know how she should respond. She really would have liked to say, "Splendid! Wonderful!" But she could not bring herself to answer. She wanted to raise the matter of supporting the family. She was numb and speechless.as she pondered the proposal. How could she raise this awkward matter of money?

Bob saw that Mee See did not respond. She seemed to be hesitating. He wondered if he had done the right thing to propose so soon after they had met and said, "What do you think?"

Mee See didn't know that Bob already knew of her illness and her situation. She felt that she had to tell Bob about herself first and said, "You are not aware that I have been ill. I have a heavy responsibility at home. That was why I needed to see a specialist doctor to help me analyse and sort out some of the issues affecting me."

Bob didn't tell her that he already knew about her situation. He was glad that she had been honest. He continued, "Tell me! Tell me about yourself. Tell me all your worries. Let's work together to resolve them. Your worries are my worries. Your problems are my problems."

The incident with Felo came back to haunt her. She could not ruin the chance this time by frightening Bob away by having to support all four children and a mother. She replied, "I have a daughter and a mother at home. They live in Macao where my daughter is studying English at a Catholic school. Living is more affordable in Macao."

Bob smiled and comforted her, "Move them over to Hong Kong so they can live with us. Your daughter is my daughter. I will bring my son from London. We should be living together. I want to take care of you. I can support your whole family. I don't want you to work at the Hollywood Bar anymore."

Mee See hadn't imagined that Bob would be so straight forward, she added, "I also have three other boys that I promised to look after for my brother. They prefer to study Chinese in Macao. My mother looks after all the children living at my sister, Mee Jing's property rent free. I work in Hong Kong to send money home to raise the children."

Without giving a second thought, Bob said, "This is a very heavy responsibility. No wonder you are worried. You're amazing! How have you done this all by yourself. Well, from today onwards, your family is my family. Your responsibility is my responsibility! Since your mother needs to look after Mee Jing's property, and the boys like to study Chinese, why don't we leave the boys and your mother in Macao? Let me send the money to support them. Move your daughter to Hong Kong to live with us. We can find her a good English school to continue her schooling. Do you think that would work?"

If Mee See had known Bob's response, she would not have lied about the boys! However, she could not change her story now. From then on, she would not have to work at the Hollywood Bar! She didn't believe this was happening to her!

Suddenly Mee See realised the reason Bob took her to Victoria Peak was to propose to her. They forgot how late it was and started planning their new life together. They could both visualise their happiness. With Bob by her side to lead the way, Mee See found a new direction in life.

Mee See could not wait to break the news to Ah Lin about her upcoming wedding to Bob Sayers. She wanted Ah Lin to be her bridesmaid. Mee See and Bob wanted Bob Hughes and Ah Lin as their witnesses at the wedding ceremony. Ah Lin was overjoyed to hear the news, and said,

"Oh Mee See Chair, this is the best thing that can happen to you both! The first day we met Bob, I thought he was interested in you. However, I knew one of the sisters had been spreading rumours that you still suffer from a mental illness. I was so scared that she might snatch Bob away from you! I am so happy for you."

Ah Lin took Mee See by the hands and said seriously, "I have never been a bridesmaid before. However if you tell me what to do, I will not disappoint you!" Ah Lin hesitated. Her insecurity overwhelmed her and added, "Being a witness at your wedding is an important position. I don't have an education, I can't even write my name. How can I stand with Bob Hughes as the witness at your wedding? I dare not take up such an important role."

Mee See insisted, "You are my very best friend and you have always been there for me. I might be in the Ching Shaun Mental Hospital if it wasn't for you. I am forever in your debt. This time, I insist on you being my witness, you are the only person in the world who is suitable for this role. All you have to do is to stand by me, look pretty, and sign your name on my marriage certificate."

Ah Lin was embarrassed and said, "Let's not talk about saving your life, being in debt, and all that nonsense. You have forgotten; you have helped me many times too. All I know is we are closer than blood sisters. One big problem is I never knew how to write my name. I can't sign with a thumb print on your wedding certificate! Ha ha ha! "

The two good friends huddled together laughing. Mee See taught Ah Lin how to write her real name. It was the first time Ah Lin had seen her name written properly. She learned each stroke and dot carefully and found her name fascinating. In the following weeks, she practised every time she was on her own. She was determined to write her name perfectly on this occasion.

With Bob supporting the family, Mee See resigned from the Hollywood Bar.

Doris was very happy about the forthcoming wedding and said, "Bob and I always thought that you two would make a good match! Would you continue to help me calculate and pay the wages for the sisters?"

Mee See was honoured to be asked to continue calculating the wages for the sisters, and said, "It would be my pleasure to continue to work on the wages. I am sure that Bob will be agreeable too. I am in your debt for everything that you have done for me. I will not forget your kindness."

Doris responded, "Please don't mention it. Bob is a good man. He is responsible and kind. We are glad to play matchmakers. We want to drink to your happiness at your wedding."

Full Recovery

Mee See decided that it was the last appointment with Dr. Sal Chee at the Royal Queen Elizabeth Hospital. She brought along a nice present for the doctor. She looked immaculate with her bright eyes and her hair was shiny and well groomed. She wore face powder, rouge and light lipstick, and a new European style skirt with a matching top. Mee See looked stunning as she walked into the consultation room.

Dr. Sal Chee was surprised. She had never seen her with makeup and dressed so modern and stylish. Dr. Sal Chee greeted Mee See happily, "Oh Mee See, you have recovered very well. You do look so attractive. I have never seen you so happy!"

Mee See could not contain herself, she smiled broadly and said, "That's so right. I am getting married next week. I have this present for you. Thank you for your kind attention to my recovery. You have never charged me for the service. I don't know how I can thank you enough."

Dr. Sal Chee wanted to tell Mee See that it was their Chief Medical Officer, the well-known Dr. Wong Nan Ku who was her consulting physician. However, she had made a pledge never to disclose about Dr.

Wong's involvement without his permission. Dr. Sal Chee wished Mee See happiness and good health. She also wished her and her future husband a very happy marriage. Mee See said her final farewell. Dr. Sal Chee completed the final patient record to report to Dr. Wong.

Ah Ku buried his feelings in his heart. He didn't get another chance to meet with Mee See.

Approval from All

Bob wanted to meet Siew Fen and the children. He went to Macao with Mee See to pay his respects to her mother. The children were at school at the time. Bob wanted to let Siew Fen know his intention to support the family.

Bob had been working in Hong Kong for two years and had learned some Cantonese words from his Chinese foremen. He bowed his head low to show respect and used Cantonese and said, "Ah Tai, lee how ma?[68](亞大,妳好嗎?)"

Siew Fen, not prepared for Bob speaking in Cantonese, was surprised and did not catch what he said. Once it was clear, she burst out laughing and said "Aw ho! Aw ho! Yau sum la! [69](我好! 我好! 有心啦!)

Bob explained to Siew Fen through Mee See, "I would like to marry Mee See. I don't want her to work so hard. From now on, let me support the family."

Siew Fen nodded in agreement and approval. It was a surprise to meet Bob who had such an open and sincere manner.

That night Bob took the whole family to the 'Smiling Buddha' seafood restaurant for dinner. Initially the children were shy when they met this

---

[68] Ah Tai, lee how ma? 亞大,妳好嗎? Chinese greeting meaning Ah Tai, how are you?
[69] Aw ho! Aw ho! Yau sum la! 我好! 我好! 有心啦! Chinese response to greeting - I am well! I am well! Thanks for your kind regards!

tall foreigner, Uncle Bob, for the first time. They dared not come forward to greet him, and all mumbled their greetings softly. Bob was friendly and played jokes with the children to put them at ease. Before long, all the children were playing with Uncle Bob in spite of the language barrier. Yau Mui, in particular, even tried out her newly acquired language skills to converse with Uncle Bob in broken English.

Siew Fen observed that Bob was obviously very caring to Mee See and her children. Above all, he was respectful to her. He was genuine in his offer to support the family. He valued everything that was important to Mee See. Siew Fen felt good about their forthcoming wedding, and she was comforted that at last Mee See had found the right man.

Bob had won Siew Fen's approval.

§   §   §

Mee See and Bob took Luk KuChar and husband to a yum cha lunch and to invite them to the forthcoming wedding. Luk Ku Chenng had attended Cambridge University to study economics before coming home to manage his father's business. The men enjoyed talking about the British weather, the Commonwealth and the city of London. Luk KuChar recalled attending East Bridge College (東橋學校) to learn English with Mee See and Mee Jing. She rekindled her English language skill after all those years.

Luk KuChar got Mee See on the side and asked in Chinese, "Would you consider letting Yau Mui move to our home and be our daughter? I personally guarantee she will be treated as our flesh and blood. We promise to raise her with the best education we can provide. This way, you will have one less child to support. Do you think that will work?"

Mee See kept her voice down and replied in Chinese that Bob wanted to bring Yau Mui to Hong Kong to send her to an English school. He would not agree with such an arrangement as he really liked Yau Mui. Luk KuChar accepted Mee See's explanation and settled for the fact that Yau Mui could not be her foster daughter.

Luk KuChar and Luk Ku Chenng thought Bob was such a good match for Mee See.

§ § §

Bob was very eager to meet all of Mee See's siblings and to invite them to the wedding. The incident of Wing Chung stealing Mee Jing's gold nugget had never been resolved. Their last encounter had ended in a fight. Having seen Wing Chung's bad temper and his unreasonable approach to life, Mee See was worried Wing Chung and Mee Jing might have an argument at the wedding and that would spoil the day for all.

Since leaving Canton, Wing Chung and Yee Hong lived in a wooden hut in a shantytown on the hillside. It was the only accommodation they could afford. He sold small goods near the shantytown. One year, fire swept through the shantytown killing a number of people who were trapped in their wooden huts. Luckily, the couple escaped the fire safely but they lost everything they possessed. The government resettled all the shantytown residents into Ngau Tau Kok (牛頭角) resettlement apartment blocks and provided funds to restart their livelihood.

Wing Chung was ashamed to show his sister and the future English brother-in-law his shabby residence so he would rather meet them at the end corner of the block of resettlement flats where they lived. Bob drove to pick them up and took them to a Chinese restaurant for yum cha.

Wing Chung met Bob who was six foot tall, thin, with kind light brown eyes, and a broad smile with friendly gestures. As he watched his sister laughing, chatting, and interpreting for Yee Hong and himself, she seemed to be fluent in the language with Bob. Wing Chung couldn't help but wish that he, too, could join in the conversation in English. He admired this capable elder sister, whom he had always held in high esteem.

Wing Chung spoke Chinese to talk to Bob, "Gosh! Now I know how good it is to have learned English. We had the chance to study English with the French nuns in Canton. It really was Wing Yu's fault! He took me out of school to play around instead of studying hard. Otherwise I am sure, I too could be clever like my sister here, conversing in English."

Mee See thought Wing Chung hadn't changed. After all these years, he still didn't take ownership of his actions, and attributed his life's failures to others. She did not interpret his entire conversation to Bob, but told Bob that Wing Chung was disappointed that he could not converse in English with him.

Bob answered Wing Chung in fluent Cantonese Chinese, "Ng yield gun la! Aw ton na kon chun mum ju tuck la![70] (唔要緊哪! 我同你講中文就得哪!)"

Wing Chung and Yee Hong were so surprised that Bob could speak such fluent and colloquial sentences in Cantonese Chinese. They laughed at Bob's strange accent, and were impressed with this future brother-in-law. They thought that Bob was humorous and easy to get along with.

Wing Chung felt uncomfortable to be in the presence of police inspectors, senior officers, and English navy personnel who were invited to the wedding and decided not to attend the wedding. His excuse was that Yee Hong was too shy to attend such a grand occasion as she would not feel comfortable in front of so many European people. He also told Mee See that his business was not good. He could not afford the new clothes for the occasion.

Mee See and Bob accepted their apology.

When they were leaving, Mee See quietly slipped a number of hundred bills to Wing Chung. She felt she had fulfilled the responsibility of being the elder sister.

---

[70] Ng yield gun la! Aw ton na kon chun mum ju tuck la![70] 唔要緊哪! 我同你講中文就得哪! – Doesn't matter ! I can speak Cantonese with you!

§ § §

Mee See invited Mee Jing and Mr. Hong to dinner to introduce Bob. They told them the good news and invited them to attend their upcoming wedding, Mee See wanted to explain to Mee Jing that they have chosen Ah Lin as her bridesmaid and witness for the wedding ceremony and wanted to make sure her sister was not offended by this arrangement.

Mr. Hong had, over the years, conducted business with European business contacts. Mr. Hong had heard that Bob was interested in law and order and community security, he admired Bob for joining the voluntary police force which was such a good deed for the community of Hong Kong. The men talked agreeably about public order and law compliance. Mee Jing was happy for the opportunity to use her English language skills with Bob. It was a chance to show off her command of the language in front of Mr. Hong, who enjoyed watching Mee Jing playing hostess to Bob ensuring Bob knew the ingredients of each Chinese dish. Mr. Hong was amazed at how well she could converse in English. It was a talent he didn't know she had. The two couples enjoyed each other's company over a scrumptious and extravagant dinner.

Mee Jing, could not contain her happiness as she was eager to tell her sister her good news. Smiling and looking at Mr. Hong, and said, "We are going to have a baby soon!"

Mee See remembered that Mee Jing had always planned to have a son as soon as she arrived in Hong Kong so that she could secure her standing in Mr. Hong's household hierarchy and assure a share of his inheritance. Now that she was pregnant, Mee See earnestly hoped that she was carrying a boy.

Mee See took Mee Jing's hand and said happily, "That is the best news! You must rest well!"

Mee Jing continued, "When we came home from Singapore, I discovered that I was pregnant. We are so happy about it. I have not been well lately, that's why I have not been in contact with you. I am a lot better now."

Mee See replied, "The last few months have been a nightmare for me. I had what the doctor described as a mild nervous breakdown. Luckily the doctors at Royal Queen Elizabeth Hospital gave me special medication. I was within a week of being sent to the mental hospital! Thank goodness I am better now." She took a deep breath and continued, "Bob knows about my illness, and he still wants to take care of me and the family. In fact, that really was the best medicine!"

Mee Jing was happy about the good news and chuckled, "Good job your nervous breakdown is over. However, this time, I am afraid I cannot be your bridesmaid! You have to find someone else."

Mee See said, "That's fine. Ah Lin can be my bridesmaid. She and Bob Hughes will be our witnesses at the wedding."

Mee Jing answered quickly, "Ah Lin has no education. She is illiterate! She may be suitable as your bridesmaid, but how can she be your witness? She is not good enough to be standing with Bob Hughes as your witness! Have you considered it carefully? Bob is really a good man, he will marry you and he will even support your four children and Ah Tai. "

Mee See replied, "All she has to do as a witness is to sign her name on the marriage certificate. There is really no big deal. I have shown Ah Lin how to write her name. She has been practising since. Actually, she writes her name very well!"

Mee See spoke in Chinese quietly on the side with Mee Jing, "I have listened to your advice and told Bob that I only have Yau Mui and promised to raise the three boys of our eldest brother. After we get married, he wants to take me to London to bring his son David home. Then, he plans to have everyone, including the boys, live together in Hong Kong." Mee See continued to tell Mee Jing, "Bob is so generous. He has accepted all the children as children of our family. If I had known he was so kind, I would not have needed to lie to him! Now I have to continue this story. I hope you will too."

Mee Jing agreed quietly, "Of course. I will continue the story with Bob and Mr. Hong."

Mee Jing spoke in English so that Bob could share in the conversation, "Well, this is a good coincidence. I was planning to sell the property in Macao and buy one in Hong Kong because the rental return is much better here. I shall sell the Macao block of flats while you two go to England. It will be just the right time to move the family to Hong Kong to join Bob and his son. Ah Tai can decide to live with me or you. This plan will work well."

Mee Jing and Mr. Hong liked Bob a lot. They thought Bob was such a humorous and caring person. They were happy for Mee See now she had Bob to take care of her and the family.

Felo's Return

One morning Bob took Mee See to the Hollywood Bar to work on the payroll for the sisters. They were happily discussing their upcoming wedding when they arrived to find Doris looking concerned and Ah Lin looking serious. They gestured toward the side office where a visitor was waiting. As usual Bob opened the door courteously, stood back, and let Mee See step in. Mee See froze as she walked in. Her eyes locked with a pair of deep blue eyes. She recognised the face with an uninhibited smile, long lost but never forgotten. Felo leaped to his feet on catching the sight of Mee See and moved forward with open arms to give Mee See a warm bear hug saying, "So happy I found you at last. I arrived in Macao from Lisbon yesterday, Ah-Pak told me you work in Hong Kong now and I jumped on the next ferry to come looking for you first thing this morning."

Mee See was taken aback. Recollecting herself she turned around to find Bob standing behind her observing Felo's warm greetings and waiting to be introduced. Mee See stepped back closer to Bob to introduce the two men of her life, "Bob this is Felo, my very good friend from Lisbon." Turning to Felo, Mee See said, "Felo this is my fiancé Bob Sayers from London, now settled in Hong Kong."

The two men stepped forward to shake hands courteously, exchanging pleasantries.

Smiling friendlily, Bob said warmly, "Mee See's good friend is my good friend too. How long will you be staying, and where are you staying?"

With a reserved smile, Felo returned, "I will be staying at the Central Hotel in Macao for a couple of weeks."

A few awkward silent moments elapsed as each tried to kick off a conversation.

Ah Lin came in with a couple of San Miguel beers for the men and a cup of English Breakfast tea for Mee See. She uttered quietly under her breathe in Chinese to Mee See, "I couldn't warn you ahead of time."

Bob suggested to everyone, "It is lunch time, how about I organise some lunch for us all? Will you stay for lunch Felo?" Bob took leave from Felo then kissed Mee See on her cheek saying, "I shall be back presently." Bob was most considerate, he wanted to give Mee See and Felo a chance on their own to catch up.

Ah Lin followed Bob saying, "Let me help you order the food from next door."

Felo and Mee See sat down together on the bench seat. Felo missed Mee See all the time he was back in Lisbon. He reviewed his intention for this trip was to rekindle his marriage plan with Mee See and to organise the migration papers to take Mee See's family to Lisbon. He was hoping that Mee See would consider his offer.

Never in her wildest dreams did Mee See imagine that she would ever meet Felo again. It was too sudden for Mee See to fathom a proper response for Felo's marriage proposal. There was no room for consideration with her forth-coming wedding with Bob. Mee See appreciated Felo's proposal. However she had to tell him that the wedding was taking place in the next fortnight.

The disappointment was overwhelming for Felo. He reached to hold Mee See's hand silently and knew that he had missed out on the opportunity of getting Mee See to come back to Lisbon with him. They both knew that this would be their final farewell.

There was a knock at the door before the door opened, in walked Ah Lin and Bob followed by the restaurant waiter delivering lunch. Bob walked in as Felo withdrew his hand into his pocket and got up, "Well, it's time I leave now so I won't miss the ferry back to Macao."

Bob smiled and said earnestly, "Please do stay to have lunch with us."

Felo already got up and awkwardly he outstretched his arms for a friendly hug with Mee See whispering in her ears, "I will never forget you."

With a lump in his throat, Felo had a warm handshake with Bob and said, "I have to move on now. Take care of Mee See. I wish you both lots of happiness."

Wedding

Siew Fen decided to let the tenants look after the children in Macao while she attended the wedding ceremony.

Mee See and Bob were very busy planning for the wedding. They found that they had the same attitude to problem-solving. They did some tasks together and others separately. They began to know each other better and grew to understand each other's values, beliefs and approach to life.

Ah Lin and Mee See chose a tailor to make several outfits for the wedding day. To save on expenses, Mee See hired the white lace-wedding gown from the photograph shop instead of having one made. Bob used his near new dinner tuxedo for the wedding day.

They held the wedding ceremony in the Hong Kong Registry office. Outside the Registry office there were a dozen of Bob's good friends from the Royal Navy dressed in their naval outfits. They used their swords to form a guard of honour for the newlyweds. Bob took Mee See by the hand to walk under this guard of honour to enter the registry office. They had a simple but solemn wedding ceremony with Bob Hughes and Ah Lin as witnesses. After the ceremony the newlyweds walked through the guard of honour. As they walked out, the sisters threw coloured confetti, lucky rice, and silver and gold paper shapes of stars, the sun and moon. A number of friends blew whistles and horns and applauded. There was such a joyous atmosphere surrounding the newlyweds. Photographers took pictures of the wedding to capture the memory of this happy occasion. Pictures were taken with friends and relatives in the garden outside the Registry Office. The sisters rushed to wish Mee See good fortune and wished them both good health and happiness. They all wanted a picture with the lucky couple. Secretly, the sisters were envious and wished that their turn would come one day.

Ah Lin was so glad that she had had plenty of practice at writing her name. She wrote her name perfectly. She was grateful for the chance to sign Mee See's marriage certificate. Being the witness at this wedding had given Ah Lin the confidence which she never had before. Ah Lin was very helpful and attentive to Mee See throughout the day and night.

The wedding banquet had fifty tables at the Police Social Club. Doris brought all the sisters from the Hollywood Bar. Many of the volunteer police friends came to the celebration. A number of Bob's colleagues from HMS Tamar; naval officers and senior engineers attended this important day. Mee Jing and Mr. Hong, Luk KuChar and Luk KuCheung, Sam Kufu and his wife and their children, Sai YeMa and her daughter attended this joyous occasion. There was live music and the Master of Ceremonies kept everyone laughing happily throughout the night. Bob Hughes gave a humorous speech as he described Bob and Mee See's courtship. Everyone had a hearty laugh at Bob Hughes' witty presentation.

It was a successful wedding party. After midnight, Mee See changed into her going away outfit. Bob and Mee See went round the circle to shake hands and thank all relatives and friends for helping to celebrate the beginning of their new journey together as a married couple. The dozen naval officers re-assembled in two rows again. They stood to attention as the guard of honour. All the sisters threw coloured confetti as the newlyweds walked hand in hand between the guard of honour for the last time before starting a new chapter in their life.

A full moon had risen in the pitch dark sky. It was bright, perfectly round, and clear, signifying a happy future. Mee See recalled the recent incidents. Life would no longer be a struggle from day to day anymore. She had found her anchor and felt as though she was ready to spread her wings freely. She was starting a brand new life with a new identity, Mrs. Mee See Sayers. She wouldn't be lonely anymore. Her future was now secure because Bob was by her side.

Mee See thought, "The moon shines from thousands of miles away, showing the way forward, tomorrow … will be a bright sunny day!

PHOTOGRAPHS – BOB SAYERS

Bob from London decided to work in HK

HMS TAMAR provided docking services for visiting war ships

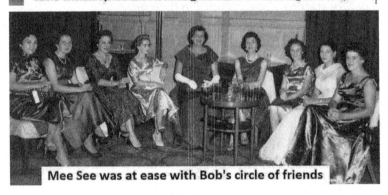

Mee See was at ease with Bob's circle of friends

Mee See & Bob at Police Ball

Bob Sayers & Mee See

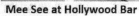

Mee See at Hollywood Bar

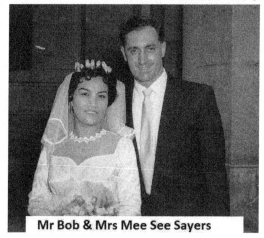

Mr Bob & Mrs Mee See Sayers

ABOUT THE AUTHOR

Phoebe Sayers - 馮友梅

It was never my intention to write a book about my grandmother and my Mummy's life. It was not as though they were movie stars or descendants of aristocrats. They were just two determined women trying to survive the best way they could under the circumstances they found themselves in through no fault of their making.

All through our childhood, my siblings and I were brought up by grandmother whilst Mummy was busy working to provide for the family. When I was young, my grandmother and Mummy talked about the good times, their extravagant life and the desperate times of years gone by. I had always been intrigued by the fact that we were meant to be wealthy beyond imagination and yet we lived in absolute poverty throughout my childhood. I had always wondered what happened to all that wealth! From their conversations, I gathered that Mummy had a hard time making ends meet whilst bringing us up and yet none of us felt deprived.

My grandmother told me a number of times that she regretted burning her life story that she had written. She told me about her life events at odd times, but I never thought of writing it down. When I reflect now, I wondered if she wanted me to fulfill her wish by writing her story for her.

When Daddy Sayers passed away, Mummy lost her will to live, I encouraged her to write down events of her and grandmother's life that stood out in her memory. I jokingly said that we would co-write a book about her life. I never dreamt it would come to fruition.

When sorting out Mummy's affairs after her passing, I found the writing she had done stuffed in a folder - there were numerous odd bits of paper containing the text she had jotted down of her memories. I decided to give up work and spent over two years collating, researching and reconstructing events from these scraps of her writing. In respect of Mummy's memory, I have kept every word of her original text, mistakes and all, in the traditional Chinese version of her life story. That book was published in Sydney in May 2012. My children and all my nephews and nieces urged me to write Mummy's story in English so they, too, could learn the early history of their exceptional grandmother and the life she lived before they were born.

I have never written any article of significance before. To embark on writing this book in honour of my Mummy was an enormous challenge that I was ill prepared for. I am grateful for the help of many relatives and friends. It was the sheer determination to do justice to Mummy's life that allowed me to persevere.

I have included a number of Cantonese words and well-known sayings that have been passed down from grandmother and Mummy. The spelling of Cantonese words does not necessarily follow the accepted Pin Yin or Wade-Giles but is roughly the phonetic spelling of how we talk in our everyday life. My grandmother and Mummy used a lot of idioms in their speech; we were exposed to them as part of our upbringing.

It has been a journey of discovery, writing Mummy's life story. Once I had set out upon the task, grandmother's tales, Mummy's scrapbook and old photograph albums unfolded the past before me. Their life story showed that we just don't know what is going to happen tomorrow and nothing is guaranteed. As we take the tribulations of today, we find the strength to move on, as tomorrow … is always another trial, another triumph!!

CPSIA information can be obtained at www.ICGtesting.com
Printed in the USA
BVOW06s1147270416

445642BV00053B/425/P